OPEN FIRE

THE FLAMES OF BETRAYAL

Chrissy Curry

HEMINGWAY
PUBLISHERS

Author's Note

There were moments in my young adult life when I felt lost, uncertain, and unsure of where I belonged—much like Cora. I still remember my mom's advice during one of those times: "Only you can decide to make a change. No one else can do it for you." Those words became my compass, guiding me through some of my darkest days. While Cora's story is fictional, the emotions, struggles, and challenges she faces are very real. Young adulthood is a time of searching—of questioning who we are and where we fit in this world. It's not always easy, but it's where we begin to discover our strength. My hope is that Cora's journey speaks to you, reminding you that you are never truly alone. That you have the power to believe in yourself, the courage to face the unknown, and the resilience to embrace new beginnings. Sometimes, a fresh start is all we need to rewrite our story.

-Chrissy Curry

What Readers Are saying?

"Sensational!"- D.C.

"Wow! You cover all the genres!"-M.W.

"Oh, WOW! It gave me goosebumps!" -K.S.

"That's beautifully written!" -S.M.

"It's gonna be a bestseller!"- S.G.

"Oh my goodness! It's riveting!"-K.W.

Prologue: A Shadow Awakened

"Every ember of the past holds the power to ignite the present."

Winter had settled heavily over the University of Delaware, blanketing the campus in thick snow that silenced even the loudest sounds. But within that silence, Cora sensed something—a discomfort lingering at the edge of her awareness, like shadows creeping just out of sight.

The cold bit into her cheeks as she wrapped her scarf tighter, glancing over her shoulder. Her friends had teased her about Vinny—her first real relationship, a whirlwind of new feelings that left her both thrilled and oddly unsettled. Vinny was her TA for the final term of her senior year, an intense but charming figure who had caught her attention in ways no one else had. They'd laughed at her shy smiles, at the way her cheeks reddened whenever she mentioned him, the flush of excitement that made her heart race.

Yet recently, that excitement had shifted. There was something about him she couldn't place—an intensity that felt both magnetic and unsettling. She sometimes caught him watching her with a focus that felt possessive, his gaze lingering for a moment too long, his presence almost consuming. She told herself it was just nerves, the thrill of something new, but the feeling gnawed at her.

Last weekend, Vinny had invited her to his family's secluded cabin by the lake. Nestled deep in the woods, it was a world apart from campus, a place where silence felt all-encompassing. Wrapped in the warmth of the cabin, she felt as though they were cut off from the rest of the world, truly alone.

The firelight flickered across his face as he leaned close, his hands tracing along her arms and shoulders, moving lower with a growing intensity. Every touch awakened a mix of excitement and tension. In his embrace, she felt herself relax, opening up in ways she hadn't expected. His fingers explored her skin, lingering at her collarbone, the curve of her waist, his breath warm against her neck, drawing her closer with each whispered word.

Yet as they lay together, wrapped in each other's warmth, a chill crept through her—a feeling she couldn't shake. She had sensed it for days— a faint unease, as though even in their most intimate moments, something else was there, watching them from the shadows beyond the windows.

After he'd fallen asleep, she lay awake, eyes tracing the shadows stretching across the cabin walls. Vinny's arm was draped over her, his breathing steady and slow, but her pulse wouldn't settle. A quietness surrounded the cabin that felt unnatural, as though something beyond the walls was listening, waiting. She tried to calm herself, but the unease lingered, keeping her from sleep.

When dawn broke, casting the cabin in a pale light, she finally forced herself to get up. She dressed quietly, feeling relieved to return to campus, ready to return to routine. But as she gathered her things, she noticed something missing: her apartment keys.

She remembered setting them on the side table by the couch, but now they were nowhere to be found. A rush of anxiety washed over her. Those keys were more than just a practical necessity; they represented a sense of security and normalcy, a tether to her life outside the intense world Vinny had drawn her into. Unable to ignore the feeling, she convinced her friends to drive back to the cabin with her later that evening to retrieve them. It was supposed to be a quick trip, a chance to put her mind at ease.

But as they approached the cabin, their car headlights illuminating the snow-covered path, Cora's breath caught. A figure moved by the trunk of an old, beaten-up sedan, struggling with something heavy—something that looked like a body. She squinted, her pulse pounding as she recognized the figure.

Vinny.

Her friends sat beside her in stunned silence, eyes wide with horror as they watched Vinny hoist what looked like a body into the trunk. His movements were mechanical, his face blank and haunted, as if he were under some dark spell. They remained frozen, unable to speak, each too terrified to shatter the silence.

In a few minutes, Vinny disappeared, his car rolling down the isolated road, leaving only fresh tire tracks and the haunting memory of his empty stare. Cora felt her heart sink, unable to reconcile what she had just seen. Her mind whirled with questions and dread as her friends drove them back, none daring to speak, haunted by the inexplicable scene.

The days following Vinny's disappearance passed in a blur. He was officially reported missing, but authorities turned up nothing—no leads, no clues, nothing to explain his sudden absence. They searched the lake and nearby woods, but all they found were footprints and tire tracks leading nowhere.

Cora tried to move on, but the image of Vinny's hollow, vacant stare haunted her. The reality of what she'd seen began to sink in, filling her with a deep, unshakable dread. She knew she should report it, share the truth, but something kept her silent—a fear she couldn't name.

Two days later, her inbox chimed with a new email. She opened it cautiously, her fingers trembling. A single image filled her screen—a photo of her, alone by the lake, looking over her shoulder as if sensing something behind her. In the background, barely visible, a dark shadow lingered, watching.

Beneath it was a single line: "Once open to the flames, nothing escapes."

Her stomach turned as she stared at the message, the words searing into her mind. The intimacy of the photo was unnerving, the sense of someone lurking close enough to capture her in such a vulnerable moment. Her friends tried to brush it off as a prank, a strange coincidence, but she knew better. She closed her laptop, feeling exposed, as if eyes were still on her.

Each day afterward brought a new reminder of that presence—her scarf left neatly at her door, a faint scent on her pillow, strange phone calls in the dead of night with no answer on the other end, only silence. The feeling of eyes on her became an uninvited guest, a reminder that someone was watching her every move.

One night, as she lay in bed, she cracked the window slightly, hoping the cold air would calm her racing mind. But as she drifted toward sleep, her heart stopped at the sound of breathing—low and steady, just outside. She froze, every nerve on edge, pulse thundering as she realized the sound wasn't her imagination. It was real, intimate, dangerously close.

She lay paralyzed, her gaze fixed on the window. The steady breathing continued, low and rhythmic, as though whoever was out there was waiting, watching. Her pulse raced as she strained to hear every sound, her mind flooded with fear. Her fingers clenched the blankets, desperate to keep herself from moving, to remain silent, hoping that whatever lurked outside would simply disappear.

The hand came first—a gloved hand pressing against the glass, smudging the frost as it traced slow, deliberate lines along the pane. She could barely make out the shadowy figure beyond, but it was close enough to make her blood run cold. She lay there, immobilized, feeling the weight of her vulnerability pressing down on her.

After what felt like an eternity, the shadow withdrew, vanishing into the night. She let out a shaky breath, her body still rigid with terror. She had never felt more exposed, more utterly alone, her safety slipping further away with every passing day.

Her past had always held shadows—unresolved mysteries, her mother's death casting a pall over her life. But now, with Vinny gone and the stalker creeping closer, her entire reality began to unravel. The unease that had once felt distant now invaded every moment, turning her world into a maze of threats she couldn't see but could feel all around her.

Each day brought new, disturbing reminders of that unseen presence—notes left on her desk in her apartment, the faint scent of cologne in her bathroom, small objects moved or replaced with no explanation. Each note bore the same phrase: "Once open to the flames, nothing escapes."

Even her friends, who had tried to reassure her, began to distance themselves, unable to comprehend the intensity of her fear. She was left alone, haunted by the invisible eyes that watched her from the shadows.

One evening, as she walked back to her apartment, she caught sight of it again—a shadow reflected in a shop window, hovering a few paces behind. She held her breath, her pulse racing as she watched the figure linger, a silhouette without a face, a dark promise that refused to leave her.

She turned, but the street was empty. The shadow had vanished, leaving only the echo of her own breathing. In that moment, she understood this wasn't a prank or a coincidence. It was a threat, a promise of something far darker, something that had seeped into her life, threading its way through her past, coiling around her present.

And so, the prologue to her new life had begun—not with warmth or joy, but with a chill that settled deep in her bones. A warning she couldn't ignore, an unwelcome promise that the shadows of her past were stirring again. She could feel them closing in, inch by inch, with every step she took—and she had only begun to sense just how close they truly were.

Somewhere, in the dark, a phone buzzed quietly. Her name lit the screen.

Table of Content

A Return to Ashes

"To return is to face the ghosts we left behind."

The bell above the bar door jingled sharply, cutting through the low hum of conversation and the faint clinking of glasses. A gust of cold air swept through the room as the door swung open, sending a ripple of murmurs through the small, packed space. Cora instinctively pulled her jacket tighter, the chill reminding her of how far she felt from the warmth of certainty. Happy Hour was in full swing at Jack's Ale House, a cozy, unassuming bar nestled in Pine Brook Hill's historic mountain district.

Heads turned briefly as a young woman stumbled in, her chest heaving as if she had run the entire way. Her eyes darted around the room, landing briefly on Cora and her friends before she quickly ducked behind a cluster of high-backed chairs near the entrance.

Cora, mid-sip of her drink, froze. MJ, seated beside her, arched a brow and muttered, "Well, this just got interesting." Before Cora could respond, the door jingled again, this time admitting a tall, lean man with tousled hair and a grin that seemed almost too charming. His gaze swept the room until it landed on the woman.

"There you are," he said, his voice light but carrying an edge of possessiveness. He sauntered over to her, ignoring the curious glances from other patrons.

The woman gave a coquettish smile. "James, you're such a flirt," she chided, though her tone betrayed more amusement than reproach. The man pushed away a chair that was pulled out from its table and motioned for her to come to him.

James closed the gap between them, sliding an arm around her waist. "What can I say, Auriela? You keep me chasing after you. A quest I'll surely take on any day." His grin widened as he leaned in to kiss her, his hand lingering in a way that drew more attention than it probably should have. There wasn't an eye in the bar that wasn't focused on this scenario.

Cora turned away, focusing on her drink. MJ, however, watched the exchange with a mixture of amusement and disdain. "Now that," he whispered, "is a couple two drinks away from a very public breakup."

Cora couldn't help but laugh, but the sound died in her throat as James suddenly turned toward their table. His gaze landed on her, and for a moment, the easy charm in his expression shifted into something sharper. He looked her up and down, his eyes lingering a beat too long.

"Well, who's this little beauty?" James said, his tone playful but carrying an undercurrent that made Cora's skin crawl.

Auriela swatted his arm lightly, laughing. "Oh, stop. Leave that one alone. She's not for you." She turned to Cora with a conspiratorial wink. "He's harmless, I promise."

Cora forced a smile, her grip tightening around her glass. MJ, sensing her discomfort, leaned forward and placed a protective hand on her arm. "Actually, we were just leaving," he announced, his voice cool and firm.

"Oh, come on," Auriela said, pouting and playing with her long blonde hair. "You look fun! We were going to invite you to our game night this weekend!"

Cora hesitated, but the way James's eyes lingered on her made the decision easy. "Thanks, but I think we're busy," she said quickly, standing up.

"Another time, then," James said, his grin returning, though it didn't quite reach his eyes. He shrugged slightly and looked across the room, clearly unconvinced.

The moment they stepped outside, MJ let out a dramatic sigh. "Well, that was gross," he declared, flipping his scarf over his shoulder with a flourish.

Cora couldn't help but laugh, though her nerves still buzzed. "You're not wrong."

"I'm never wrong," MJ said with mock seriousness, looping his arm through hers. "And I'll tell you this: if that guy so much as breathes in your direction again, I'll be personally introducing him to my stiletto heel. Size eleven. Pointy as hell."

Cora smirked, but her thoughts drifted back to the way James had looked at her—like he was peeling her apart with his gaze. It wasn't flattering. It wasn't even remotely subtle. Her skin still crawled from it.

MJ nudged her gently. "Earth to Cora. You okay, love? You're doing that thing where you spiral silently, and it's freaking me out."

"I'm fine," she lied, her voice a bit too tight.

"Liar," MJ said bluntly, steering her toward a nearby bench. "Sit."

Cora sighed but obeyed, sinking onto the cold wood. MJ perched beside her, his sharp eyes scanning her face. "You know, it's okay to feel a little unmoored. You're back in Creepyville, your Gram's gone, and the locals are apparently amorous weirdos." He leaned closer, dropping his voice to a whisper. "If you don't want to deal with this town's freaky vibe, we can bounce. Screw the boutique, screw the inheritance. Let's take the cash and run."

Cora laughed, the sound breaking the tension in her chest. "And do what? Open a drag club in Philly?" She was relieved the subject was changing.

MJ's eyes lit up. "Finally, a good idea from you! I've been waiting for this day."

Their laughter faded into a comfortable silence, the kind only years of friendship could produce. But when MJ's hand brushed hers, his grip tightened. "Seriously, though," he said, his tone softer now. "This place...it's weird, sure. But you're not. You've never been the problem, Cora. You're magic. Don't let this place—or people like James—make you forget that."

Cora felt the sting of tears but blinked them away. "Thanks, MJ," she murmured, her voice barely above a whisper.

The sky had been a rich blue as they pulled up to her grandmother's bridal shop earlier that morning, nestled in the historic business district on Boughton Street. The building looked just as she remembered it— charming with its ivy-covered walls, its large windows once filled with wedding gowns, and an air of elegance that her grandmother had lovingly crafted. Once, Gram's bridal boutique had been thriving with business, its cheery white facade contrasting with the darker tones of the buildings around it. Now, the boutique was boarded up, its windows blank, as though it were a grieving entity itself.

Cora had moved her things into the third-floor loft above, the sight filling her with a pang of regret she couldn't quite shake. Her throat tightened, the reality settling in slowly, painfully. Her grandmother, the only family she'd known for most of her life, was gone. The woman who had raised her, who had been her guide, her strength, her foundation—gone.

The private service was beautiful, a quiet gathering of faces she barely remembered, each contributing tender bouts of sympathy. Her own mother had died when she was a toddler, and she presumed her father was deceased too, as there had never been a single mention of him in all these years. Cora had asked her Gram about them once, but the conversation had been deftly redirected, and she hadn't pressed further. The finality of it all circled abruptly in her mind. She was alone. The bar seemed to close in around her as she tried to process the enormity of what that meant.

The initial thought of coming home without her grandmother waiting for her had been almost unbearable, but knowing MJ, Selah, and Jensen would be there with her made it a little more manageable. They'd always been there for each other, through every trial and triumph, and now would be no different. They had met during a 2:00 a.m. fire drill during freshman orientation, all congregating at the bench outside their dorm terrace. MJ had deemed them a friend group on the spot, and by the next morning, they were skipping orientation activities and riding the UD Dart Bus aimlessly. From that point on, they had been inseparable.

Inside the bar, familiar faces mixed with strangers, the low lighting blurring the lines between memories and the present. Her three closest college friends, all in town for Gram's services, occupied the barstools beside her, their presence the only anchor in the storm of emotions that had defined her return. The four of them had just recently walked in the University of Delaware's graduation ceremony, eager to begin new lives in different directions.

There had been a nostalgic moment on May 12, graduation day, as they walked across the lawn after the ceremony. The weather had been a picturesque 68 degrees, and Jensen's speech had been especially moving: *"Success is not final. Failure is not fatal. The courage to continue is what counts."* Graduates had mingled with family members on the green, but Cora had lingered on the outskirts, wishing her Gram hadn't been too ill to make the trip.

Though united in grief over Gram's passing, today they wore masks of determination to keep the afternoon lighthearted. It had been Gram's wish that they celebrate her life, and tonight, they tried to honor it.

Selah, ever the nurturer, was the first to break the silence. "I still can't believe she's gone," she murmured, her fingers tracing the edge of her glass. Her soft features seemed to droop under the weight of loss, her voice like a fragile thread holding back a wave of emotion. "She was like a mother to you, Cora. I always loved hearing you talk about her. Charlotte O'Clara the Third. A name for a queen," she added.

MJ, seated beside her, leaned in with his characteristic flair. "Which makes her practically my grandmother," he declared dramatically, earning a soft laugh from Selah. Dressed in his typical bold style—gold boots, an oversized scarf, and a striking maroon jacket—MJ exuded confidence that often put Cora at ease. But tonight, his humor seemed like armor, shielding him from the shared pain.

"Do you think she left me her pearls?" MJ continued, his tone light but his eyes betraying genuine affection. "Because, babe, let me tell you, I can rock a vintage look like no other."

Cora managed a weak smile, the tightness in her throat easing slightly. "I think they're in her jewelry box," she replied, her voice barely audible. "You can have them if they're there."

MJ gasped, clutching his chest theatrically. "Don't tempt me with a good time, darling. I'll be rifling through that box tomorrow morning!"

Jensen, stoic as ever, placed a hand on her shoulder. His touch was steady, grounding, and somehow heavier than usual. "She wouldn't want you to dwell on the pain. She'd want you to carry forward her legacy." His words were quiet but firm, and Cora knew he meant them.

"Legacy," Selah echoed, her voice wistful. "That building, her bridal boutique—it's all so much a part of her. You're brave, Cora, for coming back to it."

Jensen had taken Cora to meet with the attorney after the closing of Gram's service. Gram had left her everything: the building on Boughton Street, which included three floors of livable space, the business, a box of journals, and a large sum of savings. The first floor housed the bridal boutique, a renowned destination for over fifty years, even featured in *Bride Allure Magazine*. People came from all over to be fitted by Charlotte O'Clara, including movie stars of her time.

Cora remembered the layout vividly. The side door on the front walk led to the second- and third-floor lofts overlooking the business district. The main entrance steps were just a short climb from the street, and she could recall the exact time it took to run up the forty steps to make it in time for curfew. She'd grown up in that loft, the entire front room filled with floor-to-ceiling windows overlooking bustling street festivals, makers markets, and concerts.

"Brave or stupid?" Cora muttered, a flicker of self-doubt crossing her face. "Sometimes, I can't tell the difference."

She had often taken on big projects, even with the demanding course load from her major in Architecture Analytics at UD. But the prospect of running an actual business seemed entirely foreign to her.

MJ glanced over at her, breaking the silence. "You know," he began, his tone gentle, "I never got to meet your grandma, but from everything you've told me, she sounds like she was incredible. Like, old-school wisdom and sass rolled into one."

A faint smile tugged at Cora's lips as she imagined her grandmother. "She was… everything," she replied, her voice thick with emotion. "She taught me to be strong, to stand up for myself. She never took nonsense from anyone. She once told me to find love in friendship first. I thought she was nuts," she added with a soft chuckle.

Cora's mind wandered to a memory of Gram catching her in the rain with a family friend, Sebastian. The boy had been smitten with Cora, but she hadn't felt the same. Love, to her, seemed something that needed sparks first—goosebumps, electricity—not a gradual warmth from friendship.

MJ reached over and gave her hand a comforting squeeze, his usual exuberance softened in the face of her grief. "She would've been proud of you, you know? Seeing you today. You're one of the strongest people I know, Cora."

The words touched her, a bittersweet warmth filling her chest. "Thanks, MJ. I just… I don't know how I'm going to do this without her."

The group fell silent, the weight of Gram's absence hanging in the air like an unwelcome guest. But then MJ, ever the master of breaking tension, smirked. "Speaking of legacy, what's the deal with those journals she left you, babe? You mentioned keys, secrets, intrigue—come on, give me something juicy."

Cora hesitated, her fingers tightening around her glass. "They're locked," she admitted, her voice tinged with frustration. "I haven't opened them yet."

MJ gasped dramatically. "Locked journals? Hidden keys? This is starting to sound like a steamy romance novel, and I live for it."

Jensen chuckled softly, but his eyes remained on Cora, studying her with quiet concern. "You should read them," he said. "Maybe there's something in them that can help you figure out what comes next."

"What if I'm not ready for what's inside?" Cora replied, her voice barely above a whisper. She stopped moving the glass, sliding it away from her. She wasn't sure if she meant the journals or the memories they held.

The sound of glasses clinking and soft murmurs filled the space between them, yet Cora felt the weight of her friends' gazes. Each of them was a mirror, reflecting her back at herself in ways she wasn't ready to confront. She stared down at the condensation pooling around her glass, trying to find answers in the patterns.

"I think you're underestimating yourself," Selah said gently, breaking the silence. Her green eyes were full of warmth, a steady presence Cora had leaned on countless times before. "Gram wouldn't have left you the boutique if she didn't believe you were capable."

MJ leaned in, a playful smirk on his lips but an uncharacteristic seriousness in his eyes. "Listen to Selah, babe. You're one of the most capable people I know. And trust me, I've seen a lot of questionable decisions. You're not one of them."

Cora smiled faintly, though her chest still felt heavy. "It doesn't feel that way. This town… it's always felt off to me. Like there's something I can't quite place." She looked up, meeting MJ's eyes. "I stayed away for a reason."

Jensen, who had been quiet, finally spoke. "That doesn't mean it can't change. You've changed, Cora. Maybe this town isn't the same place you remembered four years ago."

The door to the bar swung open again, bringing another blast of cold air. A group of locals walked in, their laughter filling the space as they greeted the bartender. Cora's gaze drifted to them, a pang of longing hitting her unexpectedly. She used to envy that sense of belonging, of being part of something bigger. But Pine Brook Hill had never felt like home—it had always been a place she wanted to escape.

"Gram loved this town," she murmured, more to herself than anyone else. "She saw something in it that I never could."

"Maybe it's time to find out what that was," Selah suggested. Her voice was soft, almost hesitant, as if she was treading carefully around Cora's fragile emotions.

Cora sighed, running her fingers through her hair. "Maybe," she admitted. "But it's hard to let go of all the reasons I left." On the outside looking in, her childhood had looked perfect. Gram had made her a lovely home, and Cora had been composed and ready to take the world by storm. But this town had left doubts in her mind, and she had chosen a college as far away as possible.

MJ grinned, his playful tone returning. "Well, if anyone can figure it out, it's you. And if not, I'll just dress up as Gram and run the boutique myself. Think of it—MJ's Blissed Up Bridal Boutique." He struck a dramatic pose, drawing laughter from the group.

Cora shook her head, her smile more genuine this time. "You'd scare off all the brides."

"Or attract the right kind," MJ shot back with a wink.

MJ kept them entertained with stories, filling the quiet spaces with his humor. He described his wild adventures in Philly, his dreams of performing on Broadway someday, and his plans to bring his flair for drama to Colorado. Cora found herself laughing despite the sorrow weighing on her heart.

Her thoughts drifted back to her grandmother, memories weaving through her mind like a patchwork quilt of love, laughter, and lessons learned. She missed her so deeply that it felt like a physical ache. The guilt she carried about never visiting enough ate at her, yet MJ's presence was a constant reminder that she wasn't alone.

Their laughter eased some of the tension, but the underlying questions lingered. What if Gram's journals held answers she wasn't ready for? What if Pine Brook Hill hadn't changed at all, and she was setting herself up for disappointment?

As if sensing her hesitation, Jensen nudged her gently. "You don't have to figure everything out tonight. One step at a time, Cora." Jensen was always looking for something tangible he could do, something he could offer. It was hard for him to stand by without giving her a solution, and his heart ached for her.

She nodded, appreciating his steady reassurance. But deep down, she knew that the answers she sought wouldn't come easily—and that confronting them would be far harder than she was ready to admit.

Jensen paid for the tab as the four of them wandered out, arm in arm, into the cold, unexpectedly coming across another inviting tavern. Colorado in the spring was a time of blooming wildflowers and green landscapes. However, spring also yielded cooler weather, extending the life of winter activities. Memories of the first snowfall shimmered in Cora's mind as they walked along the scalloped sidewalks, each wrapping their coats tighter against the chill.

The door to the newly renamed Hillside Tavern swung open with a soft creak, allowing a sharp gust of cold air to snake its way inside. The late afternoon sun cast long shadows over the polished wood floors, signaling the transition into evening. It was still Happy Hour, still a time when the small-town locals mingled with strangers passing through, and the tavern bustled with subdued energy.

Cora glanced up from her drink, her fingers lightly grazing the condensation on her glass. Selah had just joined the table, slipping into the chair beside Jensen, her warm smile immediately softening the edges of the day. Jensen leaned back, his calm demeanor as steady as ever, a reassuring presence amid the swirling uncertainty.

"Does it feel surreal?" Selah began, her voice quiet but deliberate. "Being back here… after everything."

MJ let out a dramatic sigh, resting his chin in his palm. "I'll say. This town is like stepping into a time capsule. Nothing I envisioned except the number of cobwebs on the library door."

"You went to the library?" Jensen raised an eyebrow, his lips quirking in amusement.

"No, but I saw it on the way here, and trust me, it's seen better days," MJ retorted, eliciting a chuckle from Selah.

Cora offered a faint smile, though her thoughts remained anchored to the weight of the day. "I just can't believe Gram's gone," she said softly, her voice breaking slightly. The words felt foreign in her mouth, as if saying them aloud made them more real.

Jensen leaned forward, his gaze steady. "She was an amazing woman, Cora."

Selah nodded in agreement. "She left you the boutique because she believed in you. You are going to do amazing things."

Selah liked to think that Cora had inherited the strength and courage to build something beautiful out of this devastating opportunity. She quietly considered how fortunate she was to have three siblings, even if they were far apart. She couldn't imagine the intensity of Cora's solitude and wished she could take her pain away.

Cora swallowed hard, her throat tightening. "I just… I don't know if I'm ready for this. Coming back here, facing everything I've been avoiding for years—it feels like too much."

The door opened again, another wave of icy air brushing past them. The bartender glanced up, offering a nod of recognition to the newcomers. Cora's gaze lingered on the familiar scene of Pine Brook locals mingling and laughing, their faces a tapestry of stories she had missed out on while she was away.

"Let's be honest," MJ interrupted her thoughts, his voice tinged with both sarcasm and affection. "You've avoided this town like the plague for four years. But now, you're here. And I'm here. And we're going to face it together."

"I don't expect you to stay in Pine Brook, MJ," Cora said softly. "You already have your dream job lined up."

"Excuse me, media is so not my dream job. Plus, Pine Brook needs a bigger presence of ME. I'm talking about a Hamburger Mary's version I'd like to call *FlaminGALS* that can open some minds in this freaky town," he exclaimed, laughter rippling around the table.

Selah reached out, squeezing Cora's hand gently. "One step at a time."

"Speaking of steps," Jensen chimed in, his tone playful, "Have you thought about what you're going to do with those journals? They might be exactly what you need to make sense of everything. You owe it to yourself to read them."

Cora hesitated, her mind settling on the worn canvas bag of journals the attorney had given her that afternoon. It sat beside her in the booth, heavy with meaning she wasn't sure she was ready to confront. The small, peculiar keys the attorney had mentioned were tucked away at the bottom of a box in the loft, untouched since she'd discovered them earlier that morning. The journal titles, written in Gram's neat handwriting, came to her now: *Read When You Find Love. Read When You Are Afraid. Read When You Need Hope.*

"You owe it to yourself. You owe it to me. You owe it to this universe, girl," MJ declared as if this single act could redeem the world.

Cora managed a laugh, though it felt hollow. The weight of those journals—their potential answers and revelations—was something she wasn't sure she could carry just yet.

As their laughter settled, Jensen's expression grew more serious. "Take your time, but don't let them sit forever. Gram left them for you."

Cora nodded, though her chest tightened with the weight of unspoken truths. The journals were waiting, just like the town she had left behind. And now, both seemed intent on pulling her back into the heart of what she had been running from.

The conversation ebbed and flowed as the four friends settled into their usual rhythm, their camaraderie a comforting balm in the midst of uncertainty. Cora felt a fleeting sense of normalcy, but it didn't last long. Her mind kept wandering back to the journals, the keys at the bottom of the box, and the way everything seemed to be waiting for her to take the next step.

"Do you think she wrote them just for me?" Cora asked, her voice tentative as she traced the rim of her glass with her finger. "Or are they just... reflections of her own life?"

Selah tilted her head thoughtfully. "Maybe a bit of both. She must've known they'd help you. Your Gram always had a way of knowing what people needed. I loved the cards she used to mail to you—the advice she wrote."

MJ groaned dramatically, tossing a pretzel into his mouth. "See? This is why I need to be adopted by your family. My Gram left me nothing but guilt and a questionable casserole recipe."

Jensen snorted, shaking his head. "You'd never survive the quiet of Pine Brook, MJ."

MJ leaned forward, wagging a perfectly manicured finger. "Excuse you, Jensen. I bring the noise wherever I go."

Their laughter filled the bar, momentarily dispelling the tension that had been building since Cora's return. She was grateful for her friends, their banter reminding her of the bond they shared, but the looming weight of Gram's journals and the unspoken secrets of Pine Brook lingered just below the surface.

The bartender approached their table, a wiry man in his sixties with a friendly but weary smile. "Can I get you folks anything else?" he asked, his voice carrying the faint twang of a lifelong local.

Cora shook her head, offering a polite smile. "We're good, thanks."

As he walked away, MJ leaned in conspiratorially. "So, what's the deal with this place? It's got small-town charm written all over it, but something feels... off."

Jensen shrugged. "That's just Pine Brook for you. Population of 500. It's quiet, but it's not without its quirks."

Selah nodded in agreement. "It does have a certain... energy. Like there are stories waiting to be uncovered."

The table fell silent, the weight of her words settling over them like a heavy fog. MJ was the first to break the tension, his voice light but his expression serious. "Well, I say we rewrite the story. Starting with you, darling."

Cora managed to smile, but the unease remained, creeping along the edges of her thoughts like a shadow.

"Speaking of stories," Jensen said, his tone shifting, "Is there anything new with the Vinny situation?"

Cora stiffened, her hand tightening around her glass. "It's not something I want to talk about," she said quietly, her gaze fixed on the table.

MJ reached out, his hand resting lightly on hers. "Then we won't," he said firmly. "It stays in Delaware. We made a pact, remember?" And they had. What happened that night at the cabin was never to be brought up again.

The words hung in the air, a silent agreement that no one dared to break. But even as they moved on to lighter topics, Cora couldn't shake the feeling that Pine Brook had its own way of keeping secrets—and she wasn't sure she was ready for what it might reveal.

As the late afternoon wore on, the warmth of the bar began to feel stifling to Cora. The comforting buzz of conversation and laughter dimmed in her mind, replaced by the relentless whispers of Gram's journals and the unease lingering since her return to Pine Brook.

She pushed her chair back and stood. "I need some air," she said, brushing off Selah's concerned look.

"I'll come with you," Jensen offered, already halfway out of his seat.

"No, it's fine," Cora replied quickly. "I just need a moment."

MJ raised a skeptical brow but didn't push. "Don't wander too far, darling. We've got more stories to dissect."

Cora gave him a small smile before making her way to the door. The brisk evening air hit her like a slap, sharp and refreshing, a welcome contrast to the heavy atmosphere inside. She leaned against the cold brick of the building, letting her breath fog in front of her.

Her gaze wandered to the street, quiet except for the occasional car passing by. The town looked almost picturesque in the fading light, but the beauty felt like a mask, hiding something far less idyllic.

The creak of the door behind her made her jump. She turned to see Jensen stepping out, his expression unreadable.

"I thought you might need this." He held out her coat, a faint smirk tugging at the corners of his mouth. "It's cold enough to freeze your thoughts out here."

She chuckled softly, slipping the coat over her shoulders. "Thanks," she said as he joined her against the wall, his hands shoved into his pockets. For a moment, they stood in companionable silence, the air between them heavy with unspoken thoughts.

"You know," he said finally, his voice low, "You don't have to carry all of this alone."

Cora glanced at him, her brows furrowing. "What do you mean?"

"Whatever's been bothering you—Vinny, your Gram's death, this whole... town," he said, gesturing vaguely toward the street. "You've got us. We're here."

Her throat tightened, and she looked away, her eyes stinging. "I know. It's just... a lot. Being back here, all these memories... she was the only family I ever had." She trailed off, shaking her head.

Jensen didn't press her, but his steady presence was enough to ease the knot in her chest. Before she could say more, the sound of footsteps on the pavement caught her attention. She looked up to see a man walking toward them, his long coat billowing slightly in the wind. His face was shadowed, but there was something about his stride— purposeful, almost predatory—that sent a chill down her spine.

Jensen straightened, his eyes narrowing. "Do you know him?"

Cora shook her head, her heart pounding. The man stopped a few feet away, his gaze flicking between them before he turned and disappeared down a side street.

"Let's get back inside," Jensen said, his tone leaving no room for argument.

Cora nodded, her legs feeling unsteady as she followed him back into the bar.

The warmth of the bar wrapped around Cora like a protective shield as she stepped back inside with Jensen. The low hum of voices and clinking glasses was a stark contrast to the tension that had settled in her chest moments earlier. She scanned the room, her eyes landing on MJ, Selah, and a group of locals gathered near the jukebox.

Selah waved her over, her warm smile a soothing balm. "Everything okay out there?" she asked as Cora and Jensen approached the table.

"Just needed a breath of fresh air," Cora replied, her voice steadier than she felt. Jensen took her coat and hung it up on the hook attached to the booth.

"Jensen, our protector," MJ quipped, lifting his drink in a mock toast. "Always swooping in at the right moment."

Jensen rolled his eyes, tossing his jacket and sliding into his seat without a word. Cora followed, sinking into her chair as the weight of the day pressed down on her.

"You've been quiet," Selah said, her voice gentle. "How are you holding up, really?"

Cora hesitated, the words catching in her throat. She wanted to tell them everything—the unease that had followed her since she arrived, the unanswered questions swirling around her Gram's death, and the journals that seemed to hold secrets she wasn't ready to uncover.

Instead, she forced a small smile. "I'm okay. Just... adjusting."

MJ leaned forward, resting his chin on his hand. "Honey, adjusting doesn't look good on you. Spill."

The directness of his words made Cora laugh, a small, unexpected sound that broke through the tension. "I don't even know where to start," she admitted.

"Start with what's in that bag," Jensen said, nodding toward the small tote of journals they'd brought from the meeting with Gram's attorney. "Those things are practically glowing with importance."

Cora's gaze drifted to the tote, its presence both comforting and foreboding. She reached for the top journal, her fingers brushing over the worn leather cover. The title was embossed in elegant gold script: *When You're Lost, Find Your Way Home.*

"That one seems fitting," Selah said softly, her eyes filled with understanding.

Cora flipped over the journal, examining the back, the pages stiff with age. The faint scent of her grandmother's perfume wafted up, bringing a rush of bittersweet memories.

"Gram used to say everything had a place and a purpose," she murmured, her fingers trailing over the handwritten words. "I just wish I knew what she meant by that." The idea that her Gram had planned for this, that she'd left these journals as a guide, was both comforting and overwhelming.

MJ leaned closer, peering at the journal over her shoulder. "Maybe she meant this. These journals."

"You don't have to do it alone," Jensen said, his voice steady. "We're here. Whatever's in those journals, we'll figure it out together."

The sincerity in his words brought a lump to Cora's throat. She blinked back tears, grateful for their presence, their support.

As the group fell into a comfortable silence, the door to the bar swung open, letting in a rush of cold air. Cora glanced up instinctively, her breath catching as she recognized the man from earlier.

He stood in the doorway, his sharp gaze scanning the room until it landed on her. His lips curved into a smirk that sent a shiver down her spine.

"Who the hell is that?" MJ whispered, his tone sharp.

Cora couldn't tear her eyes away as the man stepped inside, his movements deliberate, predatory.

"I don't know," she whispered, clutching the journal tightly to her chest, wondering where she'd seen his face before.

The man's presence shifted the atmosphere in the bar. Conversations faltered, and the low hum of voices dimmed, as though the air itself had grown heavier. All eyes turned toward him. He wasn't overly tall, but something about the way he carried himself—his sharp suit, his neatly styled hair, and the casual confidence in his stride—commanded attention.

MJ leaned closer to Cora, his lips barely moving as he muttered, "That guy's giving big city villain vibes. You know, the one who smiles but has a knife in his pocket."

Cora wanted to laugh, but her throat was too tight. The man's eyes stayed locked on hers as he moved through the room with a calculated ease, like he already owned the space.

"Hey, can I help you?" Jensen's voice cut through the tension, steady but firm. He stood, his broad frame blocking the man's direct line to Cora.

The stranger smiled, though it didn't reach his eyes. "I'm just here to grab a drink. Didn't mean to interrupt anything." His voice was smooth, with a slight edge that made Cora's skin prickle.

Jensen didn't move, his gaze unwavering. "The bar is over there." He nodded toward the far end of the room, where a few locals sat nursing their beers.

The man chuckled softly, raising his hands in mock surrender. "Relax, big guy. I'm just passing through," he said, his stare fixed on Cora.

"Hello, I'm Declan. And you... you're Cora," he stated, holding out his hand for a swift handshake. His gaze lingered for a moment before he turned and sauntered to the bar, casting one last look at her over his shoulder.

"Creepy," MJ said once the man was out of earshot. He took a sip of his drink, his brow furrowed. "What's with the serial killer chic?"

Selah placed a comforting hand on Cora's arm. "Are you okay?"

Cora nodded, though her heart was still racing. "Yeah. I just... I don't know. Something about him feels off."

"You're not wrong," Jensen muttered, his eyes following Declan as he ordered a drink. "He's too polished for a place like this. Doesn't belong. How does he know your name?"

Selah frowned. "Maybe he's just passing through, like he said."

"Or maybe he's looking for something—or someone," MJ added dramatically, waggling his eyebrows.

"Enough," Cora said, her voice firmer than she felt. She didn't want to dwell on the stranger or the unease he'd brought with him. She turned back to the journal in her lap, focusing on the familiar comfort of her Gram's handwriting.

The words on the cover blurred as her thoughts spiraled. She couldn't shake the feeling that the man's arrival wasn't random—that it meant something she couldn't yet understand.

Her phone buzzed on the table, breaking her reverie. She picked it up, frowning at the unknown number flashing on the screen.

"Are you going to answer that?" Selah asked.

Cora hesitated before hitting decline. "Probably just a spam call."

But when the phone buzzed again moments later, the same number appearing, her stomach twisted.

"Ignore it," Jensen said, his tone protective. "If it's important, they'll leave a message."

Cora nodded, setting the phone face down on the table. Still, the uneasy feeling lingered, gnawing at the edges of her mind.

From the bar, Declan raised his glass in her direction, a small, almost imperceptible smirk playing on his lips.

The four of them stepped out into the brisk night air, pulling their jackets tighter as they made their way back to Cora's loft. Every so often, they glanced over their shoulders, as though the bad vibe from the bar might have followed them.

As Cora looked up into the night sky, her gaze landed on a hospital billboard. The bold lettering read: *Dr. Declan Atler, Pine Brook's Most Prominent Surgeon.* She stared at his face, now smiling and polished, in the advertisement above her.

A soft laugh escaped her lips at the discovery. For the moment, she allowed the innocent findings to curtail the untamed emotions churning inside her.

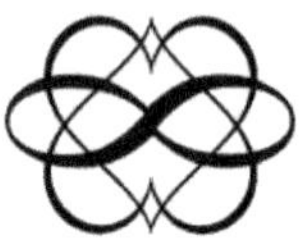

A Spark Ignited

"A single spark can awaken desires we never knew existed."

Inside the loft, the scent of lavender and old wood greeted them as the door clicked shut behind them, sealing off the chill of the night. Cora paused in the entryway, her laughter from the unexpected billboard discovery still lingering faintly in the air. But as her gaze swept across the familiar space, the levity slipped away. The soft glow of antique lamps illuminated the room, revealing a space frozen in time—exactly as Gram had left it.

The warmth of the loft wrapped around her like a comforting embrace, but it couldn't chase away the hollowness of her absence. The walls were alive with Gram's presence, adorned with her vibrant paintings—florals and dioramas, each a treasure in its own right. Cora's eyes landed on a favorite, a floral arrangement in bold strokes, and she could almost hear Gram's voice telling the story behind it. Charlotte O'Clara, her indomitable Gram, had always claimed that art wasn't meant to be confined. She'd spend hours on a canvas only to walk out onto Boughton Street and gift it to the first person who admired it.

Several of Gram's inspired pieces now graced the walls of local businesses, a legacy of generosity and artistry. Cora's gaze lingered on the signature: two intertwined C's, one forward, one backward, encircling an O—the infinity symbol, a mark of permanence in a fleeting world.

For a moment, the loft felt impossibly big, the weight of the past pressing in. But there was no time to dwell. Her friends' voices pulled her back to the present, their laughter weaving its way through the space as they settled in.

MJ wandered in, toeing off his boots and draping himself dramatically over the velvet couch. "Darling, this loft is everything," he said, his voice echoing slightly in the high-ceilinged room. "If you don't turn it into some bohemian paradise, I'll disown you."

Selah scanned the room, her gaze thoughtful as she took in the memories embedded in every corner. She remained standing as Jensen filled the doorway, his broad shoulders slumped at first but relaxing into a light snicker.

Cora let out a small laugh, but her focus was drawn to the corner of the room where a stack of boxes sat, each one carefully labeled in her grandmother's familiar handwriting. She crossed the room and knelt beside the boxes, her fingers trembling as she traced the words on one: *For Cora—When You're Ready.*

MJ sat up, his expression softening. "What's in them?"

"I don't know. I didn't notice these this morning," Cora murmured. "Maybe more journals? The attorney said the four he gave me were just the beginning. The keys were in this one," she added, pointing to the small box off to the right.

She opened the lid of the nearest box. Inside were rows and rows of journals, each bound in leather and adorned with intricate gold embossing. She lifted one, running her fingers over the title: *Read When You Find Solace.* Her breath caught, and for a moment, the room seemed to tilt around her.

MJ moved to her side, peering over her shoulder. "More journals? Are you kidding me right now? This is like some Nicholas Sparks-level shit," he said, though his voice held a rare note of reverence. He reached into the box, pulling out another journal: *Read When You Need Silence.* He let out a low whistle. "Your Gram was a queen. And apparently a prophet."

Cora laughed softly, tears pricking at the corners of her eyes. "She said she wanted me to have these, but I didn't realize there were so many. She spoke about them once or twice." She remembered one Christmas when Gram had wrapped a red leather journal for her, pairing it with a feathered brown pen. The memory softened her, and she exhaled, looking up at the ceiling before returning her gaze to the boxes.

"Well, looks like we've got some reading to do," MJ said, his voice dipping into a teasing drawl. "You want the one about love, or should we start with *Read When You're Aroused as Hell?* Because I'm telling you right now, I'm choosing violence if there's no scandalous content in these."

Cora rolled her eyes, the heat rising in her cheeks. "You're ridiculous."

MJ grinned, unrepentant. "And yet, you adore me. Now, pick a journal. Let's crack open one of Gram's little secret lives."

As Cora thumbed through the stack, her mind wandered to the secrets Gram might have kept. Her grandmother had always been a pillar of strength, but there was so much about her life that Cora didn't know. The journals felt like a doorway into a world she was only beginning to understand.

MJ leaned back on the couch, his legs splayed lazily as he watched her. "You realize this is exactly the kind of shit I live for, right? Drama, secrets, maybe a little scandal... If there's a chapter in here about Gram's torrid love affair with the town's mayor, I'm framing it."

Cora snorted, shaking her head. "You're impossible."

"And you wouldn't have it any other way," MJ replied, winking. His playful smirk softened as he added, "Seriously, though, take your time with these. Your Gram left them for you for a reason."

As Cora clutched the first journal to her chest, a faint chill brushed over her, the kind that came with knowing something monumental was about to begin.

The journal lay open on Cora's lap, its worn pages carrying the faint scent of eucalyptus and something darker, older. The handwriting was elegant, looping in a way that felt familiar yet distant. The title at the top read: *Love is both a haven and a storm. Find the strength to survive both.*

Cora traced the words with her finger, her mind buzzing with questions. What had Gram been thinking when she wrote this? Was it meant for her, or simply a reflection of her own life?

MJ leaned over her shoulder, reading aloud in a dramatic tone. "Ooh, cryptic. I like it. Your Gram was serving fortune cookie realness but make it literary."

They spent the evening sorting through her grandmother's belongings, occasionally pausing to share a laugh or shed a tear over old photos and keepsakes. MJ's humor was a steady balm to Cora's sadness. Every time she'd start to get lost in a memory, he'd pull her back with a joke, his laughter filling the quiet space and making the shop feel alive again.

At one point, MJ found an old photo of her grandmother in her twenties, posing with a sly smile in front of the shop. He held it up with a grin. "She was a knockout! No wonder you turned out so gorgeous. It's clearly in your DNA."

Cora laughed, wiping her eyes as she took the photo from him. "She had this incredible spirit," she murmured, looking at the image fondly. "She wasn't afraid to stand out, to make a statement. I always wanted to be more like her."

MJ nudged her playfully. "Oh, you've got more of her in you than you think, babe. Don't sell yourself short."

As evening descended, they decided to take a break, settling on the window ledge overlooking the cobblestone street below. Cora watched the street grow quiet, the last rays of sunlight casting a warm glow over the buildings. MJ leaned back beside her, stretching his legs, his presence a steady anchor.

"Do you think it'll feel strange, staying here?" she asked, glancing around the loft above the shop where her grandmother had lived for so many years.

MJ shrugged, a small smile tugging at his lips. "Strange? Maybe. But I like strange. Besides, we've got each other. And I call the second-floor loft—I'll be your personal drama queen in residence."

Cora chuckled, grateful for his humor. "I'm not sure this town is ready for you, MJ."

He raised an eyebrow, feigning offense. "Babe, this town doesn't know what it's been missing. I'm here to shake things up."

They laughed, and for a fleeting moment, the weight of her grief felt a little lighter. The future was uncertain, and the loss of her grandmother loomed large, like an empty space in her heart. But with MJ by her side, she felt a spark of hope, a quiet promise that she could begin to rebuild.

The loft felt quieter than usual that night, the kind of quiet that pressed against Cora's chest and made her heart race. MJ had given way to the couch, scrolling through his phone with exaggerated boredom while muttering insults about the town's lack of nightlife. As they sat in silence, Cora's gaze drifted back to the loft window by the fire escape, where a shadow seemed to flicker in the dimming light. She squinted, wondering if it was just her imagination—or something more. A chill crept up her spine, and she glanced over at MJ, who hadn't seemed to notice.

She hesitated, then crossed the room and sank onto the couch next to MJ. He wrapped an arm around her shoulders, pulling her close in a way that was both protective and comforting.

"You're safe," he said softly. "And I'm going to stay here with you. We can rebuild the shop together."

She took a deep breath, her voice softening. "You're seriously giving up the media job in DC for me?"

MJ smirked, pulling her in a little closer. "I didn't want that damn job anyway. Edmon Global must carry on without me."

"You're ridiculous," Cora replied, laughing despite herself.

MJ tilted his head dramatically. "You know, though," he began, his tone playful now, "if this were a horror movie, this would be the part where I strip down to my fabulous lingerie and go investigate the creepy noise."

Cora snorted, the sound breaking through her unease. "You'd make it about five minutes."

A faint sound pulled her from her thoughts—a rustling, like fabric brushing against the doorframe. Her heart stilled as she turned toward the door. For a moment, she considered calling Jensen, but the thought felt irrational. *It's nothing,* she told herself. *Just your imagination.*

Still, after moments of hesitation, she moved cautiously toward the door, her hand hovering over the doorknob. She pressed her ear against the wood, holding her breath as she strained to hear. The sound came again, this time softer, almost deliberate.

Her pulse quickened. "Hello?" she called, her voice trembling slightly.

Silence.

Cora hesitated before turning the lock and cracking the door open. The hallway leading to the steps below and beyond was empty, the faint hum of the building's heater the only sound. She let out a shaky breath, closing and locking the door again.

Back inside, she leaned against the door, her heart still racing. She clutched the journal tighter, the weight of the day's events pressing heavily on her chest. Declan's lingering gaze, the cryptic message, the unsettling sound outside—it all swirled together, leaving her feeling off balance.

Cora set the journal on the table and moved back to the couch, curling up with a throw blanket as she tried to calm her thoughts. The loft felt too quiet now, the shadows too long. She closed her eyes, willing herself to sleep, but the unease stayed with her, coiling tightly in the pit of her stomach.

And somewhere, out in the quiet town, someone was watching.

A Flame Beckons

"Some flames offer warmth; others burn without mercy."

The loft seemed colder the next morning, the sunlight streaming through the windows doing little to dispel the unease that had taken root overnight. Cora stood at the kitchen counter, her hands wrapped tightly around a mug of coffee, seeking warmth that eluded her. The eerie quiet of the loft felt unnatural, the shadows stretching like echoes of the previous night's disquiet. She hadn't slept well—if at all.

Her thoughts were a tangled mess, fraying at the edges with the cryptic journal entry, the unsettling noises she'd convinced herself were nothing, and the lingering weight of Declan's presence. Each thought added a new thread of tension, tightening the knot in her stomach.

The loft creaked softly as the wind pressed against the windows, and Cora's fingers tightened on her mug. The warmth seeped into her palms, grounding her as she heard MJ coming down the hall. Somewhere in the back of her mind, the unease coiled tighter—a quiet reminder that the shadows weren't just outside.

The journals sat untouched on the coffee table, their leather bindings gleaming faintly in the morning light. She had spent most of the night tossing and turning, the words inside the journal she had opened playing on a loop in her mind: *Strength doesn't mean never falling. It means getting back up, even when the world feels too heavy.*

MJ appeared in the doorway, his hair tousled and his usual dramatic flair muted by sleep. "Good morning, Glory," he said, making his way to the coffee pot. He must have noticed the tension in her posture because, as he sat, he patted the space beside him. "Come here. Sit. Breathe."

Cora hesitated before joining him. "Do you think she ever felt this way?" she asked suddenly.

"Who, your Gram?" MJ followed her gaze to the journals. "Felt what way?"

Cora struggled to find the words. "Like... like someone was always watching her. Like the walls were closing in."

MJ frowned, his playful demeanor shifting. "I don't know, babe. But if she did, she handled it like a queen. And so will you."

He reached for the top journal, flipping it open to the first page. The words were written in her grandmother's elegant script: *To my dearest Cora, who will one day find the strength I always knew she had.*

MJ let out a low whistle. "Damn, your Gram knew how to write. Are we sure she wasn't secretly an author?"

Cora smiled faintly, her fingers brushing the edge of the journal. "She always said she'd leave me the answers I needed. I just didn't think it would be like this."

MJ leaned closer, his breath warm against her ear. "Well, if there are any steamy love letters in here, you'd better let me read them first."

Cora rolled her eyes, but her smile grew. For the first time all morning, she felt a flicker of hope. Her hands trembled slightly as she turned the pages of the journal. Each entry was a glimpse into a life she only partially knew, filled with wisdom and heartbreak she couldn't yet fathom. MJ, sitting cross-legged beside her, leaned in closer, his curiosity palpable.

"Love isn't always the answer," MJ read aloud, his voice dropping an octave for dramatic effect. "But it is always worth the risk." He paused, eyebrows raised. "Okay, Gram was a poetic bad bitch. I'm obsessed."

Cora chuckled despite the heaviness in her chest. "She always had a way with words."

"Clearly," MJ said, his gaze scanning the page. "But seriously, this is deep. Like, deeper-than-the-Delaware-River deep. Did she ever talk about her past relationships?"

Cora shook her head, her brow furrowing. "Not really. She was always private about that stuff. But maybe she was trying to tell me something— about love, about life. I just wish I'd asked her more when I had the chance."

MJ reached over, squeezing her knee gently. "Babe, you're doing what you can now. And besides, it's not too late to start asking questions. Maybe the answers are hidden in these pages," he said with a sly grin.

Cora flipped to the next entry; the ink slightly smudged as if written in a rush: *The things we leave unsaid can be the heaviest burdens to carry.*

The words hit her like a punch to the gut, her thoughts immediately drifting to Vinny. She hadn't spoken his name in months, hadn't dared to bring up the memories that still haunted her. But Gram's words seemed to urge her forward, to confront the things she'd buried.

A sharp buzz at the door made her jump, the mug in her hands nearly slipping through her fingers. She set it down carefully and moved toward the door, her heart racing. She relaxed slightly when she heard Selah's voice over the camera speaker, her expression warm but concerned as she buzzed her in.

"Morning," Selah said as Cora opened the door. She stepped inside, her sharp eyes immediately scanning the room. "You look like you didn't sleep."

Cora managed a faint smile, closing the door behind her. "Rough night. Just... a lot on my mind."

Selah placed a hand on her arm, her touch steady. "I checked on flights to Dallas. I haven't booked anything yet. My firm is completely fine with me delaying my start date by a week if you need me to. How are you holding up?"

Cora hesitated, her gaze drifting toward the journals. "It's just... the shop, the journals, everything. It feels like too much all at once."

"You don't have to do it all at once," Selah said gently. "Take it one step at a time. And if you need help, you've got us."

Cora nodded, the tension in her chest easing slightly. "Thanks, Selah. That means a lot."

Selah smiled, her expression softening. "That's what friends are for. Now, how about we tackle some of this together? I'm pretty good at organizing chaos."

Cora laughed softly, the sound breaking through the heaviness in the room. "I'd like that."

As the two of them settled onto the couch, the journals spread out before them, Cora felt a flicker of hope—small but steady. The weight of Gram's secrets still loomed, but with Selah by her side, it felt a little more manageable.

Selah picked up a journal labeled *Read When You Need Clarity*, her fingers brushing over the embossed title. "This one's practically begging to be opened," she said lightly, glancing at Cora with a teasing smile. "Think you're ready for a little clarity?"

Cora paused, her fingers fidgeting with the edge of her sweater. "Not yet," she admitted, her voice soft. "I think I need to sit with all this for a little while longer."

Selah set the journal down gently, her expression understanding. "That's okay. You'll get there. No rush."

The sound of the door buzzer interrupted their conversation, the noise startling both women. Cora exchanged a glance with Selah, her brow furrowed.

"Did you order something?" Selah asked, her voice tinged with curiosity.

Cora shook her head, standing and moving toward the door. The buzz came again, more insistent this time. Her pulse quickened as she checked the camera feed. Through the distorted glass, she could just make out a figure holding a bouquet of flowers.

"It's Declan," she murmured, her voice betraying a mix of surprise and unease. She hesitated for a moment before pressing the intercom. "Hello?"

The figure straightened, and Declan's voice came through, warm and confident. "It's me, Declan Atler. I hope I'm not intruding. I just thought I'd stop by and check in after yesterday."

Cora hesitated, glancing back at Selah, who raised an eyebrow but said nothing. With a deep breath, Cora buzzed him in. "Come on up."

Cora stood by the door, her heart racing as Declan's footsteps echoed up the stairs. When he reached the loft, she opened the door slowly, her voice cautious but polite. "Hi."

"Hi," Declan replied, his smile easy and disarming. "I brought these for you." He held out the bouquet—a beautiful arrangement of chiffon roses, peonies, and baby's breath wrapped in rustic burlap. The colors were soft and warm, a perfect match for the loft's muted tones.

Cora's breath caught as she accepted the flowers, her fingers brushing against his. "Thank you," she said softly, her cheeks flushing. "They're beautiful."

"You're welcome," Declan said, his gaze lingering on her for a moment before shifting to take in the loft. "This place is incredible. The woodwork alone gives it so much character."

Cora smiled faintly, her nerves easing slightly under his praise. "It was my grandmother's. She had an eye for detail."

Declan nodded, his expression thoughtful. "It's clear she poured a lot of love into this place. You're lucky to have something like this—a piece of her to hold onto."

Behind them, Selah cleared her throat pointedly. "Well, Cora, I think that's our cue to head out," she said, her tone light but firm. "Text me if you need anything."

Cora shot her a grateful look. "Thanks, Selah."

Selah smiled as she and MJ brushed past Declan as they left. "Nice meeting you," she said, her tone polite but distant.

As the door clicked shut behind her, an almost tangible silence settled over the room. Cora turned to Declan, still holding the bouquet. "Have a seat," she offered, gesturing toward the small dining table.

Declan moved to the table with easy confidence, his presence commanding but not overbearing. "I didn't mean to interrupt anything," he said, his gaze flicking briefly to the journals scattered on the coffee table. "It looked like you were busy."

"Just... organizing," Cora replied vaguely, setting the bouquet down and searching for a vase. She kept her back to him as she spoke, grounding herself in the simple task. "It's been a lot to process—getting the shop ready, going through Gram's things."

"You're handling it all really well," Declan said, his voice warm and sincere. "Your Gram would be proud."

The words hit Cora unexpectedly, stirring a mix of gratitude and grief. She turned back to him, the vase now holding the flowers. "Thank you," she said softly. "It means a lot to hear that."

They lapsed into a comfortable silence for a moment, the weight of the conversation lingering but not unpleasant. Cora took a seat across from him, her hands clasped in her lap as she struggled to steady her nerves.

"So," Declan said, his voice lightening as he leaned slightly forward. "How are you liking the town so far? Any surprises?"

Cora gave a soft laugh, her shoulders relaxing a fraction. "It's... different," she admitted. "A little quieter than I'm used to, but there's something charming about it."

Declan nodded, his expression thoughtful. "It grows on you. But I can imagine it's a lot to take in, especially with everything you've been juggling."

"It is," Cora said, her voice tinged with honesty. "But I'm getting there."

Declan's gaze lingered on her, his eyes warm and searching. "Have you introduced yourself to the other small business owners on your block? There's a First Friday event coming up. Our hospital always sets up a welcome table on Colfax Court."

Cora met his eyes, something in his tone sparking both curiosity and caution. "I'll keep that in mind," she said carefully.

Another pause stretched between them, not awkward but charged with unspoken thoughts. Finally, Declan broke the silence, his smile returning. "Well, I should let you get back to it," he said, rising to his feet. "But if you ever need anything—whether it's with the shop or just someone to talk to—I'm around."

Cora stood as well, walking him to the door. "Thanks for stopping by," she said, her voice genuine. "And for the flowers. They really are beautiful."

Declan lingered for a moment, his hand resting lightly on the doorknob. "So are you," he said, his tone soft but deliberate.

Cora's cheeks reddened as she tried to process his words. Before she could respond, he gave her a small smile and stepped outside, the door clicking shut behind him.

Cora stood there for a moment, her hand still resting on the doorknob. Declan's presence seemed to linger in the air, his words replaying in her mind. She wasn't sure what to make of him, but one thing was clear—he was unlike anyone she'd ever met.

She turned back to the journals on the coffee table, her gaze settling on the one labeled: *Read When You Feel Conflicted.* With a deep breath, she picked it up, her fingers grazing the leather cover as she flipped it open.

The words on the first page seemed to speak directly to her: *The heart often leads where the mind fears to follow. Trust in your strength, even when the path feels uncertain.*

Cora let out a shaky breath, the weight of the day catching up to her. Declan's arrival, Selah's support, the mysteries of the journals—all of it felt like pieces of a puzzle she was just beginning to understand. For now, all she could do was take it one step at a time.

She set the journal down, her gaze drifting to the window. Outside, the town lay quiet under the fading light of evening, but the unease from the night before hadn't fully left her. Somewhere, in the shadows of this quiet place, something—or someone—was waiting.

Cora sat on the couch, her legs curled beneath her, staring at the journal still open on the coffee table. The soft hum of the heater filled the loft, but the quiet seemed to press against her, amplifying the unease that lingered in her chest.

Her phone buzzed on the coffee table, jolting her from her thoughts. She reached for it, her pulse quickening when she saw the same unknown number flash across the screen. The message was short, almost cryptic:

Be careful who you trust.

She stared at the words, her breath catching. The unease from the night before came rushing back, heavier and more tangible. Her gaze darted around the room, her eyes lingering on the locked door and curtained windows. Everything appeared secure, but the message made her feel exposed, as though unseen eyes were watching her every move.

Her first instinct was to call Jensen, but she hesitated. How could she explain this without sounding paranoid? *It's probably just a prank,* she told herself, though the reasoning felt hollow.

Setting the phone down, she stood and began pacing the room, her thoughts racing. The town's quiet charm was beginning to feel less like serenity and more like a carefully constructed façade. And the message—simple, chilling—seemed to confirm it.

A sharp buzz at the door made her freeze, her heart pounding. She moved cautiously toward the intercom, her hand hovering over the speaker. "Who is it?" she called, her voice trembling slightly.

"It's me," Jensen's familiar voice replied, steady and calm.

The tension in her chest eased slightly, and she quickly buzzed him in. Moments later, Jensen stepped into the loft, his sharp eyes scanning the room as though searching for unseen threats.

"You look like you've seen a ghost," he said, his tone calm but laced with concern.

Cora hesitated, debating how much to tell him. Finally, she handed him her phone, the message still glowing on the screen. "I got this a few minutes ago," she said quietly.

Jensen read the message, his jaw tightening. "Same number as before?"

She nodded, wrapping her arms around herself. "Do you think it's just someone messing with me?"

Jensen's expression darkened, his protective instincts kicking in. "Maybe, but we're not taking any chances. I'll look into it."

Cora exhaled shakily, grateful for his steady presence. Jensen moved to the window, peering out into the darkness. After a moment, he turned back to her, his voice firm but reassuring. "Stay vigilant. If anything else happens, call me immediately. And don't go anywhere alone until we figure this out."

"I won't," Cora promised, her voice barely above a whisper. His conviction grounded her, easing the chaos swirling in her mind.

As Jensen left, promising to keep her updated, Cora locked the door behind him, leaning against it as the weight of the evening pressed down on her. She glanced at the journal still lying open, its words a quiet echo of Jensen's reassurance: *The heart often leads where the mind fears to follow. Trust in your strength, even when the path feels uncertain.*

The loft grew quieter as the night deepened, the shadows stretching across the room with the flicker of the streetlights outside. Cora sat by the window, her knees pulled to her chest, her thoughts tangled with the events of the day. Declan's lingering words, the cryptic message, and the weight of Gram's journals all pressed against her, each demanding her attention.

Her phone buzzed again. She froze, her breath hitching as she reached for it. The screen lit up with another message from the unknown number:

You don't know who's watching.

The words sent a shiver down her spine, her fingers trembling as she locked the phone and placed it face down on the table. She stood, pacing the room as unease coiled tightly in her chest. This wasn't just a prank—it felt deliberate, targeted. And for the first time since arriving in town, she felt genuinely afraid.

Cora grabbed her phone and dialed Jensen's number. He answered on the second ring. "Cora?"

"I got another message," she said quickly, her voice barely above a whisper. "It said, 'You don't know who's watching.'"

There was a pause on the other end before Jensen spoke, his tone firm and steady. "Lock your doors and stay put. I'm coming over."

"Jensen, you don't have to—" she started, but he cut her off.

"I'll be there in ten minutes," he said firmly. "Don't open the door for anyone but me."

The line went dead, leaving Cora standing in the middle of the loft, the weight of his words pressing down on her. She double-checked the locks on the door and windows, her heart pounding in her chest. The silence felt oppressive now, the shadows in the room stretching and twisting with every flicker of light.

She sat back on the couch, her arms wrapped tightly around herself. The journal beside her seemed to beckon, its presence both a comfort and a challenge. With trembling hands, she opened it again, her eyes scanning the page: *Courage doesn't mean the absence of fear. It means facing the unknown, even when fear threatens to consume you.*

The words settled over her like a fragile shield, offering a sliver of strength as she waited. Minutes felt like hours, the quiet ticking of the clock on the wall marking time in agonizing increments.

A sharp buzz at the door shattered the silence, making her jump. She moved cautiously toward her intercom, her heart hammering in her chest. "Jensen?" she called, her voice shaking.

"It's me," he replied, his tone calm but urgent.

She unlocked the door and buzzed him up quickly, relief washing over her when she saw him standing there. Jensen stepped inside, his presence immediately grounding her. He scanned the room with a practiced eye before turning back to her.

"Are you okay?" he asked, his voice softer now. They stood in silence for a moment, her head tilted back as she tried to calm herself.

Cora nodded, though her hands were still trembling. She took a moment to explain. "I don't know what's going on, Jensen. These messages, the noises outside—it's like... it's like someone's trying to mess with me."

"They won't," he said firmly, his jaw tightening. "Whoever this is, we'll find them. I promise." His energy shifted as he reached out and touched her wrists, grounding her from spiraling further.

Cora exhaled shakily, her fear easing slightly under the weight of his conviction. Jensen moved to the window, peering out into the darkness. After a moment, he turned back to her.

"Stay vigilant," he said, his gaze steady. "If anything else happens, call me immediately. And until we figure this out, don't go anywhere alone."

"As long as the street-level door is locked and the fire escape is bolted, no one can get in," Jensen added, his tone steady. "You're safe here."

"Okay," Cora whispered, her voice small but steady.

Jensen's expression softened as he stepped closer. "You're stronger than you think, Cora. Don't let this shake you. Will MJ be back soon?"

His words echoed those in Gram's journal, and for the first time that night, she felt a flicker of hope. "Yes, he and Selah just ran out to the movies. Thank you," she said, her voice firmer now.

As Jensen left, Cora locked the door behind him, leaning against it as the weight of the evening pressed down on her. She glanced at the journal still lying open on the table, its words a quiet reminder of the strength she needed to find.

Outside, the town lay still under the blanket of night, but Cora couldn't shake the feeling that somewhere, in the quiet shadows, someone was watching. The mysteries of Gram's journals, the messages, the strange tension in Declan's gaze—it all felt like fragments of a life she was only beginning to understand.

She sat down in the kitchen, gripping the table for support, her hands frozen in place. She thought about all the times she and Gram sat there, the markings etched into the oak bringing back tender memories.

With a deep breath, she closed the journal and set it aside, her resolve hardening. Whatever was coming, she would face it. She owed that to herself—and to Gram.

Later that evening, the loft felt warmer than usual, the lingering scent of vanilla candles filling the air as Cora stretched out on the couch. MJ was in his room, humming along to a playlist of sultry jazz, leaving her alone with her thoughts—and the persistent memory of Declan.

Her phone buzzed, startling her. She grabbed it from the coffee table, her pulse quickening when she saw the message come through:

It's Declan. Can't stop thinking about you. Coffee tomorrow? 3 PM, Pearson's Coffee House? Or maybe something stronger?

Her breath caught, the simple text igniting a flicker of excitement in her chest as she saved his number on her phone. She knew she shouldn't reply, knew MJ would lecture her for hours if he found out. But her fingers moved almost of their own accord, typing out a response:

I'll think about it.

Not a commitment, but not a refusal either.

She set the phone down, closing her eyes as she tried to steady her racing heart. But her mind betrayed her, conjuring images of his intense gaze, the subtle smirk that hinted at secrets she wasn't sure she wanted to uncover.

Her body ached with a mix of anticipation and frustration, her thoughts spiraling into forbidden territory. She imagined his hands on her, firm and commanding, the heat of his breath against her neck as he whispered things that made her shiver.

"Snap out of it, Cora," she muttered, shaking her head as if it would clear the images.

Just then, MJ's voice called from down the hall. "You better not be texting Mr. Midnight Seduction!"

Cora laughed, though her cheeks burned with guilt. "I'm not!"

"Good," MJ replied, though the sound of footsteps suggested he wasn't convinced.

She sighed, pulling a blanket over herself. But even as she tried to refocus, the phantom touch of Declan's hands lingered, making her wonder if she was already in too deep.

A Fire Rekindled

"Once desire is kindled, it refuses to be extinguished."

The next morning, sunlight filtered through the loft's windows, casting a golden glow across Cora's bare legs as she curled up on the couch, coffee cradled in her hands. Sleep had been elusive, her dreams teasing her with fantasies that felt all too real. Declan's hands lingered in her thoughts—strong, confident, deliberate—and the memory of them against her skin sent a ripple of heat through her body.

She'd texted him, against every ounce of her better judgment, and now his silence sat like a challenge, daring her to wonder if he was as dangerous as he seemed.

From down the hall, MJ shuffled into view, his silk robe gaping slightly to reveal a toned chest. His sharp eyes caught hers immediately, his smirk knowing. "Morning, babe," he drawled, pausing in the doorway like he'd caught her in a guilty act. "You look like someone who spent the night fantasizing about her sexy stalker."

Cora's cheeks flushed, though her lips twitched. "I didn't." The denial sounded weak even to her, and MJ's laugh said he wasn't buying it.

"Uh-huh." He sauntered over, dropping onto the couch beside her, his arm draping lazily across the back. "You can lie to yourself all you want, but you can't lie to me. I saw the way you looked at him last night— like you were ready to let him pin you against the wall and show you what those hands are really capable of."

Heat shot through her, settling low in her stomach, and she buried her face behind her mug. "You're impossible," she muttered, her voice muffled by steam and mortification.

"Impossible? Sure. But wrong? Never." MJ grinned, pulling her phone from her hands.

"MJ!" she protested, lunging for the phone.

"Relax, I'm just scrolling!" he teased, holding it out of her reach. "Ooh, there's his message. Simple, flirty, leaves room for interpretation. Classic bad-boy move. Are you swooning yet?"

Cora snatched the phone back, glaring at him. "I don't need your commentary, thank you."

MJ laughed, flopping back onto the couch. "Alright, fine. But if you're going to do this, do it right. Wear something that screams, 'I'm interested but not desperate.' And for God's sake, make him work for it."

Cora rolled her eyes, though her heart raced at the thought of seeing Declan again.

The morning air was crisp, carrying the scent of pine and freshly brewed coffee as Cora, Selah, and MJ strolled through the outdoor market. Stalls lined the cobblestone streets, bursting with vibrant flowers, handmade jewelry, and freshly baked goods.

"I swear, this town was made for Pinterest," MJ quipped, adjusting his scarf dramatically.

Cora chuckled, her mood lighter than it had been in days. "You're impossible."

"Impossibly fabulous," he corrected, flashing her a grin.

As they stopped at a booth displaying delicate silver necklaces, a deep voice cut through the chatter behind them. "Excuse me, but the silver necklace with the brown jasper stone would certainly match those deep honey-colored eyes of yours."

Cora turned, startled to see Declan standing a few feet away. His dark, slightly tousled hair and piercing blue eyes seemed to see straight through her. He exuded confidence, his fitted leather jacket hinting at an edge beneath the charm.

"Oh?" she said hesitantly, tucking a strand of hair behind her ear.

He smiled, the corners of his mouth quirking up in a way that felt both disarming and dangerous.

MJ, who had been watching silently, stepped forward, his expression unreadable. "Girl, I just saw that billboard. Now, I am smitten," he whispered, his tone light but with an unmistakable edge.

Declan's gaze flickered briefly to MJ before settling back on Cora. He stepped closer, his presence magnetic yet unsettling, his voice calm but deliberate. "This market is one of my favorite parts of Pine Brook. The handcrafted treasures, the energy—it's a passion of mine." He turned back to Cora. "And it's even better now."

Cora felt the heat rise in her cheeks at the compliment, her mind scrambling for a response. "Well, I hope you enjoy your day. It really is a beautiful place."

"It's getting better by the minute," Declan replied, his tone low and warm.

MJ cleared his throat, breaking the moment. "Cora, didn't we have to check out that pottery stall over there?"

Cora blinked, snapping out of her daze. "Right. Yes. Nice seeing you again, Declan."

"The pleasure's all mine," Declan said, his gaze lingering on her as they walked away.

As soon as they were out of earshot, MJ grabbed her arm. "Red flag. Huge, waving, flaming red flag," he whispered urgently.

"MJ," Cora said, exasperated. "He was just being nice."

"Nice? Babe, that man wasn't just being nice. He was being a walking, talking rom-com villain," MJ declared, tossing his straw bag dramatically over his shoulder.

Selah interjected, her tone even. "He seemed harmless, MJ." She examined a silk scarf with vibrant colors of blues and golds, seemingly unbothered.

"Harmless?" MJ scoffed. "He's practically dripping with 'I have a dark secret and a mysterious past' vibes. And let's not forget the leather jacket."

Cora chuckled softly, though she couldn't deny the strange pull she felt toward Declan. His presence lingered in her thoughts long after they left the market.

By the time they returned to the shop, the morning's encounter had settled into the back of Cora's mind, a faint hum of curiosity she couldn't quite shake.

MJ, however, was less inclined to let it go. "I'm telling you, babe, that man radiates 'complicated.' If he so much as looks at you again, I'm breaking out the mace."

Cora laughed, unlocking the shop door. "You're being dramatic."

"Am I?" MJ countered, following her inside. "Look, I get it. He's tall, dark, and brooding. But trust me, those types come with warning labels."

Inside the shop, the air was cool and still, the faint scent of lavender lingering from a diffuser on the counter. Cora flicked on the lights, illuminating racks of dresses and vintage lace gowns. The inventory was a mix of old and new—a blend of timeless elegance and modern trends.

Cora worked methodically, organizing dresses by style and size, but her thoughts kept drifting back to Declan. His piercing gaze, the way his voice seemed to wrap around her—it was magnetic, yet unsettling.

The bell above the door jingled, cutting through the quiet hum of Cora's thoughts. She glanced up, her heart skipping a beat when she saw Declan standing in the doorway. His expression was casual, but there was a confidence in the way he carried himself that made her pulse quicken.

"Hope I'm not interrupting," he said, his voice smooth as his gaze swept over the shop.

MJ, who had been perched on a stool with a clipboard in hand, froze mid-note. His eyes narrowed as he took in Declan's presence. "You again," he muttered under his breath.

Cora sucked in a breath, trying to steady herself. She quickly stepped forward, forcing a polite smile. "Declan. What brings you here?"

"I was in the area," he replied, his gaze lingering on her for a moment longer than necessary. "Thought I'd stop by and see what all the fuss is about."

Her cheeks flushed as she struggled to think of a response. "We're not officially open yet, but feel free to look around," she said, gesturing toward the racks of dresses.

Declan's lips curved into a faint smile as he stepped further into the shop. "It's... charming. Feels like a place with history." His tone was warm, but there was an edge to his words that made Cora's stomach flutter with unease.

MJ, clearly unimpressed, cleared his throat loudly. "Cora's grandmother built this place. Every inch of it has her touch."

Declan nodded, his attention shifting back to Cora. "You must be proud to carry on her legacy."

Cora hesitated, unsure how to respond. "I'm just trying to figure it all out," she admitted, her voice quieter than she intended.

"You'll figure it out," Declan said, his tone steady. "It's a big responsibility, but I can tell you're up for it."

MJ rolled his eyes so dramatically Cora was surprised they didn't get stuck. "Well, thanks for stopping by," he said, his tone dripping with faux politeness. "Don't let the door hit you on the way out."

Declan chuckled softly, clearly amused by MJ's hostility. "I'll take that as my cue." He turned to Cora, his gaze softening. "It was nice seeing you again. I'll be around if you ever need anything."

Cora nodded, her throat tight as she watched him leave. The bell jingled softly as the door closed behind him, leaving an almost palpable silence in his wake.

"Babe," MJ said, spinning to face her. "I am begging you—don't fall for this guy. He's practically wearing a neon sign that says 'danger.'"

"He's just being friendly," Cora insisted, though her heart was still racing.

"Friendly?" MJ raised an eyebrow, leaning against the counter. "That man is plotting how to make you the next headline in a true-crime podcast."

Cora laughed despite herself, but the truth was, Declan's presence had left her both intrigued and uneasy.

The afternoon sun cast long rays through the shop's windows, illuminating dust motes that danced lazily in the air. Cora stood at the counter, her hands gripping the edge as she stared at the rest of the day's to-do list.

"Alright, Cinderella, let's make some magic happen!" MJ burst through the back door, a large roll of fabric in one arm and a paint swatch booklet in the other.

Cora raised an eyebrow. "You've been busy."

"You know me," MJ quipped. "Always ten steps ahead of fabulous."

He unrolled the fabric on the counter with a flourish. "Voila! I'm thinking drapes for the fitting rooms—something dramatic, yet tasteful. Thoughts?"

Cora smiled faintly, shaking her head. "MJ, I love you, but can we take this one step at a time?"

"Fine," he relented, though his grin didn't waver. "But only because I know you secretly love my vision."

As MJ busied himself in the back of the shop, Cora took a moment to wander through the aisles. She found herself drawn to the small display in the corner, where her grandmother had always showcased her favorite pieces.

One dress in particular caught her eye—a vintage lace gown with delicate beadwork along the bodice. It was one of Gram's earliest creations, and seeing it now filled Cora with a strange mix of pride and longing. Her fingers grazed the fabric, and for a brief moment, it felt like Gram was there with her, guiding her.

As they locked up the shop and headed upstairs to the loft with her invoice binder, the unease hadn't faded. Cora double-checked the locks on the doors and windows, her movements careful and deliberate.

"You okay?" MJ asked, leaning against the kitchen counter as she secured the last latch.

"Yeah," she lied, though her chest felt tight. "Just... paranoid, I guess."

MJ walked over, placing a reassuring hand on her shoulder. "You're safe here, babe. No one's getting past me."

She smiled faintly, grateful for his unwavering support.

That afternoon, the loft felt quieter than usual. Cora sat at the kitchen table, flipping through one of her grandmother's old recipe books, though her mind wasn't on the pages in front of her.

"Alright," MJ said, breaking the silence as he emerged from his room in his silk robe and fuzzy slippers, his hair wrapped in a towel turban. "We need to talk."

Cora glanced up, arching an eyebrow. "About?"

"Declan," MJ said dramatically, pouring himself a glass of wine and sliding into the seat across from her. "That man is trouble, and you know it."

Cora sighed, leaning back in her chair. "You're reading too much into this. He's just being nice."

MJ snorted. "Nice doesn't look at you like he's mentally undressing you, babe. I've seen that look before, and trust me, it's not about making friends."

A flush crept up Cora's neck at the memory of Declan's lingering gaze. She didn't want to admit it, but MJ wasn't entirely wrong. There had been a charge in the air between them, something unspoken but undeniably there.

"He's intense, I'll give you that," she said cautiously.

MJ smirked knowingly. "Intense is putting it mildly. That man wants to set you on fire."

Cora rolled her eyes, though her pulse quickened at the thought. "I'm not interested in setting anything on fire, thank you very much."

"Liar," MJ teased, swirling his wine. "You're curious, and curiosity is the first step toward bad decisions. Coffee date or no coffee date?"

Cora laughed despite herself, throwing a crumpled napkin at him. But later, as she tussled through vendor invoices for the bridal shop, her mind wandered back to Declan—the way his voice seemed to wrap around her, the way his eyes lingered just a second too long.

A Heart Scorched

"Love can burn as brightly as it consumes."

By late afternoon, the invoices lay forgotten on the counter, replaced by the nervous energy coursing through Cora as she found herself at the café. She sat by the window, fingers absently tracing the rim of her latte mug, her reflection faintly visible in the glass. The fitted blouse she'd chosen clung to her just right, and her dark jeans hugged her curves, giving her a confidence she hadn't realized she needed—confidence she'd need if she was going to sit across from Declan without giving away how deeply he unsettled her.

She glanced at the door, her nerves tightening with every second it remained closed. Her heart drummed a steady beat, anticipation coiling in her chest with every glance at her phone's clock. Would he show? Would she regret it if he didn't?

Finally, the door swung open, and the cool air from outside swept into the café along with him. Declan's presence was magnetic, his eyes scanning the room with purpose until they locked on hers. The smile that spread across his face sent a rush of warmth through her, and her stomach flipped in response, betraying the calm façade she'd tried so hard to maintain.

He moved toward her with the kind of ease that commanded attention, his shirt clinging to his frame in a way that left little to the imagination. The faint, intoxicating hint of his cologne trailed him as he stopped in front of her table, his gaze never wavering.

"Cora," he said, his voice low and smooth, wrapping around her name like a velvet ribbon. "I hope I didn't keep you waiting."

For a moment, she couldn't find her words. He was stunning—more than she remembered—and his presence filled the small space between them, amplifying the tension she'd tried to push aside.

"No," she managed, a slight tremor in her voice. "You're right on time."

Declan slid into the chair across from her, his movements fluid and deliberate. Even in the casual setting, his presence commanded the room. "I wasn't sure you'd say yes," he admitted, his gaze locking with hers.

"Well, I like to keep people guessing," she replied, surprising herself with the boldness in her tone.

Declan chuckled, the sound rich and intoxicating. "I can respect that."

The aroma of freshly roasted coffee filled the room, mingling with the quiet hum of conversations around them. As they talked, Cora found herself drawn in by his charm. He spoke with confidence, his words carefully chosen, but there was an underlying edge to him—a dangerous allure that made her pulse race.

At one point, his fingers brushed hers on the table, lingering just long enough to send a jolt through her body. She glanced up to find him watching her, his blue eyes dark with intent.

"Careful," he murmured, his voice dropping to a near whisper. "You might make me think this is more than just coffee."

Her cheeks flushed as Declan's words hung in the air between them, heavy and charged. She dropped her gaze to her coffee, struggling to steady her racing heart.

"Maybe it's more than just coffee," she said softly, barely recognizing the boldness in her own voice.

Declan leaned back slightly, his lips curving into a slow, deliberate smile. "I like your honesty."

The tension between them was palpable, each glance and subtle shift in posture feeding the fire growing between them. Cora couldn't help but notice the way his fingers drummed lightly on the table, the controlled energy behind every movement.

"So, tell me," he said, his voice dropping a note lower. "What else brings you back to this town? It doesn't seem like the kind of place you'd choose willingly."

Cora hesitated, the weight of her grandmother's memory settling over her. "Family," she said simply, her fingers tracing the edge of her cup. "It was her shop, her home. My home. I grew up here before I left for college. I'm just trying to figure out what to do with it all."

Declan's gaze softened, though the intensity didn't waver. "It's a lot to take on. But from what I've seen, you're more than capable."

The compliment sent a flutter through Cora's chest, and she glanced up to find him watching her intently. His eyes seemed to hold unspoken promises—a mixture of understanding and something darker, something thrilling.

"Thank you," she murmured, feeling the heat in her cheeks deepen.

Declan reached across the table, his fingers brushing hers once more. "Sometimes, stepping into the unknown is the only way to find where you truly belong." The warmth of his touch spread through her like wildfire, and for a moment, she forgot to breathe.

The café seemed to shrink around them, the world outside fading into the background. Declan's presence was magnetic, his voice like velvet as he continued to draw her in.

"Tell me something," he said, his tone softer now, almost intimate. "What's keeping you here? Is it just obligation, or is there something else?"

Cora hesitated, her mind flashing to the loft, her grandmother's journal, and the lingering sense of unease she hadn't been able to shake since returning. "I'm not sure yet," she admitted. "There's a lot I haven't figured out."

Declan nodded, his expression thoughtful. "Sometimes the answers come when you least expect them. And sometimes... they come from the most unexpected places."

His words carried an undercurrent of something deeper, something that made her heart race and her skin tingle. She opened her mouth to respond, but the words caught in her throat when he leaned forward, his hand resting lightly on hers.

"Cora," he said, his voice a low murmur that sent shivers down her spine. "I know we just met, but I can't shake the feeling that there's something here. Something worth exploring."

A gasp escaped her lips, her thoughts swirling in a chaotic mix of desire and doubt. "Declan, I don't even know you," she said, her voice trembling slightly.

"Then let's fix that," he replied, his lips curving into a smirk that was equal parts charm and danger. "Let me show you who I am."

The weight of his words settled over her, and for a moment, she felt herself leaning into the heat of his gaze, the promise of something she couldn't quite name.

The sound of a chair scraping nearby broke the spell, and Cora pulled her hand away, her cheeks burning. "I should go," she said quickly, standing and grabbing her bag.

Declan didn't stop her, but his eyes followed her every movement. "I'll see you again, Cora," he said, his voice a quiet promise.

The cool evening air greeted Cora as she stepped out of the café, her thoughts racing faster than her feet could carry her. Declan's words echoed in her mind, stirring emotions she wasn't ready to name. She reached her car and gripped the steering wheel for a moment, her chest rising and falling as she tried to calm the storm within her.

The door swung open abruptly as MJ slid into the passenger seat, his arms laden with shopping bags and his expression immediately suspicious. "Spill," he demanded, slamming the door shut behind him.

Cora jumped, startled by his sudden arrival. "Jesus, MJ, give me a second to breathe!"

"No time for breathing. I saw you leave the café looking like you'd just walked out of a romance novel. So, what happened? Did he ask to run his hands through your hair or, better yet, tie you up and—"

"MJ!" Cora's cheeks burned as she swatted his arm.

He cackled, leaning back in the seat. "Oh, honey, I knew it. That man's got you twisted, hasn't he? Girl, you need to form a safe word and NOW!"

Cora didn't answer, which only made MJ's grin widen.

"Alright, let me guess. He said something smooth, touched your hand, and now you're imagining him showing up at the shop after hours for a little... private fitting?"

Cora covered her face with her hands, groaning. "You really are utterly impossible."

"Impossible and accurate," MJ said smugly. "Seriously, though, what's your plan? Are you going to keep playing coy, or are you actually thinking about seeing him again?"

Cora hesitated, the memory of Declan's smirk making her stomach flutter. "I don't know, MJ. He's... complicated."

"Complicated is just a nice way of saying 'bad idea,'" MJ shot back, his tone sharp but affectionate. "Look, I get it. He's hot, he's mysterious, and he probably smells like leather and sin. But you've got to be careful, babe. Guys like him don't just walk into your life without leaving a mess."

Cora sighed, leaning her head back against the seat. "You think I don't know that? I'm not blind, MJ. I can feel the red flags waving in my face. But... there's something about him."

MJ's expression softened slightly, though his concern remained. "I get it. Sometimes the heart wants what the brain knows is stupid. But promise me you'll at least think about it before you jump in headfirst."

She nodded, her lips pressing into a thin line. "I will. I promise."

Satisfied for the moment, MJ reached over and patted her knee. "Good. Now, let's get back to it. Then, I need to shower and mentally prepare for the inevitable drama this man is going to bring into our lives."

As the late afternoon progressed, they threw themselves into work, reorganizing the shop and brainstorming ideas for a soft reopening. Cora appreciated the distraction, though her thoughts continued to drift back to Declan.

"Alright, enough work," MJ announced, clapping his hands together. "Time for dinner. My treat."

Cora raised an eyebrow. "Your treat? What's the occasion?"

MJ smirked. "Celebrating our survival. Plus, I need to scope out the town's dining options. A queen has standards, you know." His dramatic flair pulled a laugh from her, and for the first time that day, she felt a little lighter.

As they locked up the shop and stepped outside, the fresh air filled her lungs. But as they walked toward MJ's car, Cora couldn't shake the feeling that someone was watching from the shadows. She glanced back, her heart pounding. The street was empty.

For now.

Dinner with MJ was a welcome distraction, but the unease never left Cora entirely. The diner was cozy, filled with the chatter of locals and the comforting aroma of fresh coffee.

MJ leaned back in the booth, sipping a strawberry milkshake. "Alright, so the shop? A work in progress. The loft? Cozy, but definitely needs some personal touches. And you?" He pointed his straw at her. "Still too damn tense."

Cora smiled faintly, stirring her coffee. "I'm fine."

"Liar." MJ's tone was teasing, but his eyes were serious. "You've been a bundle of nerves since we got here. Talk to me, babe. What's going on?"

She hesitated, her fingers curling around her mug. "I just... I feel like something's off. Like someone's watching me."

MJ frowned, setting his milkshake down. "You think it's something to do with Gram?"

"I don't know," Cora admitted. "Maybe. Or maybe I'm just paranoid. I've been on edge since Gram died. It's probably nothing."

MJ reached across the table, giving her hand a reassuring squeeze. "Whatever it is, we'll handle it."

Cora nodded, grateful for his support. But as they paid their bill and stepped out into the evening sunlight, the uneasy feeling returned. The street was quiet, the small-town charm almost too perfect.

As they walked toward the car, Cora's eyes scanned the surroundings, searching for something—anything—that might explain the gnawing sense of dread.

And then she saw it.

A figure stood across the street, partially obscured by the shadows of an alleyway. Their face was hidden, but their posture was unmistakable: rigid, watching, waiting.

Cora's breath hitched. "MJ," she whispered, her voice barely audible.

"What is it?" MJ followed her gaze, his expression shifting from casual to alert.

The figure didn't move, their presence a stark contrast to the idyllic surroundings. Cora felt frozen, her feet rooted to the spot.

"Stay here," MJ said firmly, starting to step off the curb.

"No!" Cora grabbed his arm, her voice sharp. "Don't. Let's just go."

MJ hesitated, his jaw tightening. "Cora—"

"Please," she insisted, her eyes pleading with him.

He relented, guiding her toward the car. But even as they climbed inside and drove away, Cora couldn't stop glancing at the rearview mirror.

The figure was gone.

Back at the loft, the tension between them was noticeable. MJ paced the living room, his usual humor replaced with frustration. "You can't ignore this, Cora. If someone's stalking you, we need to go to the police."

Cora shook her head, her arms wrapped tightly around herself. "And tell them what? That I think someone's watching me?"

MJ stopped pacing, his expression softening. "Babe, you don't have to have all the answers. But you can't keep pretending nothing's wrong."

She looked away, her thoughts spiraling. "I just... I need time to figure this out."

"Alright," MJ said, his tone reluctant. "But promise me one thing. If it happens again—anything—you tell me immediately."

Cora nodded, though the uneasy feeling in her chest didn't ease.

As they drove through the quiet streets, her mind kept drifting back to Declan. His voice, his touch, the unspoken intensity that seemed to linger in the air between them—it all felt too much and not enough at the same time.

The weather in Pine Brook had become unpredictable, spring snow flurries had begun to grace the windshield as they drove in silence, both lost in thought.

Later that night, as she lay in bed, her body restless against the sheets, Cora found herself reaching for her phone. Her fingers hovered over the screen, her heart pounding as she debated whether to text him.

Her thumb brushed the edge of the keyboard, but before she could type a word, she set the phone aside, turning over with a frustrated sigh. Sleep didn't come easily, and when it did, it was filled with dreams of dark eyes, rough hands, and whispered promises she wasn't sure she wanted to keep.

A Truth Revealed

"Truth often lies hidden in the shadows, waiting for the lights to uncover it."

The next morning, the shop was alive with the hum of activity, but even the bustle couldn't drown out the thoughts swirling in Cora's mind. She adjusted mannequins, rearranged displays, and flipped through inventory lists, her hands moving with purpose while her thoughts betrayed her. She could still feel the heat of Declan's gaze, the weight of dreams she hadn't invited but couldn't shake.

She exhaled sharply, pressing her palms to the counter as if grounding herself in the present. *Work,* she thought. *Work was the solution.* But no amount of tasks could keep her from replaying the sound of his voice—low, smooth, wrapping around her name like a caress.

"Oh, dear God, that man is captivating," she muttered under her breath before snapping her focus back to the display she was rearranging.

MJ, of course, wasn't about to let her off the hook. "You're awfully quiet today," he remarked, his voice teasing as he perched on the counter with an iced coffee in hand, the cup sweating onto the glossy surface. "Thinking about someone?"

Cora froze mid-motion, the mannequin's sash slipping through her fingers. "No," she said, a little too quickly, her voice betraying her.

MJ's smirk widened, his eyes narrowing knowingly. "Liar," he sang, swirling the straw in his drink. "I just came back from the cutest coffee shop across the street, and let me tell you, even their mochas aren't as sweet as the look you're trying to hide right now."

Cora's face flushed, her hands moving faster as she adjusted the sash with unnecessary precision. "You're impossible," she muttered, but MJ wasn't about to be distracted.

"Oh, I'm very possible," he quipped, leaning closer. "But you know what's impossible? Pretending that your head isn't full of one very sexy surgeon."

Before Cora could respond, the bell above the door jingled. She looked up, her breath catching when she saw him.

Declan stepped inside, his leather jacket slung over one shoulder and a confident smirk on his lips. "Busy day?" he asked, his voice as smooth as ever.

Cora straightened, trying to mask the flutter in her chest. "Getting by," she replied, her tone casual as she fiddled with a display.

MJ slid off the counter, crossing his arms. "Oh, look. It's the walking distraction. Don't you have a massive surgery to perform?"

Declan chuckled, his gaze flicking to MJ. "Nice to see you too."

Cora shot MJ a warning look, but he ignored it, moving to stand protectively beside her. "What brings you by, Declan? Another coffee invitation?"

"Actually," Declan said, his eyes locking with Cora's, "I wanted to see if you'd join me for dinner tonight."

The question hung in the air, and for a moment, Cora forgot how to breathe. She adjusted her belt nervously, her hands fidgeting as she avoided his gaze.

MJ scoffed loudly, breaking the spell. "Wow. Straight to dinner. Bold move, Leather Jacket."

Declan smiled, unbothered. "Think about it. I'll be at Le Verve at eight. If you decide to come, the invitation's open."

As Declan turned to leave, MJ muttered under his breath, "The audacity."

When the door closed behind him, MJ whirled around to face Cora. "Please tell me you're not actually considering this," he begged, setting his coffee down with a thud.

"It's just dinner," Cora said, though her voice lacked conviction. Declan's scent lingered in the room—a mix of woodsy cologne with a faint citrus edge.

"Babe," MJ said, pinching the bridge of his nose. "Dinner with that man isn't *just dinner*. It's the prelude to every bad decision ever made."

Cora sighed, leaning against the counter. "I don't know, MJ. There's something about him... he makes me feel..."

"Like a moth to a flame?" MJ interrupted, his tone exasperated.

"Alive," Cora finished, her voice barely above a whisper.

MJ's expression softened, though his concern was still evident. "Cora, I get it. He's exciting. Dangerous. But you've been through so much already. Are you sure this is what you need right now?"

Cora didn't answer. She wasn't sure of anything anymore. That evening, as she stood in front of her closet, her heart raced with indecision. She pulled out a sleek black dress, the kind that clung in all the right places, and held it up against herself.

"What are you doing?" she muttered, shaking her head as if trying to snap herself out of a daze.

But the pull was undeniable. Declan's voice, his touch, the way he looked at her—it was a siren song she couldn't resist.

At exactly 7:45, she grabbed her coat and stepped out into the crisp night air. Her heels clicked against the pavement as she walked to her car, each step echoing her conflicted thoughts. By the time she reached the restaurant, her nerves were frayed. She hesitated outside, her hand hovering over the door handle.

Through the glass, she saw him seated at a corner table, his eyes already fixed on her as if he'd known she would come.

Declan rose as she entered, his broad shoulders cutting an imposing figure. "You came," he said, his voice low and warm.

"You made it hard to say no," Cora replied, offering a small smile as she slid into the seat across from him.

Le Verve exuded elegance, with its low lighting, plush seating, and the faint hum of soft jazz. Cora felt slightly underdressed, though the way Declan's gaze swept over her erased any self-consciousness.

Declan signaled the waiter, who appeared instantly to pour them wine. "I took the liberty of ordering something special," he said, his tone carrying that effortless confidence that both irritated and intrigued her.

"Bold of you," she teased, though her stomach flipped as their eyes met.

Declan smirked, leaning forward slightly. "I get the feeling you like bold."

Her cheeks warmed, and she reached for her wine glass to cover her reaction. "So," she said, steering the conversation to safer ground, "what made you choose this place?"

"I thought it suited the occasion," he replied, his gaze lingering on her lips. "Besides, I wanted somewhere intimate. Somewhere I could get to know you without distractions."

Cora's breath hitched at the way his voice dipped, each word carefully measured and charged with intent. She knew she should feel wary, yet she couldn't deny the way her body reacted to him—heat pooling low in her stomach, her skin prickling with awareness.

As the waiter placed their plates on the table, Declan's fingers brushed hers under the tablecloth. The subtle touch sent a jolt through her, her heart racing as his hand lingered, warm and steady.

"Relax," he murmured, his lips curving into a teasing smile. "It's just dinner."

But it didn't feel like just dinner. Every glance, every movement carried an undercurrent of something deeper, something unspoken yet impossible to ignore.

"Tell me something," Declan said, his tone conversational but his gaze intense. "What's your biggest fear?"

The question caught her off guard. She set down her fork, her brows knitting together. "That's... a bit personal for a first dinner."

Declan chuckled, his fingers toying with the stem of his wine glass. "Fair enough. Let me start, then." He leaned back slightly, his expression unreadable. "I'm afraid of being forgotten. Of leaving nothing behind."

His honesty surprised her, and for a moment, the mask of confidence he wore slipped, revealing a vulnerability that tugged at something inside her.

"What about you?" he pressed gently.

Cora hesitated, her fingers curling around her glass. "I guess... I'm afraid of failure. Of not being enough."

Declan's gaze softened, his hand reaching across the table to rest lightly on hers. "You're more than enough, Cora. You just don't see it yet."

Her breath caught, her pulse hammering as his thumb brushed over her knuckles. The intimacy of the moment made her dizzy, the restaurant around them fading into the background.

"Declan..." she began, her voice trembling slightly.

"Shh," he murmured, his eyes darkening as they locked with hers. "You don't have to say anything."

His hand lingered, his touch a promise of things unsaid, and for the first time in a long time, Cora felt herself wanting to let go.

The tension between them was electric, filling the space between their joined hands. Cora's mind screamed at her to pull away, to maintain a sense of control, but her body betrayed her, leaning into the warmth of Declan's touch.

"Tell me more about yourself," Declan said, his voice a low murmur that sent shivers down her spine. "What keeps you up at night, Cora?"

The question was simple, but the way he asked it made her stomach flip. "Lately?" she replied, forcing herself to sound casual. "Packing up my grandmother's life, trying to figure out what comes next."

Declan's thumb brushed over her knuckles, a small but deliberate motion that made her skin tingle. "You're doing something incredible," he said, his gaze unwavering. "Most people would crumble under the weight of that, but you... you're still standing."

His words hit a nerve, unearthing emotions Cora hadn't even realized she'd buried. She looked away, her throat tightening. "I don't feel strong," she admitted, her voice barely above a whisper.

"You don't have to," Declan said, his voice soft but firm. "You just have to keep going."

The intensity of the moment was broken by the waiter returning to clear their plates, and Cora took the opportunity to pull her hand away, her cheeks burning.

As the waiter left, Declan leaned back, his smirk returning. "I didn't mean to get so serious," he said, his tone lighter now. "But I meant what I said. You're impressive, Cora."

She didn't know how to respond, so she settled for a small smile. But as their eyes met again, she felt the pull of him stronger than ever, a force that both excited and terrified her.

As the evening wore on, Declan continued to peel back Cora's layers with his questions, each one drawing her further into his orbit. He had a way of making her feel seen, but it was the kind of gaze that made her question what he was really looking for.

"Why do I feel like you're studying me?" she asked at one point, her voice tinged with both curiosity and unease.

Declan chuckled, the sound low and rich. "Maybe I am," he admitted, his lips curving into a smirk. "Or maybe I just can't help myself."

The weight of his words hung in the air, and Cora felt her pulse quicken. She reached for her wine, the liquid warmth doing little to steady her nerves.

"What about you?" she asked, trying to shift the focus. "What keeps you up at night?"

Declan's smirk faded, replaced by something more serious. "A lot of things," he said after a moment. "Mistakes I've made. People I've hurt. Things I can't take back."

The honesty in his voice surprised her, and she found herself leaning forward. "Do you regret them?"

"Some," he replied, his gaze dropping to his hands. "But others... I think they were necessary. Sometimes you have to hurt to grow."

Cora nodded, her heart twisting at the vulnerability in his words. She wanted to ask more, to understand him better, but the look in his eyes stopped her. There was a depth there, a darkness she wasn't sure she wanted to uncover.

"I should go," she said suddenly, the words tumbling out before she could stop them.

Declan leaned back, his expression unreadable. "If that's what you want," he said, his tone neutral.

But as she stood to leave, his fingers brushed her wrist, a soft, lingering touch that sent a shiver down her spine. "Goodnight, Cora," he murmured, his voice like a promise.

The loft was quiet as Cora finally retreated to her room, the weight of the evening pressing down on her like a heavy blanket. She changed into a loose tank top and shorts, her movements mechanical as her mind raced with thoughts of Declan.

Her phone buzzed on the nightstand, breaking the silence. She hesitated, her heart pounding as she reached for it. It was Declan.

Goodnight, Cora. I meant every word tonight. You're extraordinary.

Her fingers hovered over the keyboard, her chest tightening as she debated whether to respond. Before she could decide, another message appeared.

Sweet dreams. I'll be seeing you.

The words sent a shiver down her spine, both thrilling and unsettling. She set the phone down, her hand trembling slightly as she lay back against the pillows. The soft glow of the bedside lamp cast shadows on the walls, but even in the warm light, she couldn't shake the feeling that she wasn't alone.

A faint creak echoed from the living room, and she sat up abruptly, her pulse spiking. "MJ?" she called out, her voice unsteady.

No response.

She slid out of bed, her bare feet padding softly against the wooden floor as she moved toward the door. The loft was dark, the faint hum of the refrigerator the only sound.

Her breath caught as she spotted a shadow near the fire escape window—a silhouette that didn't belong.

The figure moved slightly, and her blood ran cold.

"Who's there?" she whispered, her voice barely audible over the pounding of her heart.

The shadow didn't answer. Instead, it lingered for a moment longer before disappearing into the night, leaving behind a single thought that screamed in her mind:

She wasn't safe. Not anymore.

A Wound Exposed

"Some scars ache not from the wound, but from the memory of its creation."

Cora woke with the unease of the night still clinging to her. The loft was quiet in the light of morning, but the memory of the shadow near the window lingered, her skin prickling as though it hadn't left. She pushed the thought aside as best she could—there was too much to do at the shop to let her imagination run wild.

The Bridal Shop had become her haven, a space where routine kept her grounded. Selah and Jensen had settled into Dallas, their calls and texts a comforting reminder that they were thriving. Meanwhile, MJ was her anchor, his energy a welcome distraction as she poured herself into the upcoming grand opening.

That morning, as sunlight spilled into the shop, Declan had stopped by unexpectedly. His presence filled the room as he casually invited her and MJ to his estate for a poolside barbecue on Sunday. The invitation had been simple, but something about the way his gaze lingered on her made the air feel charged.

Memories of Gram drifted in and out as Cora leaned against the counter. The quiet shop seemed to echo with the stretch of days until the weekend. Sunday felt far away—too far—and Declan's visit had left a hum of anticipation she couldn't quite shake.

She was lost in thought when MJ sauntered over, snapping her back to the present with his signature dramatic flair.

"I'm ordering takeout tonight," MJ announced, pulling a water bottle from his bag and taking a long sip. "Pizza and margaritas in a can from Potzy's next door. And then—I'm taking a glorious bubble bath in your Gram's clawfoot tub. Don't bother me unless it's an emergency."

Cora gave him a once-over, raising a skeptical brow. "Bubble bath? You've got all the luxury in the world, and you're swooning over canned margaritas and my Gram's tub?"

MJ smirked, tossing the water bottle cap onto the counter. "Babe, luxury is all about the vibe. And Potzy's margaritas? Total vibe."

Cora laughed softly, shaking her head. But as MJ prattled on about bath salts and playlist options, her mind drifted back to Declan. His smile, his invitation, the way he seemed to fill every inch of space around him. She thought about him far more than she wanted to admit, and with Sunday still days away, she wasn't sure how she'd keep herself from falling deeper into the pull of him.

"Cora, have you completely lost your mind?" MJ exploded, throwing his hands in the air as he began pacing the room like a thunderstorm on the verge of breaking. "Why does this feel like a 'Swimwear Optional' kind of invite? Are we seriously letting Dr. Midnight Seduction strut into our lives and sweep you off your feet like some bad rom-com cliché?"

He paused mid-step, turning to her with a pointed look. "And don't you dare tell me it's 'just a barbecue.' We both know it's never just anything with a man like him."

Cora rolled her eyes, though she couldn't quite suppress the heat rising in her cheeks. "It's just a casual invitation, MJ. Relax."

"Relax?" MJ threw back, clutching his chest theatrically. "This is how it starts, babe. First, he gets you to show up in a bikini that barely covers your dignity. Next, he's leaning against the edge of a pool, whispering sweet nothings while you forget how to string two coherent thoughts together. And before you know it—bam! You're head over heels, and I'm stuck cleaning up the emotional debris."

Cora sank into a chair, her head in her hands. "I don't know what I'm doing, MJ. He's... intense."

"Intense?" MJ barked out a laugh. "Babe, that man is a walking, talking red flag parade."

She looked up at him, her expression conflicted. "But there's something about him. He's confident, but there's... I don't know. A vulnerability, maybe? Like he's hiding something."

"Yeah, like a basement full of ex-girlfriends," MJ shot back, his arms flailing dramatically.

Cora couldn't help but laugh, though her mind was still reeling from Declan's visit. She could still feel the heat of his gaze, the weight of his presence pressing against her like a phantom touch.

"I don't trust him," MJ said firmly, plopping onto the couch in the bride booth beside her. "And I don't want you getting hurt."

Cora nodded, leaning her head against his shoulder. "I know you're looking out for me, MJ. I appreciate it."

"Good," he said, wrapping an arm around her. "Because if he shows up again, I'm throwing glitter bombs and calling the cops."

The following day, Cora awoke to sunlight streaming through the loft's windows, cutting through the haze of her restless sleep. MJ was already in the kitchen, clattering dishes and humming to himself.

"Morning, Sleeping Beauty," he called without looking up. "Do you think they start making corn fritters around ten in the morning at the square?"

"Morning," Cora replied, her voice groggy as she poured herself a cup of coffee. The rich aroma offered momentary comfort.

MJ leaned against the counter, smirking. "Let me guess—you dreamed about Mr. Midnight Seduction, didn't you?"

Cora rolled her eyes, though her cheeks warmed. "Can we not call him that?"

"Fine," MJ relented. "But only if you admit that he's got you all twisted up inside."

She sipped her coffee, avoiding his gaze. "I don't know what you're talking about."

"Oh, please," MJ scoffed. "I saw the way you looked at him. Like a blind dog in a meat market, babe. And we all know how that ends."

Her phone buzzed on the counter, cutting through their banter. She glanced at the screen, her stomach flipping when she saw a message from Declan:

Hope you're having a good morning. Thinking about our conversation. Would love to see you on Sunday.

MJ leaned over her shoulder, his eyes narrowing. "Oh, hell no. He keeps texting you? Do we even know how he got your number?"

Cora bit her lip, her fingers hovering over the keyboard. "He's just being polite. He's a surgeon—maybe he has access to everyone's information."

"Polite, my ass," MJ muttered. "This man is playing the long game, and you're falling for it."

Ignoring MJ's protests, Cora typed out a quick reply:

Thanks, you too. Maybe I'll see you on Sunday.

"Vague. Safe," she said aloud, more to herself than MJ.

"Babe, there's nothing safe about that man," MJ said, throwing his hands up. "But fine, I'll shut up. For now. Let's head on down to the shop. We need a diva diversion. Maybe I'll try on our clearance gowns."

Cora couldn't shake the flutter of excitement in her chest, even as she tried to focus on the day ahead. She busied herself with tasks at the shop—coordinating deliveries, updating promotional events, and reorganizing displays—but her mind kept wandering back to Declan. His voice, his touch, the way he made her feel seen in a way she hadn't experienced before lingered, making it impossible to focus fully.

"Are you even listening to me?" MJ's voice cut through her daze, sharp and laced with irritation.

"Huh?" Cora blinked, her cheeks flushing as she realized he was staring at her expectantly.

MJ groaned dramatically, throwing his clipboard onto the counter. "Babe, I know that look. You're picturing all six feet of him pinning you against a wall and whispering sweet nothings in that gravelly voice, aren't you?"

Cora's mouth opened, but no words came out. The heat rising in her neck betrayed her.

"Oh my God, you are!" MJ laughed, though there was an edge of frustration to it. "Listen, I get it. He's gorgeous, he's mysterious, and that jawline could cut glass. But seriously? The man screams danger."

Cora pushed off the counter, her movements quick and defensive. "It's not like that, MJ. It's just... curiosity."

"Curiosity? Babe, curiosity doesn't make you blush like that," MJ teased, stepping closer. "I'm telling you, this is how it starts. A stolen glance, a lingering touch... and then bam! You're naked on a desk with your panties in his pocket."

Cora let out a nervous laugh, her face burning as MJ's words painted a vivid picture she couldn't shake. "Look," she said, her tone firm despite the rush of images in her head. "I'm not some naïve girl who's going to fall headfirst into trouble."

MJ raised an eyebrow, his lips quirking into a smirk. "You say that now, but let me know when he's got you pinned against the bridal rack whispering about how he can't resist you."

Her stomach fluttered at the thought, and she turned away quickly, pretending to busy herself with the price tags.

"So, are we going to this sinister soiree or not? I can't decide which swimsuit I'll wear, but I do know that my fur slipper heels will be accompanying me," MJ said as he filed the daily invoices.

Cora glanced half-heartedly at the advertisements for her grand opening, distant and unfocused. Declan's name echoed in her mind, his voice weaving through her thoughts like an uninvited guest. There was something else about him, something she couldn't quite name. His stoic confidence, the way he seemed to look at her like she was the only person in the room—it all felt different.

Cora inhaled a slow breath and released it. "Maybe we shouldn't go," she said softly, tilting her head toward MJ, second-guessing her suggestion almost as soon as she'd made it.

MJ went quiet as he absorbed her words. Finally, he shrugged, his voice lighter but firm. "No, let's go. We'll go and see what this man is all about. Let's wrap up our day, though. I'm getting hangry, and I'm about to take it out on these magazines," he added with a wave, his dramatic flair returning.

They closed up the shop and headed back to the loft, falling into the daily routine that had become second nature. The comforting rhythm of their partnership was a balm to Cora's restless thoughts, yet Declan's presence hovered in her mind like a shadow she couldn't shake.

She shook her head, focusing back on the conversation with MJ, though the truth lingered in the back of her mind, taunting her with questions she wasn't ready to answer.

What was this man doing to her?

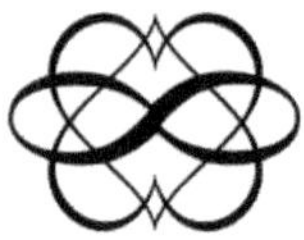

A Secret Laid Bare

"Secrets demand light, even as they seek to remain hidden."

The next few days passed in a blur of meetings with reporters, photographers, and interviews, every moment pulling Cora closer to the grand reopening of Boughton Bridal. The whirlwind of preparation left little time to think, which she was grateful for—at least until Sunday arrived.

Now, the warm glow of the late afternoon sun bathed Declan's sprawling estate in golden light, casting a radiant sheen over the deck and the pool's rippling surface beyond. The mingling scents of jasmine and sea salt hung heavily in the air, wrapping around Cora like an intoxicating veil as she leaned against the railing. The polished wood was cool beneath her fingers, grounding her even as her thoughts threatened to drift.

Declan stood beside her, close enough that the heat of his presence seeped into her skin. When his hand brushed hers, the deliberate contact sent a shiver through her—a spark impossible to ignore. He wore confidence effortlessly, his tailored linen shirt open at the collar, the faintest hint of cologne teasing her senses. His eyes reflected the golden light, and Cora found herself drawn into their intensity, unable—and unwilling—to look away.

Today was different. Declan wasn't just hosting a barbecue; he was throwing a garden gala, a sophisticated affair that felt like a glimpse into his carefully curated world. Guests mingled on the deck and in the garden below, glasses of champagne catching the sunlight as laughter floated through the air.

Cora tried to relax, to blend into the elegance around her, but a weight sat heavy in her chest. This wasn't her world. She'd stepped into something polished and refined, and though Declan had invited her into it, she felt unsteady, as though the ground beneath her might give way at any moment. Her emotions churned, untrained and unruly, threatening to spill over despite the poised exterior she tried to maintain.

"You're somewhere else," Declan said softly, his voice cutting through the hum of the evening.

Cora glanced at him, her lips curving into a faint smile. "Just thinking."

"Dangerous habit," Declan replied, his tone teasing but edged with curiosity. "Care to share?"

Cora hesitated, her fingers tightening on the railing. How could she put into words the storm brewing inside her? The pull she felt toward him, equal parts exhilarating and terrifying? "I'm just... overwhelmed," she admitted finally. "Everything feels like it's moving so fast."

Declan moved closer, his arm brushing hers. "That's not always a bad thing," he murmured, his gaze dropping to her lips. "Sometimes, it's good to let go. To just... feel."

The warmth of his voice, the promise in his words—it all made Cora's chest tighten. She turned to face him, her breath catching as he closed the distance between them. His hand came up to cup her cheek, his thumb brushing over her skin with a tenderness that belied the intensity in his eyes.

"Declan..." she began, but her voice faltered as he leaned in, his lips capturing hers in a kiss that was both gentle and demanding. The world seemed to tilt, her senses narrowing to the feel of his mouth on hers, the heat of his body against her.

Her hands found his chest, the fabric of his shirt smooth beneath her palms as she pushed slightly, her mind warring with her body. "Wait," she whispered, pulling back just enough to catch her breath.

Declan's gaze searched hers, a flicker of uncertainty crossing his face. "Too fast?"

Cora nodded, though her pulse thundered in her ears. "I just... I don't know."

Declan exhaled softly, his hand falling from her cheek. "Of course," he said, his voice steady but quieter. "I don't want to rush you, Cora. I just..." He trailed off, his gaze drifting to the horizon. "You make it hard to hold back."

His words sent a flush through her, a warmth that settled low in her belly. She bit her lip, unsure how to respond. Declan's intensity was magnetic, his presence like a force she couldn't escape—but it also scared her, the way it pulled her so completely.

They stood in silence for a moment, the tension between them palpable. Finally, Declan reached for her hand, threading his fingers through hers with a gentleness that surprised her. "I'll wait," he said simply, his tone softer now. "As long as you need."

Cora looked down at their joined hands, her heart aching with a mixture of emotions she couldn't untangle. She nodded, the words she wanted to say sticking in her throat.

As the sun dipped lower, painting the sky in hues of amber and rose, the sound of laughter drifted from inside the house—a reminder of the party unfolding beyond the deck. Declan's thumb brushed over her knuckles, a small gesture that sent shivers up her spine.

"Come back inside," he said, his voice coaxing. "Let me show you how good it feels to just let go."

Cora hesitated, her body and mind at war. But as she looked into his eyes, the shadows of doubt receded just enough for her to nod. "Okay," she whispered, her voice barely audible.

Declan's smile was slow and devastating, his grip on her hand firm but unyielding as he led her back inside. The deck door slid shut behind them, sealing off the cool evening air as they stepped into the warm glow of the house. The scent of wine and soft music filled the space, wrapping around them like a cocoon.

The party was in full swing, and the low hum of laughter and conversation filled the air, mingling with the soft strains of jazz that drifted from the speakers. Glasses clinked, and the scent of wine and fresh-cut roses added a decadent warmth to the space. It was the kind of effortless elegance that felt worlds away from Cora's everyday life.

Declan led her toward a quiet corner near the bar, his hand resting lightly on the small of her back. The warmth of his touch lingered even as he pulled away to pour them both a glass of wine. His movements were smooth and deliberate, as if he had done this a hundred times before.

"For you," he said, handing her the glass with a small smile. His dark eyes seemed to flicker with something unreadable as they met hers. "You look like you could use this."

Cora took the glass, her fingers brushing his briefly. "Thanks," she murmured, her voice soft.

"Tell me," Declan said, leaning against the bar as he studied her, "How do you feel about the soft opening coming up for the shop? Everything falling into place? Most people wouldn't have the guts to take on something so... personal."

Cora hesitated, the question catching her off guard. She swirled the wine in her glass, her gaze drifting to the floor. "Yes, I think we are ready. All of those long days and late nights are coming to fruition, thanks to MJ. It all just feels right," she said finally. "Gram poured so much of herself into it. It's just my turn now to bring her dream back to life."

Declan nodded, his expression thoughtful. "That kind of commitment says a lot about you, you know."

Cora glanced up at him, a faint blush creeping into her cheeks. "I don't know about that. It feels more like stubbornness half the time."

Declan chuckled, the sound low and warm. "Stubbornness isn't a bad thing. It's what makes people fight for what they care about."

His words struck a chord, and for a moment, the noise of the party faded into the background. Cora felt herself drawn into his orbit, the intensity of his gaze pulling her closer. But just as quickly as the moment formed, it was broken by a burst of laughter from the other side of the room.

Cora turned her attention to the group gathered near the grand piano, where a striking woman in a deep red dress was holding court. Her laughter rang out like a bell, her presence commanding the attention of everyone around her.

Declan followed her gaze, his expression shifting. "Ah, that's Evelyn," he said, his tone unreadable. "She's a... friend."

Cora raised an eyebrow, her curiosity piqued. "A friend?" she echoed.

Declan smiled, though it didn't quite reach his eyes. "Nothing to worry about," he said lightly, but there was a tension in his voice that made Cora wonder. "Come on, let's get some fresh air."

Without waiting for her response, Declan guided her toward the sliding doors that led back out to the balcony. The cool evening breeze was a welcome relief from the heat of the party, and Cora took a deep breath, letting it wash over her.

Declan leaned against the railing, his gaze fixed on the horizon. "Sometimes, all the noise gets to be too much," he said, his voice quieter now. "Out here, it's easier to think."

Cora joined him, her hands resting on the railing as she looked out at the city lights twinkling in the distance. "Do you bring a lot of people out here?" she asked, her tone teasing.

Declan turned to her, a slow smile spreading across his face. "Only the ones who matter," he said simply.

Cora's breath caught at the sincerity in his voice, her heart fluttering in her chest. She looked away, her pulse racing as she tried to steady herself. Declan had a way of making her feel like she was the only person in the room.

The balcony offered a quiet reprieve from the hum of the party, the cool breeze carrying the faint scent of jasmine and wine. Cora leaned against the railing, her glass in hand, as Declan turned his full attention to her. His gaze was steady, searching, and it made her pulse quicken despite herself.

"You keep surprising me," Declan said, his voice low and thoughtful. "Most people would've backed away from what you're doing—stepping into your Gram's shoes, taking on the shop, the weight of it all."

Cora tilted her head, a faint smile playing at her lips. "You think so?"

He nodded, his expression softening. "I do. It takes strength to build something from emotional loss. Not everyone has that in them."

His words landed heavily, and for a moment, Cora couldn't find her voice. She took a sip of her wine, letting its warmth settle her nerves. "Sometimes, I wonder if I do," she admitted quietly. "If I'm just pretending to have it all together."

Declan's hand brushed lightly against hers where it rested on the railing, the touch deliberate but gentle. "Pretending or not, you're doing it," he said. "That's what matters."

The sincerity in his tone made her chest tighten, a mix of gratitude and confusion swirling within her. She looked up at him, her breath catching at the intensity in his gaze. "You're easy to talk to," she said softly, surprising herself with the admission.

Declan smiled, his hand lingering against hers. "Good," he replied. "Because I want to know more about you, Cora. All of you."

The openness in his voice was disarming, and Cora felt a flicker of vulnerability rise to the surface. She wasn't used to this—someone seeing her, really seeing her. It was terrifying and intoxicating all at once. Before she could respond, the sliding door behind them opened, and a burst of laughter spilled out onto the balcony. Evelyn stepped outside, her red dress shimmering under the soft lights. Her sharp gaze flicked between Declan and Cora, a knowing smile curving her lips.

"Well, well," Evelyn said, her voice honeyed and smooth. "I was wondering where you'd disappeared to, Declan."

Declan straightened, his hand slipping away from Cora's as he turned to face Evelyn. "Just catching some air," he said, his tone even.

Evelyn's smile widened as her eyes settled on Cora. "And who's this divine beauty?"

Cora felt the weight of Evelyn's attention and straightened slightly, meeting her gaze. "Cora," she said simply, extending a hand. "I run the bridal shop downtown."

"Ah," Evelyn said, her tone was carrying a hint of amusement as she shook Cora's hand. "I've heard about you."

There was something in the way she said it that set Cora on edge, but she kept her expression neutral. "All good things, I hope," she replied lightly.

"Of course," Evelyn said with a wink, before turning her attention back and leaning into Declan. "Well, don't stay out here too long. People are asking about you," she whispered placing a quick kiss on his cheek. With that, she disappeared back into the house, her presence leaving behind a tension that lingered between Cora and Declan.

"So, a friend of yours?" Cora asked, her tone carefully neutral.

Declan exhaled, his hand rubbing the back of his neck. "Something like that," he said. "Evelyn's... complicated."

Cora raised an eyebrow but decided not to press. "Seems like she has a lot to say."

Declan smiled faintly, though it didn't quite reach his eyes. "She usually does."

The moment felt heavier now, and Cora wasn't sure what to make of the shift in Declan's demeanor. She turned back to the railing, her thoughts swirling as the city lights twinkled in the distance.

"Don't let her get in your head," Declan said softly, stepping closer to her. "She has a way of stirring things up, but it doesn't mean anything."

Cora glanced at him, her gaze searching. "Doesn't it?"

Declan's jaw tightened slightly, but his voice remained steady. "Not to me."

The weight of his words hung in the air, and Cora wasn't sure if she believed him—or if she wanted to. But as the cool breeze swept over the balcony, carrying with it the faint hum of the party inside, she realized that whatever was happening between them was only beginning. Cora felt the tension in the air as Declan's words settled over them, his presence both grounding and unsettling. She turned her gaze back to the skyline, the soft glow of the city lights offering a momentary distraction from the whirlwind of emotions swirling inside her.

"I'm not used to this," she said finally, her voice barely above a whisper.

Declan leaned against the railing, his shoulder brushing hers. "This?"

"Any of it," she admitted, turning to face him. "The attention, the compliments, the... intensity."

Declan's lips curved into a small smile, his dark eyes locking onto hers. "You get used to it," he said softly, his voice carrying a note of amusement. "Or maybe you don't. But that doesn't mean it's bad."

Cora exhaled, her pulse quickening under the weight of his gaze. "I'm not sure what to make of you," she confessed, her cheeks flushing with the honesty of her words.

Declan chuckled, the sound low and warm. "I'll take that as a compliment."

Before she could respond, the sliding door opened again, this time revealing MJ, his vibrant energy immediately breaking through the tension. "There you are!" he exclaimed, stepping onto the balcony with a flourish. "I've been looking everywhere for you, darling."

Cora let out a breath, grateful for the interruption. "MJ, I thought I'd lost you!"

"I'm here to save you from broody stares and cryptic conversations, obviously. Did you really think I was going to stay hidden at this bubbly barbeque?" MJ said, shooting a pointed look at Declan. "You, sir, need to share the spotlight."

Declan smirked, his demeanor lightening. "I'll leave you to it, then," he said, stepping back. "Don't let him boss you around too much, Cora." With a final glance at her, he slipped back inside, leaving Cora and MJ alone on the balcony.

MJ waited until the door slid shut before turning to her, his expression softening. "You okay, love?"

Cora nodded, though her heart still raced. "Yeah. Just... trying to figure him out."

"Declan?" MJ asked, his tone laced with curiosity. "Oh, he's gorgeous, I'll give you that. But he's also trouble. I can smell it."

Cora laughed softly, though her chest tightened at the truth in his words. "It's complicated," she admitted.

"It always is," MJ said, wrapping an arm around her shoulders. "But just remember, you don't have to dive in headfirst. Take your time."

Cora leaned into him, grateful for his unwavering support. "Thanks, MJ."

"Anytime, darling," he replied, pressing a kiss to her temple. "Now, come on. Let's find the dessert table before Evelyn eats all the good stuff."

"Oh, I see you have met Evelyn, huh?" Cora replied, not amused.

"Yassss, girl. Let's go discover the tea on that one, shall we?" MJ pronounced fluffing up his floral swim cami with impertinence.

Cora let him lead her back inside, the warmth of the party enveloping her once more. But even as she laughed at MJ's antics and let herself get lost in the rhythm of the evening, a part of her couldn't shake the feeling that Declan was watching her, his presence lingering like a shadow in the back of her mind.

The evening stretched on, the warmth of the party wrapping itself around Cora like a velvet cocoon. She moved through the crowd with MJ at her side, his bright laughter and quick wit drawing people to them like flies on a cobweb. But no matter how many conversations she found herself pulled into or how seemingly effusive Declan's world appeared to be, her mind kept wandering back to the balcony, to the look in Declan's eyes, to the way his presence seemed to linger like a phantom touch on her skin.

Across the room, she caught a glimpse of him. Declan stood near the bar, a glass of something dark in his hand, his posture relaxed but commanding. He was laughing at something Evelyn had said, but even from a distance, Cora could feel the pull of his gaze, magnetic and unrelenting.

"You're staring," MJ whispered, leaning close enough that his breath tickled her ear.

Cora snapped her attention back to him, her cheeks flushing. "I wasn't."

MJ raised an eyebrow, his lips curving into a knowing smile. "Darling, you might as well be on fire. Go talk to him before you combust."

"I don't think—"

"Cora," MJ interrupted, his voice softening. "Look. You're allowed to want this. Him. Whatever it is. You don't have to have all the answers right now."

His words settled over her like a balm, soothing the swirling doubt in her chest. She nodded slowly, her gaze drifting back to Declan. He was alone now, his focus shifting to the drink in his hand. Before she could second-guess herself, she took a step forward, then another, until she was standing in front of him.

Declan looked up, his dark eyes lighting with something unreadable as he saw her. "Cora," he said, his voice warm and familiar. "I was wondering where you'd gone."

"I was just..." She trailed off, unsure how to finish the sentence. Instead, she gestured toward his glass. "What are you drinking?"

Declan smiled, his gaze never leaving hers. "Whiskey. Want to try?" Before she could respond, he offered her the glass, his hand brushing hers as she took it. The simple contact sent a jolt through her, her pulse quickening as she raised the glass to her lips. The whiskey was smooth, warm, and unexpectedly sweet, much like the man in front of her.

"Good?" he asked, his voice low.

Cora nodded, her cheeks flushing. "Surprisingly."

Declan stepped closer, his proximity sending a wave of heat through her. "I think that's what I like most about you," he said softly. "You're full of surprises."

Cora's heart was pounding as his words sank in. The noise of the party faded into the background, leaving only the steady thrum of her pulse and the intensity of his gaze. "Declan..." she began, her voice trembling slightly.

He reached out, his hand brushing lightly against her arm, his touch deliberate but unhurried. "Tell me to stop," he murmured, his voice like a caress. "And I will."

Cora swallowed hard, her thoughts a tangled mess of desire and caution. But when she looked into his eyes, she saw the vulnerability hidden beneath the confidence, something inside her shifted. She didn't want him to stop. Not tonight.

She shook her head, her voice barely audible. "Don't."

The single word was all the permission he needed. Declan leaned in, his lips brushing against hers in a kiss that was as soft as it was electrifying. Cora felt herself melt into him, her hands finding their way to his chest as he deepened the kiss, his touch both tender and demanding.

The world around them seemed to dissolve, leaving only the warmth of his body against hers, the taste of whiskey and something darker on his lips. Her heart raced, every nerve ending in her body alight with sensation as his hands settled on her waist, pulling her closer.

When they finally broke apart, Cora was breathless, her skin flushed and her mind spinning. Declan rested his forehead against hers, his voice a low whisper. "You're dangerous, Cora."

She laughed softly, the sound shaky but genuine. "I think that's supposed to be my line."

Declan's lips curved into a slow smile, his eyes dark with something that sent a shiver down her spine. "Not tonight."

Cora's pulse was still racing as Declan's hands lingered at her waist, his touch both grounding and electric. She wasn't sure if it was the whiskey or the way his gaze seemed to strip her bare, but she felt her reservations dissolving, replaced by something raw and undeniable.

"Come with me," Declan said softly, his voice more of a request than a command.

Cora hesitated, her breath catching. "Where?"

He tilted his head toward the far end of the room, where a secluded hallway led to the quieter parts of the house. "Just away from the noise. Somewhere we can talk."

She searched his face for any hint of ulterior motive but found only sincerity—and a hint of something darker, smoldering beneath the surface. Against her better judgment, she nodded.

Declan took her hand, his grip firm but gentle as he led her through the crowd. The warmth of his touch spread up her arm, setting her nerves alight. She barely noticed the curious glances as they passed, her focus entirely on the man in front of her. The hallway was dimly lit, the noise from the party fading into a distant hum. Declan stopped at a door, opening it to reveal a small, private lounge. A fire crackled in the stone hearth, casting flickering shadows across the room. The scent of leather and wood polish hung in the air, rich and comforting.

Declan let go of her hand, turning to face her as the door clicked shut behind them. "Better?" he asked, his voice low.

Cora nodded, her heart pounding. "Much."

He stepped closer, his movements slow and deliberate, giving her time to back away if she wanted to. She didn't. Instead, she stood her ground, her breath hitching as he reached up to tuck a strand of hair behind her ear.

"You have no idea what you do to me," he murmured, his voice thick with emotion. "The way you look at me, the way you make me feel—it's like I'm losing control, and I don't even care."

Cora's chest tightened, her body caught between the pull of his words and the heat of his proximity. "I'm not sure I know what I'm doing," she admitted, her voice barely above a whisper.

Declan smiled faintly, his thumb brushing against her cheek. "You don't have to. Just… feel." His lips found hers again, this time with more urgency. The kiss was enrapturing, his hands threading through her hair as he pulled her closer. Cora surrendered to the moment, her fingers curling into his shirt as the firelight danced around them.

Declan's touch moved to her back, his fingers tracing slow, deliberate patterns that sent shivers cascading through her. His lips left hers to trail along her jawline, his breath warm against her skin. Cora tilted her head back, her eyes fluttering shut as she let herself get lost in the sensation.

"Declan," she whispered, her voice trembling with need and uncertainty.

He pulled back just enough to meet her gaze, his own filled with an intensity that made her knees weak. "Say the word, Cora," he said, his voice low and gravelly. "Tell me what you want."

Cora hesitated, her heart pounding so loudly she was sure he could hear it. Her body burned with a need she couldn't quite name, but her mind still held onto a sliver of doubt, of fear. She took a shaky breath, her fingers brushing against his chest. "I want..."

The words caught in her throat, but the look in Declan's eyes told her he already knew. He leaned in, pressing a kiss to her forehead that was so tender, it left her breathless. "You don't have to say anything," he murmured. "I'll wait for you."

The tension in Cora's chest eased slightly, the weight of his words grounding her. She looked up at him, her cheeks flushed and her emotions a whirlwind. "Thank you," she whispered, her voice trembling.

Declan smiled, his thumb brushing against her cheek. "You're worth waiting for."

The moment stretched between them, heavy with unspoken promises. And as the fire crackled in the grate, Cora realized that whatever was happening between them was far more than she'd anticipated. It was exhilarating, terrifying—and she wasn't sure she wanted it to stop. Cora found herself unable to look away, her breath reposed as his thumb brushed against her cheek one last time before he stepped back, giving her the space she hadn't realized she needed.

Declan poured them each a glass of wine from a small tray by the fireplace, the rich ruby liquid catching the firelight. "I wasn't sure how tonight would go," he admitted, handing her a glass. His tone was softer now, almost hesitant. "You've been hard to read, Cora."

She took the glass, her fingers brushing his briefly. The touch sent a ripple of warmth through her, even as her mind scrambled for a response. "It's not intentional," she said finally, her voice steady but quiet. "I'm just... figuring things out."

Declan nodded, his gaze unwavering. "I get it. You've been through a lot. The shop, your Gram—it's a lot to carry.."

Cora sipped her wine, the rich taste grounding her. "It's more than that," she confessed. "Coming here, meeting you... it's like everything I thought I knew about my life is shifting. And I don't know if I'm ready for it."

Declan's expression softened, and he set his glass down on the mantle before stepping closer. "No one's ever ready for the things that matter most," he said, his voice low. "Sometimes, you just have to take the leap and trust yourself to land."

His words struck a chord, echoing the thoughts she'd been trying to bury. Cora's chest clenched, her emotions swirling in a way that felt both petrifying and intoxicating. She looked up at him, her voice trembling as she spoke. "And what if I fall?"

Declan's smile was small but genuine, his hand finding hers with deliberate care. "Then I'll be there to catch you." The simplicity of his words, the sincerity in his tone—it unraveled something inside her.

Cora exhaled shakily, her grip tightening on his hand as she let herself lean into the moment. The warmth of the fire, the weight of his gaze, the soft pressure of his touch—it all made her feel seen in a way she hadn't realized she was craving.

Declan lifted her hand to his lips, pressing a kiss to her knuckles that sent shivers up her spine. "You don't have to decide everything tonight," he said softly. "But whatever you're ready to give, I'll take."

Cora's heart raced, her pulse thundering in her ears as she stared into his eyes. There was no mistaking the desire in his gaze, but there was also patience, a quiet strength that steadied her even as she felt herself unraveling. She placed her glass down on the small table beside her, her movements slow and deliberate. Taking a deep breath, she stepped closer, closing the distance between them. Her hands found their way to his chest, her fingers brushing against the fabric of his shirt as she tilted her head up to meet his gaze.

"I don't want to overthink this," she said, her voice barely audible. "I just want to... feel."

Declan's breath plunged, his hands settling on her waist with a gentleness that belied the intensity in his eyes. "Are you sure?" he asked, his voice rough.

Cora nodded, her cheeks flushing as she leaned into him. "I'm sure."

His lips found hers again, the kiss slower this time, deeper. Cora melted into him, her hands sliding up to his shoulders as the world around them faded into nothingness. Declan's touch was firm but careful, his fingers tracing lazy circles along her back as he pulled her closer. Every nerve ending in her body seemed to come alive, the firelight casting them in a golden glow as they moved in perfect sync. Declan's lips left hers to trail along her jawline, his breath warm against her skin as he murmured her name like a promise.

Cora's hands tangled in his hair, a soft gasp escaping her lips as he pressed kisses to the sensitive skin just below her ear. "Declan..." she whispered, her voice trembling with need and uncertainty.

He pulled back slightly, his forehead resting against hers as he cupped her face in his hands. "We can stop anytime," he said, his voice thick with restraint. "You call the shots."

Cora shook her head, her fingers brushing against his jawline as she met his gaze. "I don't want to stop."

The weight of her words seemed to ignite something in Declan, his lips finding hers once more with renewed intensity. The fire crackled softly in the background, a steady rhythm to the wild, electric current that flowed between them. Cora gave herself over to the moment, the warmth of his touch, the press of his body against hers, and the quiet promise that hung in the air.

For the first time in a long while, she felt truly alive.

The warmth of the fire painted their skin in golden hues, the flickering light catching in Declan's eyes as they deepened their gaze. Cora's breath came in shallow gasps, her hands gripping his shoulders as his lips explored the curve of her neck. Each kiss sent waves of heat cascading through her, her body leaning into him as if it knew what it wanted before her mind could catch up.

Declan's hands moved slowly, deliberately, tracing the shape of her waist as if committing every inch of her to memory. His touch was firm but reverent, igniting a fire under her skin that made her shiver. "You're incredible," he murmured, his voice husky against her ear, the words sending a thrill down her spine.

Cora's fingers slid up into his hair, tangling in the dark strands as she pulled him closer. She could feel the strength of his body pressed against hers, his warmth wrapping around her like a sheathe. Her own inhibitions began to dissolve, replaced by a heady mix of need and curiosity.

"I can't stop thinking about you," he confessed, his voice raw as his lips brushed against her collarbone. "Every moment, every look—you're all I see, Cora."

His words were both a confession and a promise, and they sent her heart racing. She tugged his face back to hers, capturing his lips in a kiss that was hungrier now, less restrained. Declan responded in kind, his hands sliding down to grip her hips, pulling her flush against him.

Cora gasped at the sensation, her skin tingling as their bodies pressed together. The air between them felt electric, charged with an intensity that left her dizzy. She could feel every movement, every shift, the heat of him seeping into her as his lips left hers to blaze a trail down her throat. Her head tilted back, her breath muffled as his teeth grazed her skin, just enough to send a spark of pleasure coursing through her. Declan's hands slid beneath the hem of her shirt, his fingers splaying across the bare skin of her back. His touch was warm and commanding, a perfect balance of control and tenderness.

"You feel amazing," he whispered, his voice a low growl that sent shivers racing through her. "I want to know every part of you."

Cora's own hands began to explore, sliding down his chest and feeling the hard lines of his muscles beneath the fabric of his shirt. She tugged at it, her boldness surprising even herself. Declan helped her, pulling the shirt over his head and tossing it aside without breaking their connection. Her eyes roamed over him, taking in the sharp lines of his jaw, the defined planes of his chest, the way the firelight played across his skin. He was breathtaking, and the hunger in his gaze as he looked at her made her feel powerful, wanted.

Declan's hands moved to her waist again. He paused, his eyes searching hers for permission. Cora nodded, her chest rising and falling with shallow breaths as he lifted the fabric and discarded it beside his own. For a moment, they simply stood there, the space between them charged with anticipation. Declan reached out, his hands cupping her face as he pressed his forehead to hers. "You're beautiful," he said, his voice barely above a whisper. "Every part of you."

Cora felt her heart swell at his words, the vulnerability in his tone grounding her even as her body burned with desire. She leaned into him, her hands finding their way back to his chest as their lips met once more, the kiss deepening with every passing second.

Declan's lips claimed hers again, this time with more urgency. His hands, warm and steady, trailed down her sides, igniting a fire wherever they touched. Every inch of Cora's body felt alive, her senses heightened as she pressed herself closer to him, craving the contact that his presence promised.

His kisses grew bolder, trailing from her lips to the hollow of her throat, where his teeth grazed her skin just enough to make her gasp. Declan's grip on her waist tightened, pulling her firmly against him as his mouth explored the curve of her shoulder, his breath hot and deliberate. Cora's fingers slid over his chest, marveling at the hard surface of muscle beneath her fingertips as her own body responded to every subtle shift of his. Her inhibitions crumbled under the intensity of the moment, and she let herself surrender to the sensation. Declan's hands moved lower, his touch firm but patient as his fingers brushed against the waistband of her jeans. He paused, his lips hovering just above hers as he whispered, "Tell me if this is too much."

Cora gasped, her chest rising and falling as she met his gaze. There was nothing but sincerity and desire in his eyes, a combination that both steadied her and sent her pulse racing. "Don't stop," she said softly, her voice trembling with need.

"You're incredible," Declan murmured, his lips brushing against her ear as his hands roamed freely now, his touch igniting every nerve in her body. Cora felt herself melt into him, their movements growing more synchronized, more urgent. The warmth of the fire in the hearth paled in comparison to the heat building between them. Declan guided her gently backward until her knees hit the edge of the couch. He lowered her carefully onto the cushions, his body following hers with a grace that made her breath catch.

Cora's back arched instinctively as Declan's lips traced a line down her collarbone, his hands anchoring her as he explored every curve with reverence. She couldn't think, couldn't speak—every part of her was consumed by the sensations he stirred within her. His movements were deliberate, his touch firm yet tender, and it left her feeling utterly undone. She let herself get lost in the moment, the weight of his body grounding her even as her mind spun. Declan's hands found hers, threading their fingers together as his lips captured hers once more. It was a kiss full of promises, of unspoken words and raw emotion, and it left her trembling beneath him.

"Cora," he murmured, her name like a prayer on his lips. "You drive me crazy."

Her lips curved into a faint smile as she looked up at him, her chest rising and falling with shallow breaths. "Good," she whispered, her voice trembling but full of certainty. "Because you do the same to me."

Cora's pulse thundered in her ears, her senses alive with every touch, every breath shared between them. His lips left hers to explore the curve of her neck, the hollow at the base of her throat, each kiss deliberate and unhurried. Cora's breath steadied, her fingers gripping his shoulders as he pressed her gently against the cushions, his body a steady weight over hers.

"You're invigorating," he murmured, his voice rough with desire. "I don't think I've ever wanted anything as much as I want you." The raw honesty in his words made Cora's heart race.

Her hands moved to his face, her fingers brushing against the stubble on his jaw as she guided his gaze to hers. "Then don't stop," she whispered, her voice trembling with both vulnerability and certainty.

Declan's gaze darkened, his restraint slipping as his lips claimed hers with renewed fervor. The kiss deepened, his hands exploring her with a mix of gentleness and urgency that left her breathless. Cora felt herself yielding to him completely, her body arching into his as her mind emptied of everything but the sensations he evoked. He shifted, his hands sliding down to her hips as he pressed a trail of kisses along her collarbone, his breath hot against her skin. Cora's hands tangled in his hair, a soft moan escaping her lips as his lips found the sensitive curve of her shoulder. Every touch, every kiss felt like a promise, an unspoken declaration of the connection they were building.

"You're incredible," Declan murmured against her skin, his voice a husky blend of awe and desire. His hands tightened on her hips, grounding her even as the intensity of his touch sent shivers racing through her.

Cora's mind was spinning as she tried to hold onto the moment. She wasn't sure when her fears and doubts had slipped away, but in this moment, they felt distant, insignificant. All that mattered was him—the weight of his body, the heat of his touch, the way he made her feel like the most beautiful, desired person in the world.

"Declan," she whispered, her voice trembling as her hands slid down his back, her touch bold and searching. "I—"

He silenced her with another kiss, his lips capturing hers in a way that left her utterly breathless. "You don't have to say anything," he murmured against her lips. "Just feel."

Cora let herself go, her body and mind surrendering to the moment as Declan's touch became bolder, more insistent. The fire crackled softly in the background, a rhythm to their movements as they explored each other with a hunger that had been building since the moment they'd met. Every touch, every kiss, every whispered word felt like a piece of a puzzle falling into place. And as the night stretched on, Cora found herself wondering if this—this connection, this intensity—was what she had been missing all along.

The fire in the fireplace crackled, its warm light flickering across the room, illuminating the depth of emotions and the growing connection between them. Declan's lips left a burning trail down Cora's neck, each kiss igniting a fire that consumed her entirely. His hands moved with purpose, memorizing every curve, every soft line, as though he were committing her to memory.

A Betrayal Foreseen

"The flames of betrayal often smolder long before they ignite."

The morning light had given way to the gentle hum of the shop, its warmth replaced by the familiar rhythm of her work. Cora sat at her desk, the quiet ticking of the clock punctuating the stillness. In her lap rested her grandmother's journal, its worn leather cover soft beneath her fingertips. It felt like an anchor, holding her steady when the ground beneath her threatened to shift.

It had been four days since she'd seen Declan, four days since his presence had filled the air around her, leaving an ache she couldn't quite shake. She'd tried to drown herself in the preparations for the grand opening—adjusting displays, perfecting inventory lists, and tweaking every detail of the event. But the weight of his absence lingered, seeping into the spaces between her thoughts, no matter how hard she worked to silence it.

The shop was finally starting to look like a reality, not just a dream. The scent of fresh paint lingered in the air as workers moved around the space, installing shelves and hanging light fixtures. Cora stood at the entrance, her notebook in hand, jotting down last-minute adjustments as her vision came to life.

Selah arrived a day earlier, her usual whirlwind of energy filling the space. She carried a carton of coffees and a bag of pastries in one hand and fabric samples in the other.

"I brought reinforcements," she announced with a grin, setting everything on the makeshift counter.

"Thank you, Sweet Baby Jesus, for delightful confectionery—and you!" exclaimed MJ as he darted forward to hug her.

Cora laughed, the sound light and genuine. "You're a lifesaver," she said, grabbing a coffee and taking a sip. "I don't think we've stopped moving since sunrise."

Selah studied her for a moment, her smile softening. "You look good, Cora. Lighter. Like you're finally starting to breathe again."

"I think I am," Cora admitted, her voice steady but tinged with emotion. "It's still overwhelming, but it feels... right."

Selah nodded, pulling out the fabric samples and spreading them across the counter. "Let's make it perfect," she said. "Gram would've loved this."

Cora's chest tightened at the mention of her grandmother, but the ache felt comforting. "I hope so," she said softly. "This is as much for her as it is for me."

"I am seeing a full-on drag show to break open this cup of tea to the locals!" MJ declared, spinning on his heels flamboyantly as he pointed to the open space in the center of the shop.

As the workers packed up for the day, a familiar figure appeared at the edge of the door. Declan. His sharp suit and polished demeanor stood in stark contrast to the casual energy of the shop's construction site. Cora's heart skipped as he approached, his expression calm but unreadable.

"Cora," he said, stopping a few feet away. "I hope I'm not interrupting."

She straightened, her notebook clutched tightly in her hands. "Declan. I'm sorry I never called you back. It's been so busy here, wrapping things up," she said, her tone careful.

"I heard you were getting close," he said simply, leaning in to kiss her cheek. "I wanted to see it for myself."

Cora hesitated, unsure how to respond as she fought the urge to just run to him. "It's coming along," she said finally. "I've been working on it every day."

Declan nodded, his gaze sweeping over the space. "It looks... incredible. You've done well."

"Thank you," Cora said softly, though the words felt heavy.

Declan's jaw tightened slightly, his tone softening. "I just wanted to say that I'm so proud of you. And if you ever need anything... you know where to find me."

Cora nodded, her chest tightening as she watched him leave. The encounter was brief but poignant, a bittersweet reminder of the inner confusion she battled.

That evening, as Cora sat on her bed, she replayed the encounter in her mind. Declan's words had been kind, but they carried an undertone of sadness that lingered in her chest. She opened a journal, her fingers tracing the familiar lines of her grandmother's handwriting: *Sometimes, the hardest choices are the ones that open our eyes and our hearts. But beginning something new is always worth the risk.*

The words brought a faint smile to her lips, the ache in her heart easing slightly. She felt torn—a longing for Declan's touch mixed with an unsettling confusion about his place in her life.

Later that night, Selah suggested a walk along the nearby park trail. The air was cool and crisp, the faint rustle of leaves creating a peaceful backdrop. They walked in comfortable silence for a while before Selah finally spoke.

"You seemed a little shaken earlier," she said gently. "Everything okay?"

Cora nodded, her hands tucked into her jacket pockets. "Declan stopping by the shop..." she admitted. "It wasn't bad, just... unexpected."

Selah frowned slightly but kept her tone even. "How do you feel about it?"

"I don't know," Cora said honestly. "It's like seeing him just tugs at my heart. But do I even really know him? We had a beautiful night together, and now I feel even more confused—like it's all happening so fast. And at the same time, I don't want to lose him. He makes me feel alive."

Selah's expression softened, her voice filled with quiet conviction. "Here's what matters. You're building something incredible, Cora. A new legacy. Take your time with Declan. Don't let anyone—or any feelings— pull you out of focus."

Cora looked at her, her chest tightening with gratitude. "Thank you," she said softly. "For always reminding me of that."

The shop's grand opening was fast approaching, and the anticipation filled Cora with equal parts excitement and trepidation. Each day brought her closer to completing the vision she had poured her heart into. The shop no longer felt like a project—it was becoming a part of her, a testament to the choices she had made and the woman she was becoming.

Selah arrived early that morning with a box of bagels and coffee in hand. "Thought you could use a proper breakfast," she said, setting the box down on the counter of the nearly completed shop.

Cora laughed softly, the tension in her chest easing as gratitude warmed her. "You know me too well," she said, grabbing a bagel and taking a bite.

Selah leaned against the counter, her gaze warm and steady. "You've done something amazing here, Cora. I hope you know that. I'm so glad I could be here to witness it."

Cora looked around the shop, the sunlight streaming through the windows and illuminating the freshly painted walls. "It still feels surreal," she admitted. "But it feels right."

Selah nodded, her voice soft but firm. "Because it is. And you've earned every bit of it."

MJ arrived just after noon, his arms overflowing with decorative items for the shop's final touches. "We need this place to scream *'Cora,'*" he declared, spreading everything out on the counter with a flourish.

Cora smiled, her heart swelling as she watched her friend's enthusiasm. "I think it's getting there," she said. "It finally feels like mine."

MJ nodded, his tone softening as he pressed both hands dramatically to his chest. "Because it is. Now, look at me getting all sentimental. Gram would be so proud."

Cora blinked back tears, her voice trembling as she said, "I hope so. This was her dream, too."

"It was," Selah added gently, her tone thoughtful. "But you've made it your own. That's what she would have wanted."

Later that evening, as Cora locked up the shop, she stood for a moment at the entrance, the cool metal of the keys grounding her in the moment. The space behind her was quiet, but it felt alive with possibility. She thought of the moments that had brought her here—the doubts, the heartbreak, the choices she had made—and felt a swell of pride.

Back at her loft, she opened the journal again, her eyes scanning the familiar lines of her grandmother's handwriting: *"Starting over is never easy. It's messy, painful, and sometimes it feels impossible. But the life you build from it is always worth the fight."*

The words resonated deeply, their truth wrapping around her like a warm embrace. She closed the journal, her heart steady as she prepared for what lay ahead.

That night, Selah suggested they take a walk along the cobbled streets. The cool night air brushed against their skin as they strolled beneath a canopy of stars, the mountainous backdrop evoking a sense of awe and wonder. The world felt vast and peaceful—a reminder that there was always space to breathe, to grow.

"You're quiet again tonight," Selah said gently, breaking the comfortable silence.

Cora smiled faintly, her gaze fixed on the star-dappled sky. "Just thinking," she said. "About everything. About how far I've come."

Selah's lips curved into a soft smile. "You should be proud of yourself," she said. "You've done something incredible, Cora."

Cora turned to her, her chest tightening with gratitude. "I am proud," she said softly. "But I couldn't have done it alone."

Selah reached for her hand, her touch warm and steady. "You're never alone," she said. "I will always be just a phone call away."

As they walked back to the loft, Cora felt a sense of calm settle over her. She was building something that was hers—something that reflected her strength, her choices, and her dreams.

And that was enough.

A Bond Shattered

"What was once binding can also become suffocating."

The walk back to the loft had felt like the closing of a chapter—a quiet acknowledgment of how far she'd come. Cora let the rare sense of calm wash over her, the thought of building something truly hers softening the edges of her usual worries. The future still loomed with uncertainty, but for once, it didn't scare her. She was creating a life that reflected her strength, her choices, and her dreams.

By morning, the calm had been replaced with a nervous buzz as the shop officially opened its doors. Cora stood near the entrance, smoothing the fabric of her dress and straightening a nearby display for the third time. But as customers began to filter in, their excitement spilling into the shop like a tidal wave, her nerves gave way to something else entirely: pride.

The air was alive with energy throughout the day, the warmth of the shop wrapping around each guest like an embrace. The carefully curated displays, the intimate lighting, and the personal touches she'd poured herself into had drawn in more people than she could have imagined.

Every approving smile, every word of praise seemed to breathe life into the space, turning it into more than a shop—it was a reflection of her.

Selah stayed close, her steady presence an anchor as she helped restock displays and answered questions from curious customers. Cora watched her friend move effortlessly through the shop, fielding compliments with a smile and redirecting conversations whenever Cora looked overwhelmed. By the time the last group left, the shop was quiet again, the buzz of the day giving way to the faint hum of the overhead lights.

Selah leaned against the counter, her grin infectious as she turned to Cora. "You survived your first day."

Cora laughed, the sound lighter than she expected. She leaned beside her, exhaustion settling into her limbs like a familiar friend. "Barely," she admitted, though the warmth of her smile made it clear she didn't regret a single second. "I can't believe how many people showed up."

"Of course they did," MJ chimed in, appearing from the back of the shop with a triumphant flourish. "You built something real. Something people want to be part of."

That evening, Selah insisted on a celebratory dinner at a cozy bistro downtown. The three of them—Cora, Selah, and MJ—sat at a small table near the window, the soft glow of candles casting warm light across their faces.

"To Cora," Selah said, raising her glass. "For having the courage to start over and the strength to keep going."

Cora's cheeks flushed as she clinked her glass with theirs. "Thank you," she said softly. "For being here. For everything."

As they ate, laughter filled the air, the weight of the past few months momentarily lifting. For the first time, Cora felt like she was truly celebrating—not just the shop's success, but the choices that had led her here.

Excusing herself to the restroom, Cora slipped away for a moment to gather her thoughts. Inside, a woman with a sharp, dark bob stood near the corner, her gaze lingering too long on Cora's reflection in the mirror. Something about her felt familiar—too familiar. A chill prickled the back of Cora's neck, but she forced herself to remain calm, quickly freshening up before returning to her table without a word.

As she sat back down, her phone buzzed, lighting up the screen. A chill ran through her as she read the message:

Yes, you are still being watched.

Cora made no mention of the ominous text to anyone. Today had been a good day, and she refused to let anything—or anyone—steal her sense of contentment in the moment.

Back at her loft, she sat by the window, a letter attached to a dozen gorgeous red roses from Declan resting on her desk. She picked it up, rereading the words he had written, her emotions a mixture of sadness and closure.

"You looked happy—truly happy. Congratulations."

Declan's acknowledgment of her happiness felt bittersweet. It was a reminder of what they had shared and the emotions she was now ready to face.

Cora tucked the letter into her journal, her grandmother's words surrounding it like a protective shield: *The choices we make can enlighten and free us. It is always worth the risk.*

She closed the journal, her heart feeling lighter. Declan's chapter in her life was just beginning, and she was determined to allow it to guide her toward clarity and strength.

Reaching for her phone, she typed a message to him:

Please come see me tomorrow. I have some things I'd like to say to you. The roses were just beautiful—thank you.

Declan replied quickly:

I'd love to.

The following day, Cora returned to the shop early, the quiet space filled with the scent of fresh flowers and polished wood. She moved through the shop, adjusting displays and straightening fabric swatches. Each task felt deliberate, grounding her in the present.

Selah arrived mid-morning, a coffee in each hand. "Ready for day two?" she asked, her smile easy.

"Ready," Cora said, her voice steady. "Yesterday was amazing. I still can't believe how well it went."

Selah leaned against the counter, her gaze warm. "You've built something incredible, Cora. And it's just the beginning. I fly out tomorrow, but I want to spend as much time with you as I can."

As the day unfolded, Cora noticed how natural it felt to work alongside Selah. Their dynamic was effortless, their years of friendship evident in every unspoken gesture. Selah anticipated her needs before she voiced them, and her quiet encouragement steadied her when doubts crept in.

By evening, as they locked up the shop together, Cora turned to her, her heart swelling with gratitude. "You've been here every step of the way," she said softly. "I don't know how to thank you."

"You don't have to thank me," Selah replied, her voice steady. "I just want to see you happy."

Cora's gaze lingered on her, the warmth of her words settling over her. "I think I'm getting there," she admitted. "For the first time in a long time."

Just then, Declan approached the shop, his figure framed against the soft glow of the streetlights outside the bridal shop's door.

"I'll meet you at the loft, Cora," Selah said, brushing a quick hello to Declan before disappearing down the sidewalk.

Cora turned to him, her heart racing. "Declan, I… I don't know what to say. I miss you. How are you?" She fumbled for the right words, her emotions a jumble.

Declan stepped closer, his expression soft yet purposeful. "My Cora," he said, his voice low. "Don't say a word. Come here and let me hold you."

Together, they walked hand in hand, exchanging light chatter about the time that had passed and sharing promises of a new beginning. For Cora, this meant taking on one more risk—something her Gram seemed to guide her toward in every quiet moment of reflection.

That night, as Cora sat in her loft, she flipped through her notebook, her pen moving steadily across the pages. Each sketch and note were steps toward the future she was building—a future that felt entirely hers.

The sound of her phone buzzing broke her focus. It was a message from Jensen:

"How does it feel to be the town's newest success story?"

Cora smiled as she typed back:

"Exhausting but worth it. I can't believe this is my life."

Jensen's reply came quickly:

"Believe it. You're amazing. I wish I could have been there."

Cora set the phone down, her heart swelling with gratitude. For the first time, she felt like she could see the road ahead clearly—and it was a road she had chosen for herself.

For the first time, she felt that the risks she'd taken weren't just worth it—they were necessary.

The shop was quickly becoming a hub of activity in the town, drawing in customers who appreciated its charm and personal touch. Every visit brought Cora closer to the community she was rebuilding, and each interaction strengthened her belief that she had made the right choice.

One afternoon, a middle-aged woman lingered near the front display, her fingers brushing over a swatch of fabric. She turned to Cora, her expression warm and curious. "This place feels special," she said. "Like there's a story behind it."

Cora smiled, her chest tightening with emotion. "Thank you," she said softly. "It means a lot to hear that."

"It shows," the woman continued. "You've poured your heart into this, haven't you?"

"I have," Cora admitted, her voice steady. "Every bit of it."

The woman nodded, her gaze kind. "It's beautiful. And so are you—for creating something like this."

As the woman left, Cora stood by the door, her heart full. Each small moment like this felt like confirmation that she was on the right path.

Cora had met other independent business owners in the district and set up collaboration events with them, each fueled by a shared passion to grow alongside one another. The community had welcomed her with open arms, and she quickly became a member of the Women's Business Development Center, the Chamber of Commerce, and the Entrepreneurs' Organization. The steady support reminded her she wasn't alone in this journey, and for that, she was profoundly grateful.

That evening, Declan stopped by the shop just as Cora was closing up. He leaned casually against the counter, his easy smile a constant source of reassurance. "Busy day?" he asked, watching her as she restocked a display.

"Busy, but good," Cora replied, her voice light as she rearranged fabric swatches. "It's starting to feel like home."

Declan nodded, his tone thoughtful. "That's because it is. You've made it yours."

Cora paused, her hand resting on a bolt of fabric as she turned to look at him. "You always know what to say," she murmured, her voice trembling slightly.

Declan's smile widened, his gaze steady and unwavering. "It's easy when it feels so natural," he said simply. Then, his tone shifted slightly, carrying a playful edge. "Listen, the hospital is throwing a fundraiser next week. I'd love to throw a sexy satin dress on you and parade you around—if you're up for it."

Cora grinned, tossing her hair with a flirtatious smile. "Well, that sounds enticing. And I think I have just the dress."

The following weekend, MJ insisted on throwing a small gathering at the shop to celebrate its success. Twinkling lights and fresh flowers transformed the space into a cozy, magical venue.

"Tonight isn't just about the shop," MJ declared, raising a glass as a small group of close friends gathered around. "It's about Cora—about her strength, her courage, her sass, and her ability to rebuild something totally badass! You're amazing, and we're all so proud of you."

Cora blushed, tears pricking at her eyes as the group cheered. "Thank you," she said, her voice trembling with emotion. "For believing in me— even when I didn't."

"You're unstoppable," MJ said, wrapping her in a tight hug. "And I pity the fool that ever tries to come at you."

After the celebration, Cora sat alone in the shop, the soft glow of the lights casting warm patterns across the walls. The space was quiet now, but it felt alive with possibility. She opened her journal, her grandmother's words echoing in her mind like a steady heartbeat: *"Strength doesn't come from certainty. It comes from moving forward, even when you're afraid."*

Cora smiled faintly, her chest tightening with emotion. She had been afraid—terrified, even—but she had moved forward anyway. And now, she could see the life she was building taking shape, one deliberate choice at a time.

Later that night, Declan and Cora took a walk, the cool night air brushing against their skin. The world felt vast and peaceful, the stars above shining brightly as they strolled in comfortable silence, their footsteps echoing softly on the cobblestones.

"You've been smiling more lately," Declan said, breaking the quiet. His voice was soft but certain, the kind of tone that made her heart flutter.

Cora glanced at him, her heart swelling at the simplicity of his observation. "It feels good to smile again," she admitted, her voice tinged with honesty. "For the first time in a long time, I feel like I'm where I'm supposed to be."

Declan stopped walking, turning to face her. His dark eyes held hers with an intensity that sent a shiver down her spine. "That's because you are," he said softly, his voice steady and resolute. "And you're only going to keep growing."

Cora's cheeks flushed, a warmth spreading through her chest. Gratitude and something deeper stirred within her. "Thank you," she said, her voice trembling slightly. "For being here. For believing in me."

Declan reached out, his fingers brushing lightly against hers before taking her hand. "Always," he replied, his tone filled with quiet conviction.

They continued walking, hand in hand, the world around them fading into the background. For the first time, Cora felt a sense of balance—between fear and courage, uncertainty and hope. She was creating something real, something hers. And with Declan beside her, the path ahead felt less daunting, filled with possibility.

A Promise Broken

"Not all promises are meant to be kept; some are meant to free us."

The night was an affair of elegance and extravagance, the kind Cora had only ever seen in movies. The grand event hall stood illuminated against the evening sky, its towering glass walls reflecting golden lights strung across the entrance. A red carpet stretched from the street to the doors, flanked by manicured hedges and flickering lanterns that cast soft shadows on the pavement.

Guests arrived in pairs and groups, their laughter and chatter blending into a symphony of sophistication.

Cora stood near the entrance, her midnight-blue dress clinging to her curves in all the right places, the silky fabric shimmering with every movement. She adjusted the strap nervously, her other hand gripping a sequined clutch that felt heavier than it should.

Beside her, Declan exuded effortless confidence, his tailored black suit accentuating his broad shoulders and sharp jawline. His hand rested lightly on her back, his touch steady, grounding her.

"You look perfect," he murmured, leaning closer so only she could hear. His breath tickled her ear, sending a shiver down her spine.

Cora glanced up at him, her chest tightening at the confidence in his gaze. "Let's hope you're right," she replied, forcing a smile.

As the grand doors swung open, they stepped inside, the cool air of the hall greeting them like a whispered invitation.

Cora's breath hitched as she took in the scene:

Chandeliers dripped from the vaulted ceiling like crystal waterfalls, their light scattering shimmering patterns across the black-and-white checkered floors.

Towering floral arrangements of white roses and deep red dahlias framed the room, their scent mingling with the crisp tang of champagne and the faint smokiness of expensive cigars.

Women in glittering gowns laughed behind jeweled masks of formality, their smiles sharp and practiced.

Men in bespoke suits exchanged lingering handshakes, their conversations full of power plays and hidden agendas.

Cora felt like she'd stepped into a different world—a world where power and wealth danced together under golden chandeliers.

Declan led her through the crowd with the ease of a man who had done this a hundred times before. Every few steps, someone stopped him to exchange greetings, their smiles widening when they saw Cora at his side.

"So, this is the woman who's managed to tame Declan," an older gentleman said with a chuckle, shaking Cora's hand. His overpowering cologne—a cloud of cedar and leather—made her stomach churn. His gaze flickered over her, assessing. Sizing her up.

"I didn't think anyone could."

Cora managed a polite smile, though her cheeks warmed under the weight of the attention. Declan's hand tightened slightly on her back, a small but deliberate reassurance.

"She's more than capable," he said smoothly, his smile warm but firm. "I'm the lucky one."

The conversation moved on, but the words lingered with Cora as they made their way further into the hall.

Declan stopped briefly to greet another group, his charm slipping into place like second nature. His voice was smooth, practiced—as if he belonged here effortlessly.

Cora took the opportunity to scan the room. Her gaze landed on a familiar figure near the bar.

Evelyn.

She was glowing under the soft lights, her gold dress shimmering like liquid sunlight. A laugh escaped her lips as she leaned into conversation, her posture relaxed, magnetic.

Cora hesitated. She had never truly figured Evelyn out. There was something enigmatic about her—an undeniable allure, a quiet power that made people lean in when she spoke.

For a moment, as she watched Evelyn tilt her head back in laughter, the tension in her chest eased.

"Declan, I see Evelyn," Cora murmured, offering him a small smile. "I'm going to say hello."

Declan nodded, his eyes softening. "I'll come find you in a bit," he said, pressing a light kiss to her temple before turning back to his conversation.

Cora made her way toward Evelyn, her heels clicking softly against the polished marble.

The moment she arrived, Evelyn enveloped her in a warm hug, her laughter bubbling over like champagne.

"Look at you," Evelyn said, pulling back to admire her. "You look like a queen."

She gestured to the man beside her. "This is Elias."

Cora smiled, nodding a hello. "So do you."

"Don't let her fool you," Elias interjected, his tone teasing as he glanced at Evelyn. "She's been stealing champagne off passing trays all night."

Evelyn swatted at him playfully, her eyes glimmering with mischief. "Guilty as charged."

Cora laughed, the sound easing some of the lingering tension in her chest. "How's the party so far?" she asked, accepting a flute of champagne from a passing waiter.

"Glamorous, overwhelming, and full of people I'll never see again," Evelyn replied, her tone conspiratorial. "Exactly how I like it."

Elias nodded toward the crowd. "And Declan's in his element."

Cora followed his gaze, her eyes landing on Declan, who stood among a group of sharply dressed men, his presence commanding without effort. He laughed at something one of them said, his hand resting lightly on the back of a chair. There was something magnetic about him—the way he drew people in with ease—but there was also a distance, a guarded edge that made him feel just out of reach.

"Cora, right?"

A warm voice pulled her attention.

She turned to find a young man standing nearby, dressed impeccably in a tailored suit, his smile easy and inviting.

"I'm Ryder," he said, extending a hand. "Declan's intern."

Cora blinked, startled by his familiarity. "Yes, that's me," she said, shaking his hand. "It's nice to meet you."

"Likewise," Ryder replied, his gaze lingering on her a moment longer than necessary as he cast an appraising glance. "Declan talks about you all the time."

Cora's cheeks warmed. She glanced toward Evelyn, who arched an amused eyebrow but said nothing.

"Does he?" she asked, keeping her tone light.

Ryder nodded, his smile widening. "He does. But I don't think words do you justice."

The compliment caught her off guard, sending an unexpected flutter through her stomach.

"Thank you," she said softly.

Ryder's gaze shifted to the dance floor, where couples swayed to the soft strains of the orchestra.

"Do you dance?" he asked suddenly, his tone playful. "Because I could use a partner, and Declan seems preoccupied."

Cora hesitated, glancing toward Evelyn, who gave her an encouraging nod.

"Why not?" she said finally, setting her champagne flute on the bar.

Ryder grinned, offering his hand. "Perfect."

With effortless confidence, he led her to the dance floor, weaving through the glistening crowd as the orchestra's melody swelled.

Under the glow of chandeliers, the marble beneath their feet shimmered, the lights reflecting in soft golden hues.

Ryder placed a hand lightly on her waist, his touch firm but respectful. His other hand held hers gently.

"Shall we?" he asked, his grin playful.

Cora let out a small breath, still adjusting to the unfamiliar attention.

"Lead the way."

Ryder stepped into the rhythm effortlessly, his movements precise, assured.

Cora followed, surprised by the natural ease between them. It felt as if they had danced together a hundred times before.

She laughed softly, her nerves ebbing as she allowed herself to be swept into the music.

"You're a good dancer," she remarked.

"My mother insisted," Ryder replied, his tone light with amusement. "She said knowing how to dance was nonnegotiable if I wanted to survive events like this."

He leaned in slightly, smirking. "But honestly? I'd rather be in my white tank and bib overalls. I'm country."

He laughed, wearing his confidence like a second skin. "Drives my mother crazy."

Cora chuckled, her smile widening. "She was right about the dancing."

They twirled through the crowd, their steps effortlessly in sync.

The fabric of her dress whispered against the floor with each turn, the soft swish blending with the melody of the waltz.

For a moment, the tension of the evening melted away, replaced by the simple, intoxicating joy of the dance.

"You seem more relaxed now," Ryder observed, his voice quieter as they continued their dance.

Cora glanced up at him, her smile faltering slightly. "Is it that obvious?"

Ryder chuckled, his grip on her hand tightening just enough to steady her as they turned. "A little. But you're doing great. These events can be... overwhelming."

"That's an understatement," Cora said, shaking her head. "It's like stepping into a different world."

Ryder's smile softened, his gaze searching hers. "It is. But you belong here, you know."

The words caught her off guard, leaving her momentarily speechless. Before she could respond, Evelyn's laughter rang through the ballroom, drawing Cora's attention.

She turned her head just in time to see Gage—one of Declan's shareholders—leaning in close, whispering something into Evelyn's ear. Whatever he said made her laugh, the sound light but unguarded.

Then, Gage's hand brushed against Evelyn's arm, a lingering touch that made Cora's stomach twist. Before she could fully process what she was seeing, Gage tilted his head and pressed a slow, deliberate kiss to Evelyn's lips, his hand lingering at her waist.

Cora's breath hitched. That wasn't a casual kiss.

She stumbled slightly, her focus breaking.

Ryder caught her with a firm grip. "You okay?" he asked, concern flickering across his face.

"Yeah," Cora said quickly, but her gaze darted back to Evelyn.

Her friend looked startled, her expression a mix of shock and something unreadable.

The dance ended just as the orchestra's final note hung in the air, followed by a round of polite applause.

Ryder released her gently, his eyes still searching hers. "Thank you for the dance," he said warmly. "You're a natural."

Cora barely registered his words. "Thank you," she murmured.

"Who was that tall drink of water you were waltzing with, *Mon Chérie?*"

MJ's voice cut through the moment as he materialized at her side, his expression gleaming with mischief.

"That was Ryder, Declan's intern," Cora replied absently, smoothing her gown.

MJ arched a brow. "Well, where do I find me one of those?"

Adjusting the swallow tails on his coat with a flourish, he sauntered away into the crowd before she could respond.

Cora barely heard him. Her focus remained locked on Evelyn, who was now walking away from Gage, her movements stiff and uncharacteristically restrained.

Something wasn't right.

"Cora."

Declan's voice snapped her back to reality. She turned to find him approaching, his expression unreadable but laced with amusement.

"I saw you dancing just now," he remarked.

"Yes," Cora said quickly, slipping her hand into his. "I met Ryder."

Declan studied her, his gaze sharp but giving nothing away. Then he nodded, his grip tightening slightly, a subtle reassurance.

"Let's get some air."

Declan guided Cora toward the expansive terrace, where the cool night air provided relief from the intensity of the ballroom.

Beyond the infinity pool stretching toward the terrace edge, the city lights twinkled against the water's glassy surface. The faint scent of jasmine and freshly cut grass carried on the breeze, mingling with the distant notes of music drifting from inside.

Cora leaned against the terrace railing, gripping the cool metal as she inhaled deeply.

"It's beautiful out here," she murmured, her voice nearly lost to the hush of the evening.

Declan stepped beside her, his presence steady, grounding.

"It is," he replied, though his gaze remained fixed on her, not the view. "But you seem distracted."

Cora hesitated, the weight of what she had seen pressing against her.

"I'm just... worried about Evelyn," she admitted finally, glancing at him. "I saw something earlier. She didn't seem like herself."

Declan's brow furrowed slightly. "What did you see?"

"Gage kissed her," Cora said, her voice low. "And it wasn't... casual. It felt like more."

Declan exhaled sharply, his jaw tightening.

"Gage can be... forward," he said carefully. "Evelyn has been known to put herself in uncomfortable positions."

Cora nodded, her chest tightening. "I just want her to be okay."

Declan reached for her hand, his grip gentle but firm.

"You two have bonded, I see."

Before Cora could respond, a commotion stirred inside—the sudden rise of voices cutting through the night's tranquility.

Declan's expression darkened as he straightened, his hand slipping from hers.

"Stay here," he said firmly. "I'll check it out."

Minutes later, he returned, his demeanor notably more relaxed.

"Looks like they just announced the highest donation," he said with a small smirk. "Our evening can come to a close—if you wish."

Cora smiled softly, her fingers brushing against the fabric of his jacket.

"I never thought you'd ask."

A Heartbound Choice

"When the heart is bound, every choice feels like a gamble."

The scotch sat untouched beside Declan as he leaned back in his leather chair, the soft glow of the desk lamp casting shadows across his face. Cora consumed his thoughts, an obsession that had grown with every passing day. The way she moved, the sound of her laughter, and her defiant independence—all of it drove him mad with desire.

She had built her shop with a determination that both impressed and infuriated him. Cora was fire wrapped in a frame so delicate it almost seemed like a contradiction. But to Declan, that fire wasn't something to admire from a distance—it was something to claim. She was his, and no amount of independence would change that.

He closed his eyes, his mind drifting to a vision of her that had haunted him for weeks. She was in their home, standing barefoot in the kitchen, her long legs on display beneath one of his grey t-shirts. The fabric brushed her thighs as she moved, swaying to music only she could hear. Her hair was messy, tumbling over her shoulders in soft waves, and her cheeks were flushed.

She didn't see him watching her, her movements unguarded and sensual. Declan imagined stepping into the room, the sound of his shoes on the marble floor catching her attention. She would turn, startled at first, but her lips would curve into that playful smile that always disarmed him.

"Good morning," she would say, her voice husky from sleep.

But he wouldn't respond with words. Instead, he'd close the distance between them in a few swift strides, his hands finding her waist as he backed her against the counter. Her laughter would fade into a soft gasp as he pressed his lips to her neck, his fingers sliding beneath the fabric of the shirt.

"You're mine," he would murmur, his voice rough with need. "Always mine."

The thought sent a shiver through him, his pulse quickening as he envisioned her melting into his touch, her breath hitching as he traced the curve of her thighs. In his mind, he lifted her onto the counter, her bare legs wrapping around him as she whispered his name, her voice trembling with desire.

Declan opened his eyes, his jaw tight as he reached for the small velvet box on his desk. Inside was the ring—a diamond that was bold yet timeless, much like Cora herself. Tonight, he would make her understand. She wasn't just a fleeting thought or a passing infatuation. She was his, and he needed to make her his in every way.

He picked up his phone, typing a quick message to the limo driver:

She's at the shop. Make it smooth. No delays.

His lips curved into a satisfied smile as he imagined the driver holding the sign that read, *"My Cora."* It was bold, possessive, and intentional. He wanted her to know, without a doubt, that she belonged to him.

Declan sent another message, this one to Cora:

The limo is for you. I'll see you soon.

He leaned back in his chair, the weight of the evening ahead settling over him. The scavenger hunt was meticulously planned, each stop chosen to reflect their connection. At the final stop, his estate, he would be waiting. The image of her stepping out of the limo, her eyes wide with curiosity, sent a rush of anticipation through him.

He wouldn't wait long once she arrived. He imagined her surprise as he pulled her into the limo, his hands gripping her waist as he silenced her questions with a kiss. She would gasp her body soft against his as he pressed her into the leather seat.

The thought alone sent heat coursing through him. Tonight, Cora would say yes. She would be his, fully and completely, and nothing would stand in the way of that.

The limo pulled up to the curb in front of Cora's shop, its sleek black exterior gleaming under the afternoon sun. MJ noticed it first, peering out the window with exaggerated curiosity. "Uh, Cora?" he called, stepping away from the bridal display he'd been rearranging. "Are you expecting someone? Because that screams VIP."

Cora glanced up from the shipment of fabric she was sorting, her brow furrowing. "What are you talking about?"

MJ waved her over, practically bouncing with excitement. "Come see for yourself!" She walked to the front of the shop, the bell above the door chiming softly as she stepped outside. The driver stood next to the car, a small sign in his hand that read, *"My Cora."*

MJ burst into laughter, clapping his hands together. "Oh, he did *not*," he said, his grin wide. "Who needs subtlety when you've got this?"

Cora's phone buzzed in her pocket. She pulled it out to see a text from Declan:

The limo is for you. I'll see you soon.

Her heart skipped, her stomach twisting with a mix of anticipation and nerves. Declan had always had a flair for the dramatic, but this? This was on another level.

MJ leaned against the doorframe, smirking. "Well, Cinderella, your carriage awaits. Go on, before the driver starts playing violins."

Cora rolled her eyes but couldn't suppress a small laugh. "You'll hold down the fort?"

"Obviously," MJ replied, waving her off. "Now get out of here before I start crying over how damn romantic this is."

She shook her head, stepping toward the limo. The driver opened the door for her with a polite nod, and she slid inside, the cool leather interior wrapping around her like a swathe. The car pulled away smoothly, leaving MJ grinning in the doorway as he watched her go.

The first stop on the scavenger hunt was a quaint little gift shop tucked into a quiet corner of downtown. The bell above the door chimed as Cora stepped inside, her curiosity growing with each step. The shopkeeper greeted her with a warm, yet hesitant smile, handing her a small, delicately wrapped box. "This is for you," she said, her tone conspiratorial.

Cora unwrapped the gift carefully, revealing a charm bracelet. Each charm represented a moment she and Declan had shared—a small coffee cup for their first date, a book for their late-night conversations, a rose for the first bouquet he had given her.

Her phone buzzed again, another text from Declan:

Stop two is waiting. Don't keep me waiting too long, my love.

The limo whisked her to the next location, a small bookstore that smelled of paper and ink. The shopkeeper slowly handed her a hardcover book of poetry, its pages filled with handwritten notes from Declan in the margins.

At the third stop, an art gallery, she received a painting—a swirling abstract piece that captured the emotions she had shared with Declan over the months.

As the hunt continued, Cora began to notice something. A man sitting in a café across the street, a woman browsing in the shop beside her— they lingered a moment too long, their eyes following her as she moved. It wasn't threatening, but it wasn't subtle either. A prickle of unease crept up her spine, the sense that she was being watched growing with each stop.

By the time the limo pulled through the gates of Declan's estate, her emotions were a tangle of curiosity and apprehension. The grounds were bathed in the warm glow of twilight, the sprawling gardens alive with the scent of flowers. The driver opened the door, and she stepped out, her breath catching at the sight before her. A white-clothed dinner table sat in the garden, surrounded by candles and an explosion of blooms. Declan stood nearby, his silhouette sharp and commanding against the setting sun. But before she could take it all in, Declan was in front of her, his hands gripping her waist as he pulled her against him.

"You took your time," he murmured, his voice low and rough.

"Declan—"

Her words were silenced as his mouth claimed hers, his kiss urgent and possessive. The air around them seemed to thrum with electricity as his hands slid up her back, pulling her closer.

"Get in," he said, his voice husky as he motioned toward the open limo door. Cora barely had time to process before he was guiding her inside, the door shutting behind them with a soft click. They were soon sealed into the intimate confines of the limo. The driver had barely taken his seat when Declan moved, overcoming the gap between them with a predatory intensity. His hands were on her waist, pulling her into his lap as though the space between them was unbearable.

"You drive me mad, Cora," he growled, his lips brushing against her ear. "I couldn't wait a second longer."

Cora gasped, her hands gripping his shoulders as he tilted her head back, his mouth descending on hers with a hunger that left no room for hesitation. His kiss was possessive, claiming her completely as his hands roamed her body, sliding up her thighs and under the fabric of her dress. The soft leather seat cradled them as he pushed her back, his weight pressing her down as he whispered, "Do you have any idea what you do to me?"

His lips left hers, trailing hot kisses down the column of her neck. Cora found herself gasping for breath, her fingers tangling in his hair as he explored her with a fervor that bordered on desperation. The limo rocked slightly as he adjusted her beneath him, his hands gripping her hips as though he couldn't get enough of her.

"I need you," he murmured, his voice rough with desire. "Right now. Right here."

Cora's cheeks flushed, the heat of his words sending a thrill through her. "Declan," she whispered, her voice trembling with a mix of hesitation and need. He silenced her with another kiss, his hands sliding higher, finding the edge of her lace and pushing it aside. The intimacy of the moment was electric, the confined space amplifying every sensation as they lost themselves in each other.

The limo driver kept his gaze firmly ahead, his professionalism unwavering despite the heat radiating from the backseat. Outside, the estate's manicured gardens passed in a blur, but neither of them noticed. For Declan, the world had narrowed to Cora—her soft gasps, the way her body arched into his touch, the heat between them that refused to be ignored. The limo's plush interior seemed to shrink around them, the heat of their bodies and the tension between them filling every corner. Declan's lips moved down her neck, his breath hot against her skin as his hands explored her curves with a deliberate hunger. The dress she wore shifted beneath his touch, the fabric giving way as his fingers traced every line of her body.

"Do you have any idea how long I've been waiting for this?" he whispered against her collarbone, his voice rough with desire. "You make me lose control, Cora."

She couldn't answer—not with the way her heart was racing, as his hands slid under the hem of her dress, finding the bare skin of her thighs. Her back arched instinctively, pressing her closer to him as her fingers tangled in his hair.

"Declan," she managed to whisper, her voice trembling with a mix of anticipation and need. His lips found hers again, this time softer but no less intense, his kiss filled with a possessive tenderness that sent a shiver down her spine. His hands gripped her hips, pulling her firmly onto his lap, their bodies fitting together as though they had been made for this moment.

"I've imagined this," he murmured against her mouth, his words sending heat pooling in her core. "Every curve, every sound, every gasp... you're mine, Cora. Always mine."

His hands roamed freely now, sliding up her back and pulling her closer as he deepened the kiss. She could feel the intensity of his need, the way his body pressed against hers as though he couldn't bear the thought of even an inch of space between them.

"Declan," she whispered again, her voice barely audible over the sound of their mingled breaths.

"Say it," he demanded softly, his hands stilling as his gaze locked onto hers. His eyes burned with intensity, his voice low and commanding. "Say you're mine."

Cora inhaled sharply, her chest rising and falling rapidly as she met his gaze. "I'm yours," she said softly, the words trembling but certain. "I'm always yours."

A low growl escaped him, his lips capturing hers in a kiss that was both tender and raw. His hands moved with purpose now, sliding the fabric of her dress higher as he explored her with an intensity that left no doubt of his desire. Time seemed to blur in the confined space of the limo, the world outside forgotten as they lost themselves in each other. The driver kept his gaze fixed firmly ahead; his character unyielding despite the heat emitting from the back of the limo.

Declan's whispers grew softer, his voice filled with reverence as he murmured her name against her skin. Every touch, every kiss was a promise, a declaration of his obsession, his need, his unwavering claim on her. The world outside the limo faded completely, leaving only the electric connection between them. Declan's hands roamed freely now, his touch alternating between firm and featherlight, leaving trails of heat along her skin. His lips traced a slow path down her neck, his breath hot against her collarbone as he whispered, "You drive me to the edge, Cora. Every part of you makes me lose control."

Her body responded instinctively, her back arching against the plush seat as her fingers tightened in his hair. The thin fabric of her dress bunched around her hips, and she could feel the heat radiating from him, a raw need that mirrored her own.

"Declan," she murmured, her voice trembling with desire and hesitation.

His hands slid higher, brushing over lace that did little to shield her from his touch. "You're perfect," he said roughly, his lips brushing the sensitive spot just below her ear. "Every inch of you, mine."

She gasped as his teeth grazed her skin, a shiver coursing through her as he pressed closer. His body surrounded her, his weight grounding her as his touch sent waves of pleasure rippling through her.

His hands were relentless, exploring her curves, tugging at the barriers between them until there was nothing left. She felt exposed, vulnerable, but the intensity in his gaze made her feel worshipped, cherished in a way that stole the air from her lungs.

"Look at me," he commanded softly, his hands framing her face as his eyes bore into hers. "I want you to remember this. Every touch. Every word. Because I'll never let you go, Cora. You're mine."

Her chest rose and fell rapidly, her body trembling beneath him as she whispered, "I'm yours."

The declaration sent a spark through him, and he kissed her again, deeper this time, his hands gripping her hips as he guided her closer. The limo rocked slightly as he moved against her, his control fraying with every soft sound that escaped her lips.

Their movements grew frantic, their breaths mingling as they lost themselves completely. The heat between them was all-consuming, leaving no room for doubt, no space for hesitation. Declan's hands tightened on her waist, pulling her closer as his lips traced every inch of her skin, his whispers a blend of reverence and possession.

The air in the limo was thick with the remnants of their shared intensity, their breaths still uneven as they remained pressed against each other. Declan's hands rested on her hips, his fingers tracing lazy circles over her skin as if unwilling to break the connection between them. The flush on Cora's cheeks deepened as she shifted slightly, her dress askew, her heart still racing from the heat of the moment.

He leaned back against the seat, his eyes dark and filled with satisfaction as he studied her. "You undo me, Cora," he said, his voice low and rough. "Every time, you leave me wanting more."

She laughed softly, her fingers brushing over his jawline. "You're insatiable," she replied, her voice trembling with a mix of teasing and lingering desire.

Declan's lips curved into a wicked smile. "Only when it comes to you." He reached out, smoothing a strand of hair from her face. "But tonight isn't over yet."

Her brow furrowed slightly as she adjusted the strap of her dress. "What else do you have planned?"

Declan's hand slid over hers, his grip firm yet gentle. "You'll see," he said cryptically, his gaze holding hers. "But first, you need to catch your breath."

The limo pulled to a smooth stop, the driver stepping out to open the door. Cora blinked, the cool night air hitting her skin as Declan stepped out first, extending a hand to help her. As she stepped out, her breath caught in her throat. The estate's expansive gardens had been transformed into something out of a dream. Twinkling lights hung from the trees, casting a warm glow over the scene. A small table draped in pristine white linen sat in the center, surrounded by cascading floral arrangements. The soft hum of instrumental music floated through the air, blending with the gentle rustle of the breeze.

"This is... stunning," Cora whispered, her voice filled with awe.

Declan stepped closer, his hand sliding around her waist as he guided her forward. "Only the best for you," he murmured. "You deserve all of this and more."

Her heels clicked softly against the stone path as they approached the table, its surface adorned with elegant place settings and flickering candles. But before they could sit, Declan paused, turning to face her fully.

"There's something I need to do first," he said, his tone shifting to something softer, more vulnerable.

Declan knelt before her, pulling a small velvet box from his pocket. The glow of the lights reflected in his eyes as he opened it, revealing a diamond ring that caught the light like fire.

"Cora," he began, his voice steady but filled with emotion. "You've turned my life upside down in the best way. You challenge me, push me, make me want to be better every day. I don't just want you in my life— I need you. Marry me. Be mine in every way that matters."

Cora's heart pounded, her vision blurring slightly as her emotions swirled. The life she had been building—the independence she had fought so hard for—stood at odds with the overwhelming pull she felt toward him.

"Yes," she whispered, her voice trembling. "I will."

Declan's smile widened, his relief and joy evident as he slid the ring onto her finger. He rose to his feet, pulling her into his arms and pressing a kiss to her lips.

"You won't regret this," he murmured against her mouth. "I'll make sure of it."

Cora smiled faintly, her fingers brushing over the ring. As they moved to sit at the table, the mountains stretching out before them, she couldn't shake the mix of elation and uncertainty settling in her chest.

Declan pulled out a chair for Cora, his movements deliberate, as if orchestrating a moment too perfect to be left to chance. The soft glow of the candles illuminated her face, highlighting the lingering flush on her cheeks. She slid into the seat, her fingers brushing over the edge of the white linen tablecloth as she tried to steady her racing thoughts.

The table was adorned with an elegant spread—delicate plates of hors d'oeuvres, a bottle of champagne chilling in an ornate silver bucket, and small floral arrangements that mirrored the explosion of blooms surrounding them. The estate's gardens stretched out before them; the distant mountains bathed in the silver light of the moon.

Declan sat across from her, pouring two glasses of champagne with practiced ease. His eyes never left hers as he slid one glass toward her, his lips curving into a faint smile.

"To us," he said, raising his glass. "To the life we're going to build together."

Cora hesitated for a moment before lifting her glass, her voice soft as she replied, "To us."

The clink of their glasses felt final, like a promise sealed under the watchful glow of the stars. She took a sip, the bubbles bursting softly against her lips, and tried to ignore the swirling mix of emotions tightening in her chest.

He leaned forward, his elbows resting on the table as his gaze swept over her. "You're quiet," he remarked, his tone gentle but probing. "What's on your mind?"

"Declan," she began softly, her voice trembling. "I need you to understand something. I've worked so hard to get where I am. To have something that's mine."

He didn't pull his hand away, but his jaw tightened slightly. "I know," he said, his tone measured. "And I admire that about you. Your strength, your ambition—it's part of why I love you."

"But?" she pressed, her eyes searching his.

"But I don't want it to come between us," he admitted. "I don't want your independence to feel like distance. I want us to build something together—something that's ours."

She absorbed his words. She wanted that too—wanted him—but the thought of losing herself in the process terrified her.

Declan rose from his seat, his chair scraping softly against the stone patio as he stepped around the table. He reached for her hand, guiding her to her feet with a tenderness that left her breathless.

"I know you're afraid," he said, his voice low. "Afraid of what this means, of what you might lose. But I promise you, Cora, you won't lose yourself. Not with me. I'll give you the world and still leave room for you to take what's yours."

Tears pricked at her eyes as she searched his face, the vulnerability in his gaze disarming her. "And if I need space?" she whispered. "If I need to hold on to what I've built?"

"Then I'll give you that too," he said without hesitation. "Because I'd rather fight to stay in your life than risk losing you altogether."

Her lips trembled, the weight of his words sinking into her. "I want to believe that," she said softly.

"Then let me prove it," he replied, his hand sliding around her waist as he pulled her against him. "Starting now."

Her heart ached at his words, the sincerity in his voice pulling her closer to him even as a flicker of doubt crept into her thoughts. This moment felt like a dream, but the weight of her independence—the life she had been building—pressed heavily against it.

Declan's hand rested on the small of Cora's back as he guided her toward the edge of the garden, the soft glow of the estate lights casting their shadows across the stone path. The silence between them wasn't awkward but charged, heavy with the weight of what had just transpired. The ring on her finger caught the light, a brilliant reminder of the promise she had just made—a promise that both excited and terrified her.

He stopped near a low stone wall that overlooked the sprawling grounds and the distant mountains. The view was breathtaking, the kind of serene beauty that made the world feel still. Declan stood behind her, his arms circling her waist as he pulled her back against his chest.

"Do you know what you mean to me, Cora?" he murmured against her ear, his voice low and intimate.

She leaned into him, her fingers brushing against his forearms. "Tell me," she said softly, her words almost a challenge.

"You're everything," he said simply, his lips grazing her temple. "Everything I've ever wanted. Everything I didn't know I needed."

Her emotions swirling as his words settled over her. She turned in his arms, her hands resting on his chest as she met his gaze. The intensity in his eyes left her feeling both exposed and cherished.

"You make it sound so easy," she whispered, her voice trembling. "But it's not. I've worked so hard to find myself, to have something that's mine. And I'm afraid of losing that."

Declan's hands cupped her face, his thumbs brushing over her cheekbones. "You're not losing anything," he said firmly. "You're gaining me. Us. And I'll make sure that what's yours stays yours. Always."

Her heart ached at the conviction in his voice, the way his words felt like both a promise and a plea. She wanted to believe him, to trust that he could give her the space she needed without losing the connection that bound them together.

As the night deepened, they moved to a nearby bench, the cool stone a grounding contrast to the warmth between them. Declan pulled her close, his arm draped over her shoulders as they sat in comfortable silence. The stars above twinkled faintly, their light reflecting in Cora's eyes as she traced the ring on her finger.

"You've turned my world upside down," Declan said after a while, his voice breaking the quiet.

Cora smiled faintly, her fingers brushing over his. "You make it sound like I've done something monumental," she said, her tone teasing but gentle.

"You have," he replied, his gaze serious. "You've made me see what matters. You've made me want to be better—for you, for us."

Her chest tightened at his words, the sincerity in his tone disarming her. She turned to him, her lips curving into a soft smile. "Then I guess we'll have to figure this out together."

Declan leaned in, his forehead resting against hers. "We will," he said softly. "Because I'm not letting you go."

His lips found hers in a kiss that was slow and deep, filled with a reverence that left her breathless. As the night stretched on, the weight of her fears began to lift, replaced by the quiet hope that maybe, just maybe, they could build something extraordinary together.

A Silent Reckoning

"Reckoning arrives not with fury, but with the quiet resolve of truth."

The engagement party was in full swing, laughter and the clinking of glasses creating a symphony of celebration around her. Yet, to Cora, it all felt surreal—like she was floating through someone else's dream. A kiss from the night before lingered on her lips, a ghost of emotions that left her chest both light and heavy. It had been slow, deep, and filled with a reverence that made her wonder if there was truly hope for something extraordinary. But tonight, surrounded by the glitz and glamour of Declan's world, the quiet hope that had blossomed now felt fragile, as if it could shatter under the weight of the evening.

Declan's family had been welcoming, their smiles polished, and their words carefully measured. His mother, a poised woman with sharp eyes and a voice that carried a passionate grace, had kissed both her cheeks. "Welcome to the family," Nadine Atler presumed in a tone that was more observation than warmth. "And your parents? Are they here?" she asked peaking around Cora.

"No, my mother died when I was two. I was raised by my Gram here in Pine Brook and she passed away 5 months ago so it's just me," Cora stated trying her hardest to appear standing tall.

"Well, my goodness you little thing. You have certainly been through a lot." Nadine said shaking her head in disbelief. "What was your grandmother's name, Cora?" Nadine pressed.

"Charlotte O'Clara. She owned the bridal shop downtown and she left it to me, so I am now the owner." Cora nervously announced.

"Oh, yes. I knew Charlotte. We had a mutual friend, Vayna." Nadine declared as she smoothed out her hair nervously.

Oliver Atler had shaken her hand firmly, offering nothing more than a short but approving nod.

But it was Declan's younger brother, Gareth and older sister Bree, who lingered in her mind. Gareth had been charming, with the same easy smile and eyes as Declan, but there was something beneath the surface— a glint of mischief or danger that made her uneasy. "Big shoes to fill, huh?" he'd said with a wink as he passed her at the bar. Bree casually slapped him across his back and they both escaped to the patio.

Now, standing by the edge of the pool with Selah, MJ and Jensen at her side, Cora sipped her champagne, her fingers brushing against the cool metal of the ring on her finger. The weight of it felt heavier than it should, as though it carried the expectations of a life she wasn't sure she was ready to embrace.

MJ had just witnessed the awkward exchange between Declan's parents and Cora. "Oh, Cora? Will you ever, I mean EVER adapt to these new surroundings? I mean, I could." He said laughing and playing with his hair mimicking Declan's mother.

"You're hopeless, MJ," Cora spatted losing some champaign at the impression he just gave.

"You haven't said much," Selah said gently, her arm brushing against Cora's. "What's going on in that head of yours?"

Cora glanced at her, her lips curving into a faint smile. "Just trying to take it all in," she admitted. "It feels... fast."

Selah nodded, her gaze steady. "It is fast. But it's your life, Cora. You don't have to justify it to anyone—not even yourself."

Cora exhaled, her shoulders relaxing slightly. "It's just... a lot to process. Declan, his family, all of this," she said, gesturing to the opulence around them. "I don't know if I fit here."

Selah placed a hand on her arm, her grip firm but reassuring. "You fit wherever you decide to fit," she said simply. "And if this is what you want, then own it."

Jensen, who had been quietly observing the interaction, spoke up. "Declan seems like a good guy," he said, his voice even. "But if he ever makes you doubt that, you've got people who will remind him exactly who you are."

Cora laughed softly, the sound breaking through the tension in her chest. "Thanks, Jensen. That means a lot."

Across the pool, Declan appeared, his eyes locking onto hers instantly. The intensity in his gaze made her stomach flutter, a mixture of nerves and excitement that she hadn't yet learned to tame. He made his way to her, his movements smooth and purposeful, and within moments, he was at her side.

"Stealing you for a moment," he said, his voice low and warm as his hand found hers. Selah and Jensen exchanged a glance, their smiles faint but knowing as they stepped back, leaving the two of them alone.

"Well, I have to go get ready for my late-night rendezvous with my new lavender queens. I will see you all bright and early tomorrow when we meet to finalize the low-down on this shindig," MJ mumbled gracefully bowing out and walking back up to the house.

Declan led Cora to a quieter corner of the patio where the lights were dimmed, the sounds of the party fading into the background. He turned to face her, his hands slipping to her waist as he pulled her closer. "You've been in your head," he said softly, his thumb brushing against her hip.

Cora looked up at him, her lips parting as she tried to find the right words. "It's just... a lot," she admitted, her voice trembling. "All of this. You. Us."

Declan's gaze softened, and he leaned down, his forehead resting gently against hers. "You don't have to have all the answers right now," he murmured. "I'm not going anywhere."

The sincerity in his voice sent a shiver through her, and she closed her eyes, letting herself rest in the comfort of his presence. "I'm scared," she whispered, the words slipping out before she could stop them.

Declan tilted her chin up, his dark eyes meeting hers. "Good," he said softly. "That means it's real."

His lips found hers then, a kiss that was slow and deep, full of promises she wasn't sure either of them could keep but that she wanted to believe in anyway. The world around them seemed to fade, leaving only the warmth of his touch, the steady beat of her heart, and the quiet thrill of stepping into the unknown.

The party began to dwindle as the night wore on, the guests departing one by one until only a few close friends and family remained. MJ had returned to the loft in time to catch the nightlife of the bustling downtown for Pride Fest. Cora found herself back at the edge of the pool, Declan's arm around her shoulders as they watched the water ripple in the breeze.

"You've changed everything for me," Declan said quietly, his voice carrying the weight of a confession. "And I don't think I can ever go back to the way things were."

Cora looked up at him, her chest tightening as she saw the vulnerability in his eyes. She reached up, her fingers brushing against his jaw. "Neither can I," she admitted softly.

Declan stepped aside to casually take a private phone call and later as they stood there, the lights casting their reflections in the water, Cora realized that, for better or worse, her life had shifted irrevocably. The path ahead was uncertain, but for the first time in a long time, she felt timid, yet alive—reckless, excited, and ready to see where it would take her.

The quiet was shattered moments later by the sound of someone calling her name. She turned to see Selah approaching, her expression a mix of relief and anxiety. "Cora," she said breathlessly. "We need to leave. Now."

Cora's heart lurched as she stepped closer, her hand reaching for Selah's. "What happened? Are you okay?"

Selah hesitated, glancing back toward the hall. "I'm fine," she said quickly, though her voice was tight. "But MJ—he was in the loft, and there was... there was a fire."

"A fire?" Cora repeated, her chest tightening with panic. "Where is he?"

"They're trying to put it out, but it's spreading fast," Selah said, her voice trembling. "I don't know where he is, Cora."

Without thinking, Cora started toward the terrace doors, her heart pounding. "I have to find him."

"Cora, wait!" Selah called after her, but Cora didn't stop. The world around her felt like a blur as she moved through the diminishing crowd, her focus narrowing to the single thought pulsing in her mind: MJ needed her.

The night felt endless, the chaos around the loft both deafening and surreal. Flames licked at the night sky in furious waves, their orange glow casting stark shadows across the faces of firefighters and paramedics rushing between trucks. Cora stood frozen by the ambulance, her dress torn, her skin streaked with soot. The world moved around her, fast and fragmented, but she was stuck in a haze of fear and disbelief.

MJ lay on the stretcher, his breathing shallow and labored. The rise and fall of his chest were erratic, each breath a fight. His usually vibrant presence, the energy that had always filled every room he entered, was eerily quiet now. Cora's hands trembled as she reached for him, her fingers brushing against his soot-streaked arm.

"MJ," she whispered, her voice breaking. "You're going to be okay. Just hold on, okay?"

His eyes fluttered open for a brief moment, a faint smile tugging at his lips. "Drama Queen... to the end," he rasped, his voice barely audible.

Cora let out a shaky laugh, her tears spilling over. "You don't get to joke about that," she said, her voice trembling. "Not right now."

Declan appeared beside her again, his presence steady. His hand rested lightly on her shoulder, grounding her even as her emotions spiraled. "Cora," he said gently, his voice low and firm. "He's in good hands. They'll do everything they can."

"But what if it's not enough?" she said, her voice rising, the panic clawing at her throat. She turned to face him, her eyes wide and brimming with tears. "I can't lose him, Declan. He's... he's my family."

Declan's expression softened, a flicker of pain crossing his face as he removed his suit coat and wrapped it around her, "I know," he said quietly walking away to acquire more information.

Slowly, an officer began to walk in Cora's direction with a determined stride as Jensen and Selah followed suite.

"Sebastian?" Cora said, trying to blink the tears away so she could believe what she was seeing.

"Cora, hello. I am so glad to see you are ok. I saw the name and address come up on my scanner. It was you. How are you holding up?" Sebastian asked with a deeply rooted concern.

Sebastian and Cora had a bond through their adolescent years, connected by family. He once professed his love to Cora after traveling 1800 miles and appearing in the lounge of Cora's dorm one rainy night just before he was accepted into the police academy. But she did not feel the same as he did back then, and it tore at her thinking she had lost him forever.

Cora ran into his arms and fell into him broken with despair as Selah and Jensen stepped to the side to allow them privacy. The weight of his words, the unspoken history between them, pressed down on her like a tidal wave. She swallowed hard, her chest aching as she looked at him.

"Why now?" she whispered, her voice trembling. "Why are you here now? I've been home for six months now. I had no idea you were here."

Sebastian's gaze didn't waver. "Because I never stopped caring," he said simply. "Not when you left, not when everything fell apart. And I couldn't stand the thought of you facing something like this alone."

His words cracked something inside her, the emotions she'd been holding back spilling over. Cora covered her face with her hands, her shoulders shaking as the sobs overtook her. Sebastian stepped closer, his arms wrapping around her gently but firmly, offering the support she so desperately needed.

"It's okay," he murmured against her hair, his voice steady despite the emotion in it. For the first time that night, Cora let herself break. The fear, the grief, the weight of everything she'd been carrying—it all came crashing down. Sebastian held her through it, his familiar presence unwavering, his quiet strength anchoring her even as the world around them burned.

The fire continued its relentless assault, consuming everything in its path. Cora's eyes remained fixed on the stretcher as the paramedics worked tirelessly to stabilize MJ. The sharp beeping of machines and the clipped commands of the medics blurred together, creating a soundtrack of urgency that matched the chaos in her mind.

Selah appeared beside her, her own face streaked with ash, her hands trembling as she clutched at Cora's arm. "He's strong," Selah said, her voice trembling but resolute. "He'll pull through. He has to."

Cora turned to her, the tears still falling freely. "What if he doesn't?" she asked, her voice cracking under the weight of the words. "What if this is it?"

Selah shook her head fiercely, her grip tightening. "Don't go there, Cora," she said, her tone firm despite the quiver in it. "He's not done fighting."

Declan's voice cut through the moment; his tone sharp as he approached them. "We need to move," he said, his eyes darting between Cora and Selah. "This fire isn't under control yet. It's not safe here."

"I'm not leaving him," Cora said immediately, her voice stronger now. "I can't."

Jensen hesitated, his jaw tightening as he looked at her. "The paramedics are taking him to the hospital," he said finally. "We can follow."

Cora nodded, her chest tightening as she turned back to MJ. "I'll see you soon," she whispered, her voice trembling as she placed a gentle hand on his. "Just hang on, okay?"

The medics began moving the stretcher toward the waiting ambulance, and Cora felt a piece of her heart break as she watched them go. Selah wrapped an arm around her, guiding her toward Declan, who reached for her hand. His grip was strong and steady, but it wasn't enough to quiet the storm raging inside her.

The night felt like it had stretched into eternity, the smoke pressing against Cora's senses as she stumbled toward the ambulance. Declan's grip on her arm was firm but distant, his voice calling out to first responders as they moved through the scene. The glow of the flames in the distance seared into her mind, a reminder of everything she couldn't unsee.

Cora stopped short as a stretcher passed by, her heart seizing as she recognized MJ's form lying motionless beneath the oxygen mask. His usually vibrant energy was absent, his chest still, his skin pale and streaked with soot. "No," she whispered, her voice trembling as her legs gave way beneath her. "No, no, no."

Selah caught her before she fell, her own face streaked with tears. "Cora," she said urgently, her voice breaking. "They said he was—" She couldn't finish, her words dissolving into a sob.

Cora shook her head, breaking free from Selah's grip as she stumbled toward the paramedics. "He's not gone," she said desperately, her voice rising. "He can't be. Let me see him. Please."

One of the paramedics stepped forward, his expression a mixture of sympathy and professionalism. "Miss," he said gently, placing a hand on her shoulder. "We did everything we could. I'm so sorry."

The words hit her like a blow, the air rushing from her lungs as she stared at him, her mind refusing to process the meaning. "No," she said again, her voice barely above a whisper. "You're wrong. He's just unconscious. He needs help."

Declan appeared beside her, his face pale but resolute as he took her hand. "Cora," he said softly, his voice steady despite the emotion in it. "He's gone."

Cora turned to him, her chest heaving as she shook her head. "No," she said fiercely, tears streaming down her face. "He's not gone. He's MJ. He's... he's MJ."

Her knees buckled, and Declan caught her, his arms wrapping around her as she sobbed into his chest. The world around her dissolved into noise and disarray, but all she could hear was the sound of her own grief, raw and unrelenting.

The rest of the night passed in a haze. Cora sat in the back of Declan's car, her gaze fixed on the streaks of ash and soot on her dress. Selah sat beside her; her own face streaked with tears as she gripped Cora's hand tightly. Declan drove in silence, his jaw set as he navigated the darkened streets.

By the time they reached Declan's estate, the weight of the night had settled over Cora like a suffocating blanket. The loss of MJ felt like a void she couldn't begin to fill, his laughter and energy echoing in her mind with every step she took. She went straight to bed, unable to deal with everything that happened.

The morning after the fire felt like a blur. Cora sat in the corner of Declan's expansive living room, her knees pulled to her chest, her eyes red and swollen from crying. The quiet was unbearable, broken only by the faint hum of a news report playing in the background. Images of the fire flickered across the screen, the bridal shop and her loft reduced to smoldering ruins, the headlines naming it one of the most devastating fires the city had seen in years.

Selah sat nearby, her face pale as she scrolled through her phone, searching for updates. She hadn't said much since they left the scene the night before, her usual energy replaced with somber stillness. Declan entered the room with two steaming mugs of coffee, setting one in front of Cora. He crouched beside her, his hand brushing lightly against her arm.

"Have something," he said gently, his voice soft but firm. "You need to keep your strength up."

Cora shook her head, her gaze fixed on the floor. "I can't," she murmured.

Declan's jaw tightened slightly, but he didn't push. "You can't stop living, Cora," he said quietly. "MJ wouldn't want that."

The mention of MJ's name broke something inside her, and tears spilled down her cheeks once more. She wiped them away quickly, as she tried to breathe through the overwhelming grief. "He's gone," she whispered, her voice cracking. "And everything else... the shop, my home—it's all gone too."

Declan sat beside her, his hand resting on hers. "Not everything," he said firmly. "You still have people who care about you. You have me. You have our future."

His words were sincere, but they felt like a weight she wasn't ready to carry. She glanced at him, her voice trembling. "I don't know what to do."

Later that afternoon, Declan and Selah insisted on taking Cora to the remains of her shop. She resisted at first, but eventually relented, feeling a pull to see what was left of the place that had been her dream—and Gram's legacy. The scene was devastating. The storefront, once warm and inviting, was now charred and lifeless. Blackened beams jutted out at odd angles, the smell of smoke still thick in the air. Cora stood frozen, her hand covering her mouth as tears welled in her eyes.

"This was everything," she whispered, her voice shaking. "Gram's dream... my dream."

Declan stood beside her, his expression solemn. "Dreams don't die with buildings," he said softly. "They change, but they don't die. You can rebuild, Cora."

She turned to him, her tears spilling over. "How? I've lost everything, Declan. The shop, MJ, my home..." Selah leaned in to hold her dear friend, her stance wobbly with emotion she tried to hold in.

Declan stepped closer, his hands reaching out to hers. "You haven't lost everything," he said firmly. "You still have me. Move in with me. Let me help you."

Cora stared at him, catching the sincerity in his eyes. "Move in with you?" she repeated, her voice barely above a whisper.

"Yes," he said, his tone unwavering. "You don't have to do this alone. Let me be there for you." As Declan's words settled over her, a familiar voice cut through the air, making her freeze.

"Cora."

She turned to see Sebastian approaching, his uniform still streaked with soot from the night before. His blue eyes met hers, filled with concern and something deeper—something unspoken. "I was hoping I'd find you here," he said, his voice soft but steady. "I wanted to check on you."

Cora's chest tightened at the sight of him, the memories of their past rushing back in a wave. "Sebastian," she said, her voice trembling. "I... I didn't expect to see you."

Sebastian's gaze flicked to Declan briefly before returning to her. "I couldn't just leave," he said simply. "Not after what happened."

Declan stepped forward, his posture stiff as he extended his hand. "Declan," he said curtly. "Cora's fiancé. I don't believe we've formally met."

Sebastian hesitated for a moment before shaking his hand. "Sebastian," he said evenly. "Old friend."

The tension between them crackled, and Cora felt the weight of their gazes on her. She looked down, her thoughts spinning. "Thank you for everything last night," she said quietly, addressing Sebastian.

"You don't have to thank me," Sebastian replied, his tone softening. "I just want to make sure you're okay."

"I don't know if I'll ever be okay," Cora admitted, her voice cracking. "I don't even know where to start."

Sebastian stepped closer, his expression earnest. "You don't have to have all the answers right now," he said. "But if you need anything—anything—I'm here."

Declan's hand slipped to Cora's waist, a subtle but firm gesture. "She's not alone," he said, his tone steady but pointed. "I'll make sure of that."

Cora's gaze darted between them, as the unspoken tension hung heavily in the air. She didn't know what to say, didn't know how to reconcile the pieces of her life that felt like they were crumbling around her. But as she looked at the man who had been her past and the one promising her a future, she knew one thing: the path ahead would not be simple.

The drive back to Declan's estate was quiet, the silence between Cora, Declan, and Selah heavy with unspoken words. Cora stared out the window, her reflection distorted by the rain that had begun to fall, each drop streaking the glass like a tear she couldn't shed anymore. The smoldering remains of her shop and the weight of MJ's absence pressed against her chest, leaving her feeling hollow.

Selah broke the silence first, her voice soft but insistent. "Cora, you don't have to decide anything right now. Take your time."

Cora nodded faintly; her gaze still fixed on the passing streets. "Time doesn't fix everything," she murmured, her voice trembling. "It doesn't bring people back."

Selah reached for her hand, squeezing it gently. "No, but it helps you figure out how to move forward. And when you're ready, you'll know."

Declan remained quiet, his hands gripping the steering wheel as he navigated the winding roads to his estate. His jaw was tight, the tension in his posture a stark contrast to the calm he usually exuded. When they pulled into the long driveway, the gates opening automatically to reveal the sprawling grounds, Cora felt an odd sense of detachment. The grandeur of Declan's world felt overwhelming now, a sharp contrast to the simplicity of what she'd lost.

Inside the estate, Declan led Cora to the sitting room, the soft glow of the fireplace casting a warm light across the polished wood and plush furniture. He motioned for her to sit, his gaze steady but full of concern.

"Cora," he began, his voice low and measured. "I know you're going through more than anyone should have to bear. And I know you feel like everything is falling apart."

She looked up at him, her eyes glassy. "It is," she said simply. "Everything I had—everything I was trying to build—it's all gone."

Declan crouched in front of her, taking her hands in his. His touch was firm, grounding. "Then let me help you rebuild," he said. "Move in with me. Let me take care of you."

Cora stared at him, her chest tightening as his words sank in. "Declan, I don't know if I can," she said quietly. "I don't even know who I am without the shop, without... without him."

Declan's expression softened, his thumb brushing against the back of her hand. "You're still you, Cora. And you don't have to figure this out alone. You've been carrying so much on your own for so long. Let me lighten the load."

The tears she thought she'd run out of threatening to fall again. "I don't want to feel like I'm giving up."

"You're not," he said firmly. "You're choosing to move forward. And sometimes that means letting someone else help."

The fire crackled softly in the background as hours passed by while Cora considered his words. She didn't want to be here—not like this, not under these circumstances. But the weight of everything she'd lost was too much to carry alone, and Declan's offer felt like the only solid ground she had left.

The sound of a knock at the door broke the moment, pulling both their attention. Declan frowned, standing to answer it. Cora stayed seated, her body too heavy to move, her thoughts too jumbled to care who might be on the other side.

When Declan returned, Sebastian followed, his presence filling the room with a quiet intensity. His uniform was gone, replaced by a simple button-down and jeans, but his eyes held the same piercing focus as before.

"I wanted to check on you," he said, his gaze locking onto Cora. "I'm worried about you."

Cora nodded slowly, her throat tightening. "Thank you," she said softly, her voice barely audible.

Sebastian hesitated, glancing at Declan before stepping closer. "I know you're overwhelmed," he said. "And I know I'm coming out of nowhere after all these years, but I meant what I said. If you need anything, anything at all, I'm here."

Cora looked down at her hands, her beautiful diamond ring glistening in the light, her mind spinning. The weight of Sebastian's words, the sincerity in his voice, clashed with the solidity of Declan's offer. She felt torn between the life she thought she was building and the one she might have to embrace out of necessity.

"You've always been there for me," she said finally, her voice trembling. "Even when I didn't deserve it."

Sebastian's brow furrowed, and he knelt in front of her, his hands hovering over hers but not touching. "Don't say that, Kitten" he said, his voice firm but kind. "You've never deserved anything but the best, Cora. And I know... I know I didn't handle things the way I should have back then, but I'm here now."

Declan's posture stiffened slightly, his jaw tightening as he watched the exchange. "She's not alone," he said, his voice measured. "I'm here for her too."

Cora looked between them, her chest aching with the weight of their words. The fire crackled in the silence, the decision looming over her like a shadow. She didn't know where to go from here, but she knew one thing: nothing would ever be the same.

The silence in the room was suffocating, the crackle of the fire the only sound as Cora sat between Declan and Sebastian. Her fingers twisted nervously in her lap, her thoughts spinning in a thousand directions. The weight of both men's presence pressed down on her, each offering something different—stability, familiarity, promises of a future she wasn't sure she was ready to accept.

Sebastian broke the silence first, his voice low but steady. "Cora, I know this is a lot. And I know it's not the right time, but I can't leave without saying it."

Cora's eyes flicked up to meet his, her breath catching at the intensity in his gaze. "Sebastian..."

"I never stopped caring about you," he said, his voice thick with emotion. "Not in college, not after everything fell apart. And seeing you like this, going through all of this... it's killing me. I just need you to know that I'm here for you—not just now, but always."

His words hit her like a wave as tears welled in her eyes. She opened her mouth to speak, but no words came. The depth of what he was saying, the vulnerability in his tone, left her reeling.

Declan's voice cut through the moment; his tone measured but edged with tension. "Sebastian, I think Cora's been through enough for one night."

Sebastian's jaw clenched, but he didn't look away from Cora. "I'm not trying to add to her burden," he said quietly. "I just need her to know the truth."

Cora's hands trembled as she looked between them, the tension in the room palpable. "I can't do this," she said finally, her voice breaking.

"You don't have to do anything," Sebastian said softly. "I just needed to say it."

Declan stepped closer, his hand resting lightly on her shoulder. "Cora," he said gently, his voice softer now. "You don't have to face any of this alone."

Her chest ached as she looked up at him, the sincerity in his gaze both comforting and overwhelming. "I don't know where to start," she whispered, her voice trembling.

"With what feels right," he said simply. "The rest will follow."

That night, after Sebastian left, the weight of the day pressed down on Cora like a physical force. She sat in the quiet of Declan's living room, the fire burning low in the hearth as she stared at the ring on her finger. Everything about her life felt like it was in pieces, but Declan's offer had been clear, steady—a lifeline she wasn't sure she could refuse.

He entered the room quietly, his presence grounding as he sat beside her. "You don't have to decide tonight," he said softly. "But I meant what I said. You don't have to carry this alone."

Cora turned to him, her eyes brimming with tears. "I've already lost so much," she said, her voice trembling. "I can't lose myself too."

"You won't," he said firmly, his hand covering hers. "You're stronger than you realize. And whatever comes next, I'll be here."

The certainty in his tone settled something inside her, and she nodded slowly. "Okay," she whispered. "I'll move in."

Declan's relief was visible, his hand tightening around hers. "You won't regret this," he said, his voice filled with quiet conviction.

But as Cora sat there, her heart heavy with grief and uncertainty, she couldn't help but wonder if she was stepping toward stability—or losing herself entirely.

Later, as she stood in the master bedroom, Cora traced her fingers along the edge of the dresser, her thoughts circling back to Sebastian. His words lingered in her mind, a reminder of a time when things had felt simpler, when life hadn't carried the weight of everything she'd lost.

She looked out the window at the darkened grounds, the faint glow of the city lights in the distance. The world felt vast and empty, and she felt like a small, untethered piece drifting through it. Moving in with Declan was a choice—a step forward. But as she closed her eyes and leaned her forehead against the cool glass, she couldn't shake the feeling that part of her was still standing in the ruins of what she'd lost.

The morning sunlight streamed through the tall windows of Declan's estate, casting soft golden rays across the room. Cora sat at the edge of the bed, her hands folded in her lap as she stared at the floor. Her suitcase was still unopened, sitting neatly in the corner—a reminder that she was here, but not fully present.

The silence was heavy, broken only by the faint rustle of the trees outside. Moving in with Declan seemed like the only option last night, but in the clarity of daylight, the decision weighed on her. It felt like surrender, like she was letting the fire take more than just her shop and MJ—it was taking her sense of self.

A soft knock at the door pulled her from her thoughts. Declan stepped inside, his expression calm but watchful. He held a tray with coffee, toast, and fresh fruit, setting it on the small table by the window. "You didn't come down for breakfast," he said gently. "I thought you might need some time."

Cora managed a faint smile, though her chest still ached with the weight of everything. "Thank you," she said quietly.

Declan sat in the chair across from her, his hands resting on his knees as he studied her. "I know this is hard," he said. "But you don't have to go through it alone. Whatever you need, I'll make sure it happens."

Cora looked at him, her eyes filled with tears. "I don't even know what I need," she admitted, her voice trembling. "I feel like I'm drowning."

Declan leaned forward, his hand covering hers. "Then let me be your lifeline," he said softly. "We'll take it one step at a time."

Later that afternoon, Selah arrived, her presence a burst of warmth that cut through the heavy air of the estate. She pulled Cora into a tight hug, her arms strong and reassuring. "You're allowed to feel all of it," she said softly. "The grief, the anger, the confusion—it's all valid."

Cora nodded, her voice breaking as she whispered, "I don't know how to start over."

"You don't have to know right now," Selah said firmly. "You just have to take it one day at a time. And you have people who will hold you up when you can't."

They moved to the garden, where the soft rustling of leaves and the gentle hum of bees filled the air. Selah poured them both tea, her movements calm and deliberate. "What do you need right now?" she asked, her voice steady.

Cora thought for a moment, her fingers curling around the warm mug. "I need to find something that feels like mine again," she said finally. "Something that's not... all of this."

Selah nodded, her gaze thoughtful. "Then we'll figure that out. You're not stuck, Cora. You will be able to move forward."

The days began to blur together at Declan's estate. The routine of waking up to the smell of freshly brewed coffee and walking the manicured gardens felt foreign to Cora, as though she was living someone else's life. The weight of everything she had lost pressed down on her chest, leaving little room for the spark she once felt for the future.

Selah had been visiting frequently, her laughter and reassurance a temporary balm for Cora's grief. But even with her closest friend nearby, the emptiness lingered. Declan was attentive, his gestures of support unwavering, but Cora couldn't shake the feeling that she was adrift, unmoored from who she used to be.

It was a week after the fire when Declan insisted on taking Cora back to the site of her shop. "You can't move forward without really facing it," he said gently, his hand resting on hers as they drove through the city.

When they arrived, Cora stepped out of the car, her heart tightening as she took in the blackened remains of the building. The structure that once housed her dreams was now a hollow shell, its windows shattered, the air still carrying a faint scent of smoke.

Declan stayed back, giving her space as she moved closer. Her heels clicked against the cracked pavement, the sound echoing in the eerie quiet. She reached out, her fingers brushing against the charred brick. Tears welled in her eyes, spilling over as the weight of the loss became undeniable.

"I worked so hard for this," she whispered, her voice trembling. "It was supposed to be my future."

Declan approached cautiously, his arms wrapping around her shoulders. "This isn't the end, Cora," he said softly. "You can rebuild. You'll come back stronger."

Cora leaned into him, her tears soaking into his jacket. "It doesn't feel that way right now."

"It will," he promised, his voice firm. "You just have to let yourself heal first."

As they drove back to the estate, Cora stared out the window, her thoughts swirling. Declan reached over, his hand covering hers. "I meant what I said back there," he said. "You don't have to face this alone."

"I know," she said softly, her voice heavy with emotion. "I just don't know how to let go."

Declan's grip tightened, his voice steady. "You don't have to let go of what you've lost. But you can hold onto what you still have. Let me help you find that balance."

Cora turned to him, her eyes brimming with unshed tears. "I'll try," she whispered. "That's all I can do."

Declan smiled faintly, his thumb brushing against the back of her hand. "That's enough."

The days that followed felt heavy, a constant push and pull between finding solace in Declan's unwavering presence and grappling with the memories of everything she had lost. The estate was peaceful, almost unnervingly so, its quiet elegance at odds with the chaos in Cora's heart.

Selah arrived one afternoon with a bag of pastries and a determined expression. "Get up," she said firmly, setting the bag on the kitchen counter. "We're taking a walk."

Cora blinked at her from the couch, her legs tucked beneath her. "Selah, I'm really not in the mood."

"Tough," Selah replied, grabbing her hand and pulling her to her feet. "You've been cooped up here for days. You need fresh air."

Reluctantly, Cora let herself be led outside. They walked through the estate's expansive gardens, the gravel crunching softly beneath their feet. The sun was warm on their faces, the scent of blooming jasmine lingering in the air.

"I don't know what I'm doing," Cora admitted finally, her voice barely above a whisper. "Every decision feels wrong."

Selah stopped, turning to face her. "Cora, no one expects you to have all the answers right now," she said gently. "You've been through so much. It's okay to feel lost."

"But what if I never figure it out?" Cora asked, her chest tightening. "What if I don't know who I am without the shop, without MJ?"

Selah placed her hands on Cora's shoulders, her gaze steady. "You're more than the shop, more than any one thing or person. You're still Cora. And you're going to find your way."

Tears welled in Cora's eyes, spilling over as she nodded. "I don't feel strong."

"That's because strength isn't about feeling it," Selah said with a faint smile. "It's about showing up even when you don't."

That evening, Declan handed her an envelope as they sat by the fire. The paper was slightly rough at the edges, the handwriting unmistakably MJ's. "This was in the mail here at the estate," Declan explained softly. "I thought you should have it."

Cora's fingers trembled as she opened the envelope with a return address from Washington DC, MJ's mother, as she unfolded the letter. The words on the page blurred as tears filled her eyes.

Cora,

Thinking about you tonight. I don't say this enough, but I'm proud of you. For the shop, for the way you've kept Gram's dream alive, for the way you keep going even when it's hard. You're stronger than you realize, and I know you'll do amazing things.

Don't forget to laugh, even when things feel impossible. And if you ever lose your way, just look in the mirror—you'll see the woman who's capable of anything. See you soon.

Love,

MJ

The letter slipped from her hands as sobs wracked her body. Declan moved to her side, wrapping her in his arms as she cried. He didn't speak, letting her grief fill the room until the tears slowed, leaving her feeling raw but lighter.

As the days turned into weeks, Cora began to find small moments of clarity. She spent mornings walking the estate grounds, afternoons talking with Selah, and evenings sitting quietly with Declan. Slowly, she started flipping through wedding websites and began to see glimpses of a future—one that wasn't defined by what she had lost but by what she could rebuild.

One evening, as they sat in the library, Declan handed her a folder. "I've been thinking," he said. "You've talked about finding something that feels like yours again. What if we rebuilt the shop together?"

Cora stared at him, her heart twisting at the thought. "Declan…"

"Too much?" he interrupted gently. "I don't think it is. It's an investment in you, in your dream. You don't have to decide now, but I want you to know that it's possible."

She looked at him, her emotions warring as tears pricked at her eyes. "Why are you doing all of this for me?"

"Because I love you. I believe in you," Declan said simply. "And I want to see you thrive."

The days began to take on a rhythm. Morning walks through Declan's gardens gave Cora a resemblance of routine, while afternoons spent talking with Selah offered small moments of relief. Declan remained a constant presence, his steady support both comforting and overwhelming. But it was MJ's letter that lingered in her mind, his words echoing in her thoughts whenever the grief threatened to consume her.

Declan's offer to rebuild the shop hung heavily between them. The folder he had given her sat on the desk in their sitting room, untouched but ever-present. Cora couldn't bring herself to open it, the weight of the decision pressing against her chest.

One evening, she found herself sitting in the estate's library, staring at the folder as the fire crackled softly in the background. Declan entered the room quietly, his footsteps soft on the polished wood floor. He sat across from her, his expression calm but expectant.

"You haven't looked at it yet," he said gently, motioning to the folder.

Cora shook her head, her fingers curling around the edge of the chair. "I'm scared," she admitted, her voice trembling. "What if I fail again? What if it's not the same?"

Declan leaned forward, his gaze steady. "It won't be the same," he said. "And that's okay. Dreams evolve, Cora. What matters is that they're still yours."

Tears welled in her eyes, spilling over as she nodded slowly. "I don't know if I'm ready."

"You don't have to be," he said softly. "But when you are, I'll be here."

The next afternoon, Sebastian arrived unannounced. Cora met him at the door, her heart tightening at the sight of him in his casual clothes, his presence somehow both grounding and disarming.

"I wasn't sure if I should come," he said, his voice low. "But I needed to check on you."

Cora stepped outside. "I'm glad you did," she said quietly. They sat on the patio, the sun warm on their faces as the breeze rustled the leaves of the nearby trees. Sebastian leaned back in his chair, his gaze thoughtful as he looked at her.

Sebastian nodded, his expression softening. "I recovered some books from a few boxes that survived the fire, Cora. I placed them in this bag."

Cora reached for the bag as tears gently escaped her eyes. "Oh, my gosh Sebastian. These are my Gram's journals! You saved them!"

They sat in companionable silence for a while, the unspoken history between them hanging in the air. Finally, Sebastian turned to her, his blue eyes serious. "Cora, I know this isn't the right time, but I need to say something."

Her heart skipped a beat, her breath catching as she met his gaze. "What is it?"

"I still care about you," he said simply, his voice steady. "I always have. And if there's ever a chance—if you ever feel the same—I'm here."

Cora's chest tightened, her emotions swirling as she looked away. "Sebastian, I—" She paused, her voice trembling. "I don't know what I feel right now. Everything is so... complicated. I'm getting married."

He nodded, his expression understanding. "I'm not asking for an answer. I just needed you to know."

Cora's breath caught at his words, the quiet sincerity in Sebastian's voice lingering even after he had left. The weight of what he had shared pressed against her chest, mingling with the growing unease that had taken root in her life.

The estate felt too quiet that evening, the stillness amplifying the echo of his words in her mind. She wandered through the halls, her fingers brushing absently against the smooth banister as her thoughts spiraled.

Declan's charm, his insistence that everything was fine—it all felt like a carefully constructed facade, one she was beginning to see through. And now, with Sebastian's confession still fresh in her mind, the cracks in that facade seemed larger than ever.

That night, as Cora lay in bed, sleep refused to come. The moonlight streaming through the window cast soft shadows across the room, and the sound of the wind rustling through the trees outside offered little comfort. Her thoughts drifted to MJ, to her grandmother, to the promises Declan had made.

When her phone buzzed on the nightstand, the sound startled her. She reached for it, her pulse quickening as she saw Declan's name on the screen. The message was brief but direct:

We need to talk tomorrow. I'll be in my study late tonight. Sleep well.

Her chest tightened as she set the phone back down, her mind racing. Declan's requests were rarely simple, and they were never optional.

A Gilded Cage

"Not all prisons have bars; some are build with love and lies."

The next morning, the estate was bathed in golden light, but the beauty of the day did little to ease Cora's tension. Declan found her in the sitting room, his expression calm but calculating as he entered.

"I've been thinking," he began, his tone carrying the practiced charm she had come to recognize. "About us. About the future."

Cora nodded, her hands clasped tightly in her lap. "What about it?" she asked carefully.

Declan smiled faintly, his gaze steady. "I think it's time we move forward. Officially."

Her stomach churned at his words, but she forced herself to remain composed. "You mean... the wedding?"

"Exactly," he said, his tone brightening. "Why wait any longer? We've already wasted enough time."

The days that followed blurred together, the hours slipping through her fingers as Declan's plans began to take shape. He arranged meetings with planners, set appointments for fittings, and secured a date.

Cora found herself swept up in the whirlwind, her objections dismissed with his usual charm. "It's for the best," Declan had said, his tone leaving no room for argument. "The sooner we do this, the sooner we can move on with our lives."

She nodded reluctantly, her heart heavy as the weight of his expectations pressed against her. It felt like she was being pulled further into a life she hadn't chosen, each decision made for her rather than by her.

At night, as the estate grew quiet, Cora turned to her grandmother's journals for solace. The faded ink and familiar words offered a small comfort, a reminder that strength could be found even in the darkest of times.

One passage stood out to her: *Love isn't meant to cage us—it's meant to set us free. And if it doesn't, then it isn't love at all.*

Her chest tightened as she read the words, her fingers trembling as she closed the journal. The truth they carried was one she couldn't ignore, even as the wedding date loomed closer.

The day had arrived. Unwillingly.

The estate bustled with the kind of carefully orchestrated chaos that only a grand wedding could create. Florists carried cascading arrangements of roses and lilies through the halls, their perfume mingling with the scent of freshly polished wood. Caterers moved in synchronized precision, their trays laden with gold-rimmed china and crystal glasses. To anyone else, it was the vision of a perfect wedding. To Cora, it felt like confusion, a gilded cage.

Standing at the edge of the grand ballroom, Cora watched the planners and staff transform the space into Declan's dream of perfection. Every detail, from the shimmering gold accents to the custom lighting, had been carefully curated. And yet, as beautiful as it all was, it felt empty. Declan's voice carried across the room, calm and commanding as he directed the setup.

"It's all coming together beautifully, My Cora," Declan said, his tone smooth as he appeared at her side. "Exactly how I envisioned it."

Cora nodded faintly, her hands clasping tightly in front of her as she silently found herself craving for an impulsive comment from MJ. "It's stunning," she said softly.

Declan smiled, his confidence radiating. "I told you everything would be perfect. You just need to trust me."

She forced a small smile, but her chest felt heavy. The decisions, the details—it had all been Declan. Even the menu, something she had once imagined choosing together, had been finalized without her. The wedding was a masterpiece, but it didn't feel like hers.

Later that afternoon, Cora found herself in the bridal suite, her gown hanging nearby, its delicate lace shimmering in the sunlight. Selah stood behind her, holding the veil with practiced care.

"You look sad," Selah said lightly, her tone tinged with concern. "What's going on?"

Cora hesitated, her fingers brushing against the edge of the dressing table. "It's just... overwhelming," she admitted. "All of this. The wedding, the expectations. Declan."

Selah raised an eyebrow. "What about Declan?"

Cora took a deep breath, her chest tightening. "It feels like... he's making all the decisions. I don't know how to explain it, but it's like everything is being done for me, not with me."

Selah placed the veil down gently and turned to face her. "Cora, this is your wedding. It should feel like yours, not someone else's."

Cora nodded, though her throat felt tight. "It's too late, Selah. Everyone's already here. Everything's already set."

"It's never too late to choose yourself," Selah said firmly, her gaze steady as she placed the veil on Cora's hair. "But only you can decide if that's what you want."

As Selah placed the veil on her head and adjusted it over her shoulders, she caught a glimpse of herself in the mirror, her gown hanging in the background. The dress was breathtaking—delicate lace, intricate beading, and a long train that seemed to stretch into eternity. But the woman in the mirror didn't feel like her. She felt like an actress in a play, reciting lines that weren't hers.

A knock at the door pulled her from her thoughts. Declan stepped inside, his polished demeanor radiating confidence. "Are you ready?" he asked, his gaze sweeping over her approvingly.

"As ready as I'll ever be," Cora replied, her voice barely above a whisper.

"You're going to be stunning," Declan said, his smile widening. "And everything is going to be perfect. Trust me."

Cora forced a smile, her chest tightening as his words echoed in her mind. *Trust me.* But as she followed him out of the room, her unease only deepened.

The rehearsal dinner that evening was a carefully curated spectacle of elegance and charm. The estate's grand ballroom had been transformed into a glittering vision of gold and ivory. Guests mingled beneath cascading chandeliers, their laughter and chatter blending with the soft strains of a live string quartet. Cora sat at the head table; her hands folded tightly in her lap as Declan delivered his toast. He spoke with practiced ease, his voice confident as he painted a picture of their future—a future filled with ambition and success, built on the foundation of their perfect partnership.

"To the love of my life," Declan concluded, raising his glass to her. "The woman who makes everything possible." The room erupted into applause, and Cora forced a smile, her heart sinking under the weight of his words. *The woman who makes everything possible.* To Declan, it sounded like a compliment. To her, it felt like a role she didn't choose.

After dinner, Cora slipped out onto the terrace, the cool night air a welcome relief from the stifling warmth of the ballroom. The stars twinkled overhead, their soft light reflecting on the estate's manicured gardens. She leaned against the railing, her thoughts spinning as she stared into the darkness.

"You've been so quiet tonight," Selah said gently, stepping out onto the terrace. She wrapped a shawl around her shoulders, her gaze steady as she watched Cora.

"I'm fine," Cora replied automatically, though her voice wavered.

Selah frowned. "You don't seem fine."

Cora hesitated, her fingers curling around the railing. "It's just... Declan," she admitted finally. "He makes everything sound so perfect. Like he has it all figured out."

"And that bothers you?" Selah asked.

"It's not that," Cora said, shaking her head. "It's that it doesn't feel like he's figured *us* out. It feels like he's figured out *himself*—and expects me to just fit into that."

Selah placed a hand on Cora's arm, her touch grounding. "Cora, this is your life too. If it doesn't feel right, you need to say something. You deserve to be heard."

Their conversation was interrupted by Declan's voice, calm but firm. "There you are," he said, stepping onto the terrace. He offered Selah a polite smile before turning his full attention to Cora. "We should get back. Our guests are asking about you."

"I just needed some air," Cora said quietly, glancing at Selah.

Declan's smile softened, though his tone remained authoritative. "I understand. But this is our night. Let's not waste it."

Cora nodded reluctantly, following Declan back inside as Selah watched them go, her expression unreadable.

That night, as Cora lay in bed, the doubts she had been trying to suppress began to surface. Declan's voice echoed in her mind, his promises of perfection ringing hollow against the reality of their relationship. A tarnished journal sat on the bedside table, its worn leather cover catching the faint glow of the lamp.

She reached for it hesitantly, flipping through the pages until her grandmother's words stopped her cold: *I stayed too long in a life that wasn't mine, convincing myself it was enough. But in the end, it's the choices I didn't make that haunt me.*

Tears pricked her eyes as she traced the faded ink, the weight of her grandmother's regrets settling heavily over her. The parallels were undeniable, and they left her feeling trapped in a story she hadn't written.

The morning of the wedding was a carefully choreographed spectacle. The estate was alive with movement, every detail meticulously prepared to meet Declan's exacting standards. The grand ballroom gleamed with golden accents, the cascading floral arrangements filling the space with the scent of roses and lilies. To everyone else, it was perfection. To Cora, it felt like a stage set for a performance she wasn't sure she wanted to star in.

In the bridal suite, Cora sat in front of the mirror, her makeup artist brushing the final strokes of highlighter along her cheekbones. The wedding dress hung nearby, its intricate lace and flowing train as breathtaking as the first time she'd seen it. But as she stared at her reflection, the woman looking back at her didn't feel like herself.

Selah entered, her presence a welcome relief. "How's the bride?" she asked, her tone light but laced with concern.

Cora forced a smile. "Perfect," she said, though her voice trembled slightly.

Selah frowned, pulling up a chair beside her. "You don't have to say that," she said softly. "How do you really feel?"

Cora hesitated, her gaze dropping to her lap. "Like I'm being swept along," she admitted. "Like this isn't my life anymore."

Selah reached for her hand, her grip firm but reassuring. "Cora, you have to listen to yourself. If this doesn't feel right, it's okay to stop."

Cora shook her head, tears welling in her eyes. "I'm marrying him, Selah. Everything's already in motion."

The wedding itself was a blur of music, vows, and applause. Cora stood at the altar, her hands clasped tightly around Declan's as he recited his vows with polished perfection. The guests beamed, the cameras clicked, and the officiant's voice carried through the air with practiced ease.

"You may now kiss the bride," the officiant declared, and the room erupted into cheers as Declan leaned in, his kiss brief but confident.

As they walked down the aisle together, Cora's smile felt frozen, her chest heavy with a mixture of emotions she couldn't untangle. She glanced at Selah in the front row, whose concerned expression was a stark contrast to the sea of smiling faces.

Declan leaned close to her as they exited the ballroom. "You did beautifully," he said softly. "Everything was perfect."

Cora nodded, but the weight in her chest only grew heavier. The applause, the laughter, the endless compliments about the ceremony all blurred together, the voices merging into a cacophony she couldn't escape.

That night, as they danced beneath the glittering chandeliers of the grand reception hall, Declan's grip on her waist felt both grounding and constricting. His smile never faltered, his charm on full display as he guided her effortlessly across the floor. "You're everything I ever wanted," he whispered as the music swelled, his voice low but firm.

Cora forced herself to smile, the corners of her lips trembling as she replied, "And you've given me everything I could have dreamed of."

But the words felt hollow, a script she had rehearsed too many times to believe anymore.

A Flame of Doubt

"Doubt is the ember that weakens the strongest fire."

The days after the wedding passed in a blur of travel arrangements, congratulations, and meticulously planned itineraries. Declan's excitement was palpable as they boarded the private jet, his hand resting possessively on hers.

"Wait until you see the villa," he had said, his eyes lighting up. "It's going to be perfect."

Cora nodded, her smile tight as she leaned back against the plush seat. She told herself to feel grateful, to embrace the life they were starting together, but the quiet voice in the back of her mind wouldn't be silenced: *Is this what I really want?*

The late afternoon sunlight streamed through the suite's wide-open windows, bathing the space in a golden glow. The soft sound of the waves crashing against the cliffs below mixed with the faint hum of life in Santorini.

Cora stepped into the suite, her cheeks flushed and her skin glowing from the day's adventures. Her summer dress swayed lightly with each step, and the oversized sun hat she wore cast playful shadows across her face.

She set her bags down on the small chaise near the window, running her fingers through her hair as she glanced around. "That was perfect," she said, her voice filled with a soft kind of contentment, her mind at ease and rest assured she had made the right choice to marry him. "This is the perfect honeymoon."

Declan followed her inside, his khaki shorts and deep blue button-up slightly rumpled from their excursion. The color of his shirt made his piercing blue eyes seem even sharper, and they tracked her every movement as though she were the only thing in the room. He let the door swing shut behind him, his lips curving into a faint smile as he watched her.

"You're stunning," he murmured, his tone low and reverent.

Cora turned, arching a brow at him as she removed her hat and placed it on the chaise. "I'm sunburned and sweaty," she teased, her lips fluttering into a small smile.

"You're perfect," he countered, stepping closer. His fingers brushed a stray lock of hair from her face, his touch lingering for just a moment too long.

Declan moved to the small bar in the corner of the suite, pouring two glasses of chilled white wine. The faint clink of glass against glass broke the quiet rhythm of the room as he walked back to her, handing her one of the glasses.

"Before dinner?" she asked, tilting her head as she accepted it.

"Before everything," he replied, his voice deep and warm.

Cora laughed softly, sipping the wine as she followed him out onto the balcony. The view took her breath away—a sweeping panorama of Santorini's whitewashed buildings cascading down the cliffs, their stark beauty framed by the endless blue of the sea. The fading sun painted the scene in shades of gold and pink, making it feel like a dream.

Declan leaned against the railing, his posture relaxed but his gaze intense as it lingered on her. "It's hard to believe anything could be more beautiful than this view," he said, his voice dropping. "But here you are."

She flushed, her fingers tightening around the stem of her glass. "You're insufferable," she teased, though her tone was soft.

"And you're irresistible," he countered, his lips twitching into a faint smile.

As they stood together, sipping their wine, Declan reached into his pocket, his fingers brushing against a small box. He hesitated for a moment before pulling it out, his expression shifting into something more serious.

"I wanted to give you this. I had it made for you," he said, his voice quiet but filled with intention.

Cora turned to him, her brows knitting slightly as her curiosity piqued. "What is it?"

Declan opened the box to reveal an infinity diamond necklace, the delicate pendant gleaming in the fading light. The heart intertwined in the design caught her attention, their subtle elegance alluring.

"It's beautiful," she murmured, her voice trembling slightly.

Declan stepped closer, lifting the necklace from the box. "Turn around," he said softly, his tone a mixture of command and reverence.

Cora complied, her heart racing as he brushed her hair aside. The cool metal of the necklace against her skin sent a shiver down her spine, his fingers lingering just a moment longer than necessary as he fastened it.

"To me, this means everything," he whispered, his lips grazing her ear.

She smiled, her fingers brushing against the pendant. "It's just a necklace," she said lightly, unaware of the significance it held for him.

Declan's eyes darkened briefly, a flicker of something unreadable crossing his face before he leaned in, pressing a kiss to her bare shoulder. "You'll understand eventually," he murmured, his voice filled with an intimacy that sent heat pooling in her chest.

The sun dipped lower on the horizon as Declan's hands lingered on Cora's shoulders. He stepped closer behind her, the warmth of his body pressing against her back. The cool metal of the infinity diamond necklace still rested against her collarbone, a delicate contrast to the heat building between them.

"You drive me mad," he murmured, his voice rough as his lips brushed against the curve of her neck.

Cora's glass began trembling slightly in her hand. "Declan," she whispered, her voice wavering with a mix of hesitation and anticipation.

He reached around her, taking the glass from her hand and setting it on the nearby table. His fingers intertwined with hers as he turned her to face him, his intense blue eyes locking onto hers. "You're breathtaking," he said, his tone low and commanding. "Do you have any idea what you do to me?"

Her cheeks flushed, her pulse quickening as his gaze swept over her. Her summer dress clung to her curves, the fabric whispering against her skin as the breeze teased its hem. Her lips parted to respond, but the words never came—his mouth was on hers before she could speak, his kiss demanding and possessive.

Declan's hands slid down her sides, his fingers brushing against the soft fabric of her dress before finding her hips. He pulled her closer, their bodies pressed together as his lips moved against hers with an urgency that left her breathless. Cora gasped softly, her hands gripping the front of his deep blue button-up shirt as she tried to steady herself. The crisp fabric shifted beneath her touch, and she let her fingers trail up to his collar, undoing the first button.

"You've been teasing me all day," Declan murmured against her mouth, his hands sliding to the small of her back. "Do you have any idea how hard it was not to touch you?"

Her laughter was soft, breathless. "Teasing you? I thought I was snorkeling and biking like an innocent tourist."

"Innocent?" he said with a dark chuckle, his lips trailing down her neck. "Cora, the way you look in this dress, there's nothing innocent about it." She shivered as his hands moved lower, the fabric of her dress inching up beneath his touch. The cool air brushed against her exposed thighs, sending a thrill through her as she leaned into him, her body arching against his.

Declan's lips moved across her shoulder, his teeth grazing her skin in a way that made her gasp. "I saw the way the driver looked at you today," he murmured, his voice rough with possessiveness.

Her brow furrowed slightly. "What are you talking about?"

"At the snorkeling stop," he said, his tone darkening as he kissed the hollow of her throat. "He couldn't take his eyes off you. And all I could think about..." He paused, his lips curving into a faint smile against her skin. "...was what it would look like if he kissed you."

Cora froze, her eyes widening. "Declan—"

"I imagined it," he continued, his hands tightening on her hips as he guided her back against the railing. "Him leaning in, his hands on your waist, your lips parting for him."

Her cheeks flushed, heat pooling in her core as his words ignited something she couldn't quite name. "And you thought about that... while we're here?"

He pulled back slightly, his gaze locking onto hers with an ominous gloom. "I thought about it." His voice softened, his hands cupping her face. "Is that so wrong?"

He kissed her again, the intensity of it leaving no room for argument. His hands roamed freely now, sliding up her back and pulling her closer as he deepened the kiss. The sun dipped below the horizon, the fading light casting their entwined forms in shadows as Declan lifted her effortlessly onto the edge of the balcony railing. Cora gasped, her legs wrapping around his waist instinctively as her hands clutched at his shoulders. The crisp cotton of his shirt shifted beneath her fingers, and she tugged at the buttons, pushing the fabric aside to reveal the warm skin of his chest.

"You're driving me crazy," she murmured, her voice trembling as his lips moved down the curve of her neck.

"Good," he growled, his hands sliding beneath the hem of her dress. "Because I want you to feel exactly what I feel."

The night air swirled around them, the soft rustle of the breeze mingling with their ragged breaths as Declan claimed her with a fervor that left her breathless. The cool marble of the balcony railing pressed against Cora's back as Declan leaned into her, his lips tracing the line of her jaw before moving lower. Her hands trembled as they slid over his chest, her fingers brushing against the warm skin revealed by his open shirt.

"You have no idea how badly I've wanted this," Declan murmured, his voice rough and low. "How many times I've imagined having you like this, completely at my mercy."

"Declan," she whispered, her voice trembling with a mixture of desire and hesitation as the back of her dress hung slightly over the railing.

His lips brushed against her ear, his breath warm and teasing. "Say it," he murmured, his hands sliding to her hips. "Say you're mine."

"I'm yours," she replied softly, the words barely audible over the sound of her pounding heart.

His mouth captured hers again, his kiss deep and possessive as his hands moved with increasing urgency. The straps of her dress slipped from her shoulders, the fabric pooling around her waist as his lips trailed down her collarbone. Her soft gasps began mingling with the sound of the waves crashing far below.

"You're beautiful," he said, his voice thick with desire as his hands roamed her body. "Every part of you."

Cora's head fell back, her chest rising and falling as she surrendered to the moment. The cool night air brushed against her skin, a sharp contrast to the heat radiating between them. Declan's movements were both deliberate and desperate, his touch igniting a fire that left her breathless.

"You've undone me, Cora," he admitted, his lips moving against her neck. "Every look, every touch—it's like you've burned yourself into my soul."

Her cheeks flushed at his words, her body trembling as his hands slid beneath her dress, finding the soft curve of her waist. "You say that like it's a bad thing," she managed to tease, though her voice trembled with the intensity of the moment.

Declan chuckled softly, the sound low and wicked. "Oh, it's the best thing that's ever happened to me," he said, his hands tightening on her hips as he pulled her closer. "But it's also maddening. Do you know what it's like to want someone as much as I want you?"

She could feel the raw hunger in his touch, the way his body pressed against hers with an urgency that left no doubt of his desire. Her hands slid to his back, her fingers curling into the fabric of his shirt as she whispered, "Then take me, Declan."

An orange hue lit up the sky, the fading light casting their entwined forms in shadows that danced with the flicker of the beacons around them. His lips found hers again, slower this time, as though savoring every second. His hands moved with purpose, tracing the curves of her body as if committing every inch of her to memory. The soft fabric of her dress gave way beneath his touch, exposing more of her skin to the cool night air and the warmth of his hands.

"You're everything, Cora," he murmured, his lips brushing against her temple. "And I'll spend the rest of my life making sure you know it."

Her heart was pounding as his words sank in. The intensity of his gaze left her feeling both vulnerable and cherished, the depth of his desire matching her own. She pulled him closer, her hands sliding to his jaw as she whispered, "Show me."

The passion between them burned brighter, every touch, every whispered word igniting a fire that refused to be extinguished. Declan's movements became more deliberate, his focus entirely on her as he guided her into a rhythm that left her gasping. The world around them faded, leaving only the sound of their breathing, the crash of the waves, and the steady hum of their connection.

The stars above twinkled faintly, their light casting a soft glow over the balcony as they gave themselves over to the moment. Declan's whispers became softer, his voice filled with reverence as he murmured her name against her skin. Every kiss, every touch was a reminder of his unwavering devotion, his need to claim her completely. The night wrapped around them like a velvet curtain, the breeze carrying the salty tang of the Aegean Sea. Declan's hands slid down Cora's body, the deliberate pressure of his touch making her gasp softly.

"Every inch of you," he murmured, his voice low and thick with desire as his fingers traced the edge of her dress. "You undo me, Cora."

"Declan..." she whispered, her voice trembling with need.

He silenced her with a kiss, deep and commanding, his mouth moving against hers with a hunger that left her breathless. His hands roamed her body, sliding beneath the fabric of her dress to trace the bare skin of her back. She arched into him, the feel of his warm hands against her cool skin sending a shiver racing down her spine.

"You've driven me crazy all day," he said against her lips, his voice a rough growl. "The way you moved, the way you laughed—it's been torturous not to touch you."

Her cheeks flushed, heat pooling in her core as his words ignited something primal within her. "Then touch me," she whispered, her voice trembling but certain.

He didn't need to be told twice. "You're mine," he murmured against her skin, his voice thick with possessiveness as his hands explored her with an unrelenting hunger. "Every part of you, Cora."

Her body responded to him instinctively, her head falling back as she surrendered to the moment. "Always," she whispered, her voice trembling.

"You're perfect," he said, his voice a mix of reverence and need. "And I'm going to show you exactly how much you mean to me."

The rhythm between them was unrelenting, each movement a declaration of the connection that bound them together. Declan's lips found hers again, his kiss slow and deliberate as his hands guided her into a rhythm that left her gasping. The world around them disappeared—the stars, the waves, the faint hum of Santorini—all of it faded, leaving only the fire that burned between them.

Her fingers slid beneath the open fabric of his shirt, her touch exploring his chest as he whispered her name like a prayer. "Cora," he murmured, his voice rough and unsteady. "You drive me insane."

Her body trembled beneath his touch, her head falling back as his lips moved lower, tracing a path across her chest. Her hands braced against his shoulders, her soft moans mingling with the sound of the waves far below.

"Declan," she gasped, her voice breaking as her body arched into his.

He pulled back just enough to meet her gaze, his eyes dark and filled with intensity. "I want you to remember this," he said softly, his hands tightening on her hips. "Every moment. Every touch. Because this is only the beginning."

The passion between them reached a crescendo, their movements frantic yet deliberate as they claimed one another completely. The intimacy of the moment was electric, their breaths mingling as they lost themselves in the rhythm of their connection. The stars above twinkled faintly, their light casting a soft glow over their entwined forms as they gave themselves over to the moment. Declan's whispers became softer, his voice filled with reverence as he murmured her name against her skin. Every kiss, every touch was a reminder of his need to possess her, to claim her in every way.

As their passion subsided, the world around them slowly came back into focus—the soft rustle of the breeze, the distant sounds of the town below, the faint glow of the lanterns around them. Declan pressed his forehead against hers, his breath ragged as he whispered, "You're everything to me, Cora."

Her hands cupped his face, her fingers brushing against his jaw as she smiled faintly. "I love you," she replied softly, her voice filled with a quiet certainty that left no room for ambiguity.

The soft hum of the waves below slowly returned to their awareness as the intensity of their connection ebbed, leaving behind a quiet intimacy. Declan pressed his forehead to Cora's, his hands still resting on her hips, holding her as though she might disappear if he let go. His breath mingled with hers, both of them unsteady, their chests rising and falling in tandem.

"I'll never get enough of you," Declan murmured, his voice a low rasp as he brushed his lips against her temple. "You'll always leave me wanting more."

Cora smiled faintly, her fingers tracing lazy circles against the bare skin of his chest beneath his open shirt. "You have a way of making me forget everything else," she whispered, her voice soft but tinged with warmth.

Declan tilted her chin up, his piercing blue eyes locking onto hers. "Good," he said, his tone firm but tender. "Because when I'm with you, nothing else matters."

Her cheeks flushed, the intensity of his gaze leaving her breathless. She leaned in, her lips brushing against his in a kiss that was slower this time, less urgent but no less consuming. The breeze played with the edges of her dress, the fabric teasing against her legs as his hands roamed her body once more, his touch reverent yet possessive.

They lingered on the balcony, the glow of the lanterns casting warm light over their entwined forms. Declan reached up, his fingers brushing against the infinity diamond necklace that now adorned her neck. The pendant sparkled faintly in the moonlight, catching his attention and holding it.

"This necklace," he began, his voice low as he traced the delicate chain. "It's not just a piece of jewelry."

Cora tilted her head, her lips curving into a curious smile. "What do you mean?"

Declan hesitated for a moment, his thumb brushing over the pendant as he spoke. "The infinity heart... it's a symbol. To most, they represent love, eternity, connection. But in certain circles, they also signify something more... open."

Her brow furrowed slightly, her gaze searching his. "Open?" she asked, her voice tinged with curiosity.

"It's a subtle mark," he explained, his tone careful. "A way of saying there's room for more. That the connection we share isn't confined or ordinary."

Cora's cheeks flushed as she absorbed his words, her fingers brushing against the necklace. "You're saying this means something more to you than it does to me."

"To me, it's everything," Declan said simply. "But to you, it's whatever you want it to be. For now."

She smiled faintly, her fingers trailing along his jaw. "You're full of mysteries, Declan," she teased lightly, though her voice held a note of sincerity.

"And I plan to unravel them with you," he replied, his hands sliding to her waist as he pulled her closer. "But not tonight. Tonight is just about us."

The stars continued to dance across the sky as they stood together, the intimacy between them unbroken. Declan's hand moved to her cheek, his thumb brushing against her skin as he gazed at her with an intensity that made her heart skip.

"You're everything I never knew I needed," he said softly, his voice filled with reverence. "And I'm going to spend the rest of my life proving it to you."

Cora's emotions swirled as she searched his face. There was something in his gaze—something raw and unyielding—that made her feel both cherished and claimed. "You're impossible," she whispered, her lips curving into a soft smile.

"And you're irresistible," he countered, his tone teasing but filled with affection.

As the night deepened, Declan led her back inside the suite, his arm draped around her shoulders as he guided her toward the bed. The room was still bathed in the soft glow of the lights outside, the curtains swaying gently in the breeze. He stopped near the edge of the bed, his hands resting on her waist as he leaned in to kiss her again, this time slower, more deliberate.

"You're not tired, are you?" he asked against her lips, his tone laced with amusement.

"Not even close," she replied, her voice a whisper as her hands slid beneath the open edges of his shirt.

Declan smirked, his lips curving into a wicked grin. "Good. Because I'm not finished with you yet."

The lanterns outside swayed gently in the breeze, casting golden light across the room as Declan pulled Cora closer. The straps of her summer dress were loose, the fabric barely clinging to her as his hands slid down her back, his touch slow and deliberate. She let out a soft gasp as his lips found the hollow of her throat, pressing kisses there that left her skin tingling.

"You undo me," he murmured, his voice thick with reverence as his hands roamed her body.

Her fingers tangled on the edges of his open shirt, tugging it down his arms until it fell to the floor. Her hands moved over his bare chest, her touch exploring his body as her breath quickened. "You say that like it's a bad thing," she teased, though her voice trembled with anticipation.

Declan chuckled low in his throat, his lips curving into a wicked smile against her skin. "It's the best thing," he admitted, his hands tightening on her waist as he guided her back toward the bed.

She smiled faintly, her cheeks flushed as her dress slipped lower with every step. The cool sheets brushed against the backs of her legs as she sank onto the edge of the bed, her heart racing as Declan knelt in front of her.

His hands found her ankles first, sliding her shoes off and discarding them carelessly to the side. His lips pressed soft, teasing kisses to her calves, moving higher with every touch. The delicate way he touched her contrasted with the dark intensity in his eyes, leaving her breathless.

Her hands found his hair, her fingers threading through the dark strands as her body responded to his every touch.

"Declan..." she whispered, her voice trembling as he pushed the fabric higher, his lips following the path of his hands.

Declan smiled faintly, his lips curving into something softer as he leaned in to capture her mouth again. His kiss was slow and deliberate, his hands roaming her body with an intensity that left no part of her untouched.

"You're everything to me," he whispered against her ear, his voice trembling slightly as his body pressed against hers.

Her hands slid down his back, her touch igniting a fire that left him trembling. "Then show me," she said softly, her words both a challenge and a plea.

Declan's response was immediate, his body moving against hers in a rhythm that left her gasping. Every kiss, every touch, every whispered word was a revelation—a reminder of how deeply he needed her. The intimacy of the moment was overwhelming, a blend of passion and tenderness that left her feeling unraveled. The sounds of the town below faded, the world narrowing to just the two of them. The soft rustle of the sheets, the warmth of their bodies, and the steady hum of their connection created a symphony that was theirs alone. Declan's hands framed her face as he kissed her again, slower this time, his touch filled with a reverence that made her heart ache.

The room was silent save for the faint hum of the breeze outside and the steady sound of their breaths mingling. The warmth of Declan's body pressed against Cora's, the crisp sheets beneath her a sharp contrast to the fire still burning between them. His hands moved slowly now, his touch less urgent but no less deliberate as he traced lazy circles along her hip.

Cora tilted her head, her fingers brushing against the infinity necklace still fastened around her neck. "It feels like you planned all of this," she said softly, her voice teasing but warm.

Declan smiled faintly, his lips pressing to her shoulder. "Every moment," he admitted, his voice rough. "Because I knew exactly how I wanted tonight to go—with you in my arms, wearing nothing but that necklace."

Her cheeks flushed as she looked at him, her smile growing. "I suppose it worked," she teased, her fingers brushing against his jaw.

"It always does," he replied, his tone low as he leaned in to kiss her.

The kiss deepened, the world narrowing once again to the space between them. The intimacy between them shifted into something softer, more reflective, as they lay tangled together. Declan's fingers brushed through her hair, his gaze fixed on her as though committing every detail to memory.

"I could stay like this forever," he murmured, his voice filled with reverence.

Cora smiled faintly, her hand resting lightly on his chest. "You say that now," she teased. "But wait until I start stealing all the blankets."

Declan chuckled, his lips curving into a rare, unguarded smile. "You can take everything, as long as you stay right here."

The moonlight filtered through the open curtains, casting their entwined forms in a silvery glow as they lay together. Cora rested her head against Declan's chest, listening to the steady rhythm of his heartbeat as her own began to slow.

"Thank you," she said softly after a moment.

Declan's hand stilled in her hair, his brow furrowing slightly as he looked down at her. "For what?"

"For today. For all of it," she replied, her fingers brushing against the infinity pendant. "You have a way of making everything feel... unforgettable."

His lips pressed into her hair, his voice a low rumble. "That's because you're unforgettable, Cora. And I'll spend every day reminding you of that."

As the night deepened, the quiet intimacy between them lingered, the weight of their connection leaving no room for doubt as they ordered in dinner. Declan's possessiveness, his intensity, and the raw vulnerability he showed only when they were alone made her feel both cherished and claimed. And later as she drifted off in his arms, the faint sound of the waves lulling her to sleep, she knew that this moment would stay with her forever.

The turquoise waters of Santorini sparkled under the glistening sunlight, the island's whitewashed buildings standing in stark contrast to the deep blue sky. The setting was idyllic, a picture-perfect backdrop for their honeymoon.

The flying dress photoshoot had been Declan's idea. "It'll be stunning," he'd said, arranging for a renowned photographer to capture the moment. Cora stood on a cliff overlooking the sea, the dramatic red fabric of the dress billowing around her in the breeze.

"Hold your pose," Declan called from the sidelines, his voice firm. "And tilt your chin a little higher. It needs to look effortless."

Cora tried to comply, her heart sinking with each adjustment. The photoshoot felt oddly more like a performance for Declan than a celebration of their honeymoon. When the photographer finally called for a break, Cora slipped away to a quiet corner of the cliff, her chest tight.

"You looked incredible out there," Declan said, approaching her. He placed a hand on her arm, his smile wide. "These photos are going to be iconic."

Cora forced a smile, though her throat felt tight. "I hope so."

That evening, they dined at an exclusive cliffside restaurant, the candlelit setting as romantic as it was breathtaking. Declan ordered wine, his charm effortlessly drawing the attention of their waitress. At first, Cora dismissed it as harmless, but as the evening went on, Declan's interactions with the waitress became harder to ignore.

When Cora returned from the restroom, she found him leaning close to the waitress, his hand lightly brushing her arm as he laughed at something she'd said. The young woman's cheeks flushed, her smile shy but flattered.

Cora's chest tightened, a mix of hurt and anger bubbling to the surface. She stepped forward, her voice trembling. "Declan, can I talk to you?"

He straightened, his expression shifting quickly. "Of course," he said smoothly, excusing himself from the table.

Once they were alone, Cora's voice wavered as she spoke. "What was that?"

"What was what?" Declan replied, his tone calm but clipped.

"With the waitress," Cora said, her hands trembling. "The way you were with her... it didn't feel right."

Declan sighed, his jaw tightening. "Cora, you're overreacting. I was being polite. That's all."

"It didn't feel polite," Cora said, tears welling in her eyes. "It felt like... something else."

Declan's tone dropped, his voice low but firm. "You're tired," he said. "Let's not turn this into something it's not. It's our honeymoon, my love."

Cora stared at him, her heart breaking as utter confusion in their relationship became undeniable.

The rest of the evening in Santorini passed in strained silence. Declan's flirtation with the waitress replayed in Cora's mind, each moment sharpening the doubts that had been building inside her for months. She sat on the balcony of their suite, the soft glow of the moon reflecting off the turquoise waters below. The idyllic setting, once a symbol of their honeymoon's promise, now felt suffocating.

Declan joined her on the balcony, his presence filling the space. He handed her a glass of wine, his expression unreadable. "You've been reserved, darling," he said softly.

Cora took the glass, her fingers curling around the stem. "There's a lot on my mind," she replied, her voice trembling slightly.

Declan leaned against the railing, his gaze fixed on her. "Are we still talking about the waitress?" he asked, his tone measured.

"I can't stop thinking about it," Cora admitted. "It wasn't just the waitress, Declan. It's... everything. The wedding, the photoshoot, the decisions. Sometimes I feel like I'm just a piece in your perfect picture."

Declan's jaw tightened, and he exhaled sharply. "That's not fair, Cora. I've done everything to make our life extraordinary. For both of us."

"But it doesn't feel like my life," she said, her voice breaking. "It feels like yours."

Declan's expression hardened. "You're exhausted," he said firmly. "You're letting your emotions cloud your judgment. We'll talk about this when you're thinking more clearly."

Cora stared at him, her heart sinking. "You don't see it, do you?" she whispered. "You don't see me."

The flight back from Greece was silent. Cora sat by the window, staring at the clouds as they soared over the ocean. Declan worked on his laptop beside her, his focus unbroken. The weight of their unspoken tension pressed against her chest, leaving her breathless.

When they landed, Declan turned to her, his voice calm but firm. "We'll figure this out," he said. "We always do."

Cora nodded faintly, though her heart wasn't in it. She felt a deep coil in their relationship as her emotions heightened the more she thought about it.

Back at home, Cora found solace in the journals that had become her guide through uncertainty. She flipped through its pages late one night, the glow of the bedside lamp illuminating her grandmother's handwriting. Her breath caught as she came across a passage she hadn't noticed before: *Henry was the kind of man who saw you for who you were, not who he wanted you to be. He taught me that courage isn't about fearless—it's about stepping into the unknown, even when it terrifies you.*

The name struck her like lightning. Henry Tate. Sebastian's grandfather.

Cora's heart raced as she traced the faded ink, the connections between her grandmother's story and her own life suddenly coming into focus. Henry had been a pivotal figure in her grandmother's journey—

someone who had reminded her of her strength, her worth. And now, Sebastian was doing the same for her.

The next morning, Cora picked up her phone, her hands trembling as she dialed Sebastian's number. He answered on the second ring, his voice steady and warm. "Cora?"

"I found something in Gram's journal," she said, her voice breaking. "Your grandfather's name. Henry. She wrote about him."

Sebastian was silent for a moment before replying, his tone filled with curiosity. "What did she say?"

"She wrote about how he helped her find herself," Cora said softly. "And I think... I think I need to understand more about him. About what they shared."

Sebastian's voice softened. "I'll help you," he said simply. "Whatever you need."

Cora exhaled as tears slipped down her cheeks. "Thank you," she whispered. "I don't know what I'm doing, but... I know I need to figure it out."

A Storm Within

"Some storms rage around us; others rage within."

Sebastian's steady presence was becoming a lifeline, a grounding force in the chaos of her thoughts. For the first time in weeks, the future felt like it held possibilities instead of just shadows. But the enormity of what lay ahead—untangling the web Declan had spun around her, finding her way back to herself—was daunting.

That night, as Cora sat in the quiet of their room, her mind drifted to her grandmother's journals. She flipped through the worn pages, searching for guidance among the lines of wisdom she had come to depend on. One passage stood out: *The most dangerous lies are the ones we tell ourselves. Truth can hurt, but it also frees.*

Her chest tightened as she read the words, their truth cutting through her like a blade. Her mind veered off to the business event tomorrow. They were boarding the private jet for a conference in Georgia first thing in the morning. She knew what she had to do next, even if the path ahead felt impossible.

The sprawling Atlanta estate was nothing short of breathtaking. Towering glass walls framed the skyline like a work of art, while inside, the chandeliers cast a golden light over the polished marble floors.

Cora stepped into the grand foyer, her heels clicking softly against the marble. The Surgeon's Conference was a huge success, and an exclusive afterglow was being held at a mansion in Buckhead. The hum of conversation, the clinking of champagne glasses, and the occasional burst of laughter surrounded her, creating an atmosphere of opulence and ease.

She smoothed her hands over the delicate fabric of her dress, the warmth of Declan's hand resting on her lower back, grounding her as he guided her further into the room. "Relax," he murmured, his voice low but firm. "You belong here."

Cora gave him a faint smile, but her fingers tightened slightly around her clutch. The truth was, she wasn't sure if she did. The room was filled with people who exuded wealth and confidence, their sharp smiles and watchful eyes taking in everything. Sheer curtains hung elegantly in doorways leading to separate rooms, yielding her to a territory of the unknown. And yet, with Declan beside her, she felt like she might be able to pretend, at least for tonight.

They hadn't made it far into the room before a man in a tailored suit approached, his grin wide and his hand outstretched. "Declan!" he exclaimed, clasping Declan's hand firmly. "Good to see you, man. And who's this vision?"

Declan's smile was smooth, practiced. "The former Cora Jacobs, now my wife," he said, his tone warm.

The man's eyes lit up as he turned his attention to Cora. "Ah, so you're the one everyone's been talking about. Declan hasn't stopped talking about you," he said, glancing down briefly at her diamond infinity necklace.

Cora flushed, looking briefly at Declan, who met her gaze with an easy smile. "It's nice to meet you," she said, her voice steady despite the flutter of nerves in her chest.

"Likewise, I'm Sylas," the man replied, giving her a friendly nod before excusing himself to greet another guest.

As they continued through the room, Cora caught snippets of conversations—discussions of investments, politics, and travel that felt worlds away from her everyday life. It was overwhelming, but Declan's presence at her side kept her grounded.

"Having fun yet?" Declan asked, his tone teasing as he handed her a glass of champagne.

Cora took a sip, the cool, bubbly liquid calming her nerves. "It's a lot to take in," she admitted. "But it's... exciting."

Declan's smile widened. "Good. That's the point."

Before she could respond, a familiar voice called out her name. "Cora!" Evelyn's vibrant energy cut through the hum of the party as she approached, her arms outstretched. "Darling, you look divine."

Cora laughed, relief washing over her as Evelyn pulled her into a hug. "What are you doing here?" she asked, stepping back to look at her.

"Networking, of course," Evelyn replied with a wink. Then her gaze shifted to Declan, and her smile tightened. "Declan. Always a pleasure."

"Evelyn," Declan said, his tone polite but cool.

The tension between them was subtle but unmistakable, and Cora's stomach twisted as she glanced between them. "Am I missing something?" she asked, her voice light but pointed.

"Not at all," Evelyn said smoothly, her gaze flicking back to her. "Now, come with me. There's someone I want you to meet."

Cora hesitated, her eyes meeting Declan's. "I'll find you later?" she asked softly.

Declan nodded, his smile returning. "Of course."

Evelyn wasted no time whisking her away, her arm linked with hers as they moved through the crowd. "So," she began, her tone low, "How are things with Mr. Perfect?"

Cora frowned, glancing up at her. "Declan's been great. Why do you ask?"

Evelyn sighed, her expression softening slightly. "I'm just looking out for you, love. He's charming, sure, but there's something about him that doesn't sit right with a lot of people."

Cora's chest tightened. "Evelyn, he's been nothing but kind to me," she stated as a half-truth, not wanting to confess the raw illusion of her new life.

"Maybe," Evelyn said, her lips pressing into a thin line. "But don't let his charm blind you to who he really is."

Together they walked past a small line of people waiting to get through a set of sheer curtains leading into the study.

Cora opened her mouth to respond, but before she could, Declan appeared at her side.

His gaze flicked briefly to Evelyn before settling on her. "Mind if I steal her back?" he asked smoothly.

Evelyn's smile didn't reach his eyes. "Be my guest."

The tension between them was palpable as Declan led Cora away, his hand resting on her back once more. "What was that about?" he asked, his tone light but edged with curiosity.

Cora sighed, shaking her head. "Evelyn's just... intuitive."

Declan's lips curved into a small smile. "I can respect that. But she should know you're in good hands."

Cora's heart fluttered at his words, but a flicker of doubt remained. She pushed it aside, letting herself get lost in the rhythm of the party as Declan guided her toward the balcony.

The cool night air enveloped them as Declan slid the balcony door closed, sealing off the hum of the party behind them. The view from the terrace was breathtaking—Atlanta's skyline glittered like a sea of stars, the distant hum of the city a soothing counterpoint to the tension brewing inside Cora.

Declan leaned against the railing, his hands resting casually on the smooth metal, but there was nothing casual about the way his gaze locked onto hers. "This party is... different," he said softly, his voice cutting through the silence.

Cora hesitated, her arms folding protectively across her chest. "Definitely," she admitted, glancing away. "The doorway curtains. What do they mean?"

Declan stepped closer, his movements slow, deliberate. "It's an opening, Cora. It's an avenue to see what you want to see, be who you want to be," he said without pressing as he traced the infinity necklace lightly.

Cora met his gaze, her chest tightening under the weight of his sincerity. "Is there something between you and Evelyn?" she asked finally, her voice trembling slightly.

Declan exhaled, his jaw tightening as he looked out over the city. "I'm not surprised you would ask that," he said quietly. "Evelyn cares about you. That's a good thing, but she tends to cause her own problems which is the least of my worries."

"Then why does it feel like there's something between you two that you're not telling me?" Cora pressed, her heart pounding as she took a step closer.

Declan's lips pressed into a thin line, his gaze darkening as he turned back to her. "Because there is," he admitted, his voice tinged with frustration. "But it's not what you think."

"Then tell me," Cora said, her voice firmer now. "I deserve to know."

Declan hesitated, his hand running through his hair as he struggled for the right words. "Evelyn doesn't think I'm good enough for you," he said finally, his tone raw. "And maybe she's right. My past isn't spotless, Cora. I've made mistakes. I've hurt people."

Cora's breath caught at the vulnerability in his voice, her own doubts momentarily silenced.

"Declan..."

He took a step closer, his hand reaching for hers. "But I'm not that man anymore," he said, his voice steady. "When I'm with you, I feel like I can be better. Like I can be the man you deserve."

Cora stared at him, her heart aching at the honesty in his words. Her hand tightened around his, her voice trembling as she spoke. "I don't need you to be perfect, Declan. I just need you to be real."

A faint smile tugged at his lips as he brought her hand to his chest, pressing it over his heart. "Then I'll do my best," he said softly. "For you."

The moment stretched between them, heavy with unspoken promises. But before Cora could respond, the sliding door opened, and Evelyn stepped onto the balcony, her expression unreadable.

"Am I interrupting?" Evelyn asked, her tone light but edged with tension.

Cora stepped back instinctively, her hand slipping from Declan's as she turned to face Evelyn. "No," she said quickly. "We were just talking."

Evelyn's gaze flicked between them, her jaw tightening briefly before she plastered on a smile. "Good," she said smoothly. "Because I wanted a word with you, Declan."

Declan's expression shifted, his easy charm replaced by something harder, more guarded. "Of course," he said, his tone polite but clipped.

Cora looked between them, her stomach twisting as she sensed the undercurrent of hostility. "Evelyn..." she began, but she held up a hand.

"It's fine, love," Evelyn said, her smile softening slightly as she looked at her. "Go back inside. I won't keep him long."

Cora hesitated, her gaze lingering on Declan. He gave her a small nod, his lips curving into a faint smile. "Go ahead," he said softly. "I'll be right behind you."

Reluctantly, Cora turned and slipped back inside, the warmth of the party a stark contrast to the tension on the balcony. She glanced back through the glass as she saw Evelyn and Declan facing off, their postures tense.

The party felt distant now, its hum of laughter and music muffled as Cora stood just inside the glass doors, her gaze fixed on the balcony. Evelyn and Declan were facing each other, their postures rigid, the tension between them visible even from where she stood. She couldn't hear their words, but the sharpness in their movements, the way Declan's jaw clenched, and Evelyn's hands gestured wildly, spoke volumes.

Cora's chest tightened, her fingers fidgeting with the strap of her dress. She wanted to step back outside, to insert herself between them and force whatever this was to stop, but something held her back. Perhaps it was the fear of what she might hear—or the realization that this was a confrontation they both needed.

The glass door slid open suddenly, breaking her thoughts. Declan stepped inside first, his expression a storm of restrained anger and something deeper, something she couldn't quite place. He stopped when he saw her, his gaze softening just slightly.

"Cora," he said, his voice low. "I need a minute."

Without waiting for a response, he moved past her, disappearing into the crowd. Evelyn followed moments later, her expression equally stormy as she ran a hand through her hair. Her usual flair was gone, replaced by a rawness that made her stomach twist.

"What happened?" Cora asked, her voice trembling as she stepped closer.

Evelyn let out a sharp laugh, shaking her head. "What always happens with men like him," she said bitterly. "He wants you all to himself, and anyone who tries to get in the way? They're a problem."

Cora frowned, her heart pounding. "That's not fair, Evelyn. Has he done anything to you?"

Evelyn's eyes met hers, and the hurt in her gaze made her breath catch. "I just don't want you to get hurt, love," she said softly. "And I can see the way he's pulling you in, sweeping you off your feet. But where is this really going? Do you even know?"

Cora's throat tightened, her thoughts swirling. She didn't have an answer, not one that felt honest. "I don't know," she admitted quietly. "But that's for me to figure out."

Evelyn sighed, her shoulders sagging. "I know. I just... I care about you, Cora. That's all."

"I know you do," she said, her voice softer now. "But I need to figure this out on my own."

Evelyn nodded reluctantly, her hand brushing her briefly before she turned and disappeared into the crowd. Cora watched her go, her chest heavy with the weight of the evening.

Cora found Declan near the edge of the pool, his posture rigid as he stared into the rippling water. She approached cautiously, her heels clicking softly against the stone patio.

"Declan," she said, her voice hesitant.

He turned, his expression softening when he saw her. "Hey," he said, his voice quieter now.

Cora stepped closer, the warmth of the nearby pool a stark contrast to the cool tension between them. "What happened out there?"

Declan sighed, running a hand through his hair. "Our friend has a lot to say about me," he said, his tone clipped. "And none of it's good."

Cora frowned, her heart aching at the frustration in his voice. "Evelyn's just...She feels the need to protect me for some reason."

"That much is obvious," Declan said with a faint, humorless laugh. He turned to face her fully, his gaze searching for hers. "But what about you, Cora? Do you trust me?"

The question hit her like a wave, her breath catching as she struggled for an answer. Did she trust him? She wanted to—God, she wanted to—

but the doubts Evelyn had planted, the secrets that still lingered between them, made her hesitate.

"I don't know," she admitted finally, her voice trembling. "I want to, but.. I don't know if I can keep up."

Declan's jaw tightened, but he nodded, his expression softening. "I get it," he said quietly. "And I don't want to push you. But I need you to know—I'm not going anywhere. I'm all in."

Their quiet moment was interrupted by a man's voice shouting an announcement from inside the mansion. "It's time, my friends! Step into the doorway of a curtained room and see what you came for!" Declan turned to Cora with a tender hand and began to guide her indoors as she trembled at his side.

Inside the mansion, people began to gather in doorways as Declan brushed by with Cora at his side. "I want to show you something, My Cora," Declan said with a reverence.

Cora felt her chest tighten, the weight of his words both comforting and terrifying. She nodded slowly, her fingers brushing against his.

He walked up to a curtained room and stood behind Cora so she could see the activity going on inside. He brushed her hair aside and began placing small kisses on her neck as they both watched a man and a woman begin to undress.

"Declan, what is going on?" she whispered in complete shock, her hands trembling and grasping for her clutch.

"In our world, My Cora, we can be anyone we want to be," he stated with an intense longing.

"I don't feel comfortable watching this," she whispered with a confusion like no other. "Please take me back to the hotel," she begged, silently wishing for the night to end.

"Yes, my darling. We can leave anytime you wish," he complied with one last kiss to the back of her neck.

They walked out the back door, passing the pool on their way to the car. The moon hung low over the Atlanta estate, its silver light casting a soft glow on the water as the pool rippled with faint reflections of the string lights draped above.

Cora's gaze lingered on the scene, the serene beauty of the estate clashing with the quiet unease that had settled in her chest. Declan walked beside her, his presence as commanding as ever, but her thoughts felt distant, untethered. The evening had been flawless on the surface—charming conversations, warm laughter, and the kind of effortless elegance that came naturally to Declan. But beneath it all, she had felt the cracks growing wider.

The car ride back to their hotel had been quiet, the hum of the engine a backdrop to the silence between them. Declan had scrolled through his phone, his attention focused elsewhere, while Cora stared out the window, the glow of the city fading into the distance.

That night, she had laid awake, her thoughts restless as she replayed the evening in her mind. Selah's text had come just after midnight:

How are you holding up? Call me if you need to talk.

Cora hadn't replied, her fingers hovering over the screen before setting the phone back on the nightstand. The weight of her silence pressed against her chest as she stared at the ceiling, the moonlight casting faint patterns across the room.

The flight back to Colorado was just as quiet. The hum of the plane's engines filled the silence between Cora and Declan, their seats side by side yet worlds apart. Cora leaned her head against the cool window, her eyes fixed on the endless expanse of clouds below. Declan sat beside her; his posture relaxed as always, the faint glow of his laptop screen illuminating his sharp features. His fingers moved quickly over the keyboard, his focus entirely elsewhere.

Cora closed her eyes, exhaling softly as she let the quiet wrap around her. The moments of stillness were rare, and while they gave her space to think, they also magnified the questions she didn't yet have answers to: *Is this the life I want? Is this who I want to be?*

Her thoughts drifted back to the past few days in Atlanta, where Declan had thrived in the spotlight of the American Surgeon Association Conference. The event had been a whirlwind—a showcase of power, wealth, and intellect that left her feeling both out of place and mesmerized. Declan had commanded the room effortlessly, his charm and precision making him the center of every conversation.

The after-party at the mansion, though, had carried a different energy. It was lavish, yes, but there was something unspoken, almost unnerving, about the exclusivity of the crowd and what she witnessed. Cora couldn't forget the way eyes had lingered on her, as if she were being assessed. And Evelyn—poised, polished Evelyn—had been there, dipping in and out of conversations with an ease that made Cora feel like a spectator. What had Evelyn been trying to tell her about Declan?

Her fingers brushed against the infinity necklace resting against her collarbone, the cool metal grounding her. Declan had fastened it there during their honeymoon, his words still echoing in her ears: *"To me, this means everything."* She didn't fully understand its significance, but it felt heavy now, a weight she couldn't quite place.

A Whisper of Freedom

"Freedom speaks softly before it roars."

When they landed, Colorado greeted them with its crisp air and sprawling mountains. The estate felt vast and eerily quiet after the constant buzz of Atlanta. Cora stepped inside, the familiar luxury of the space both comforting and stifling. Declan set his bag down near the staircase and placed a hand on the small of her back, his touch firm but gentle.

"You should rest," he said softly. "It's been a long trip."

Cora nodded, offering him a small smile before heading upstairs. She paused halfway, glancing back to see Declan pulling out his phone. He stepped into his study, the door closing behind him as he began speaking in a low tone. The sight sent a faint prickle of unease through her.

That night, sleep eluded her. She lay in bed staring at the ceiling, her thoughts circling back to Atlanta. Declan's question from their last night there resurfaced: *"Do you trust me?"* The question had been simple, but its weight had lingered, heavy and unresolved.

She wanted to trust him. She wanted to believe that the man who had promised her the world, who had filled her days with grand gestures and moments of intimacy, was someone she could rely on completely. But the doubts Evelyn had planted, the strange energy at the party, and Declan's occasional air of detachment left her uncertain.

Her fingers found the infinity necklace again, tracing its delicate lines as she tried to quiet her mind. Declan had given it to her with such intensity, his words dripping with meaning she didn't fully understand. To her, it was a beautiful gift. But to him, it seemed to symbolize something more—something unspoken that gnawed at the edge of her thoughts.

The next morning, a sharp knock at the door startled her. She opened it to find a tall man standing there, his broad shoulders filling the frame. He was dressed casually, but the badge he held up gleamed under the morning light.

"Cora Atler?" he asked, his voice steady and professional.

"Yes," she replied, her brow furrowing.

"My name is Dax Sheridan," he said, his tone softening slightly. "I'm the lead investigator on the fire at your loft. I'd like to ask you a few questions. Are you alone?"

The name hit her like a wave, her chest tightening as she stared at him. Sheridan. She found herself wondering just where she had heard that name before.

"Of course, yes," she said after a moment, stepping aside to let him in. "Come in."

Dax's presence felt both familiar and foreign. His sharp green eyes scanned the room briefly before settling on her, his expression unreadable. They sat in the sunlit sitting room, a faint tension filling the space as he pulled out a notebook and pen.

"I understand this is a sensitive topic," he began, his voice measured. "But I need to ask—do you have any reason to believe the fire wasn't accidental?"

Cora hesitated, her thoughts flickering to Declan before she pushed them away. "No," she said quietly. "I can't think of anyone who would do something like that."

Dax nodded, his pen scratching against the paper. "And were you aware of anyone who might have had access to your loft that night?"

She shook her head. "Only MJ and I had keys. It was locked when I left. I keep my set of keys on the hook in our study."

A flicker of guilt crossed Dax's face, his pen pausing briefly. "I'm sorry for your loss," he said softly.

"Thank you," Cora replied, her voice trembling.

The conversation continued, Dax's questions probing deeper into the events surrounding the fire. But as they spoke, Cora couldn't shake the feeling that he knew more than he was letting on. His careful phrasing, the way his eyes lingered on her—it was as if he were holding back something important.

When the interview ended, Dax stood, his movements deliberate. "Thank you for your time," he said. "If anything comes to mind, please don't hesitate to reach out," placing his business card in her hand.

"I will," Cora said, watching as he walked toward the door.

As he left, her mind raced with questions she didn't know how to ask. The name Sheridan hung heavily in the air, its significance gnawing at the edges of her thoughts.

Cora stood by the window of the sitting room, watching as Dax's car disappeared down the long driveway. The lingering tension from his visit left a strange weight in the air. His name—*Sheridan*—repeated in her mind, a drumbeat of familiarity she couldn't quite place. There was something about him, the way he looked at her, that felt oddly personal, though he'd kept his demeanor professional throughout the interview.

Her fingers brushed against the infinity necklace around her neck, the cold metal grounding her as her thoughts spiraled. Dax had been thorough in his questioning, but it was clear he was holding something back. She turned the name over in her mind again. Was it just a coincidence? Or was there something more?

She sighed, leaning her forehead against the cool glass of the window. The estate, with its sprawling gardens and opulent halls, felt suffocating today. Normally, she could find comfort in its quiet luxury, but now it felt heavy, like a gilded cage she couldn't escape.

Declan's voice broke the silence, pulling her from her thoughts. "Everything okay?" he asked as he entered the room, his tone casual but curious.

She turned to face him, offering a small smile. "Yeah," she replied, her voice soft. "I just had a visitor."

"Who?" he pressed, his gaze sharp as he approached her.

"Dax Sheridan," she said, watching his expression carefully. "He's the lead detective investigating the fire. He came by to ask some questions."

Declan's brows furrowed briefly before smoothing. "And what did you tell him?"

"Nothing he didn't already know," she replied. "I told him I couldn't think of anyone who might have targeted me."

Declan nodded, his expression unreadable as he crossed the room to stand beside her. "Good. The last thing you need is more stress."

Cora studied him for a moment, her lips parting as though to say more, but she stopped herself. The tension in his jaw, the way he avoided meeting her eyes—it sent a faint ripple of unease through her.

Later that evening, Cora found herself alone in the study, one of her grandmother's journals open on the desk in front of her. The familiar scent of aged paper filled the air as her fingers traced the delicate handwriting. She often turned to these journals when she felt lost, again finding solace in the wisdom her grandmother had left behind. Tonight, the words struck a deeper chord: *Sometimes, the answers we seek aren't in the questions we ask, but in the truths we're afraid to face.*

She leaned back in her chair, her chest rising as she absorbed the meaning. The truths she was afraid to face were stacking up—her doubts about Declan, the fire, and now Dax Sheridan. Her instincts told her there was something more beneath the surface of all of it, but she didn't know where to begin.

The next day, Cora decided she needed clarity. She called Dax, her fingers trembling slightly as she dialed his number. He answered on the second ring, his voice calm and steady.

"Detective Sheridan," he said.

"Hi, it's Cora," she began, her voice wavering. "I was wondering if we could meet again. There's... something I wanted to ask you."

There was a pause on the other end, and for a moment, she worried she'd made a mistake. Then Dax's voice softened. "Of course. I'll text you an address. Can you meet me this evening?"

"Yes," she said quickly, relief washing over her.

The small café where they met was a world away from the grandeur of the estate. It was cozy and unassuming, the kind of place where people could slip into quiet corners and speak without being overheard. Dax was already there when she arrived, sitting at a table near the window. He stood when he saw her, offering a small smile.

"Thanks for meeting me," Cora said as she slid into the seat across from him.

"Of course," Dax replied, his tone kind but measured. "What's on your mind?"

Cora hesitated, her fingers toying with the edge of her coffee cup. "I wanted to ask about the fire," she said finally. "You seemed... hesitant yesterday, like there was something you weren't saying."

Dax's expression shifted, a flicker of something unreadable crossing his face. He leaned back in his chair, his fingers lacing together as he studied her. "You're perceptive," he said after a moment.

"Was there something you wanted to tell me?" she pressed, her heart pounding.

He exhaled slowly, his gaze steady but cautious. "There's something you deserve to know," he said, his voice quieter now. "But it has nothing to do with the fire."

Cora's brow furrowed, confusion and curiosity mingling in her expression. "What do you mean?"

Dax's hands tightened slightly on the edge of the table, his jaw working as though he were searching for the right words. "Cora," he began, his voice trembling slightly. "I didn't just come to the estate because of the investigation. I came because... I'm your father."

The words hit her like a thunderclap, her breath catching as the weight of them sank in. "What?" she whispered, her voice barely audible.

Dax's gaze softened, guilt and vulnerability etched into his features. "I should've told you sooner," he admitted. "But I wasn't sure how. I've known who you were for a little while now, and I didn't know how to approach you."

Cora stared at him, her mind reeling. "You're my father," she repeated, her voice trembling.

"Yes," he said quietly. "And I can't tell you how sorry I am for not being there, Cora."

The world around Cora seemed to blur as Dax's words sank in. Her father. He was her father. She stared at him, her mind racing to piece together the fragments of her life with this new revelation.

"Why didn't you tell me sooner?" she asked, her voice trembling as she tried to make sense of it all.

Dax hesitated; his gaze steady but filled with guilt. "I didn't know how," he admitted. "Your mother... she never told me. I didn't even know you existed until a few years ago."

Cora's breath hitched at the mention of her mother. "She didn't tell you?"

Dax shook his head, his expression heavy with regret. "No. Your mom and I..." He paused, running a hand through his hair. "We were complicated. She was married when we met to a man who was all wrong for her. But she and I... we connected. It wasn't supposed to happen, but it did."

Cora leaned back in her chair, the weight of his words pressing down on her. "You had an affair," she said softly.

"Yes," Dax admitted, his voice raw. "And when she found out she was pregnant, she didn't know who the father was. She was scared, ashamed. She didn't want to break up her marriage, so she left town for a while. I didn't find out until years later—after she was gone. I received a letter and DNA results in the mail. When your grandmother passed away, I knew you would come back. I'm sorry I hesitated, Cora. You didn't deserve that."

Her heart clenched, the pieces of her mother's story falling into place. "How did she die?"

Dax's jaw tightened, his hands gripping the edge of the table. "Veda drove off a mountain road when you were just two," he said quietly. "She was distraught, alone in her mind, and... she wasn't ready to face the truth. She left you to be cared for by your grandmother Charlotte. I didn't pry. Your grandmother nearly lost herself losing your mother and you saved her Cora."

The weight of his confession settled heavily between them, the quiet of the café amplifying the tension. Cora looked down at her hands, her fingers twisting in her lap as she processed his words.

"She loved you," Dax said softly, his voice trembling. "But she was scared. And I failed her. I failed both of you. She named you Cora after the weekend we spent in the Gulf of Farallones outside of San Francisco, after the beautiful coral reefs. I should have been there for her, but she tried to shut me out. She wasn't in her right mind, Cora."

Cora swallowed hard, her emotions swirling in a chaotic mess. "Why now?" she asked finally, her voice barely above a whisper. "Why tell me this now?"

Dax leaned forward, his gaze earnest. "Because I couldn't stay silent anymore. And because I think this fire—it's connected to Declan."

Her head snapped up, her eyes narrowing. "What do you mean?"

Dax hesitated, his expression grave. "We've been looking into the fire, and there are too many things that don't add up. The investigator found evidence of accelerants—this wasn't an accident, Cora. It was arson."

The word hit her like a punch to the gut, her breath catching as she tried to process what he was saying. "Arson?" she repeated, her voice trembling.

"Yes," Dax said firmly. "And we're narrowing down suspects. Declan..." He paused, his gaze searching hers. "I need to know. Did Declan have any reason to want that loft gone?"

Cora's chest tightened, her mind flashing back to the engagement party, to Declan stepping away for a phone call, to the vague unease she had felt ever since. She pictured MJ as he left, excited to hit the Pride Nightlife that night on the business district.

"I don't know," she said finally, her voice breaking. "I don't think so. But... there are things he doesn't tell me."

Dax nodded, his expression understanding but firm. "If there's anything you remember—anything that seems off—you need to tell me. This isn't just about property damage, Cora. It's about MJ. This is bigger than either of us."

Her heart clenched at the mention of MJ, guilt and grief twisting in her chest. She nodded slowly, her voice trembling as she said, "I'll think about it. I promise."

When they left the café, the air outside felt cooler, sharper, as though it carried the weight of everything that had just been said. Dax hesitated before getting into his car, his expression softening as he looked at her.

"Cora," he said quietly. "I know this is a lot to take in. And I don't expect you to forgive me right away. But I want to be here for you, in whatever way you'll let me."

She nodded, her throat tight with emotion. "I'll call you," she said softly.

Dax offered her a faint smile before stepping into his car and driving away.

The estate felt unusually quiet, the heavy wooden doors shutting behind her with a soft thud. The quiet amplified her thoughts, her father's revelation echoing in her mind: *"I'm your father."* The words carried a weight she wasn't prepared for, adding to the storm of doubts already brewing inside her.

She wandered through the halls, her fingers brushing against the cold marble banister as she ascended the stairs. The infinity necklace felt heavier than usual, its delicate chain resting against her skin like a question she couldn't answer. She passed Declan's study on the way to her room, pausing briefly at the sound of his low voice.

The door was slightly ajar, and she caught snippets of his conversation. "No, I don't want delays... Just handle it," he said, his tone sharp and clipped.

Her chest tightened as she moved away quickly, her heart pounding. Declan had always been commanding, always precise in his demands, but lately, his private conversations had taken on a different weight—a weight she couldn't ignore.

In their bedroom, Cora sat on the edge of the chaise lounge, her grandmother's journal open in her lap. She traced the faded ink, the words offering a semblance of comfort even as her mind raced: *Sometimes, the people closest to us carry the heaviest secrets. The question isn't whether we can uncover them—it's whether we're strong enough to face them.*

Her breath hitched as she absorbed the meaning, her fingers trembling slightly as she closed the journal. The idea of secrets—her father's, Declan's—pressed against her chest, leaving her feeling suffocated.

A knock at the door startled her, and she looked up to see Declan leaning against the doorframe, his blue eyes studying her intently. "You've been quiet," he said, his voice soft but probing.

"I have a lot on my mind," she replied, setting the journal aside.

He stepped into the room, closing the door behind him. "I can see that," he said, his tone low as he approached her. "You've barely looked at me since you came home. Is there something you're not telling me?"

Cora hesitated, her fingers curling into the fabric of her dress. "It's just... everything. I just really miss MJ, and now..." She stopped herself, unsure how to finish the sentence.

Declan moved closer, his hands finding her shoulders as he crouched in front of her. "And now what?" he pressed, his gaze searching hers.

"I met with the detective again," she said finally. "Dax Sheridan. He thinks the fire was arson."

Declan's jaw tightened briefly before he masked the reaction, his hands sliding to cup her face. "I'm sorry you're dealing with this," he said, his tone gentle but firm. "An arson case huh? That sounds awful."

His lips brushed against her forehead, the gesture tender but heavy with intent. Cora felt herself leaning into him, her body craving the comfort he offered even as her mind remained restless. He pulled her to her feet, his hands sliding to her waist as he studied her intently.

"Let me take care of you," he murmured, his voice dipping lower as he pressed a kiss to her temple.

His lips found hers, the kiss slow but insistent. His hands moved to the small of her back, pulling her closer as he deepened the kiss, his body pressing against hers with a deliberate intensity.

"Declan..." she whispered, her voice trembling as he guided her toward the bed.

"Let me," he said softly, his lips brushing against her neck as his hands roamed her body. "You've been carrying so much. Let me take some of it away."

Declan's hands slid along the curve of Cora's waist, his touch both deliberate and reverent as he guided her back toward the bed. The tension that had been building between them—fueled by her doubts, her father's revelations, and the lingering unease surrounding the fire— seemed to reach a breaking point. She didn't want to think anymore, didn't want to feel the weight of everything pressing down on her.

"Let me take it all away," Declan murmured, his voice low and rough as his lips found the sensitive spot just below her ear.

Cora gasped softly, her fingers clutching at the front of his shirt as she allowed herself to be swept up in his intensity. He pushed her gently onto the bed, his body following hers as he hovered over her, his hands bracketing her face.

"You're everything, Cora," he whispered, his gaze locking onto hers. "Everything I've ever wanted. Everything I'll ever need."

There was a mix of emotion and need swirling within her as his lips descended on hers. The kiss was slow at first, his mouth moving against hers with deliberate tenderness, but it quickly deepened, becoming more insistent, more consuming. Declan's hands roamed her body, his touch igniting a fire that left her trembling. He tugged at the hem of her dress, sliding it higher as his lips trailed down her neck. His fingers found the bare skin of her thighs, his touch sending shivers racing through her.

"My Cora," he murmured against her collarbone, his voice filled with a possessive edge that both thrilled and unsettled her. "I love every inch of you."

"Declan," she whispered, her voice trembling as her doubts were momentarily drowned out by the heat between them.

His lips found hers again, his kiss more urgent now as his hands continued their exploration. His touch grew more deliberate as Cora's heart raced, her body aching with both need and the faintest hint of hesitation as she surrendered to the moment. The world around them seemed to disappear, the quiet of the estate amplifying the sounds of their mingled breaths, the soft rustle of fabric, and the faint creak of the bed beneath them. Declan's movements were slow but unrelenting, his focus entirely on her as he guided her into a rhythm that left her gasping.

Her hands slid down his back, her nails grazing his skin as her body arched against his. "You undo me, Cora," he murmured, his voice rough with emotion as he pressed his forehead against hers. "You always have."

Her breath caught, her chest rising and falling rapidly as his words sank in. For a moment, the intensity of his gaze made her feel as though he could see right through her, past the doubts and fears that lingered in the corners of her mind.

As the passion between them subsided, Declan pressed a lingering kiss to her temple, his arms wrapping around her as though to shield her from the world. Cora lay still, her heart still racing as she stared at the ceiling, her mind already slipping back to the questions that had been haunting her.

Declan seemed to sense her unease, his hand sliding to her cheek as he tilted her face toward him. "Never leave me," he murmured, his voice soft but firm.

Cora forced a faint smile, her fingers brushing against his jaw. "I'm here," she said softly, though the words felt heavy on her tongue.

The rest of the night passed in quiet stillness, but the tension remained. The intimacy they had shared had momentarily dulled the edge of her doubts, but it hadn't erased them. As Declan drifted off to sleep beside her, his arm draped possessively over her waist, Cora stared into the darkness, her mind spinning with unanswered questions.

She thought of Dax, of the fire, of the unease she had felt since their honeymoon. The threads were starting to come together, but the picture they painted left her feeling more uncertain than ever.

The morning sunlight spilled through the floor-to-ceiling windows of the estate, forming long remnants across the marble floors. Cora woke slowly, the events of the previous night lingering at the edges of her consciousness. Declan's arm was draped over her waist, his breathing deep and even as he slept beside her. She shifted slightly, careful not to wake him, as her thoughts began to spiral once more. The intimacy they had shared had momentarily quieted the questions racing through her mind, but now, in the clarity of daylight, they returned with full force. Dax's revelation echoed in her ears: *"It was arson."* The way Declan had avoided her gaze when she mentioned it, the sharp tone he'd used on the phone just before—these moments clung to her like a shadow she couldn't shake.

Cora slipped out of bed quietly, grabbing one of Declan's oversized shirts from the chair and pulling it on as she padded barefoot across the cool floor. She needed space to think, to process everything without his penetrating gaze making her feel exposed.

In the kitchen, she found her phone buzzing with a message from Selah:

Hey babe, Missing you. Don't forget to breathe, okay? Call me when you can.

Cora smiled faintly, her chest tightening at the reminder that her closest friends were miles away. Selah and Jensen's departure after the wedding had left a void in her life, one that seemed to grow with every passing day. Their support had been a lifeline, but now, with them gone, she felt more isolated than ever.

Her fingers hovered over the call button, but she hesitated. Selah would sense the tension in her voice immediately, and Cora wasn't ready to explain everything—especially not about Dax. Instead, she sent a quick reply:

Miss you too. Will call soon. Promise.

The sound of Declan's footsteps pulled her from her thoughts. He entered the kitchen, his hair still tousled from sleep, the deep blue of his eyes sharp as they met hers. He smiled faintly, crossing the room to pour himself a cup of coffee.

"You were gone when I woke up," he said, his tone casual but tinged with curiosity.

"Just needed some air," Cora replied, lifting her cup to her lips.

Declan leaned against the counter, his gaze steady as he studied her. "Anything you want to talk about?"

She shook her head, forcing a small smile. "No. Just thinking about everything."

His jaw tightened slightly, but he nodded, stepping closer to place a hand on her shoulder. "Have you thought more about rebuilding the bridal shop?" he said softly. "I think a big project is just what you need to take your mind off everything."

Cora nodded but the words didn't resonate. She was lost in her own thoughts and she wasn't sure how much longer she could keep up the pretense.

Later that afternoon, Dax called, his name flashing on her phone screen like a beacon. She hesitated for a moment before answering, her voice steady. "Hi."

"Hi, Cora," Dax said, his tone warm but professional. "I just wanted to check in. Are you okay after yesterday?"

"I'm fine," she said quickly, though her voice trembled slightly.

Dax paused, his voice softening. "You don't have to be fine. I know I dropped a lot on you."

Cora exhaled slowly, her fingers tightening around her phone. "It's just... a lot to process. My whole life, I thought I knew my story, and now...everything's different."

"I understand," Dax sighed gently. "I remember the day you were born. Your mom wasn't sure if the contractions were real or not and she drove herself to the hospital in full labor. You arrived just three hours later. She said that the twenty-minute drive to the hospital was a blur. Talk about timing," he laughed at the memory, picturing Veda's beautiful turquoise eyes.

She hesitated, her chest tightening at the sincerity in his voice. "Thanks," she said softly. "I love hearing about her. I feel like Gram kept a lot of her story hidden from me."

"If she did, it was due to her own broken heart, Cora. Charlotte just wanted to give you a good, stable life and protect you as much as she could," Dax said with a calm and enduring tone.

"I get that. And she did. I had a good life with Gram. She left me all of her journals and they were miraculously saved from the fire. I have been sifting through them over these months. I feel like I am learning about Gram at a different level and yet, it gives me so much solace," Cora said to Dax with a gentle tone.

"Your mom always said Charlotte could have been a writer. I think it's great that you have them. What a blessing to have them still intact," Dax replied.

With that, they ended the conversation and Cora felt peace with the tidbits of knowledge she was slowly gaining about her life.

That evening, as the estate grew quieter, Cora found herself standing in the sitting room, staring at the large print of the flying dress photoshoot that Declan had framed and hung prominently on the wall. The image was stunning, a perfect snapshot of their honeymoon in Santorini.

The image was flawless—her dress billowing against the backdrop of Santorini's cliffs, the vibrant blue of the sky meeting the endless Aegean Sea. Declan proudly displayed it in the most visible part of the estate. It was beautiful, undeniably so, but tonight, it felt like something else. A reminder of how Declan saw her: an extension of his life, his world, his perfection

But now, as she studied it, it felt like something else—a symbol of the life Declan wanted her to have, the life he was building around her. Her hands brushed against the infinity necklace as she tried to quiet her thoughts.

The sound of Declan entering the room pulled her from her reverie. His presence was commanding as always, the sharpness of his gaze softening when it landed on her.

"Admiring my favorite piece?" he asked, his voice low as he stepped closer.

Cora offered a faint smile, her fingers dropping from the pendant. "It's stunning," she said softly. "But it feels... larger than life."

"Because you're larger than life," Declan replied, his tone carrying both affection and conviction. He stood beside her, his hand brushing against hers. "Every time I look at it, I see everything we've built. Everything we are."

Her chest tightened at his words, a mix of emotion and unease swirling within her. She wanted to believe him, to trust that his intentions were as pure as his words, but the weight of Dax's revelations and the doubts they stirred left her feeling unsteady.

The quiet tension between them was broken by the sound of her phone buzzing on the nearby console. She picked it up, her brows furrowing as she read the message from Dax:

We need to meet again. There's more you need to know about the fire—and about Declan.

Her stomach dropped, the words sending a ripple of unease through her.

Declan's gaze shifted to the phone in her hand, his expression curious. "Something important?" he asked, his tone light but probing.

Cora hesitated, her fingers tightening around the phone. "Just Selah," she lied, forcing a small smile. "Checking in from Dallas."

He nodded, his posture relaxing slightly. "Good," he said. "I was worried she'd stay here forever. You need space to focus on us."

The comment, casual as it seemed, sent a chill through her. Declan's words often carried layers of meaning, and tonight, they felt heavier than usual.

The next day, Cora met Dax at a quiet park on the outskirts of town. The air was crisp, the trees swaying gently in the breeze as they sat on a bench overlooking a small pond.

"I didn't want to alarm you last night," Dax began, his tone careful, "but there are some developments in the fire investigation that you need to be aware of."

Cora's chest tightened as she looked at him. "What kind of developments?"

Dax hesitated, his gaze steady but cautious. "We've uncovered evidence that points to arson," he said. "And the pattern of the accelerants used suggests it wasn't random. It was planned."

Her heart pounded as she absorbed his words. "Planned by who?" she asked, her voice barely above a whisper.

"We're narrowing down suspects," Dax replied, his voice steady. "But there are connections to Declan. Some of the accounts linked to his estate match transactions made just days before the fire."

The ground beneath her seemed to shift as the weight of his words sank in. "You think Declan had something to do with it," she said, her voice trembling.

"I think it's worth looking into," Dax said carefully. "And I think you need to be prepared for what that might mean."

She sat in silence, her mind racing as the pieces began to come together. Declan's sudden phone calls, the way he had handled the aftermath of the fire—it all felt connected in ways she couldn't yet articulate.

Dax reached out, his hand resting lightly on hers. "I know this is a lot," he said softly. "You've already been through so much. I'm sorry this is happening, Cora. I wish I could take it all away. I'm very worried about you."

She nodded slowly as she looked at him. "Thank you," she murmured. "For being honest with me."

"You deserve honesty," Dax replied. "And you deserve answers."

As Cora drove back to the estate, her thoughts spiraled. She glanced at the necklace in the rearview mirror, its infinity hearts catching the sunlight. What had once felt like a romantic gesture now felt like something else entirely—something heavier, more binding.

When she arrived home, Declan was waiting in the sitting room, his laptop open as he typed. He looked up when she entered, his expression softening as he stood to greet her.

"Busy day?" he asked, his tone casual.

Cora nodded, her lips curving into a faint smile. "Just went for a drive to clear my head," she replied.

He stepped closer, his hands finding her waist as he studied her intently. "Good," he said softly. "Because I need all of you tonight. No distractions."

Her breath caught at the intensity in his gaze, her doubts momentarily drowned out by the pull of his presence. The sitting room was quiet except for the faint rustle of the breeze slipping through the slightly open window.

Her thoughts drifted to Atlanta, where their whirlwind trip to the American Surgeon Association Conference had left her feeling both exhilarated and out of place. Declan had thrived in that environment, moving through the conference with effortless charm as he networked with surgeons, donors, and influential figures in the medical field.

Cora had observed from the sidelines, dressed impeccably in a deep emerald gown Declan had chosen for her. She had smiled politely during conversations, offering input when prompted, but the world around her had felt distant, foreign. It wasn't just the conference—it was the people. There was a sense of exclusivity that made her feel as though she were always on the outside looking in.

Declan had noticed her discomfort, of course. He always did. "You're doing great," he had whispered during one of the breaks, his hand resting possessively on her back. "Just smile and let me handle the rest."

She had nodded, but her unease had only grown during the after-party at the mansion. The opulence of the place was overwhelming—lavish furniture, glittering chandeliers, and rooms filled with people who seemed to know each other far too well. Conversations drifted around her, light and charming on the surface but tinged with something darker that she couldn't quite place.

And then there had been Evelyn.

Cora had noticed her at the conference, her sharp blue eyes and sleek blonde hair making her stand out even among the polished crowd. She was introduced as a neurologist presenting research on neural regeneration, her voice calm and confident as she spoke of breakthroughs and funding initiatives. She eluded a confidence that seemed hidden at Declan's summer barbeque, where they first met.

Declan had been impressed with her presentation, and Cora had watched as he engaged Evelyn in conversation, his usual charm on full display. Evelyn had matched his energy effortlessly, her demeanor polished and professional but with a flicker of something else—something that left Cora unsettled.

At the mansion, Evelyn's presence had shifted. She was no longer the poised speaker from the conference but something looser, more casual. She had floated through conversations, her laughter bright but calculated. Cora had caught her watching Declan more than once, her gaze sharp and lingering.

Evelyn had approached Cora at one point. "Declan speaks so highly of you, Cora. I don't think I have ever seen him so in love…well, except maybe Mara, but that ended tragically," she said leaving a hint of unrest.

"Oh?" Cora had replied, her voice polite but distant, never having heard of the name Mara before.

"Oh, constantly," Evelyn had said with a faint smile. "Though I imagine he's just as proud of himself. You do have a way of bringing out the best in him."

The words had felt pointed, though Evelyn's tone remained light. Cora had excused herself soon after, the strange energy of the night leaving her feeling more like a spectator in her own life.

Declan entered the sitting room now, pulling her back to the present although her mind was on replay with the conversation she had had with Evelyn. He was dressed casually, his shirt sleeves rolled up as he walked toward her.

"Who is Mara?" she asked, her tone light but tinged with uncertainty.

"Mara," he replied softly, his fingers brushing against her arm. "We were engaged," he said, stepping closer. "It wasn't—beautiful, bold, or unforgettable. Like you."

Cora forced a small smile, though the weight of his words pressed against her. "What happened?" she asked, glancing at him.

"She was a psychiatrist at the hospital," Declan said with a faint chuckle. "Sometimes a patient can't come to terms with the aftermath of a major surgery and Mara would step in to help. What she couldn't do was come to terms with her own conscious. She went into a dire mental state and the board let her go. I don't even know where she is anymore. I couldn't save her, and she couldn't save herself. Who told you about her?"

An undercurrent of uneasiness leaving her unsettled. "Evelyn. It wasn't anything bad, she just said she hasn't seen you in love like you are with me, except for Mara. You just have never spoken about her, is all," she said lightly, though the comment carried an edge she hadn't intended.

"Is this her?" she asked as she glanced across the table and picking up the *American Journal of Psychiatry* where Mara's face graced the cover. Cora froze when she saw her face, the dark bob haircut, those deep black eyes. Dr. Mara Quill. She had undeniably seen this face before, but where?

Declan's smile faltered briefly before he recovered, his hand resting lightly on her waist. "Because she isn't worth discussing, and Evelyn is correct…I am very in love with you, and yes, I thought I threw that out. They did a feature on her right before she lost her mind," he said softly.

She nodded, her fingers brushing against her light sweater. "I see," she said, her voice trembling slightly. But as Declan pulled her into his arms, his presence enveloping her, more questions she couldn't bring herself to ask lingered, heavy and unanswered. His arm wrapped around her waist, pulling her close as they stood in the study. His touch was warm, grounding, yet heavy with the possessiveness that had begun to creep into their interactions more often.

"You've been distant," he said softly, his voice low but edged with concern.

Cora looked up at him, her lips parting slightly as she searched for the right words. "Dax Sheridan, the detective…he told me that he is my father," she admitted.

Declan's jaw tightened slightly, his hand moving to brush a strand of hair from her face. "Oh, Cora, he is? How are you feeling about this?" he asked, his tone careful but probing.

She hesitated, her chest tightening as Dax's words echoed in her mind. *"Declan might be involved."* She pushed the thought away, forcing a small smile as she said, "I was shocked at first. But he has been telling me about my mom, and I like hearing about her."

Declan nodded, his fingers brushing against the infinity pendant around her neck. "Good," he said softly. "Because if it brings a smile across that beautiful face, I will welcome it."

His words felt layered, and while his tone was gentle, there was an undercurrent of something firmer beneath them. She nodded slowly, allowing him to guide her to the sofa as he sat beside her, his hand never leaving hers.

That evening, as Declan stepped into his study to take another phone call, Cora slipped outside to the garden. The air was cool, the faint scent of lavender drifting on the breeze as she walked along the stone path. The estate felt too quiet, its grandeur pressing against her like a weight she couldn't shake.

She thought of Evelyn, her sharp smile and perfectly crafted demeanor. The woman had seemed so poised at the conference, but at the mansion, there had been a shift—something more calculated in the way she moved, the way she spoke. Cora couldn't help but wonder what Evelyn had seen in Declan, what she might have noticed or known that Cora hadn't.

The sound of footsteps behind her made her turn, her heart skipping as Declan appeared in the doorway leading to the garden. He wore his usual calm expression, but his eyes were sharp, scanning her as though trying to read her thoughts.

"Fresh air?" he asked, his voice light but curious.

Cora nodded, forcing a faint smile. "Needed a moment to clear my head."

Declan stepped closer, his hands finding her waist as he studied her. "You've been doing that a lot lately," he remarked, his tone gentle but pointed.

Her pulse quickened as she shook her head. "No, I'm sorry," she said quickly. "I just... I don't know how to feel about everything..."

Declan's gaze softened slightly, his hands moving to cup her once vibrant face. "Come inside and eat something. You are beginning to wither away," he said softly noticing the slenderness in her face, "Let me take care of you."

The intensity of his words left her momentarily speechless, and she allowed him to pull her into his arms. His touch was warm, steady, and for a moment, she felt the tension in her chest ease. But as he pressed a kiss to her forehead, the unease lingering in the back of her mind refused to fade.

As Declan stepped out for a meeting, Cora found herself drawn to the sitting room once again, nestled around wooden bookshelves and lush rugs of elaborate patterns. She quietly began to scale the rebuilding of the bridal shop in her mind, anything to detour her thoughts.

Cora walked over to the magazine with Mara's face on the cover and quietly thumbed through to her article. The article was dated just two months ago. It featured her assessing psychiatric comorbidities in medical patients and addressing the psychological impact of medical diagnoses. Cora quickly googled the hospital directory and saw her name, her contact information. There it was. The phone number matched the one doing the hang-ups, the odd texting, the warnings since she arrived in Pine Brook.

The calls had gone quiet so Cora didn't report any more to the police. And, with the loft gone now, Cora hadn't paid any attention to someone stalking around in her shadows. Her life became completely consumed around Declan. Was Mara trying to warn her? Was she there that night at the bar after Gram's service? Thoughts began swirling in her head, her loose balance causing her to quiver under her knees.

That night, back at the estate, Cora wandered through the halls, her mind spinning with Dax's revelations. Declan was in his study, the soft glow of the desk lamp visible through the partially open door. She paused briefly, watching him as he typed, his posture relaxed but his expression sharp.

The sight of him sent a chill through her, the doubt in her mind growing louder. Was it possible? Could the man she had married, the man who had promised her the world, be capable of something so calculated, so destructive?

She turned away, her hand clutching onto her robe. The weight of it felt unbearable now, a constant reminder of how little she truly understood the man she had chosen to spend her life with.

The weight of Dax's words stayed with Cora, even as the estate grew quiet and the night deepened. Declan was still in his study, the faint glow of his desk lamp visible under the door as she passed by. She hesitated for a moment, her hand hovering over the doorknob, but the sharp memories of his clipped tones during phone calls stopped her.

Her phone buzzed in her pocket, breaking the stillness. She pulled it out and saw a message from Sebastian:

Just checking in. I know I haven't called a lot, but I'm worried about you. Call me when you can. I need to know that you are ok. Miss you, Kitten.

Cora exhaled, guilt and longing twisting in her chest. Sebastian had been her rock during her childhood, the person who could ground her even when everything else felt chaotic. But now, with everything swirling around her—Dax's revelations, the arson case, her own spiraling doubts, she didn't know where to begin to tell him about what she had discovered.

"Miss you too," she typed back, her fingers trembling. *"I'm fine. Will call soon."*

Declan's footsteps echoed in the hall, pulling her from her thoughts. She turned to see him entering the sitting room, his shirt unbuttoned at the collar and his expression unreadable. His eyes shifted briefly to the flying dress print before settling on her.

"You keep coming back here," he remarked, his tone light but probing.

"It's hard not to," she replied, her voice soft. "Greece was stunning."

"It's more than stunning," Declan said, stepping closer. "It's a reminder of who we are, what we've built. Don't you think?"

Her chest tightened at his words, the layers in them making her stomach twist. "It's... a lot," she said carefully. "A lot to take in."

Declan studied her for a moment before reaching out, his fingers brushing against the infinity pendant around her neck. "That's the point," he murmured. "I want you to always feel what we are. Connected. Forever."

Cora swallowed hard, her fingers curling into fists at her sides. "Forever's a big word," she said lightly, trying to ease the tension she felt growing between them.

Declan's lips curved into a faint smile, but it didn't quite reach his eyes. "Not when it's true," he said simply.

Later that night, Cora sat on the edge of their bed, her grandmother's journal open on her lap. The soft glow of the bedside lamp illuminated the pages, the familiar handwriting bringing a faint sense of comfort as she read: *Sometimes, the people we trust most are the ones who hold the deepest secrets. And sometimes, those secrets are the ones that shatter us.*

The words hit far too close to home. How did Gram know exactly what to say? She thought of Declan, of the way his smile sometimes didn't reach his eyes, of the way he brushed aside her questions with charm and carefully chosen words. The doubt in her chest grew louder, heavier until it felt like it might crush her.

The next morning, Dax called again, his voice steady but laced with urgency. "I've been looking into more records," he said. "And there's a pattern emerging. Declan's estate accounts... there's movement that coincides with the fire. We need to talk again, Cora. In person."

Her throat tightened as she nodded, even though he couldn't see her. "Okay," she said softly. "When?"

"Tonight," he replied. "I'll send you the location."

After the call ended, she sat in silence, the pieces of the puzzle swirling in her mind. Declan's phone calls, his insistence on control, the weight of the necklace around her neck—it all felt connected in ways she wasn't ready to face.

But as she stood in front of the mirror, adjusting the infinity pendant against her collarbone, she knew one thing for certain: the answers were coming. And once they did, there would be no going back.

The sun dipped lower in the sky as Cora drove to the address Dax had sent her, the winding roads and dense trees casting long shadows over the pavement. Her hands tightened on the steering wheel as she replayed their last conversation in her mind. *"Declan's estate accounts... there's movement that coincides with the fire."*

The words echoed in her ears, each repetition adding to the growing knot in her stomach. She had tried to tell herself that Declan couldn't be involved, that the man she had shared her life with wouldn't do something so calculated, so cruel. But doubt had a way of creeping in, unrelenting and insidious until it was impossible to ignore

She pulled into the small parking lot of a café on the edge of town, the neon "Open" sign flickering faintly against the gathering dusk. Dax was already there, standing near the entrance with his arms crossed, his sharp green eyes scanning the lot.

When their eyes met, he offered her a faint smile, but his expression was heavy with the weight of what he was about to tell her.

They sat in a quiet corner of the café, the hum of conversation around them blending into white noise as Dax pulled out a folder. He placed it on the table between them, his hands steady as he opened it to reveal a series of documents and photographs.

"These are financial records linked to Declan's estate," he began, his voice calm but firm. "There's a pattern here—large withdrawals made in cash around the time of the fire. And these transactions..." He tapped a finger on one of the pages. "...match payments made to a known arsonist who's currently under investigation."

Cora's breath caught as she stared at the documents, her heart pounding in her chest. "You're saying Declan hired someone to set the fire?"

Dax hesitated, his expression softening as he met her gaze. "I'm saying the evidence points in that direction," he said carefully. "But we need more to confirm it. That's where you come in."

She shook her head, her voice trembling. "I don't know anything about this. Declan never mentioned... He wouldn't—"

"Cora," Dax interrupted gently. "I need you to think. Has Declan done or said anything that seemed... off? Anything that could point to him being involved?"

Her mind flashed back to the end of the engagement party, to Declan stepping away for a phone call. She remembered the clipped tone of his voice, the way his mannerism would have brushed off any questions if she did ask.

"I don't know," she said finally, her voice barely above a whisper. "But... there are things that don't make sense. Can I ask you for a favor?"

"Anything, Cora. What can I do?" Dax asked with a gentle sincerity.

"Can you please look into Dr. Mara Quill? She is a psychiatrist at the hospital. Well, she was. I think...Declan said she had a mental breakdown, and the board fired her. But, I was getting strange text messages when I first moved here and there was someone outside of my loft a few times. I think it may have been her," Cora explained.

Dax took a deep breath and placed his hand on hers, "Cora, we know who Mara Quill is. There was a restraining order on her. She is a very unstable woman and I need to know if you are still getting messages from her."

"I am not," she replied nervously. "I haven't gotten any messages since the grand opening of the bridal shop two months ago…Oh, my gosh, it was her! I saw her when we were out celebrating at dinner that night," Cora remembered. "She had told me Declan wasn't who I thought he was."

"Well, that may just be spot on," he recoiled with determination. "But she is a precarious woman, Cora. Please do let me know if you ever hear from her again. We are investigating her in three other cases."

"So much of this is becoming clear now," Cora uttered softly, gently stirring the ice around in her tea.

"I'm sorry you are going through all of this, Kid. Maybe when this is all over, we can take it from a brand-new start," he asserted, giving her a soft wink.

"I'd like that," Cora replied, taking a moment to let it all sink in.

Dax reached across the table, his hand again resting lightly on hers. "I know all of this is hard," he said softly. "But you deserve the truth. And so does MJ. Cora, your mom was married to an unstable man, and it was an unrelenting abyss of misery for her. Please keep yourself aware. Life doesn't have to be this way for you."

Her chest tightened at the mention of MJ and her mother, guilt and grief twisting together as she thought of her friend's death and her mom's suicide. "I'll think about it," she said, her voice trembling. "I promise."

Dax nodded, his expression filled with quiet determination. "You know where to find me," he said.

As she left the café, the weight of everything pressed heavily against her chest. The drive back to the estate felt longer than usual, the winding roads blurring together as her thoughts spiraled. Declan's face flashed in her mind—his smile, his charm, the way he could make her feel like the only person in the world. But now, those memories were tainted by doubt, by the possibility that the man she had trusted most had been hiding something unforgivable.

When she arrived home, the estate was bathed in the soft glow of the evening lights. She stepped inside, the familiar scent of lavender and polished wood wrapping around her as she set her keys on the console. Declan's voice drifted from the study, low and even as he spoke on the phone.

She paused in the hallway, brushing her hand against the cold, wall as she listened.

"No delays," he said, his tone calm but firm. "I don't want excuses. Just handle it."

Her stomach twisted as she moved away, her heart pounding in her chest. The doubts that had been gnawing at her grew louder, more insistent. She made her way to her room, her hands trembling as she opened the door and sat on the edge of the bed.

Her grandmother's journal sat on the nightstand; the familiar leather cover worn from use. She opened it, her fingers tracing the faded ink as she read: *The hardest truths to face are often the ones we already know deep down. They wait for us, quiet and patient, until we're ready to confront them.*

Tears pricked at her eyes as she closed the journal, her breath hitching. She wasn't ready—not yet. But the truth was waiting for her, and she knew it wouldn't wait forever.

The house was silent as Cora sat on the edge of her bed, the journal clutched tightly in her hands. The words her grandmother had written felt like they were written for this exact moment, a reminder that she couldn't keep avoiding the truth. Declan's voice still echoed in her mind—sharp, commanding, and so deeply intertwined with the doubts she had tried to bury.

She stood, her bare feet brushing against the cool wooden floor as she moved to the window. Her mind drifted off to Sebastian and his gentle, familiar nature. She reached for her phone and stopped to graze over his name.

Declan's study light was still on, the faint outline of his figure visible through the partially drawn curtains. He was still on the phone, his gestures sharp and precise, as though he were orchestrating something that required his full attention.

Cora turned away from the window, her hands trembling as she picked up her phone. Selah's messages lingered on the screen, each one more worried than the last. Cora knew she should call her, knew Selah would be able to anchor her in the chaos, but something held her back. How could she explain everything? The arson investigation, Dax, Mara—it was too much, too tangled.

Instead, she typed out a quick reply:

I'm fine. Just need to figure things out. Will call soon, promise.

The words felt hollow, but it was all she could manage.

The next morning, Declan was waiting for her in the kitchen, a cup of coffee and egg white already prepared and waiting on the counter. He smiled as she entered, his gaze sweeping over her.

"You were up late," he said, his tone casual.

"So were you," Cora replied softly, her fingers brushing against the edge of the counter as she avoided his eyes.

Declan tilted his head, his smile faint but watchful. "Reports," he said simply. "They never end."

She nodded, taking a sip of her coffee. The silence between them stretched, the tension palpable even as they tried to mask it with small talk.

"Are you doing okay?" Declan asked after a moment, his voice gentle but probing.

Cora hesitated, her mind flashing to Dax's warnings, to the unanswered questions that had been piling up. "I'm fine," she said finally, though her voice trembled slightly.

Declan's gaze lingered on her, his expression softening as he reached out to touch her hand. "You know you can talk to me, right?"

Her chest tightened as she forced a small smile. "I know," she said.

The estate's quiet felt oppressive as Cora moved toward Declan's study. This time, she wasn't willing to retreat. Her hand hovered over the doorknob, and with a deep breath, she pushed the door open just enough to catch his attention. Declan looked up from his laptop, his sharp blue eyes narrowing slightly before softening.

"I need to talk," she replied, stepping fully into the room. Her hands tightened into fists at her sides as she steadied herself. "About everything—about the fire, MJ, and... and the way things have felt lately."

Declan's expression remained calm, though the faintest flicker of something—frustration?—crossed his face. He gestured to the chair opposite his desk. "Then let's talk," he said smoothly, closing the laptop and folding his hands in front of him.

Cora sat down, her heartbeat hammering in her chest. "Dax called me again," she began. "He's been digging deeper into the fire, and he's found... things." Her voice trembled as she searched his face for a reaction.

Declan leaned back slightly, his jaw tightening. "And what exactly did he find?" he asked, his voice even.

"He said it wasn't an accident," she said softly. "That it was arson. And that there's... evidence pointing to you."

The words hung in the air between them, heavy and sharp. Declan's eyes narrowed, his lips pressing into a thin line before he exhaled slowly. "Cora, do you honestly believe I would do something like that? That I would endanger you—or anyone else?"

She paused at the question, the sincerity in his voice making her doubt herself even as the evidence stacked up in her mind. "I don't know what to believe," she admitted. "But there are too many things that don't make sense."

Declan stood abruptly, pacing to the window. His hands clenched into fists before he turned back to her, his expression a mixture of frustration and hurt. "Do you realize what you're saying?" he demanded, his voice rising slightly. "You're questioning my integrity, my love for you, based on the words of a man who's a stranger to you."

"I'm questioning what I don't understand," Cora shot back, her voice trembling but firm. "I'm questioning why there are so many gaps—why you can't just tell me the truth."

Declan approached her slowly, his hands resting on the arms of her chair as he leaned down, his face inches from hers. "The truth," he said softly, his voice low and dangerous, "is that I have done everything for us. Everything to protect you, to build a life for us that you deserve. And you're letting someone plant doubts in your mind because they don't know what they're talking about."

Cora's breath hitched, her heart racing as she met his gaze. "Then prove it," she whispered. "Prove to me that you didn't do this."

For a moment, Declan didn't move. Then he straightened, running a hand through his hair. "I shouldn't have to prove anything to you, Cora," he said quietly, his voice carrying a note of finality. "You're my wife. You should trust me."

Her stomach twisted at his words, the weight in her chest pressing against her like a chain. "I want to trust you," she said softly. "But I can't ignore what I'm feeling."

Declan's gaze darkened, but he said nothing. Instead, he walked past her, pausing at the door. "Get some sleep," he said, his tone clipped. "You're exhausted. You barely know this man. We'll talk more tomorrow."

And then he was gone, leaving Cora alone in the study with her thoughts swirling and the truth feeling further away than ever.

The next morning, Cora woke early, her sleep fitful and plagued by dreams of fire and shadows she couldn't name. She stepped onto the balcony, the cool morning air brushing against her skin as she stared out over the gardens. Her phone buzzed in her hand, Dax's name flashing on the screen.

"Hi," she said softly, her voice still heavy with sleep.

"Cora," Dax began, his tone serious. "There's something new. It's about the transactions."

Her stomach dropped. "What is it?" she asked, her voice trembling.

"I traced one of the payments to a burner phone that was activated a week before the fire," he explained. "The phone was deactivated immediately after, but the signal matches a tower near your estate."

Her breath hitched. "What are you saying?"

"I'm saying the person behind the fire was close," Dax said carefully. "Very close."

Cora stood frozen on the balcony, Dax's words ringing in her ears. Her fingers tightened around the phone, her pulse racing as she tried to process what he was saying.

"What do you mean, close?" she asked finally, her voice trembling.

"The signal from the burner phone matches a cell tower near your estate," Dax replied. "And the timeline suggests whoever orchestrated this was keeping a close eye on you."

Cora's stomach churned, the implications of his words leaving her breathless. "You think Declan...?"

"I don't want to jump to conclusions," Dax said carefully. "But I need you to think. Has he said or done anything that seems... off? Anything that could suggest he's hiding something?"

Her mind flashed to the night before, to Declan's sharp words, his defensiveness, the way he avoided giving her direct answers. And then there were the phone calls, his insistence on control, and unanswered questions he diverted into a detour.

"There are things," she admitted, her voice barely above a whisper. "Things that don't add up."

"Cora," Dax said, his tone softening. "I know this is a lot to take in. But if there's anything—anything at all—you notice, you need to tell me. This isn't just about the fire. It's about MJ, about the life you're building. You deserve to know the truth and I want you to be safe. I am going to have Officer Tate patrolling just outside of the estate if you need security of any kind. His name is Sebastian. Declan won't even know he is there."

Tears pricked at her eyes as she nodded, even though he couldn't see her. "Ok," she said softly.

"Stay safe," Dax said. "And remember, I am just a phone call away. I am sending you Officer Tate's direct cell phone number should you need it."

As the call ended, Cora sank into the balcony chair, her hands trembling as she stared out at the sprawling estate. Sebastian. Why couldn't she tell her father that she knew who Officer Tate was all too well? The comfort of having Sebastian there brought a moment of peace to her as she thought about the life she had built with Declan—the life that had seemed so perfect was starting to feel like a house of cards. And she didn't know how much longer it could stand.

Declan found her on the front stoop later that morning, her gaze fixed on the floral gardens as she replayed the marriage proposal in her head.

"You seem rather subdued this morning," he remarked, his voice breaking the silence.

Cora turned to face him, her heart pounding. "Just thinking," she said, forcing a small smile.

Declan studied her for a moment, his gaze sharp as he approached. "You've been doing a lot of that lately," he said softly, his hand brushing against her arm. "I miss my Cora."

Her breath hitched, the weight of his admission pressing against her chest. "I'm sorry," she said quickly. "I wish I could fix all the anguish in my head."

"Your father," Declan said, his tone neutral but his expression darkening slightly. "He's been keeping you busy."

Cora hesitated, her fingers brushing against the infinity pendant around her neck. "He's trying to help," she said softly.

Declan stepped closer, his hand resting lightly on her waist. "I hope he's not making things harder for you," he said, his voice low. "You've already been through enough."

His touch was warm, steady, but it carried an edge of possessiveness that left her feeling uneasy. She forced another small smile, nodding as she stepped out of his grasp. "I'm fine," she said. "I just need some time to process everything."

Declan watched her carefully, his expression unreadable. "Take all the time you need," he said finally. "But remember, Cora—We're a team. Don't forget that. For better or for worse."

She nodded, her heart pounding as she made her way to her room. The necklace felt heavier with each step, the infinity hearts resting against her skin like a silent reminder of Declan's hold on her.

That evening, as the estate grew quiet, Cora sat at her desk with her grandmother's journal open in front of her. The words blurred on the page as her thoughts spiraled, Dax's revelations and Declan's evasiveness intertwining in a web she couldn't untangle.

Her fingers traced the faded ink as she read: *The truth often hides in the spaces we're afraid to look. But when it reveals itself, it demands to be faced.*

Her chest tightened as the weight of her doubts pressed down on her. The truth was coming, whether she was ready for it or not.

Cora sat by the window in the sitting room, her knees pulled to her chest as she stared out at the sprawling gardens. The estate was as beautiful as ever, but its grandeur felt hollow without the presence of Selah and Jensen. Their departure for Dallas had left an ache she hadn't anticipated, a sense of isolation that seemed to grow heavier each day. Selah's messages lingered on her phone, unanswered except for a few brief replies. Each one carried the warmth and concern of a friend who knew something wasn't right.

Babe, I'm worried. Please talk to me when you can.

I know you need space, but you're not alone. I'm always here.

Cora sighed, her fingers brushing against the infinity pendant at her neck. She wanted to call, wanted to pour everything out to Selah—the doubts about Declan, the fire, the weight of the secrets swirling around her. But the words felt too big, too tangled to say aloud.

Instead, she typed a quick response:

Miss you. Just trying to get through things. Will call soon.

The moment she sent it, a pang of guilt twisted in her chest. Selah had always been her anchor, the one who could steady her when the world spun too fast. But now, with so much unsaid between them, even Selah's unwavering support felt like a reminder of how far Cora had drifted from the life she thought she was building.

Declan's voice pulled her from her thoughts. He stood in the doorway, his posture relaxed but his eyes sharp as they swept over her.

"My Cora, you did not come down for supper," he began, stepping into the room.

Cora straightened, forcing a small smile. "Hello, I'm just not hungry," she said softly.

"You have to eat," he said, his tone casual but pressing as he crossed the room to sit beside her.

She hesitated, her mind flashing to Dax's revelations and the growing doubts she couldn't shake. "I know," she admitted finally.

Declan's jaw tightened briefly, but his expression remained calm. "Maybe you should see someone. There is a nutritionist at the hospital I could introduce you to. I could hire one to cook for you here at the estate. How can I help?" he asked, his hand moving to rest lightly on her knee.

Her chest tightened at his words, the sincerity in his voice clashing with the unease swirling in her mind. "I will eat," she said softly. "I'll work on it, I promise."

Declan tilted her chin up, his gaze locking onto hers. "Good," he said softly. "Because I need you, Cora. Whatever happens, whatever you're feeling, I need you here with me."

The intensity in his eyes left her momentarily speechless. "I'll try," she whispered, the words feeling like both a promise and a lie.

That evening, as Declan worked in his study, Cora slipped outside to the garden. The cool night air wrapped around her as she wandered the paths, her thoughts a chaotic swirl. The doubts she had tried to bury rose to the surface again—Dax's warnings, Declan's sharp tone, the gaps in the stories she couldn't reconcile.

She paused near the fountain, her fingers brushing against her nightgown as she stared at her reflection in the rippling water. The woman staring back at her looked the same, but inside, she felt like someone else entirely. Someone who didn't know where the truth ended and the lies began.

Her phone buzzed in her pocket, and she pulled it out to see a new message from Sebastian:

I spoke to Dax. I am right outside. I can't believe this is happening, Cora. I won't let him hurt you.

Her stomach twisted as she read the words, the weight of them settled heavily in her chest. She glanced back toward the estate, the soft glow of the lights casting long shadows over the garden. Declan's figure was visible through the study window; his head bent over his laptop, his movements precise and deliberate.

Cora exhaled shakily, her fingers trembling as she typed back:

Sebastian, I'm scared.

The reply from Sebastian came quickly:

Tonight. 8 p.m. Take a walk down the path. I'll be there. I need to see you.

Cora's fingers tightened around her phone as she read the message, her heart pounding in her chest. The tension that had been building for weeks now felt like it was about to reach its peak. She glanced toward the estate, the glow from Declan's study casting a faint light through the hallway. She had to go. She needed answers, even if she wasn't ready for what they might reveal.

The flying dress print loomed over her, its vibrant colors and perfect composition feeling more like a symbol of the life Declan had curated for her than a memory of their honeymoon. She stood before it, her fingers brushing against the edge of the frame as she whispered to herself, *"Who are you, Declan?"*

His voice broke the silence, pulling her from her thoughts. "Who am I?" he repeated, his tone light but edged with something darker.

Cora turned to see him standing in the doorway, his arms crossing as he watched her. "I didn't hear you come in," she said softly, her pulse quickening.

Declan stepped into the room, his gaze sweeping over her before landing on the print. "You've been spending a lot of time here," he remarked, his voice calm but probing. "Is there something about it that's bothering you?"

"It's beautiful," Cora replied carefully, her voice steady despite the tension in her chest. "But it feels... overwhelming sometimes."

Declan tilted his head, his lips curving into a faint smile. "It's supposed to," he said simply. "It's a reminder of what we are. What we've built."

Her chest tightened at his words, the weight of the necklace pressing against her collarbone. "What if I need more than reminders?" she asked, her voice trembling.

Declan's smile faltered, his gaze sharpening as he stepped closer. "What are you saying?"

"I don't know," she admitted, her voice barely above a whisper. "I just... I don't feel like myself anymore."

Declan's jaw tightened, but he nodded slowly. "Then let me remind you," he said softly, his hands moving to rest lightly on her shoulders as he kissed her lips. "I love you, Cora. That's all that matters."

Her body tense beneath his touch. "Is it?" she whispered, her voice breaking.

He tilted her chin up, his gaze locking onto hers. "Yes," he said firmly. "Because nothing else makes sense without that." The finality in his tone left her breathless, the doubts swirling in her mind louder than ever.

"I'm going for a walk. I'll have my phone with me," she told Declan as she grabbed her jacket and shoes.

"Don't be gone too long, My Cora," he replied with a sheer lack of concentration, focused on his phone buzzing in his hand.

Cora closed the door behind her and walked along the winding path to Sebastian's patrol car. He stepped out of the car and walked in her direction with a fierce intention.

"Cora, come here," he said as she melted into his arms crying.

"How did I get here. Seb? How is this my life? I don't even know what to think," she cried.

"I know, Kitten. It is a mess, and we are going to get you out of this," he promised as he placed his coat down for her to sit.

They sat in silence on the curb of the street. No words needed to be said. The wholesomeness of their connection was undeniable, a comfort only they could share. He put his arm around her as she wept, wishing he could take her away from it all. Sebastian's presence was steady, grounding. Cora felt the weight of her grief pressing against her chest, but for the first time in a long time, it didn't feel like it would consume her. He didn't offer hollow reassurances or promises he couldn't keep— he simply stayed. And in that quiet moment, his arm around her, the world felt a little less heavy.

The sound of a car pulling up broke the stillness, its headlights cutting through the soft glow of the streetlights. Cora glanced up, her tears glistening in the dim light as the familiar figure of Declan stepped out of the vehicle. His sharp features were unreadable as his gaze swept over the scene, his presence a stark contrast to Sebastian's quiet comfort.

"We should go," Declan said, his tone even but carrying an edge that made Cora's chest tighten.

Sebastian's arm fell away, though his gaze remained on Cora. "You okay?" he asked softly.

She nodded, her voice trembling as she whispered, "I'll…I'll be fine."

Sebastian's presence was steady, grounding. Cora felt the weight pressing against her chest, but for the first time in a long time, it didn't feel like it would consume her. He didn't offer hollow reassurances or promises he couldn't keep—he simply stayed. And in that quiet moment, his arm around her, the world felt a little less heavy.

She glanced over her shoulder, pleading, as she began to walk in Declan's direction.

A Web of Control

"Control is a web that tightens with each struggle to break free."

The next day, Cora found herself sitting across from Declan's parents in one of the most elegant restaurants she had ever seen. The contrast between the warmth of the previous night and the polished opulence of her current surroundings wasn't lost on her.

The restaurant was buzzing with muted conversation, the quiet hum of wealth and privilege weaving through the dimly lit space. Cora sat beside Declan at the long, polished table, Nadine and Oliver across from them. Nadine's warmth filled the space between them, her soft smile and genuine curiosity drawing Cora out of her thoughts.

Cora admired Declan's mother, a poised and elegant woman with a calm nature. There was something reassuring about the way Nadine carried herself, her gestures graceful, yet sincere. But as Cora studied her, a familiar ache crept into her chest—the ache of wondering about the mother she had lost.

Would her own mother have been as successful, as serene? Would they have shared a bond built on trust and love? Or would they have been strangers, separated by time and circumstance? The questions, though unspoken, lingered in her mind, adding another layer to the distance she felt from the world around her. Would she know what to say to help Cora through this unmitigated time in her life?

"You did so well with the shop," Nadine said, her voice kind as she reached for her glass. "I've seen the photos Declan shared. It was beautiful. I should have stopped in to see it for myself. I meant to. You should be proud. Will you rebuild?"

"Thank you," Cora replied softly, her cheeks flushing at the praise. "I am thinking about it. I worked so hard to keep my grandmother's dream alive. It was hard to watch it go," Cora replied.

Oliver, however, remained distant, his sharp gaze moving between them as though assessing Cora's worth in silence. His lips twitched briefly into something resembling a smile before he returned his focus to the menu. Declan's hand rested lightly on Cora's knee beneath the table, a subtle but constant reminder of his presence. She could feel his eyes on her even as he engaged in effortless conversation with his parents, his charm on full display.

But the tension in Cora's chest refused to ease, the weight of everything—Dax's warnings, the fire, the growing distance between her and Declan—pressing against her with every passing moment.

Midway through the meal, Cora excused herself, slipping away to the restroom in an attempt to collect her thoughts. The cool marble and soft lighting offered a brief reprieve from the overwhelming energy at the table, and she leaned against the counter, exhaling slowly.

The door opened behind her, and Cora glanced up to see a woman entering. Her breath caught as recognition hit her like a wave.

Mara.

Her sharp features were framed by her sleek black bob, her lips curving into a faint smile as she stepped closer. "Cora," she said, her voice smooth but carrying an edge that sent a chill down Cora's spine.

Cora straightened, her heart pounding as she turned to face her. "Do I know you?" she asked cautiously.

Mara's smile widened, but it didn't reach her eyes. "You've seen me before," she replied cryptically. "You just didn't know who I was."

Mara's eyes swept over Cora, her expression both amused and calculating. "Declan has good taste," she said lightly, though her tone carried something darker. "But you don't really know him, do you?"

Cora's stomach twisted, her fingers gripping the edge of the counter. "I think I know him well enough," she replied, her voice steady despite the unease creeping over her.

Mara let out a soft laugh, shaking her head. "You think you do," she said, stepping closer. "But Declan... he's not what he seems. He's dangerous, Cora. Little, innocent girl from Delaware... you should be careful."

Cora's breath hitched, her chest tightening as she stared at Mara. "What are you talking about?"

Mara tilted her head, her smile fading as her gaze sharpened. "Just think about it," she said softly. "Have you ever wondered why things don't add up? Why life with him is so eerie? Why he's so good at hiding things... leaving?"

Before Cora could respond, Mara turned and walked out, leaving her standing there, her mind spinning.

When Cora returned to the table, Declan's gaze immediately locked onto hers, his expression shifting as he took in the tension on her face. "Everything okay?" he asked, his tone casual but probing.

She forced a small smile, nodding as she slipped back into her seat. "Fine," she said softly.

But the rest of the dinner passed in a blur, Mara's words echoing in her mind like a warning she couldn't shake.

Back at the estate, the silence between them was heavy as Declan led her inside. The soft glow of the chandeliers cast long shadows across the ivory flooring, the quiet of the house amplifying the tension that had lingered since the restaurant.

Declan turned to her as they reached the sitting room, his gaze sharp as he stepped closer. "What happened tonight?" he asked, his voice low. "You've been distant since you came back to the table."

Cora hesitated, her chest tightening as she searched for the right words. "I... I ran into someone," she said finally. "A woman. Well, Mara. She said some strange things."

Declan's jaw tightened, his hands moving to rest lightly on her arms. "Mara? What kind of things?"

"She said you weren't what you seemed," Cora replied softly, her voice trembling. "That you were dangerous."

A flicker of something crossed Declan's face—aggravation, perhaps—but it was gone in an instant. He pulled her closer, his hands sliding to her waist as he gazed into her eyes. "Cora," he said softly, his voice steady but firm. "You can't listen to people like that. They don't know us. Besides, she is deranged."

As his words sank in, her doubts began swirling even as his touch steadied her. "I just... I don't know what to think," she admitted, her voice breaking.

Declan tilted her chin up, his lips brushing against hers. "Then don't think," he murmured. "Just trust me."

His kiss deepened, his hands tightening on her waist as he guided her toward the sofa. The intensity of his touch left her breathless, his need to pull her closer undeniable.

"Declan," she whispered, her voice trembling as his lips trailed down her neck.

"I love you, My Cora," he said softly, his voice rough with emotion. "And I'll spend the rest of my life proving it to you."

Declan's hands gripped her waist firmly, his touch grounding but insistent as he guided her backward onto the plush sofa. His lips moved against hers with deliberate intensity, deepening the kiss as though trying to erase the tension that had clung to them all evening. His fingers slid up her sides, brushing against the soft fabric of her dress. His touch was deliberate, claiming, a stark contrast to the vulnerability she had felt moments ago. He pulled back slightly, his forehead pressing against hers as his hands tightened on her hips.

"Do you know what you do to me?" he murmured, his voice rough and low.

Her chest rose and fell rapidly, her hands clutching at his shirt as she struggled to find her voice. "Declan..."

"You make me crazy," he said, his lips trailing down her neck, his teeth grazing her skin in a way that made her gasp. "Every look, every word, every second you're near me—it's not enough. It's never enough."

His hands moved lower, finding the hem of her dress and tugging it upward with deliberate slowness. The fabric whispered against her skin, as his lips claimed hers again, more urgent this time. The weight of his body pressed her into the sofa, his movements fluid yet unrelenting.

"I love you, Declan," she whispered, her voice trembling but certain.

Her words seemed to ignite something in him. His hands roamed her body, sliding over the curve of her hips and gripping her thighs with a fervor that left no part of her untouched. The strap of her dress slipped from her shoulder, and his lips followed, trailing heat along her skin.

The quiet of the estate amplified every sound—the rustle of fabric, the sharp intake of breath, the soft creak of the sofa beneath them. Declan's movements grew more urgent, his need to pull her closer, to erase every doubt, evident in every touch, every whispered word.

"You feel it, don't you?" he murmured, his lips brushing against her ear as his hands slid higher. "The way we're connected. The way we fit."

Her head fell back against the sofa, her breath catching as his touch sent waves of heat coursing through her. "I feel it," she whispered, her voice trembling as her hands slid down his back, her nails grazing his skin.

The tension that had simmered between them all evening boiled over, their movements growing frantic as they lost themselves in each other. Declan's hands framed her face, his thumbs brushing against her cheeks as his lips found hers again, his kiss both tender and demanding.

The world outside the estate faded completely, leaving only the heat of their connection and the raw intensity of the moment. Declan's body moved against hers with a precision that felt both practiced and desperate, his focus entirely on her. Her soft moans mingled with the sound of their breathing, the rhythm between them unrelenting as he claimed her fully.

When the intensity subsided, Declan buried his face in her neck, his breath ragged as he held her tightly. Cora's fingers traced lazy patterns along his back, her own breathing uneven as she stared at the ceiling.

For a moment, the quiet felt like a truce, a fragile balance between the passion they shared and the doubts that lingered in her mind. But as Declan lifted his head, his gaze locking onto hers, the possessiveness in his eyes was unmistakable.

"You're mine," he whispered again, his voice steady but edged with something darker. "Never forget that."

The silence that followed their intimacy felt heavy, the air between them thick with unspoken words. Declan's fingers traced lazy circles against her bare shoulder, his gaze fixed on her face as though studying every detail. Cora stared at the ceiling, her chest rising and falling as she tried to catch her breath.

For a moment, she allowed herself to sink into the quiet, to let the warmth of his body and the steadiness of his touch anchor her. But the doubts that had been swirling in her mind all evening refused to fade. Mara's words lingered like a shadow: *He's not who you think he is.*

Declan shifted slightly, propping himself up on one elbow as he looked down at her. "You're quiet again," he murmured, his voice low and steady. "What's going on in that head of yours?"

"I was thinking about dinner," she said softly. "Your father seems so intense."

Declan's jaw tightened briefly before he leaned in, his lips brushing against her temple. "He is. He never really has much to say about anything. He is always fixated on his business," he said quietly. "His time, his thoughts are absorbed around his work, Cora. He was never around. He was never much of a father to me; I was more of a nuisance to him than anything. Nadine and Oliver were the front to our family, while the real worth was hiding behind nannies and caretakers."

Cora sighed softly, thinking about how different their two worlds really were.

She turned her head to meet his gaze, her chest tightening at the intensity in his eyes. "Why would Mara say those things, Declan? Why would she warn me about you?"

His lips pressed into a thin line, his hand moving to cup her face as he spoke. "Because she's jealous," he said, his voice calm but edged with frustration. "She can't stand to see me happy. To see me with you. She wanted a baby. I did not. She became obsessed about it. We both wanted different things and she could not come to terms with it."

Cora hesitated, her mind flashing to Mara's cryptic warnings, the way her voice had trembled as she spoke. "But she seemed so sure," she whispered, her voice trembling. "Like she knew something I didn't."

Declan exhaled sharply, his hand sliding to her neck as his thumb brushed against her jaw. "Cora, you know me. You've seen me at my best and my worst. Do you really think I'd ever hurt you? Do you think I'd ever let anything come between us?"

Her breath slowed at his words, the sincerity in his voice cutting through the doubts that had been gnawing at her. "I don't know," she admitted finally, her voice breaking. "I don't know what to think anymore."

Declan leaned down, his forehead pressing against hers as his hand moved to rest over her heart. "Then let me make it simple," he murmured. "This life is ours, Cora. Always. And I'll do whatever it takes to protect what we have."

His words sent a shiver through her, the weight of his possessiveness both grounding and unsettling. She nodded faintly, her hands resting on his shoulders as she whispered, "Okay."

But even as she said the words, the unease in her chest refused to fade.

The next morning, Declan was up early, his side of the bed already cool by the time Cora stirred. She found him in the kitchen, dressed sharply in a deep gray suit, his phone pressed to his ear as he poured himself a cup of coffee.

When he noticed her, he ended the call quickly, setting his phone down on the counter as he smiled at her. "Morning," he said, his tone light but watchful.

"Morning," Cora replied softly, her fingers brushing against the edge of the counter as she poured herself a cup of tea.

Declan leaned against the counter, his gaze fixed on her. "What's your plan for today?" he asked, his voice casual but probing.

She hesitated, her mind flashing to Dax's message from the night before. "I'm not sure," she said finally. "Probably just some research for the shop."

He nodded, his expression unreadable. "Good," he said simply. "You need something to focus on. Something to keep you grounded."

Her chest tightened at his words, the layers in them making her stomach twist. "What about you?" she asked, her voice careful.

"Surgeries," he replied, his tone clipped. "I'll be out most of the day."

As Declan left the estate, Cora felt a strange mixture of relief and apprehension. The house felt larger, emptier in his absence, but the silence gave her room to think. She wandered through the halls, her fingers brushing against the polished banister as she made her way to the sitting room.

The flying dress print loomed over her once again, its vibrant colors and dramatic composition a stark contrast to the weight pressing against her chest. She stared at it for a long moment, her fingers curling into fists at her sides.

"It's all so perfect," she whispered to herself. "Too perfect."

Her phone buzzed in her pocket, pulling her from her thoughts. She glanced at the screen and saw another message from Dax:

Can we talk? I think we're closer to answers.

Cora's breath hitched as she read the words, the tension in her chest growing tighter. She typed back quickly:

I'm free now.

Cora arrived at the café a little after noon, her nerves already on edge as she scanned the room for Dax. He sat at the same corner table, his expression as serious as ever, the folder on the table in front of him looking fuller than before. He stood when he saw her, pulling out a chair for her as she approached.

"Thanks for coming," he said, his voice steady but tinged with urgency.

"Of course," she replied softly, sliding into the chair. "I saw Mara. I recognized her from a magazine at the estate. She was at the restaurant last night. She followed me to the restroom and stopped me. She said that Declan was dangerous."

Dax sat down across from her, his hands resting on the folder as he exhaled deeply. "That much is true. He is. And she is as well. Did she try to hurt you?" he asked.

"No, but she definitely creeped me out," Cora said as she adjusted herself in the seat.

"We've uncovered something significant," he began. "It's not just financial transactions anymore. There's a witness—someone who saw a man near the loft the night of the fire."

Cora's stomach tightened, her heart pounding as she leaned forward. "A witness?" she asked, her voice barely above a whisper.

Dax nodded, opening the folder and sliding a document toward her. "A neighbor across the street reported seeing a man parked near the loft around midnight. He stayed in the car for a while, then walked toward the building with a small bag. The description matches someone linked to the transactions we've been tracing."

Cora stared at the document, her hands trembling as she tried to process what he was saying. "Linked to the transactions..." she repeated softly. "But... Declan wasn't there that night."

"No," Dax agreed, his voice careful. "But the man described has ties to someone close to him. Someone who works for his ground's entity."

Her breath hitched as the pieces began to fall into place. "An employee at the estate? You think Declan hired him," she said, her voice trembling.

"It's looking more and more likely," Dax replied. "And if that's true, this wasn't just about the loft. It was about control. About sending a message."

The weight of his words pressed against her chest, making it hard to breathe. "A message to who?" she asked, her voice breaking.

"To anyone who might stand in his way," Dax said, his tone heavy. "Including you."

The silence between them was deafening, the hum of the café fading into the background as Cora's thoughts spiraled. She thought of MJ, of the fire, of the way Declan had dismissed her questions every time she tried to bring it up. And then there was the necklace, the constant reminder of his hold on her, his need to tether her to him.

"I can't believe this is happening," she admitted finally, her voice trembling. "If this is true... if Declan was behind it..."

"Then you need to think about your future," Dax said firmly. "Cora, I know this is hard. I know you love him. But you need to start thinking about what's best for you."

Her chest tightened at his words, tears pricking at the corners of her eyes. "How do I even begin?" she whispered.

"One step at a time," Dax replied gently. "And you don't have to do it alone. I'll be here every step of the way."

The drive back to the estate felt longer than usual, the weight of Dax's revelations pressing heavily against her chest. She pulled into the driveway, her fingers gripping the steering wheel as she stared at the sprawling house in front of her. The estate, once a symbol of beauty and stability, now felt like a cage—a gilded trap that she couldn't escape.

Declan arrived home later that evening, his presence filling the estate with a weight she hadn't noticed before. He found her in the kitchen, staring out the window as she absentmindedly stirred a cup of tea.

"I brought take-out from your favorite Chinese place downtown," he said, cutting through the quiet like a lightning bolt.

"Aw, thank you. I loved eating there with MJ," she replied softly, not turning to face him.

Declan moved closer, his hand resting lightly on her shoulder. "Ready to eat?" he asked, his voice dropping slightly.

Cora hesitated, her chest tightening as she searched for the right words. "I don't think I can eat right now," she said finally, staring out the glass doors leading to the terrace.

"You're spiraling, Cora," he said softly, his voice steady but edged with something firmer. "And it's because of the people you're listening to. People who don't know us. Who don't understand what we have."

Cora's breath caught, her chest tightening at the weight of his words. "Declan, it's not just... them," she said carefully. "It's everything. The fire, the questions, the way things don't seem to add up..."

His jaw tightened, his hand moving to her chin as he tilted her face upward to meet his eyes. "Stop," he said firmly, his voice low but commanding. "You're letting other people plant doubts where there shouldn't be any. I've given you everything, Cora. I've built a life for us. And you're going to throw it away because of what? Paranoia?"

Her stomach twisted at his words, the sharpness in his tone cutting through her like a blade. "I'm not throwing anything away," she whispered. "I'm just trying to understand."

Declan stepped back, running a hand through his hair as he exhaled sharply. "There's nothing to understand," he said, his voice rising slightly. "Everything I've done has been for you. For us. And the fact that you can't see that..." He trailed off, shaking his head.

Cora felt the tears welling in her eyes, but she blinked them away, her hands trembling at her sides. "I want to believe you," she said softly. "But things keep happening—things I can't ignore. And I don't know how to move past them."

Declan turned sharply, his eyes flashing as he moved closer. "Then let me help you," he said, his voice dropping. "Let me remind you of what we are. What we have."

His hands found her arms, pulling her closer as his lips brushed against hers. The kiss was slow at first, almost reverent, but it deepened quickly, the intensity of his touch leaving her breathless.

"Declan..." she murmured, her voice trembling as his hands slid to her waist, pulling her flush against him.

"You're mine," he whispered against her lips, his voice rough. "No one else gets to come between us. No one."

His hands moved higher, his touch igniting a fire that left her trembling. For a moment, she allowed herself to be swept up in the heat of his kiss, the strength of his presence drowning out the doubts that had been gnawing at her. But as he pressed her back against the counter, her mind flashed to Dax's warnings, to the fire, to the unanswered questions that hung over them like a storm.

"Wait," she said softly, her hands pressing against his chest.

Declan froze, his breathing heavy as he looked down at her. "What's wrong?" he asked, his voice low.

Cora hesitated, her chest tightening as she searched for the right words. "I just... I don't know," she said finally, her voice trembling.

Declan studied her for a long moment, his expression unreadable. "Fine," he said finally, his voice quiet but firm. "But don't forget what we have, Cora. Don't let other people take that away from us."

That night, Cora sat alone in their room, the infinity necklace still resting heavily against her collarbone. Her grandmother's journal lay open on her lap, the faded ink a steady presence as she read: *Sometimes, the people we think we know best are the ones who hide the deepest secrets. And sometimes, those secrets are the ones that shatter us.*

Her hands trembled as she closed the journal. The truth was looming closer, its shadow stretching over every corner of her life. And no matter how much she wanted to run from it, she knew she couldn't avoid it forever.

Declan's study light was still on as Cora stepped onto the balcony, the cool night air brushing against her skin. She stared at the faint glow through the window, her heart pounding as she thought of the phone calls, the financial transactions, the fire.

Her phone buzzed in her hand, Dax's name flashing on the screen. She answered quickly, her voice barely above a whisper. "Hi."

"Cora," Dax said, his tone steady but urgent. "There's something you need to know. I've found more evidence—it's definitive this time."

Her stomach dropped, her fingers tightening around the phone. "Definitive?" she asked, her voice trembling.

"Yes," Dax replied. "Declan's connection to the fire—it's undeniable. We need to meet again, but... you need to be careful. I don't want to talk on the phone. He's dangerous, Cora."

The words hit her like a wave, her breath catching as she stared out into the darkness. "Okay," she said softly, her voice breaking. "I'll meet you tomorrow."

Cora didn't sleep that night. She lay in bed, staring at the ceiling as Dax's words replayed in her mind: *"Declan's connection to the fire—it's undeniable. He's dangerous, Cora."* The weight of the warning pressed heavily against her chest, every whispered word and suspicious glance from Declan now taking on a sinister undertone.

When morning came, she found herself in the kitchen, her hands wrapped around a cup of tea as she stared blankly out the window. The estate's gardens, once a sanctuary, now felt suffocating. The sprawling beauty of it all only served as a reminder of how tightly Declan had woven his world around her.

The sound of footsteps broke her trance. Declan entered the room, dressed sharply in a navy suit, his phone in hand. His presence filled the space, commanding and deliberate, as his gaze found her immediately.

He crossed the room, placing his phone on the counter as he poured himself a cup of coffee. "Good morning, Cora," he remarked, his tone casual.

Cora looked at him then, her chest tightening as she tried to reconcile the man standing before her with the one Dax had described. "Declan," she began carefully, her voice barely above a whisper. "Do you ever feel like... like things aren't what they seem?"

His brow furrowed slightly, his head tilting as he studied her. "What do you mean?"

"I don't know," she said quickly, shaking her head. "Maybe it's just me overthinking."

Declan's lips curved into a faint smile, though his eyes remained sharp. He stepped closer, his hand brushing against her arm as he spoke. "You've been carrying so much, Cora," he said softly. "You're overthinking because you're exhausted. You need to let go. Trust me to handle things."

Her chest tightened at his words, the sincerity in his voice clashing with the doubts swirling in her mind. "I want to," she admitted, her voice trembling.

"Then do," Declan said firmly, his hand moving to rest on her waist. "We're a team, Cora. And we don't let anyone or anything come between us."

The intensity in his gaze left her breathless, and for a moment, she allowed herself to nod, to let his words settle over her like a fragile shield.

After Declan left for his meeting, the estate grew quiet again, the silence amplifying the tension that had been building for weeks. Cora wandered through the halls, her footsteps echoing faintly against the marble floors.

Her phone buzzed in her pocket, pulling her from her thoughts. She glanced at the screen and saw Dax's message:

12 p.m. at the park. It's safer than the café.

Cora's stomach churned as she read the words, the reality of what she was about to do sinking in. She was going to meet Dax, to confront the truth about Declan. And this time, there would be no turning back.

The park was quiet when she arrived, the faint rustle of leaves in the breeze blending with the distant sound of children laughing. Dax was waiting on a bench near the edge of the pond, his expression serious as he stood to greet her.

"Thanks for coming," he said, his tone steady.

"Certainly," Cora replied, her voice trembling slightly. "What did you find?"

Dax motioned for her to sit, his hands steady as he pulled out a small envelope. "I traced the burner phone activity to someone on Declan's payroll," he began. "A man who's been involved in similar cases before. It's more than circumstantial now, Cora. We have the evidence."

Her chest tightened as he handed her the envelope, her fingers trembling as she opened it. Inside were copies of financial records, phone logs, and a grainy photo of a man she didn't recognize.

"This man," Dax continued, pointing to the photo. "He was hired by someone with ties to Declan's estate. The timing, the money—it all lines up. Declan didn't just know about the fire, Cora. He orchestrated it."

Cora stared at the evidence, her mind racing as the weight of his words pressed down on her. "Why would he do this?" she whispered, her voice breaking.

Dax hesitated, his expression softening. "To send a message," he said carefully. "To remind people of his power. To remind you."

Her breath calmed, tears welling in her eyes as she thought of MJ, of the life that had been destroyed in the flames. "I can't believe this. He knew how special MJ was to me, what that loft meant to me. It was the only tie I had left to my childhood," she said softly. "I can't..."

"You need to be careful," Dax said gently, his hand resting lightly on hers. "Declan is dangerous, Cora. And the closer we get to the truth, the more unpredictable he'll become."

Cora nodded slowly, her chest tightening as she met his gaze. "What do I do?" she asked, her voice trembling.

"For now, just stay alert," Dax replied. "And when you're ready, we'll take the next step together."

"Ok. I can do that," she replied, fidgeting with her necklace.

"Your necklace is beautiful, Cora. Your mom used to wear a rare blue spinel stone around her neck. It is one of the rarest gemstones in the world. She got it from the Baffin Island in Canada when she was in her teens," he said tenderly.

"Declan gave this necklace to me on our honeymoon," she sighed as she stood up from the table.

She could tell that Dax really loved her mom, and she felt so much peace knowing that, as troubled as she was, she had him in her life, even if it was for a short period of time.

Cora drove back to the estate, her thoughts a whirlwind of disbelief and fear. Dax's words repeated in her mind: *"Declan didn't just know about the fire—he orchestrated it."* The weight of the evidence sat heavy in her lap, the grainy photo of the man in the envelope etched into her memory.

The towering gates of the estate loomed before her, their grandeur no longer comforting but ominous. She pulled into the driveway, her heart racing as she stepped out of the car. The house seemed to rise around her like a fortress, its silence oppressive as she pushed open the door.

Declan wasn't home yet. His absence filled the space with an eerie stillness, amplifying every creak of the floorboards as she made her way to the sitting room. The flying dress print greeted her again, its perfection mocking her with the life it symbolized—the life that felt more like an illusion with each passing day.

Her fingers brushed against the infinity necklace as she stood there, her mind swirling with questions. *How much of this was real? How much of Declan's love was genuine, and how much of it was control?*

The sound of the front door opening made her jump. Declan's footsteps echoed in the hall, his presence filling the house once again.

Cora turned to see him entering the sitting room, his expression softening when his eyes met hers.

Declan reached out, his hand brushing against her cheek as he tilted her face upward. "You've been distant," he said, his voice low but steady. "Ever since the dinner with my parents. Ever since... her."

"Mara," Cora whispered, her stomach twisting at the memory of the woman's cryptic warnings.

Declan's jaw tightened briefly, but his voice remained calm. "Don't let her get in your head," he said firmly. "She doesn't know me. Not like you do."

Cora hesitated, the weight of his words pressing against her chest. "She seemed convinced," she said carefully, her voice trembling.

Declan's lips curved into a faint smile, but it didn't reach his eyes. "Mara has always been unstable," he said softly. "She thrives on chaos, on obsessing over things she can't have. Don't let her win, Cora. Don't let her come between us."

Her fingers curled into fists at her sides as she struggled to reconcile the man standing before her with the man Dax had described. "I just... I don't know what to think," she admitted, her voice breaking.

Declan's hands moved to her waist, his grip firm but not forceful as he pulled her closer. "Then don't think," he murmured, his lips brushing against her temple. "Trust me. Trust us."

The intensity in his gaze left her breathless, and for a moment, she allowed herself to nod, to let his words wrap around her like a fragile shield. But deep down, the doubts remained, whispering louder with each passing second.

"I need to lie down," she said softly, her voice trembling.

Declan nodded, stepping back but keeping his gaze fixed on her. "Of course," he said. "You've been so stressed. Rest, and we'll talk later."

Cora forced a faint smile, her chest tightening as she turned and made her way to their room.

That night, as the estate grew quiet, Cora sat on the edge of the bed with her grandmother's journal open in her lap. The familiar handwriting brought a fleeting sense of comfort, even as her mind raced with the truths she couldn't ignore: *The people who love us most often carry the heaviest secrets. But love without trust is no love at all.*

Cora exhaled at the words, tears pricking at her eyes as she closed the journal. The love she and Declan shared had once felt unshakable, but now it felt like a fragile illusion, cracking under the weight of the secrets between them.

Declan's study light was still on as Cora stepped out onto the balcony, the cool night air brushing against her skin. She stared at the faint glow through the window, her heart pounding as she thought of the phone calls, the financial records, the fire.

Her phone buzzed in her hand, Sebastian's name flashing on the screen. She answered quickly, her voice barely above a whisper. "Hi."

"Cora," Sebastian said, his voice steady but urgent. "They are getting closer to a breakthrough. But you need to be careful. If Declan finds out what they're doing..."

"I know," she said softly, her voice trembling. "I'm being careful."

"I'm just outside the estate," Sebastian replied with a quiet pause. "Remember that time we drove out to the lighthouse and got stuck in the snow? I don't know why I was thinking about that the other day. Your hands were frozen and you missed curfew. Gram was so mad, I never thought we would get dug out," he said laughing, trying to give her an ounce of familiarity.

"Oh, my gosh, Seb. I hadn't thought about that in forever. The tires just kept spinning in your grandpa's truck. We were so cold," Cora reminisced softly, thinking about simpler times.

"Now, I wonder if your Gram and my Pops were hanging out that night," he declared with a hint of amusement.

"Now that better be written somewhere in these journals," laughed Cora. "MJ would have been all over those details. I wish you had known him. MJ would have loved you."

Cora stared at her phone long after the call with Sebastian ended, the weight of his words sinking in. She felt like the ground beneath her was crumbling, and every step forward risked sending her tumbling into a void she couldn't escape.

Her gaze drifted to the journal on her nightstand. The words she had read earlier echoed in her mind: *Love without trust is no love at all.*

She closed her eyes as she leaned back against the headboard.

The sound of the front door opening echoed through the estate, pulling her from her thoughts. Declan was home. Had he left again? His presence now felt like a storm brewing just beyond the horizon. She heard his footsteps approaching her room, each one deliberate and steady.

The door opened slowly, and Declan stepped inside, his expression calm but unreadable. He leaned against the doorframe, his gaze sweeping over her. "You're still awake," he remarked, his tone casual but probing.

"I couldn't sleep," Cora admitted, her voice soft.

Declan crossed the room, sitting on the edge of the bed beside her. "Is it everything again?" he asked, his hand resting lightly on her knee. "The fire? MJ? Or is it her?"

Her breath caught at the mention of Mara, her chest tightening as she searched for the right words. "It's everything," she said finally. "I just can't stop thinking about... how much has changed."

Declan nodded slowly, his hand sliding to cup her cheek as he met her gaze. "Change is hard," he said softly. "But it's also necessary. It shows us what we're made of. And what we're worth fighting for."

She cringed at how he always knew what to say. Why did he always know what to say? Why did he seem so perfect yet keep her masked behind uncertainty?

Cora's lips parted as she tried to respond, but the intensity in Declan's gaze left her momentarily speechless. He leaned in, his forehead pressing against hers as his hand slid to the back of her neck.

"I need you to fight for us, Cora," he murmured, his voice low and rough. "No one else matters."

Her heart pounded, her breath pulling as his words sank in. "I want to," she whispered, her voice trembling. "But..."

Declan silenced her with a kiss, his lips moving against hers with a hunger that left her breathless. His hands tightened on her waist, pulling her closer as he deepened the kiss. "No buts," he said against her mouth. "You're mine. Always mine."

His hands slid beneath the hem of her shirt, his touch igniting a fire that left her trembling. For a moment, she allowed herself to get lost in the heat of the moment, to let the doubts and fears melt away beneath the intensity of his touch. But as his lips trailed down her neck, her mind flashed to Dax's warnings, to the fire, to the secrets that seemed to linger in every corner of their lives.

"Wait," she said softly, her hands pressing against his chest.

Declan froze, his breath hot against her skin as he pulled back slightly. "What's wrong?" he asked, his voice low but steady.

"I just..." Cora hesitated, her chest tightening as she searched for the right words. "I need time to think."

His jaw tightened briefly, but he nodded, his hands dropping to his sides as he sat back. "You've been saying that a lot lately," he remarked, his tone calm but edged with frustration. "But you're still here. You're still with me. What more do you need, Cora?"

Her throat tightened as she met his gaze, the weight of his words pressing against her chest. "I need to figure out who I am in all of this," she said softly. "Because right now, I don't know anymore."

Declan's expression darkened, but he stood, his movements slow and deliberate as he stepped away from the bed. "Figure it out, then," he said quietly, his voice carrying a note of finality. "But don't forget what we've built. Don't let other people take that away from us."

He left the room without another word, the sound of the door clicking shut echoing in the silence. Cora sat still for a long moment, her hands shaking as she stared at the empty space he had left behind.

The truth was unraveling around her, piece by piece. And she knew that when it finally came together, there would be no going back.

The silence in the room was stifling after Declan left. Cora sat on the edge of the bed, her fingers toying with the infinity necklace, its weight, a constant reminder of his presence in her life. Everything felt heavier now—the estate, the necklace, the doubts swirling in her mind. She closed her eyes, her breath catching as she tried to steady herself.

Mara's warning lingered like a shadow: *"He's not who you think he is."* And now, Dax's revelations felt like the final threads unraveling the life she had built with Declan. She needed clarity. Answers. Something to break the fog of confusion that had consumed her for weeks.

The next morning, Declan's absence in the house felt both a relief and a weight. He had left early for another "meeting," his phone calls cryptic as ever. Cora wandered through the estate, her footsteps echoing softly in the vast halls.

The sound of her phone buzzing snapped her out of her thoughts. She pulled it from her pocket, her pulse quickening when she saw Dax's name on the screen.

"We need to talk," he said immediately when she answered. "There's something I haven't told you yet."

Cora's breath hitched. "What is it?"

"It's about your necklace," Dax said carefully. "I've been looking into it, and it's more than just a piece of jewelry, Cora. Declan had it custom-made by his private jeweler in Bali, and the symbolism isn't what you think it is."

Her fingers instinctively went to the pendant resting against her collarbone. "What do you mean?"

Dax hesitated, his voice lowering. "It's connected to the open relationship culture in this town. The infinity symbol with the intertwined heart—it's a symbol some people use to mark their partnerships. But it's also a claim, Cora. A way of saying you're his, no matter what happens. It's about control."

Cora's stomach churned as she processed his words, her grip on the necklace tightening. "You're saying he gave this to me as a... mark?"

"It looks that way," Dax replied. "And with everything else we've found about him, I think it's important you know what this means. Declan doesn't see relationships the way you do. To him, this might be a declaration of ownership, not love and an opening to do whatever he pleases."

Her chest tightened, the air around her feeling suffocating. "Open relationships? As in sharing? I don't know what to think of this," she said finally, her voice trembling.

Cora's mind returned to Auriella and James, the way he looked at her, the way he seemed to inhale her mere existence. *"This one's not for you,"* she had told him. She thought about the way the bar seemed to stop in its tracks when Declan first walked in that night, as if every single person knew who he was.

Cora thought back to the engagement stops in the boutiques, how the clerks seemed to plead with their looks. Were they trying to warn her? And MJ. Oh, had MJ seen something? Had he heard something? He warned her so many times about him. What did he sense?

Evelyn. The way she graced every room, consciously seeking attention. The summer barbeque. The couples standing too close, the way they touched each other leaving no room for space. The argument Evelyn had with Declan in Atlanta. *"She doesn't think I'm good enough for you,"* he had told her. Were they together? Were they a couple in this open relationship charade?

Atlanta. The sheer curtains. *"We can be who we want to be,"* Declan had said. He put her in front of that doorway where that couple started undressing. The man with the microphone, *"It's time,"* he had said. Time for what? The thoughts made her sick to her stomach. What had she gotten herself into?

Her mind was racing; everything was becoming clear to her. Every single moment in these last six months flashed before her eyes as she came to the conclusion that Dax was right. Her head began to spin as she grasped this new knowledge. Yes, this town seemed to hold onto secrets, but a society of secrets? Everyone? Where was he really going in the evenings? To other women?

"I…I have to go," Cora said softly, dropping her phone.

"But be careful, Cora. Please," Dax tried to say.

When the call ended, Cora sat in the quiet of the sitting room, the pendant still clutched tightly in her hand. Declan's words from the night before echoed in her mind: *"You're mine. Always mine."* The sincerity in his voice had felt like a comfort then, but now it felt like a warning.

The estate's beauty now felt stifling, its grandeur more like a cage than a sanctuary. Everywhere she turned, there was a reminder of Declan's control—the print, the necklace, the constant presence of his influence.

Her phone buzzed again, this time with a message from Selah:

I know you said you're fine, but I'm worried about you. Call me, okay? If you are out, text me when you get home

"Text me when you get home." It was something they said through their college years, every single time they parted, no matter what. Selah was becoming worried; Cora never brushed off her contact with her.

Cora stared at the screen, her chest tightening. She wanted to call Selah, to pour everything out, but the weight of what she was carrying felt too much to say aloud. Instead, after twenty minutes, she typed a quick response:

Miss you too. Just trying to figure things out. Will call soon.

That evening, as the estate grew quiet, Cora found herself in her room with her grandmother's journal open in her lap. The familiar handwriting brought a fleeting sense of comfort, even as her mind raced with the truths she couldn't ignore: *The truth, no matter how painful, is always the most powerful tool we have. But it demands courage to face it.*

She had avoided the truth for weeks, maybe even months, but now it was staring her in the face, demanding to be confronted. She glanced at the door to her room, her heart pounding as she thought of Declan. The man she loved, the man who had promised her the world, was hiding something. And the pieces of the puzzle were starting to come together in a way that terrified her.

The truth felt suffocating, pressing down on her with an intensity she couldn't ignore. Cora sat on the edge of the bed, her fingers tracing the infinity necklace resting against her collarbone. Dax's words repeated in her mind: *"It's a claim. A way of saying you're his."*

She had thought it was a gift—a token of love and commitment—but now, it felt like a chain, a silent reminder of how much control Declan had over her life and a lifestyle she didn't want. Her chest tensed as she thought about all the other ways he had marked her: the flying dress print displayed like a trophy in the sitting room, the curated life he had built for her at the estate, the decisions he made without consulting her.

Cora pushed herself to her feet, the silence of the estate pressing against her as she paced the room. She needed answers. She needed to know what Declan was hiding and what the necklace truly meant to him.

Later that evening, Declan returned, his presence filling the house with an intensity that left her on edge. Cora found him in the sitting room, standing before the flying dress print with a glass of scotch in his hand. His posture was relaxed, but there was a sharpness in his gaze as he turned to face her.

"You've been avoiding me," he remarked, his tone calm but edged with something darker.

"I've just been thinking," Cora replied carefully, her fingers brushing against the necklace.

Declan's eyes flicked to the pendant, his lips curving into a faint smile. "Good," he said softly. "That's what it's for. To remind you of what we are."

Her stomach churned at his words, the weight of the necklace suddenly unbearable. "What do you mean?" she asked, her voice trembling.

Declan tilted his head, studying her carefully. "It means forever, Cora," he said simply. "It means that no matter what happens, you're mine. For all infinity."

The finality in his tone left her breathless, her heart pounding as she struggled to process his words. "And what if I need space?" she asked softly, her voice barely audible.

Declan's jaw tightened briefly before he stepped closer, his hand reaching out to cup her face. "Then you take it," he said firmly. "But, you belong to me."

Her breath stiffened at his words, the possessiveness in his gaze sending a shiver through her.

His lips pressed into a thin line, his hand dropping from her face as he stepped back. "You know you belong to me," he said quietly.

Cora watched as Declan turned away, his posture tense as he walked to the bar and poured himself another drink. The silence between them was heavy, the unspoken tension thickening with every passing second.

"Why don't you tell me what's really bothering you?" Declan asked finally, his voice calm but probing. "Because I can see it, Cora. I can see it every time you look at me."

Her chest tightened, her fingers curling into fists at her sides. "I just... I don't know what to believe anymore," she admitted, her voice breaking.

Declan turned to face her, his gaze sharp as he stepped closer. "Then believe in me," he said firmly, his voice dropping. "Believe in what we've built. Because I won't let anyone tear it apart."

The intensity in his voice left her trembling, her heart pounding as she stared at him. "I want to," she whispered,

His jaw tightened, his hands balling into fists at his sides. "Then let me make it simple," he said, his voice low and steady. "You're mine, Cora. And I'm not letting you go."

The possessiveness in his tone sent a shiver down her spine, the finality of his words both grounding and terrifying.

Later that night, as the estate grew quiet, Cora sat in her room with her grandmother's journal open in her lap. The words on the page blurred as tears filled her eyes, the weight of everything pressing against her like a storm she couldn't escape: *The hardest truths are the ones we already know but are too afraid to face. They wait for us, patient and unyielding, until we have no choice but to confront them.*

Her hands trembled as she closed the journal. She wasn't ready to confront the truth, but she knew it was coming—inevitable and unstoppable.

Cora woke to the sound of faint murmurs drifting down the hallway. She sat up in bed, her heart racing as the quiet of the estate pressed against her like a weight. Declan's voice carried through the stillness, low and firm. She slipped out of bed, the cool floor grounding her as she crept toward the door.

Peering down the hall, she saw the light spilling from the study, the faint silhouette of Declan pacing as he spoke on the phone. His tone was calm but sharp, the kind of measured intensity that sent a chill down her spine.

"No excuses," he said, his words clipped. "This needs to be handled now. I don't care what it takes."

Her stomach churned as she listened, her fingers tightening around the edge of the doorframe. She didn't know what he was talking about, but every instinct told her it was connected to the fire, to Dax's warnings, to the unanswered questions that had been gnawing at her for weeks.

She stepped back into her room, her chest heaving as she tried to catch her breath. The infinity necklace felt heavier than ever, its delicate design a stark contrast to the suffocating reality it represented. Cora sank onto the edge of the bed, her head in her hands as she struggled to steady herself. The truth was there, just out of reach. She was terrified of what would happen when she finally grasped it. By mid-morning, Declan was gone again, leaving the estate eerily quiet in his absence. Cora wandered through the halls, her fingers brushing against the cool marble banister as she tried to make sense of her spiraling thoughts.

Her phone buzzed again, this time with a message from Selah:

I don't know what's going on, but I'm here when you're ready to talk. Please call me.

Tears pricked at her eyes as she read the words, her chest tightening with guilt and longing. She wanted to call Selah, to pour everything out, but the weight of what she was carrying felt too much to say aloud.

Instead, she typed a quick reply:

I'm ok, Se. I'll call soon.

Declan returned later that night, his presence filling the estate with an intensity that left her on edge. He found her in the kitchen, staring out the window as she nursed a cup of tea.

"Another surgery?" she questioned as he quickly turned towards her.

"You need to eat. You are getting too thin," he remarked, his tone light but probing.

Cora turned to face him, her chest tightening as she forced a faint smile. "I will," she said softly.

Declan studied her for a long moment, his gaze sharp as he stepped closer. "You haven't been eating at all," he said, his voice low. "What's going on, Cora?"

Her breath caught, her fingers curling into fists at her sides. "I just don't feel well," she admitted, her voice trembling. "I think I will go lay down."

Declan's hand moved to rest lightly on her shoulder, his touch both comforting and heavy. "Just rest," he said softly. "Let me handle our life. That's what I'm here for."

She winced at his words, the sincerity in his voice clashing with the doubts in her mind. "I'm trying," she said softly.

"Try harder," Declan replied, his voice dropping. "Because I'm not going to let anyone or anything come between us."

As days went by, the estate felt heavier, as though the walls themselves had absorbed the tension that lingered in every room. Cora woke early one day, her dreams restless and fragmented, filled with flashes of the fire and the weight of Declan's words.

She dressed quickly, pulling on a light sweater as she made her way down to the kitchen. The house was quiet, save for the faint sound of birds outside the window. Declan was gone again, his absence both a relief and a reminder of how much he occupied her thoughts. She knew it came with his profession, surgeries at all hours, but she couldn't shake the feeling that he was off with other women. Had Mara been a part of this secret society?

The sound of the front door opening startled her, and she turned to see Declan stepping inside, his expression calm but sharp. He set his keys down by the door and made his way to her, his gaze sweeping over her with an intensity that made her stomach twist.

His brow furrowed slightly, his gaze sharpening as he studied her. "What are you thinking about?"

"I don't know," she said quickly, shaking her head.

Declan reached out, his hand brushing against her cheek as he tilted her face upward. "You've been thinking too much," he said softly, his voice steady but edged with something firmer. "You need to trust me, Cora. Whatever's in your head, let it go."

"I want to," she whispered. "But there are so many questions, Declan. So many things that don't make sense."

His jaw tightened, and he stepped back, his posture stiffening as he crossed his arms. "Then ask them," he said firmly, his tone dropping. "If there's something you want to know, ask me."

Cora hesitated, her heart pounding as she searched for the courage to speak. "Were you involved in the fire?" she asked finally, her voice trembling.

The room fell silent, the weight of her question hanging between them like a storm cloud. Declan's expression darkened, his eyes narrowing as he stepped closer. "Why would you ask me that?" he demanded, his voice low and sharp.

"Because nothing makes sense anymore," she replied, her voice breaking. "The way you avoid talking about it—Declan, I need to know the truth."

His hands balled into fists at his sides, his gaze burning into hers. "The truth?" he repeated, his voice rising slightly. "The truth is that I've done everything for us. Everything to protect you, to build this life for you. And this is how you repay me? By questioning me?"

Her chest tightened, her breath hitching as she stepped back. "I'm not trying to accuse you," she said quickly. "I just... I need to understand."

Declan exhaled sharply, his hands moving to grip the back of the sofa as he leaned forward, his shoulders tense. "You're letting people get into your head," he said, his voice dropping. "People who don't know us. Who don't understand what we have."

Cora watched him carefully, her heart pounding as she tried to steady her voice. "Then prove them wrong," she said softly. "Prove to me that they're wrong."

Declan turned to face her, his expression softening slightly as he stepped closer. "I don't need to prove anything to you," he said quietly, his voice steady but edged with finality. "You're my wife, Cora. You should trust me."

"I want to," she whispered. "But something doesn't feel right."

Declan's gaze darkened, but he nodded slowly, his hands moving to rest lightly on her shoulders. "Then I'll fix it," he said softly, his voice carrying a quiet determination. "Whatever's wrong, I'll fix it. Because nothing—no one—comes between us."

His words left her trembling, her heart pounding as she nodded faintly. "Okay," she said softly, though the doubts in her chest refused to fade.

Cora remained in the sitting room long after Declan left, her hands trembling as she tried to collect her thoughts. His words echoed in her mind, heavy and unrelenting: *"No one comes between us."* The tone of his voice had carried a finality that left her uneasy, as though it wasn't just a promise—it was a warning.

Her phone buzzed in her lap, pulling her from her thoughts. Dax's name flashed on the screen, his call coming in just as her doubts were reaching a breaking point. She answered quickly, her voice trembling as she whispered, "Hi."

"Cora," Dax said, his voice steady but urgent. "We have everything we need now. The financial records, the burner phone activity, the witness statement—it all points to Declan."

Her chest tightened as his words hit her like a wave. "You're sure?" she asked, her voice barely audible.

"Yes," Dax replied firmly. "This isn't just suspicion anymore, Cora. It's evidence. And I'm telling you, he's dangerous. You need to get out of there."

The weight of his words pressed against her, leaving her breathless. "I don't know how," she admitted, her voice breaking. "He watches everything. He'll know."

"Then you have to be smart," Dax said, his tone softening. "Start planning. Reach out to people you trust. You don't have to do this alone."

Cora nodded faintly, tears pricking at her eyes as she whispered, "Okay."

"Call me if you need anything," Dax added. "Anything at all."

"Thank you," she said softly, her voice trembling.

As the call ended, Cora sat in the quiet of the room, her hands gripping the phone tightly. The life she had built with Declan was unraveling around her, the truths she had avoided now crashing down like a tidal wave.

Declan later found Cora in the garden, the twilight casting long shadows over the perfectly manicured hedges. She stood by the fountain, her arms wrapped around herself as she stared into the rippling water.

"Remember our engagement? Right about here?" Declan asked, his voice breaking the silence as he nodded off in the direction where the table sat.

Cora turned to face him, her chest tightening as she forced a faint smile. "Yes," she replied carefully.

Declan stepped closer, his gaze sharp as he studied her. "What's bothering you, My Cora?" he asked, his tone calm but probing.

"It's Selah," she admitted, her voice trembling as she tried to make up an excuse. "I need to see her."

His jaw tightened, but he nodded, his expression softening slightly as he reached out to brush a strand of hair from her face. "Then let's fly her up here," he said, his voice low.

"I was thinking I could go see her in Dallas, maybe for just a few days," she said softly, her fingers brushing against the infinity necklace as she tried to find a detour away from him.

"I think that is a great idea. Is she alright?" Declan asked, his hand resting lightly over hers on the pendant.

Cora hesitated, her heart pounding as she searched his face. "Yes, I just need to see her, Declan," she whispered.

Declan's expression darkened briefly before he leaned in, his forehead pressing against hers. "Then, we will make it happen," he said firmly. "I'll call the pilot, you call Selah."

His hands moved to her waist, his grip tightening as he pulled her closer. "Whatever's in your head, let it go," he murmured, his voice low and commanding. "We're stronger than this. We're stronger than them. Razi can accompany you. Go and have a nice time with your friend."

The intensity in his gaze sent a shiver through her. "Razi?" she asked softly.

Declan pulled back slightly, his lips curving into a faint smile. "He is my pilot, Cora," he said simply. "He will see to it that you get safely to Selah and he can escort you anywhere you two need to go."

Cora watched him walk back toward the house, his posture confident and unyielding. He was not going to let her go see Selah without someone watching her every move, even if she wanted to. The truth was closing in, and she knew that when it finally came to light, nothing would ever be the same.

That night, she sat on the edge of her bed with her grandmother's journal open in her lap. The words on the page seemed to leap out at her, a reflection of everything she was feeling: *There comes a point where the truth can no longer be ignored. It demands to be faced, no matter the cost.*

Her hands trembled as she closed the journal, her breath hitching. The cost of the truth felt too high, but she knew she couldn't avoid it any longer. The night wrapped around the estate like a shroud, the silence pressing heavily against Cora's chest. She stood on the balcony of her room as she gazed out at the darkened gardens below. The quiet should have brought her peace, but instead, it amplified the storm raging in her mind.

Declan's words from earlier echoed like a mantra, the intensity in his gaze, the unyielding confidence in his tone—it all felt like a cage, tightening around her with each passing moment.

Her phone buzzed on the nightstand, pulling her from her thoughts. She glanced at the screen, Dax's name illuminating the display.

"Cora," he said when she answered, his voice steady but urgent. "I've been digging further. There's one more thing you need to know."

Her chest tightened, her breath catching as she whispered, "What is it?"

"It's about MJ," Dax said carefully. "The fire wasn't just about sending a message. Declan knew MJ would be there that night."

Cora froze, the words sinking into her like a blade. "What are you saying?" she asked, her voice trembling.

"I'm saying he didn't just set the fire to destroy the loft," Dax replied. "He set it knowing MJ would be inside. This wasn't just about you, Cora. It was about eliminating someone he saw as a threat."

Tears filled her eyes, her hand trembling as she clutched the phone. "No," she whispered, shaking her head. "He wouldn't... he couldn't..."

"I know it's hard to hear," Dax said gently. "But it's the truth. And the sooner you accept it, the sooner you can protect yourself."

Her heart raced as his words sank in. Leaving Declan felt impossible, like trying to escape a web that only grew tighter the more she struggled. But staying—staying meant living under his control, his manipulation, and the weight of the truths he had hidden from her.

Her stomach churned, tears pricking at the corners of her eyes as she thought of MJ. His laughter, his kindness, his unwavering support. The thought that Declan might have been behind the fire that killed him was almost too much to bear.

Cora ended the call without another word, the weight of Dax's revelation crushing her. She sank onto the edge of the bed, her hands shaking as she stared at the floor. The man she had trusted, the man she had loved, was a stranger. And the life they had built together was built on lies and manipulation.

Her gaze drifted to the infinity necklace, its delicate design now feeling like a chain wrapped tightly around her throat. She tore it off, the cool metal slipping through her fingers as she dropped it onto the nightstand.

The sound of the front door slamming echoed through the estate, sending a jolt of fear through her. Declan was home. His footsteps were heavy, deliberate, as he moved through the halls. Cora stood, her heart pounding as she made her way to the door of her room, cracking it open just enough to see him pass.

His expression was dark, his jaw clenched as he strode toward the sitting room. She watched as he stopped before the flying dress print, his gaze fixed on it with an intensity that made her stomach twist.

He reached out, his fingers brushing against the edge of the frame before his hand balled into a fist, slamming against the wall beside it. The sound reverberated through the house, and Cora flinched, her breath hitching as she quickly closed the door.

The tension in the estate was visible; every creak of the floorboards and rustle of the wind outside magnified in the stillness. Cora sat back on the bed, her hands gripping the journal as she tried to steady herself. She flipped to a random page, the words blurring as tears filled her eyes: *Sometimes, the only way to move forward is to let go of what's holding you back— even if it means stepping into the unknown.*

The truth in her grandmother's words cut through her like a knife. She couldn't stay here. Not anymore. The man she had married wasn't the man she thought he was, and the life they had built was unraveling around her.

The next morning, Declan was quiet, his demeanor calm but strained as he moved through the kitchen. Cora watched him carefully, her heart pounding as she tried to gather the courage to speak.

"Did something happen last night?" she asked softly, her voice trembling.

Declan's gaze flicked to her, his expression unreadable. "I lost a patient today on the table," he replied, his tone clipped. "Nothing you need to worry about. Have you connected with Selah yet?"

Her chest tightened at his words, the dismissal in his tone cutting through her like a blade. "Declan..." she began, her voice barely above a whisper.

He turned to face her fully, his eyes narrowing slightly. "What is it, Cora?"

She hesitated, her throat tightening as she searched for the right words. "I just... I feel like we're slipping away from each other," she admitted, her voice breaking. "I don't know how to fix it."

Declan's expression softened slightly, his hand moving to rest lightly on her arm. "We're not slipping," he said firmly. "You're letting other people get into your head."

She stopped at his words, the intensity in his tone both grounding and terrifying. "I just want to understand," she said softly.

"Then trust me," Declan said, his voice steady but edged with finality as he glanced at her neck to see her necklace gone from her chest.

His mind began to race. "Where is your necklace, Cora?"

"I…I am cleaning it. It's upstairs on my dressing table," she said quickly.

"See to it that it finds its way back onto you," he said as he kissed her shoulder and walked out of the kitchen.

Cora sat at the breakfast table long after Declan had left the room, her untouched tea growing cold in her hands. His words echoed in her mind. The power in his voice had been unmistakable; the questioning felt less like love and more like a warning.

A Breaking Point

"Every fire reaches its crescendo before it consumes or fades."

The estate was silent again, the heavy quiet amplifying the storm inside her. She needed to leave—she had wanted to use this "Trip to Dallas" to step out of the life that had slowly become a prison. But every path forward felt fraught with danger. Declan watched everything, controlled everything, and now, with Dax's revelations, the stakes felt higher than ever.

The morning light spilled through the grand windows of the estate, emitting long shadows across the polished floors. Declan stood near the door, his suitcase resting at his feet. He looked at Cora, his blue eyes sharp and assessing, as though trying to read her thoughts.

"I'll be gone for three days," he said, his voice calm but firm. "You'll have the estate to yourself. Razi will be around; I am taking a commercial flight. Use the time to rest and clear your head."

Cora nodded, her hands clasped in front of her. "I'll try," she said softly.

He leaned in, pressing a kiss to her forehead. "Good," he said, his tone carrying an edge of finality. "I'll call you tonight."

The sound of the door closing behind him echoed through the estate, the silence that followed feeling heavier than usual. Cora stood frozen in place for a moment as she stared at the empty space he had left behind.

For the first time in weeks, she was truly alone. The thought was both liberating and terrifying. Declan's presence was commanding, even when he wasn't physically there, and now, the weight of his absence pressed against her like a phantom.

She wandered through the halls, her footsteps soft against the marble floors. The estate felt different now—larger, colder, and eerily quiet. Her fingers brushed against the banister as she descended the staircase, her gaze drifting to the sitting room where the flying dress print loomed like a silent spectator.

Her phone buzzed in her pocket, pulling her from her thoughts. It was a message from Selah:

C, I'm worried about you. Please let me know if you're okay. I'll come if you need me.

Tears filled her eyes as she read the words, her chest tightening with guilt and longing. Selah had always been her lifeline, the one person who could steady her when everything felt like it was spinning out of control. She needed to reach out to her, but she couldn't find the strength.

She typed back quickly, her hands trembling:

I'm okay. Just trying to figure things out. I'll call soon. Promise.

As the evening fell, Cora sat in her room with her grandmother's journal open in her lap. The familiar handwriting brought a fleeting sense of comfort, even as her mind raced with the truths she couldn't ignore:

When the time comes to making a choice, choose the path that leads to freedom. Even if it's the hardest one.

Her breath wavered as she read the words, the weight of them settled heavily over her. Freedom felt impossible, but staying felt even worse. The weight of her grandmother's words lingered in her mind as Cora closed the journal and placed it on the nightstand. The path to freedom felt like a distant light, flickering faintly but just within reach. She exhaled shakily, brushing a tear from her cheek as she stood and moved toward the window.

The estate's sprawling gardens stretched before her, bathed in the soft glow of the moonlight. The quiet beauty of it all had once brought her comfort, but now it felt like an illusion—a carefully constructed facade masking the cracks in her life.

Her phone buzzed again, the sound startling her in the silence. It was a message from Sebastian:

Just checking in. Call if you need anything.

Cora stared at the screen, her chest tightening. She hadn't reached out to Sebastian in days, too afraid of what Declan might think if he knew he was out there patrolling. But now, with everything closing in around her, she felt a desperate need for someone who truly understood her— someone who saw her outside of Declan's shadow.

She hesitated for a moment before typing back:

Can you come by tomorrow? I need to talk.

The response came quickly:

Of course. Anytime you need me.

The next day, the estate was quiet as usual, the stillness broken only by the occasional rustle of the breeze against the windows. Declan hadn't called since leaving on his trip, his silence both a relief and a source of unease. Cora found herself pacing the sitting room, her thoughts spiraling as she waited for Sebastian to arrive.

When the doorbell rang, she nearly jumped, her heart pounding as she made her way to the door. She opened it to find Sebastian standing there, his expression warm but tinged with concern.

"Hey," he said softly, his eyes scanning her face. "You okay?"

Cora stepped aside, motioning for him to come in. "Not really," she admitted, her voice trembling. "But I'm trying to be."

They sat in the sunlit sitting room, the flying dress print looming over them like a silent witness. Cora's hands fidgeted in her lap as she tried to find the words to explain everything.

"I don't know where to start," she said finally, her voice breaking.

"Start wherever you need to," Sebastian replied gently, his hands resting on his knees as he leaned forward.

Cora exhaled slowly, her gaze drifting to the floor. "It's Declan," she said softly. "Things haven't been... right. And now, with everything, Dax has told me about the fire, about MJ..."

Her voice trailed off, tears slipping down her cheeks as she shook her head.

Sebastian moved closer, his hand resting lightly on hers. "You don't have to worry," he said firmly. "It's almost over, Kitten. I've got you."

His words broke something inside of her, and before she knew it, she was leaning into him, her head resting against his shoulder as she sobbed quietly. Sebastian's arms wrapped around her, his touch steady and comforting as he whispered reassurances. The warmth of his presence, the strength in his embrace—it was everything she had been missing. And for a fleeting moment, she felt safe.

Cora pulled back slightly, her tear-streaked face tilting up to meet his gaze. "Thank you," she murmured, her voice barely audible.

Sebastian's hand brushed a strand of hair from her face, his touch lingering. "You don't have to thank me," he said softly. "I'm here for you. Always."

The intensity in his gaze left her breathless, and before she could stop herself, she leaned in, her lips brushing against his. The kiss was soft at first, hesitant and filled with unspoken emotion. But as Sebastian's hand moved to hold her face, it deepened, the connection between them igniting into something neither of them could ignore. For a moment, the world fell away, the weight of her doubts and fears replaced by the raw intensity of the moment. Cora's hands gripped his shirt, pulling him closer as her heart pounded in her chest.

But as quickly as it began, the reality of the situation came crashing down. Cora pulled back abruptly, her breath hitching as she stared at him, her cheeks flushed.

"I shouldn't have done that," she whispered, her voice trembling.

Sebastian shook his head, his expression filled with understanding. "It's okay," he said softly. "You're overwhelmed. I get it."

Cora stood, wrapping her arms around herself as she turned away. "I don't know who I am anymore," she admitted, her voice breaking. "Everything feels like it's falling apart, and I don't know how to stop it."

Sebastian rose, his hands sliding into his pockets as he watched her. "Then let me help you," he said firmly. "Whatever you need, I'm here."

The sincerity in his tone cut through the chaos in her mind. "Thank you," she murmured, her voice barely audible.

As Sebastian left, Cora stood at the door, watching his car disappear down the long driveway. The moment of connection they had shared left her shaken, a mix of guilt and longing swirling in her chest.

Unbeknownst to her, Declan's shadow moved behind the hidden cameras in the estate. From his hotel room, he watched every moment play out on his screen, his jaw clenched and his eyes dark with fury.

"Cora," he muttered to himself, his voice low and dangerous. *"What are you doing?"*

His laptop screen glowed faintly in the dim light as he stared at the live feed from the estate's hidden cameras. His gaze was fixed on Cora, his jaw tight and his eyes dark with anger as he replayed the scene with Sebastian in his mind. She had kissed him. Cora had kissed Sebastian in the sitting room he had built for her, under the print that symbolized their perfect life. The betrayal burned in his chest, his hands clenching into fists as he muttered to himself, *"She doesn't understand. She doesn't see. I'll make her see."*

Declan's mind raced with thoughts of control, of punishment, of how to bring her back to him. He couldn't lose her—not to Dax, not to Sebastian, not to her own doubts.

The tension in the house felt different now, sharper and heavier, as though Declan's presence lingered even in his absence. Cora sat on the edge of her bed, her hands trembling as she tried to steady her breathing. The memory of her kiss with Sebastian played on a loop in her mind, filling her with a mix of guilt and longing she couldn't reconcile.

Her phone buzzed on the nightstand, pulling her from her thoughts. It was a message from Selah:

Thinking of you. Please call me when you're ready to talk.

Cora's chest tightened as she read the words. She wanted to call Selah, to pour everything out, but the weight of her emotions felt too overwhelming. Instead, she typed a quick response:

Miss you. I'll call soon. Thinking about flying out to see you.

The lie sat heavy in her chest, but she couldn't bring herself to explain everything—not yet.

Declan's absence should have felt like a reprieve, but instead, it left her feeling more trapped than ever. The estate's quiet grandeur now felt suffocating, its beauty mocking her as she wandered through the halls. Every room carried traces of him—his meticulousness, his control, his unyielding presence.

Cora couldn't sleep, so she sat up to look over building plans on her laptop, quietly setting plans in her mind—Anything to keep the eerie quiet of the estate afar.

Her phone buzzed from across the room. She got up and walked over to her vanity.

It was Nadine.

Could you please meet me tomorrow afternoon? Blooms Coffee Bar? 4 pm?

Cora adjusted her robe and picked up her phone.

I'd love to. See you then.

The questions in her mind circling Nadine kept her up most of the night, anxiety taking its toll.

The next morning was Saturday, and a storm was brewing across the sky. Cora decided to stay in and do some more research on the shop construction. She walked lazily through the corridors of the estate, counting the hours until her meeting with Nadine, unable to concentrate on anything else.

At 3:30, she collected her things and walked out to her car. The sky had separated into a hazy grey, allowing the clouds to clear, granting hope as she drove into town.

Cora parked her car, and the late afternoon sunlight filtered through the windows of the small café, casting soft patterns on the wooden table where Cora sat. Her hands rested around a steaming cup of tea, her mind spinning as she waited for Nadine to arrive. The last time they had spoken, Nadine's voice had carried a quiet sadness, a weight that Cora couldn't ignore.

The sound of the door opening pulled her from her thoughts. Nadine stepped inside, her expression warm but weary as she made her way to the table. "Cora," she said softly, pulling her into a gentle embrace before sitting across from her. "Thank you for meeting me."

"Of course," Cora replied, her voice steady despite the tension in her chest. "It's nice to see you."

They ordered quickly, the quiet hum of the café providing a comforting backdrop as Nadine stirred her coffee absently. Her gaze drifted out the window, her lips pressing into a thin line before she spoke.

"There's something I need to tell you," Nadine began, her voice trembling slightly. "Something I've been carrying for a long time."

Cora's heart tightened as she leaned forward, her hands resting on the table. "What is it?"

Nadine hesitated, her fingers tightening around her cup. "Declan's... behavior," she said carefully. "The way he approaches relationships—it's not something he came to on his own. It's what he grew up around. It's all he's ever known."

Cora frowned, her brow furrowing as she processed Nadine's words. "What do you mean?"

Nadine's gaze met hers, her eyes brimming with tears. "Declan grew up in a world where... fidelity wasn't what it seemed," she admitted. "Open marriages, secret arrangements—it was the norm in the circles we ran in. I was part of it, too. For a long time."

Cora's breath caught, the revelation sending a jolt through her. "You mean...?"

Nadine nodded, her voice breaking as she said, "I thought it was harmless at first. A way to keep the spark alive, to maintain appearances. But it wasn't harmless—not for Declan. He grew up watching it, absorbing it. It's all he's ever understood about love."

Cora sat back, her chest tightening as Nadine's words sank in. "That's why he's the way he is," she murmured. "Why he's so controlling, so possessive."

Nadine nodded, her tears slipping down her cheeks. "You two have been having problems. I saw the intensity at dinner with you two and I blame myself," she said softly. "For not seeing what it was doing to him. For not stepping away sooner. He is our middle child; his siblings handled it much better than he did. They appear to live decent lives. Declan had always held a stronger sense of not belonging, feeling overshadowed. He was always so self-reliant, we never worried about him."

Cora hesitated, brushing her fingers against the edge of her cup. "He did more than watch, Nadine," she said finally, her voice trembling. "He is the one behind the fire. He hired someone to burn down the loft. MJ was in the way, and he... he took him from me."

Nadine's hand flew to her mouth, her expression crumpling as a sob escaped her. "Oh, my God," she whispered, her voice breaking. "Cora, I had no idea. I didn't—"

"I know," Cora said quickly, her voice softening. "But now you do. And I needed you to know the truth."

Nadine shook her head, shaming herself in disbelief.

"They are building a case against him. Dax Sheridan, well, my father, is the lead detective, and he has been keeping me informed, unofficially…" she began to explain.

Nadine stopped her and offered her a smile. "Dax is your father? Oh, Cora. He is a remarkable man. I am so happy to hear this for you."

Cora sighed as her tension released, "He will be arraigned soon, Nadine."

Nadine held her gaze for a few seconds, then set her hands on Cora's across the table. There was a moment of bestowment as they came together to try to process what the future would hold.

They finished their desserts in silence, listening to the soft hum of voices around them. When they were finished, Nadine paid for their tab and Cora stood to grab her jacket.

"Please. Keep my number, Cora. I'm here if you need anything at all," she said with a sweet sympathy.

"Thank you. I will keep you posted. Please don't contact him, he doesn't know everything. He is in Chicago but will be back in a few days. I will know more then," Cora said as she hugged her softly and turned away.

Later that night, the estate was eerily quiet. Cora sat in the library, her grandmother's journals spread out before her. The words on the pages carried a strange weight now, hints of secrets she hadn't noticed before.

Her gaze lingered on one passage, the ink faint but legible: *Love isn't always what it seems. Sometimes, it bends and twists in ways we don't understand. Henry taught me that.*

Henry had always been a comforting figure in the stories her grandmother had shared, but now, there was something deeper—a love triangle hidden in the lines of her writing.

The words hinted at choices, at struggles with fidelity, and at a life that mirrored the complications of her own. The realization sent a chill through her, the parallels too stark to ignore.

A Phoenix Rises

"From the destruction of the past, we find the strength to rise anew."

Cora sat back in her chair, her fingers brushing over the worn pages of her grandmother's journal. The inked confessions felt like a reflection of her own life, the struggles with control and love, the weight of unspoken truths. She closed the journal slowly as the storm outside raged against the windows.

The estate groaned softly under the force of the wind, the sound of branches scratching against the glass adding to the unease that had settled over her. It felt as though the storm wasn't just outside—it was within her, a relentless force breaking apart everything she had believed in.

The aftermath of the storm let in a cool breeze as Cora walked to the front door to open a window. She set the journal down, the familiar sound of Selah's car pulling into the drive brought Cora to her feet. She opened the door to find Selah and Jensen standing there, their expressions a mix of concern and frustration.

"Cora," Selah said, her voice trembling as she stepped forward. "You've been sending me these vague messages for weeks. What the hell is going on?"

Cora's throat tightened, tears welling in her eyes as she whispered, "It's Declan. There's so much I need to tell you."

Selah pulled her into a tight embrace, her arms wrapping around her friend as she murmured, "Then tell us everything. We're here now."

Cora led Selah and Jensen into the foyer, the tension between them palpable. The dim light overhead flickered faintly, casting uneven shadows on the walls. Selah glanced around the sparse room, her lips pressing into a thin line as she crossed her arms.

"Are you alone?" Selah asked, her voice tinged with disbelief.

"For now," Cora replied softly, her fingers brushing against the edge of the entry table.

Jensen stepped closer, his expression calm but concerned. "Cora," he said gently, his voice steady, "You need to tell us everything. Start from the beginning. What's going on?"

Cora exhaled shakily, her hands trembling as she gestured for them to sit. The three of them settled into the room, the small space feeling even tighter as the weight of the conversation loomed over them.

"It's Declan," Cora began, her voice trembling. "There's so much you don't know—about the fire, about MJ, about who he really is."

Selah's eyes widened, her brows knitting together in confusion. "What do you mean? What about the fire?"

Cora hesitated as she searched for the right words. "It wasn't an accident," she said finally, her voice breaking. "Declan orchestrated it. He hired someone to set it."

Selah gasped, her hand flying to her mouth as Jensen's jaw tightened, his fists clenching at his sides. "What?" Selah whispered, her voice trembling. "Cora, that's insane. Are you sure?"

"Yes," Cora said firmly, tears streaming down her cheeks. "Dax found the evidence—financial records, burner phones, a witness. It's all there. Declan wanted to send a message, and MJ... MJ got caught in the middle."

Jensen leaned forward, his expression dark. "So, he's responsible for MJ's death," he said, his voice low but sharp.

Cora nodded as she whispered, "Yes. And I should have seen it sooner. I should have known what he was capable of."

Selah reached out, her hand covering Cora's. "This isn't your fault," she said softly, her voice steady but filled with emotion. "You couldn't have known."

Cora shook her head, her tears falling freely. "He's been watching me," she admitted, her voice trembling. "There are cameras all over the main rooms in the estate. He sees everything I do, hears everything I say. Even now, I feel like he's watching."

Cora was right. Declan sat in his hotel room in Chicago, his laptop opened in front of him. The screen displayed the live feed from the hidden cameras in the estate, the small entry way now taking up the frame.

He leaned back in his chair; his jaw clenched as he listened to Cora's voice trembling through the speakers. Her words cut through him like a knife, each one a reminder of how far she had slipped from his grasp.

"She's slipping away," he muttered under his breath, his fists clenching against the armrests.

Declan's focus shifted to Selah and Jensen, their presence fueling the fire of his anger. Their support for Cora, their encouragement for her to leave him—it was all unacceptable. They were interlopers in the life he had built, threats to the control he had so carefully maintained.

Back at the estate, Cora continued to speak, her voice growing steadier with each word. "I want to leave," she said firmly, her gaze locking onto Selah's. "But, if I do, he'll destroy me. He already has."

Selah nodded, her expression fierce. "We'll help you. Whatever you need. Who is Dax?"

Cora took a step back to collect her thoughts, "He is the lead detective…his name is Dax Sheridan, and he is my father," she stated, looking up.

"Oh, Cora! That is incredible!" Selah remarked.

Jensen leaned back in his chair, his arms crossed as he studied Cora. "Does Dax know you are here alone?" he asked.

"Yes," Cora replied. "He has a police officer on all shifts watching the grounds. He's been working on the case."

"And you trust him?" Jensen asked, his tone cautious.

"With my life," Cora said simply.

As the conversation continued, Cora felt a small flicker of hope for the first time in weeks. Selah's unwavering support and Jensen's calm reassurance gave her the strength to keep going, to believe that she could find a way out of the nightmare she was living.

But that flicker of hope was short-lived.

In his hotel room, Declan closed his laptop with a sharp snap, his jaw tightening as he stood. His mind raced with plans, his anger simmering just below the surface. He couldn't let Cora slip away—not like this. He paced the room, his thoughts spiraling.

"I won't lose her," he muttered, his voice low and dangerous. *"Not to them. Not to anyone."*

The foyer felt heavier now, the air thick with the weight of Cora's confession. Selah sat beside her, her hand still resting on Cora's, while Jensen paced the small space, his brow furrowed as he processed everything she had said.

"So, he's been watching you this entire time," Jensen said, his voice low but sharp. "Even while he's away?"

Cora nodded, her gaze fixed on the floor. "There are cameras everywhere—hidden in places I didn't even think to look. He knows where I am, what I'm doing. It's like I can't escape him, even now."

Selah's jaw tightened, her eyes narrowing. "That's not just controlling, Cora. That's dangerous. He's not just keeping tabs on you—he's trying to break you."

Jensen stopped pacing, his hands resting on his hips as he turned to face Cora. "Have you seen the cameras? All of them?"

"Not all," Cora admitted, her voice trembling. "But enough to know they're everywhere. Dax pointed out a few of them before."

Jensen's expression darkened; his voice was steady but laced with frustration. "We need to get you out of here for good, Cora. Staying anywhere Declan can find you isn't an option."

Cora nodded, tears welling in her eyes. "I know," she said softly. "But where do I go? He's not just watching me—he's watching everyone around me. He'll know if I run."

Selah straightened in her seat, her expression fierce. "Then we make sure he doesn't find you," she said firmly. "We'll create a plan, something he can't predict."

Cora glanced between her friends. "And what happens if he does?" she asked, her voice breaking. "What happens if he comes after me?"

"He won't," Jensen said, his tone resolute. "Not if we stay ahead of him. Dax has the evidence to put him away, and once he's behind bars, he can't hurt you anymore."

Cora swallowed hard, the weight of Jensen's words settling over her. She wanted to believe him, but the lingering fear in her chest refused to fade.

Meanwhile, miles away in Chicago, Declan sat in his hotel room, his laptop now closed but his anger still simmering. He had replayed the live feed in his mind a dozen times, every word Cora spoke feeding the fire of his frustration. She had confessed everything—to Selah, to Jensen. She had exposed him in ways he couldn't have anticipated, and the betrayal cut deeper than he wanted to admit.

Declan stood, his hands clenching into fists as he paced the room. His phone buzzed on the nightstand, pulling him from his thoughts. He grabbed it, glancing at the screen. A message from his assistant:

Your presentation is in thirty minutes. Are you ready?

Declan stared at the message for a long moment before typing back:

Delay it.

The reply came quickly:

Sir, that's not possible. The board is waiting.

Declan exhaled sharply, his jaw tightening as he set the phone down. His focus wasn't on Chicago; it wasn't on the presentation he had spent weeks preparing. It was back home with Cora.

Back in the estate, Selah stood and began pacing, her arms crossed tightly over her chest. "We need to get Dax here," she said firmly. "If anyone knows how to handle this, it's him."

Cora nodded, her chest tightening as she pulled out her phone. She typed a quick message to Dax:

Can you come to the estate? I need help figuring out what to do next.

The reply came almost immediately:

On my way in an hour. Stay put.

Selah glanced at the phone, her expression softening. "Good," she said. "We'll figure this out, Cora. You're not alone in this anymore."

"Stay here tonight. Please. You can each take a guest room. I don't want to be alone," Cora said softly, gazing out the window.

Meanwhile, miles away in Chicago, Declan sat in the corner of the hotel conference room, his laptop open on the table in front of him. The voices of his colleagues faded into the background as his eyes remained fixed on the screen, the live feed from the estate now replaced with archived footage of the last few weeks.

He rewound the scene of Sebastian walking across the grounds, his movements deliberate as he approached Cora. The sight of them talking, their heads bent close together, sent a wave of anger coursing through Declan's chest. His jaw tightened as he paused the video, his focus sharpening on the way Cora had smiled at Sebastian.

"*She thinks she can replace me,*" Declan muttered under his breath, his hands gripping the edge of the laptop. "*She has no idea who she's dealing with.*"

The sound of his name pulled him from his thoughts. Declan turned, his assistant standing near the door with a clipboard in hand. "Sir, they're waiting for you in the conference room," she said cautiously, her eyes flicking to the laptop before meeting his gaze.

Declan forced a tight smile, closing the laptop with a deliberate snap. "Tell them I'll be there in a moment," he replied, his tone calm but clipped.

As she left, Declan leaned back in his chair, his mind racing. He needed to regain control, to remind Cora of what they had built and why she couldn't walk away. The thought of her slipping further from his grasp was intolerable, and he knew he couldn't let it happen.

He booked an early flight to head home directly after the presentation and then quickly walked out of his hotel room.

That night, as Selah and Jensen walked up to settle into their rooms, Cora sat alone in the kitchen with one of Gram's journals. Her thoughts were spinning with everything that had happened. Her fingers trembled as she flipped to a page she had read countless times: *Freedom isn't easy, but it's always worth fighting for. The hardest battles often lead to the greatest victories.*

She traced the words with her fingers, tears slipping down her cheeks. For the first time in weeks, she allowed herself to believe that victory was possible—that she could reclaim her life and leave Declan's shadow behind.

But even as the flicker of hope grew, her phone buzzed softly on the counter, pulling her back to reality. She hesitated before reaching for it, her heart sinking when she saw Declan's name on the screen. The message was short but chilling:

You can't hide from me, Cora. You know that.

Her hands trembled as she turned the phone face down, her chest tightening with fear. Declan's reach was long, but for the first time, she felt the strength to fight back.

The sound of a faint creak broke her focus. Cora froze, her heart pounding as she glanced toward the doorway. The house had been locked, Selah and Jensen just a floor above her in the guest rooms. Slowly, she stood, her breath catching as she reached for her phone.

A shadow moved just beyond the doorway, and Cora's blood ran cold.

"*Mara,*" she whispered, her voice trembling.

Mara stepped into the room, her dark bob casting shadows across her face. Her expression was sharp, her eyes wild as she stared at Cora. "You ruined everything," Mara hissed, her voice low and venomous. "You don't deserve him."

Cora's chest tightened as she took a step back, her hands trembling. "You need to leave," she said firmly, though her voice wavered. "This isn't going to fix anything."

Mara lunged before Cora could move, her hands grabbing at her arms. They struggled, the journal falling to the floor as Cora tried to break free. "He doesn't love you," Mara spat. "He never did. You don't belong here!"

Mara grabbed a knife from the kitchen counter, her eyes glossed over in a haze. The commotion brought Selah rushing into the room, her eyes wide as she took in the scene. "Cora!" she shouted, moving quickly to intervene.

Jensen appeared moments later, his posture tense as he stepped between Cora and Mara. "That's enough!" he barked, his voice sharp.

Mara whirled on him, the knife gleaming in her hand as she lunged. The blade sliced through the air, and Jensen moved to block her. A sharp gasp filled the room as the knife found its mark, Jensen stumbling back, his hand clutching his side.

Cora screamed, her hands flying to her mouth as Mara stepped back, her expression shifting from rage to panic. Before anyone could move, the sound of sirens broke through the confusion, red and blue lights flashing outside the windows.

The front door burst open moments later, Dax and three police officers stormed inside. Mara dropped the knife, her hands trembling as they grabbed her, pulling her away from the group.

"Cora!" Sebastian yelled, scanning the room for her.

"Are you ok?" Dax yelled as another officer pulled Mara away from the kitchen and into the hallway.

Cora just had one focus. She rushed to Jensen, her hands shaking as she pressed against the wound. "Stay with me," she whispered, tears streaming down her face. "You're going to be okay. Please, Jensen. I'm so sorry."

Outside, Declan's car pulled up just as the ambulance arrived. He stepped out, his expression dark as he took in the scene—police lights, paramedics, and Mara being led away in handcuffs.

"What the hell happened?" he demanded, his voice sharp.

Selah turned to him, her gaze filled with fury. "This is your fault!" she spat. "All of it. And now, it's over!"

Declan stood near the edge of the driveway, his sharp features illuminated by the flashing red and blue lights of the police vehicles. His expression was unreadable, but his clenched fists and the tension in his jaw betrayed the storm brewing beneath the surface. The chaos of the scene—officers escorting Mara into a squad car, paramedics rushing Jensen into the ambulance, and Cora's tear-streaked face—painted a vivid picture of his crumbling control.

"What happened here?" Declan demanded, his voice cutting through the noise as he stepped closer.

Selah was the first to face him, her fiery gaze locking onto his. "What happened?" she repeated, her tone sharp. "You happened, Declan! All of this—Mara, the fire, MJ—it all comes back to you!"

Declan's gaze shifted to Cora, who stood near the ambulance, her hands trembling as she watched the paramedics work on Jensen. "Cora," he called, his voice softening slightly as he took a step toward her.

Dax moved between them, his stance firm. "Stay back," he warned, his voice low and steady.

Declan's eyes narrowed, his frustration spilling over. "I just want to talk to her," he said, his tone sharp.

"You've done enough talking," Dax replied, his expression unyielding. "It's over, Declan."

Cora turned then, her tear-filled eyes meeting Declan's. For a moment, the disarray around them seemed to fade, the weight of their shared history filling the space between them.

"I trusted you," she said, her voice trembling but firm. "I believed in the life you promised me. And you destroyed it."

Declan's chest heaved as he took another step closer. "I didn't destroy anything," he said, his voice rising. "Everything I did was for us, Cora. For you."

"No," Cora said, shaking her head. "It wasn't for me. It was for you. To feed your need for control, to keep me under your thumb. But you don't own me anymore, Declan. And you never will again."

Declan froze at her words, the finality in her tone leaving him momentarily speechless. Before he could respond, the sound of heavy footsteps approached, and two uniformed officers stepped between him and the group.

"Declan Atler?" one of the officers said, his voice steady.

Declan's jaw tightened, his gaze darting between the officer and Cora. "Yes," he replied, his voice clipped.

The officer's expression didn't falter as he continued, "You're under arrest for arson and manslaughter."

The words hung in the air like a thunderclap. Declan's composure cracked as he turned back to Cora, his voice rising. "Cora, you don't have to do this," he said, his tone desperate. "Tell them it's not true. Tell them—"

"It is true," Cora interrupted, her voice firm. "And you know it."

The officers stepped forward, one of them pulling Declan's hands behind his back as they began to cuff him. Declan struggled slightly, his frustration boiling over.

"You'll regret this!" he spat, his voice low and venomous as he glared at Cora. "You'll regret all of it!"

Selah moved to Cora's side, her hand resting lightly on her arm as the officers led Declan to the squad car. "It's over," she said softly. "He can't hurt you anymore."

Cora nodded, though her chest remained tight as she watched the car disappear down the driveway. The weight of the moment settled over her, a mix of relief and grief swirling in her chest.

Dax approached then, his expression softening as he placed a reassuring hand on her shoulder. "You did it," he said gently. "You stood your ground. And now, it's time to start over."

That night, the estate was quiet, the lingering shadows of the day's events still heavy in the air. Cora sat in the library; the journals spread out before her once more. Her grandmother's words offered a sense of comfort, a connection to the resilience she had always admired.

She turned to a new page, her eyes scanning the faint ink: *Sometimes, we have to let go of the things we thought defined us to discover who we really are. It's in the breaking that we begin to rebuild.*

Cora closed the journal, her breath steady as she leaned back in the chair. The road ahead was uncertain, but for the first time, she felt like she had the strength to face it.

The next morning, Selah and Cora prepared to leave for the hospital to visit Jensen. The faint hum of the car engine filled the driveway as Selah loaded a small bag into the trunk. Cora stood inside the front door, her hands clasped in front of her as she waited.

Just as they were about to leave, a knock at the door broke the quiet. Dax answered, his expression shifting as two uniformed officers stood on the porch.

"We need to speak to Cora Atler," one of the officers said, his tone formal.

Dax frowned, glancing back at Cora before stepping aside. "What's this about?" he asked cautiously.

The officer's gaze shifted to Cora, his expression serious. "We've received new evidence related to Declan Atler's case," he said. "We'll need a formal statement."

Cora's chest tightened, but she nodded, her voice steady as she replied, "I'll do whatever it takes."

Selah placed a hand on her arm, her expression filled with quiet strength. "We'll be with you," she said firmly.

As Cora followed the officers into the foyer, the weight of everything she had endured pressed against her, but so did the glimmer of something new—freedom.

The drive to the hospital was quiet, the weight of the previous day pressing heavily on Cora and Selah. The winding roads passed in a blur, but Cora's thoughts remained sharp, replaying the events at the estate: Declan's arrest, Mara's intrusion, Jensen's injury. The chaos felt like it had barely begun to settle, and yet, for the first time in weeks, there was a faint sense of finality.

Selah glanced over at her, her expression soft but concerned. "You've been quiet," she said gently. "What's going through your mind?"

Cora exhaled shakily, her hands twisting in her lap. "Everything," she admitted. "Declan, Mara, Jensen... It's all so much. I don't know how to process it."

"You don't have to do it all at once," Selah replied, her tone steady. "One thing at a time, Cora. You've already been through the worst of it."

The hospital came into view, its gray exterior rising against the cloudy sky. Selah parked near the entrance, her movements purposeful as she turned to Cora. "Jensen's tough," she said firmly. "He's going to be okay."

Cora nodded, her chest tightening as they stepped out of the car and made their way inside. The bright fluorescent lights and the quiet hum of activity in the hospital felt disorienting after the stillness of the drive. They approached the front desk, where a nurse directed them to Jensen's room on the third floor.

When they entered, the sight of Jensen sitting up in bed, his side bandaged and his expression calm, brought an overwhelming wave of relief. "You're okay," Cora whispered, her voice trembling as she stepped closer.

Jensen managed a faint smile, his voice steady despite the exhaustion in his eyes. "Takes more than a knife to take me out," he said lightly, though his tone carried a hint of strain.

Selah crossed her arms, her brow furrowing as she studied him. "You're lucky," she said sharply. "If that knife had gone an inch deeper..."

"I know," Jensen interrupted, his smile fading. "But it didn't. And I'm still here."

Cora sat in the chair beside his bed, her hands clasping his as tears welled in her eyes. "You saved me," she said softly. "You didn't have to, but you did. And I don't know how to thank you for that."

Jensen's gaze softened, his grip on her hands steady. "You don't have to thank me, Cora," he said gently. "You're family. And we protect our own."

The three of them sat together for a while, the conversation shifting to lighter topics as the tension began to ease. Selah teased Jensen about his hospital food, while Cora smiled faintly, grateful for the reprieve from the heaviness of the past few days.

That night, as the house grew quiet, Cora sat in the library, her grandmother's journal open before her. She turned to a page she hadn't read before, the faint ink drawing her eyes to a passage that felt almost prophetic: *The truth is never easy, but it is always freeing. To live without it is to live in shadows, but to face it is to step into the light.*

As she read the words, tears began slipping down her cheeks. For the first time, she felt like she was stepping into the light, leaving the shadows of her past behind.

The moon hung low in the sky as the estate finally fell silent. Cora stood on the back porch, the cool night air brushing against her skin as she stared out at the darkened garden. The events of the day had left her emotionally drained, but the presence of Selah and Dax inside the house gave her a small sense of comfort.

She pressed her hands to the porch railing, her fingers curling around the worn wood as she let her thoughts drift. Jensen's words from the hospital replayed in her mind: *You're family. And we protect our own.*

The idea of family, of being surrounded by people who truly cared for her, felt foreign and fragile. For so long, her world had been controlled by Declan, his promises of love masking the reality of his manipulation.

But now, the walls of that control were crumbling.

Selah joined her on the porch, her footsteps soft against the wooden planks. "You're still out here," she said gently, leaning against the railing beside Cora. "You okay?"

Cora nodded, though her chest tightened as she replied, "I don't know. Everything feels... different now. Lighter, maybe. But also heavier, if that makes sense."

Selah smiled faintly, her gaze drifting to the stars above. "It makes perfect sense," she said. "You've been carrying so much for so long. Letting it go doesn't happen all at once. It takes time."

Cora glanced at her friend, her voice trembling as she said, "I don't think I'd be here without you. Without all of you."

Selah's expression softened, her hand brushing lightly against Cora's arm. "You'd have made it," she said firmly. "But I'm glad we're here with you anyway."

The two women stood in silence for a moment, the quiet of the night wrapping around them like a blanket. Inside, Dax's voice carried faintly from the library, the low hum of his conversation with the officers reminding Cora that the battle wasn't entirely over.

"What happens next?" Cora asked softly, her gaze fixed on the horizon.

Selah exhaled slowly, her arms crossing over her chest. "You rebuild," she said. "You take the pieces of what he tried to break and turn them into something new. Something better."

Cora nodded, her resolve hardening. "That's what Gram would have done," she said. "It's what she did. And now it's my turn."

The next morning, the estate was bathed in soft light as the sun rose over the horizon. Cora woke early, the faint sound of Selah moving through the house grounding her as she got dressed. The day felt heavy with expectation, a sense of finality hanging in the air.

She made her way to the kitchen, where Selah was preparing coffee. "Morning," Selah said, her voice warm but tired.

"Morning," Cora replied, her tone soft. "Did Dax leave already?"

Selah nodded, handing her a mug. "He went to the precinct early. Said he'd call if anything came up."

Cora took a sip of the coffee, the warmth spreading through her as she leaned against the counter. "It feels strange," she admitted. "Knowing he's gone but also knowing there's still so much to do."

Later that day, Cora sat in the library, her grandmother's journals spread out before her. The familiar handwriting offered a sense of comfort, a connection to the strength she had always admired.

She turned to a page she hadn't read before, the faint ink catching her attention: *The end of one chapter is the beginning of another. We carry the lessons forward, but we leave the pain behind.*

As she read the words, tears began slipping down her cheeks. For the first time, she felt ready to close the chapter of her life that had been defined by Declan and to begin writing something new.

The next morning brought golden light across the estate's sprawling grounds, filtering through the large windows of the library where Cora sat. Her grandmother's journals were spread out before her, their weathered covers a comforting presence against the polished wood of the desk. The quiet of the room felt fragile, as though the events of the past few days could break through at any moment.

Cora traced the faded handwriting on one of the open pages, her fingers brushing against the ink. The words were familiar now, their wisdom offering solace in a way nothing else could: *Strength isn't found in the absence of fear. It's found in moving forward despite it.*

She exhaled shakily, her gaze drifting to the infinity necklace resting on the table beside her. The delicate chain gleamed faintly in the morning light, but its weight felt heavier than ever. It wasn't a symbol of love anymore—it was a reminder of everything she had endured.

Minutes later, she picked up the necklace, shook her head and tossed it in the trash. When it finally vanished from sight, she felt a moment of relief.

Selah guided Cora to the sofa, her presence steady as she sat beside her. "You did it," Selah said gently, her voice filled with quiet pride. "You stood up to him. To all of it."

Cora managed a faint smile, though her chest remained tight. "It doesn't feel real yet," she admitted softly. "Like it's not over."

"It is," Selah replied firmly. "He's in custody, Cora. He can't hurt you anymore."

Later that day, Cora found herself wandering the grounds of the estate. The manicured gardens, once a source of solace, now felt like a reminder of the life she was leaving behind. The air was crisp, carrying the faint scent of lavender from the flower beds near the fountain. She paused by the bench where she and MJ used to sit, their laughter filling the quiet of the mornings as they planned their days. The memory brought a lump to her throat, the ache of his absence sharp and unrelenting.

"*I miss you,*" she whispered, her voice trembling. "*But I'm going to make you proud. I promise.*"

Back inside, Selah was waiting in the kitchen with a cup of tea. She handed it to Cora, her expression soft. "You ready to go see Jensen?" she asked.

Cora nodded, her grip tightening around the mug. "I think so," she replied. "He's done so much for me. It's the least I can do."

The drive to the hospital was quiet, the hum of the engine filling the silence as they made their way through town. When they arrived, the sight of Jensen sitting up in bed brought a wave of relief that eased some of the tension in Cora's chest.

"You're looking better," she said softly, her voice breaking as she stepped into the room.

Jensen offered a faint smile, his hand resting on the edge of the bed. "You should see the other guy," he said lightly, though the strain in his tone was evident.

Still, as she walked towards his bed, she hoped that he didn't falter their friendship, her heart aching to fix what was done. Cora sat beside him on the bed and leaned into him, resting her head on his shoulder. "I'm so glad you are alright," she smiled.

"Yeah?" he said as he played a light smile across his lips.

"Yeah," she echoed, as she nudged him playfully as he smiled.

Selah crossed her arms, her gaze narrowing as she studied him. "You're so lucky," she said firmly. "That knife could have done a lot more damage."

"I know," Jensen replied, his expression sobering. "But it didn't. And I'd do it again if I had to."

Cora sat beside him, her hands clasping his as tears filled her eyes. "Thank you," she whispered. "For everything."

Jensen's gaze softened, his voice steady as he said, "You don't have to thank me, Cora."

Jensen's words lingered in Cora's mind as she sat beside him, her fingers still lightly brushing against his hand. The hospital room was quiet except for the rhythmic beep of the monitors, the soft hum a reminder of how close they had come to losing him.

Selah pulled a chair closer, her expression softening as she glanced between Cora and Jensen. "You're too stubborn for your own good," she teased lightly, though her tone carried an edge of relief.

Jensen smirked faintly, his brow arching. "Someone had to be," he replied. "And let's face it, Selah—you needed me to keep you grounded."

Selah rolled her eyes, though the corners of her lips curved upward. "You're impossible," she muttered.

"And you love me for it," Jensen shot back, his voice warming.

Cora smiled faintly, the quiet banter between her friends easing some of the tension in her chest. For the first time in weeks, the weight of her fear felt just a little lighter.

"You two are ridiculous," she said softly, her voice trembling but steady.

"And you wouldn't have it any other way," Selah replied, her gaze locking onto Cora's. "You're part of this now, Cora. All of it. And we're not letting you go through this alone."

Cora's breath hitched, her emotions threatening to overwhelm her as she nodded. "Thank you," she whispered.

A knock at the door interrupted the moment, and they turned to see a nurse peeking inside. "Sorry to interrupt," she said gently, "but we'll need to run a few tests soon. You're welcome to come back afterward."

Selah stood, her expression soft as she nodded. "We'll head out for now," she said, glancing at Cora. "But we'll be back soon."

Jensen gave them a small wave, his smile faint but genuine. "Don't forget to bring me something edible next time," he said lightly. "This hospital food is trying to kill me."

Selah chuckled, her hand resting lightly on Cora's shoulder as they stepped into the hallway. "He's impossible," Selah muttered, though her fond smile betrayed her words.

The drive back to the estate was quiet, the late afternoon sun casting long shadows across the road. Cora stared out the window, her thoughts swirling as they passed familiar landmarks. The town felt both foreign and familiar now, a reminder of the life she was slowly reclaiming.

"You okay?" Selah asked, breaking the silence.

Cora nodded, though her chest remained tight. "I think so," she replied softly. "It just feels... strange. Like I'm standing in two worlds—the one I'm leaving behind and the one I'm trying to build."

Selah nodded, her gaze thoughtful as she replied, "That's because you are. But the world you're building? It's going to be incredible, Cora. You just have to give yourself time to see it."

When they arrived at the estate, the quiet was almost unsettling. The once-bustling halls now felt vast and empty, the absence of Declan's commanding presence leaving a hollow stillness. Cora made her way to the library, her steps slow as she entered the familiar space.

The journals sat on the desk where she had left them, their worn covers a comforting sight. She sat down, her fingers brushing against the edges as she opened one to a page she hadn't read before: *When we let go of what no longer serves us, we make space for something new—something that can truly belong to us.*

The weight of her past was heavy, but for the first time, she felt like she was ready to release it.

Selah appeared in the doorway, her expression soft as she leaned against the frame. "I ordered sushi! Still reading those journals?" she asked gently, entering with a platter of teriyaki chicken rolls, maki, and sashimi.

Cora glanced up, a faint smile tugging at her lips. "They're like a lifeline," she admitted. "They remind me of who I am—and who I want to be." She watched Selah put several pieces of sushi from a platter onto a plate.

Selah used her chopsticks to pick up a maki roll, her gaze drifting to the open page. "Your grandmother was incredible," she said. "And so are you, Cora. Don't forget that."

Cora closed the journal, her fingers lingering on the cover. "I'm trying not to," she said softly as she walked over to the couch. "But it's hard to see myself that way sometimes."

"You will," Selah replied firmly. "You've already come so far. And you've got a whole life ahead of you to figure out the rest."

The next morning, sunlight streamed through the estate's tall windows, casting warm patterns across the floors. Cora moved quietly through the house, her footsteps echoing softly in the vast halls. She had woken early, her thoughts too restless to let her sleep any longer.

Her gaze drifted to the sitting room as she passed, the flying dress print still hanging on the wall. It loomed over the space like a relic of a life she no longer recognized. She hesitated, her fingers brushing against the doorframe as she stared at the image. It had once represented everything she thought she wanted—a perfect life, carefully curated and polished to the outside world. Now, it felt like a lie, a mask that had hidden the cracks in her reality for far too long.

With a deep breath, she stepped into the room, her hands trembling as she reached for the print. The glass was cool beneath her fingers as she carefully unhooked it from the wall, setting it gently on the floor.

Selah found her there moments later, her expression softening as she took in the scene. "You're finally taking it down," she said, her tone gentle but approving.

Cora nodded, her chest tightening as she replied, "It doesn't belong here anymore. It never really did."

Selah stepped closer, her gaze steady. "What are you going to do with it?"

Cora exhaled slowly, her fingers brushing against the edge of the frame. "Let it go," she said simply.

Together, they carried the print to the garden, where Cora had already prepared a small firepit. The morning air was crisp, the faint scent of lavender from the nearby flowerbeds mingling with the promise of something new.

As the flames flickered to life, Cora held the print in her hands, her grip steady despite the emotions swirling in her chest. She stared at the image for a long moment, her reflection faintly visible in the glass.

"This isn't who I am anymore," she murmured, her voice trembling.

Selah nodded, her hand resting lightly on Cora's arm. "It's time to let it go," she said softly.

Cora placed the print into the fire, her breath hitching as the flames began to consume it. The colors and lines that had once defined her life curled and blackened, disappearing into ash.

As the smoke rose into the sky, Cora felt an unexpected sense of relief. The weight that had pressed against her chest for so long began to lift, replaced by a quiet determination.

Later that day, Cora stood outside the shop lot on Boughton Street, her hands resting on her hips as she looked at the empty space. The foundation was still solid, the bones of the building intact, but it needed work—a lot of it. The second and third floor lofts were in ruins, but much of the white brick was salvaged, a little piece of Gram left among the wreckage.

"This is where it starts," she said softly, more to herself than to anyone else. She thought back to the day she and MJ arrived and what she would give right now to have him by her side.

Dax arrived a few minutes later, his expression calm but warm as he approached. "You're really doing it," he said, his tone laced with quiet pride. He turned to Cora and offered her a hug.

Cora smiled faintly, her chest tightening as she replied, "I have to. It's the only way forward."

The two of them walked through the space together, their footsteps echoing softly. Cora pointed out where the displays would go, the fitting rooms, the register. Each word brought her vision into sharper focus, and for the first time in weeks, she felt a flicker of excitement.

As they stood near the front windows, Cora turned to Dax, her voice trembling as she said, "Thank you. For everything. I wouldn't be here without you."

Dax placed a hand on her shoulder, his expression softening. "You did this, Cora," he said gently. "All I did was give you the tools. The rest was all you."

Together, they walked out into the sunshine that glistened the cobbled walks of Pine Brook. For the first time in weeks, she felt a flicker of peace. The road ahead was uncertain, but it was hers to walk—and she was ready to take the first step.

A thunderstorm rolled through, bringing with it cooler temperatures as Cora returned to the estate one last time. The halls felt quieter now, the echoes of her past fading into the distance as she moved through the space. She stopped in the library, her fingers brushing against the spines of the books as she made her way to the desk. The journals were still there, their covers tarnished and worn but familiar. She opened one, her eyes scanning the faded ink as she read: *Freedom isn't found in the things we leave behind, but in the courage to move forward.*

As she closed the journal, her hands shook. She placed it carefully into her bag, along with the others, before turning toward the door.

Selah was waiting for her outside, the car already packed with Cora's belongings. "Ready?" Selah asked, her voice steady. She and Jensen had each taken remote jobs and planned on relocating to the Boulder area, with promises of a future together on the horizon.

Cora nodded, her chest tightening as she replied, "As I'll ever be."

They climbed into the car, the estate disappearing in the rearview mirror as they drove away. Cora stared out the window, her mind spinning with thoughts of what lay ahead.

"It feels strange," she admitted softly. "Leaving it all behind."

Selah glanced at her, her expression filled with quiet encouragement. "You're not leaving everything," she said. "You're taking the most important parts with you."

As the car moved farther from the estate, Cora pressed a hand to her chest, her fingers brushing against the spot where the infinity necklace had once rested. It was gone now, left behind with everything else that no longer served her.

The car moved steadily along the highway, the golden glow of the setting sun casting long shadows over the passing fields. Cora sat quietly in the passenger seat, her gaze fixed on the horizon. The weight of the estate's memories seemed to lessen with each mile that separated her from it.

Selah glanced over at her, her hands steady on the wheel. "You're awfully quiet," she said gently. "What's going through your head?"

Cora exhaled slowly, her hands resting in her lap. "Everything," she admitted. "It feels like I've been holding my breath for months, and now I can finally exhale. But it's terrifying too. What if I don't know who I am without all of it?"

Selah smiled faintly, her tone warm but firm. "You're stronger than you think, Cora. You've spent so much time surviving that you haven't had the chance to just be. This is your chance to figure it out—to build a life that's yours."

Cora nodded, though the uncertainty in her chest remained. "It's hard to imagine what that life looks like," she murmured. "But I want to try. I want to create something that's just mine."

"And you will," Selah said confidently. "The shop, your new place, your future—it's all waiting for you. One step at a time."

The conversation lulled, the quiet hum of the car filling the space between them. Cora stared out the window, the fading light bathing the world in hues of orange and pink. For the first time in a long time, she allowed herself to dream of the future—a life free from Declan's shadow, one built on her own terms.

They arrived at Cora's new apartment just as dusk settled over the town. The small building was unassuming but welcoming, its brick exterior softened by the warm glow of porch lights. Selah parked the car, her gaze sweeping over the neighborhood as she said, "This looks cozy."

Cora stepped out, her bag slung over her shoulder as she took in her new surroundings. The air smelled of freshly cut grass, and the faint sounds of laughter drifted from a nearby house. It felt normal in a way the estate never had—a quiet, grounded normalcy that she realized she craved.

Selah joined her, her expression softening as she said, "This is a good place to start."

"It feels... real," Cora replied, her voice trembling slightly.

"That's because it is," Selah said firmly.

Inside, the apartment was small but bright, the furniture minimal but functional. Cora set her bag down by the door, her fingers brushing against the worn fabric as she exhaled shakily.

Selah moved to the kitchen, pulling out two glasses and a bottle of wine she had brought along. "A toast," she said, handing Cora a glass.

"To what?" Cora asked, her brow furrowing.

"To you," Selah replied, her tone light but sincere. "To freedom. To starting over. And to whatever comes next."

Cora smiled faintly, her chest tightening as she clinked her glass against Selah's. "To moving forward," she said softly.

As the night wore on, the two of them talked about the future—about the shop, about the people they wanted to surround themselves with, about the kind of life Cora wanted to build. The conversation was easy, filled with laughter and quiet encouragement, a stark contrast to the heaviness of the past few weeks.

Selah left for her hotel with a quick promise to return the next day to help unpack. Cora sat alone in the quiet apartment. The stillness felt different here—not suffocating, but peaceful.

She moved to the small desk by the window, her grandmother's empty journal resting on the surface. Opening it to a blank page, she picked up a pen, her hands trembling slightly as she began to write: *Tonight, I stood on the edge of something new. It's terrifying, but it's also exhilarating. For the first time in years, I feel like this life is mine to build. And I'm ready to see where it takes me.*

The following morning, sunlight streamed through the sheer curtains of the apartment, waking Cora gently. She stretched lazily, her body feeling lighter than it had in weeks. The scent of fresh coffee drifted through the air, and she smiled faintly, remembering Selah's promise to return early.

When she opened the door, she found Selah holding two cups of coffee and a bag of pastries. "Breakfast delivery! And I think I found a place here in Pine Brook! I won't be far at all!" Selah said brightly, stepping inside.

"Oh, that's great, Se! I am so glad you are moving here," Cora said, her smile widening. She watched as her expression suddenly went soft.

"Get used to it," Selah replied, setting the bag on the counter. "Dallas doesn't need me, you do after everything you've been through."

They spent the morning unpacking boxes, the small apartment slowly beginning to feel like home. As they hung photos and arranged furniture, Cora felt the weight of her past slipping further away.

Selah paused as she hung a picture frame on the wall, her gaze softening. "You're going to do great things here, Cora," she said. "I can feel it."

Cora nodded, her chest swelling with a mix of hope and determination. "So can I," she said softly.

That afternoon, as Selah left to run errands, Cora stood by the window, her fingers brushing against the journal in her hands. She opened it to the last page she had written, her eyes scanning the words before she added a new line:

"This is the start of something beautiful."

Her chest tightened with emotion, but for the first time, it wasn't fear—it was hope.

Cora's phone buzzed on the table, bringing in a message from Nadine:

Can we meet at The Alpine Café in the morning?

Cora was hesitant but replied with a simple:

Yes, 9 am work?

The café was quieter than usual, the soft murmur of conversation blending with the clinking of porcelain cups. Cora sat at a corner table, her hands wrapped around a steaming mug of tea. The warmth seeped into her fingers, but her thoughts remained elsewhere—drifting between the events of the past few weeks and the uncertain path ahead.

When Nadine arrived, her presence was subdued, her usual poised demeanor tinged with a quiet sorrow. She approached the table slowly, her gaze meeting Cora's with a flicker of hesitation before she sat down.

"Thank you for agreeing to meet me," Nadine said softly, setting her purse beside her.

Cora nodded, her chest tightening as she replied, "I wasn't sure I would, but... there's too much left unsaid."

Nadine exhaled shakily, her fingers brushing against the edge of her cup as she studied Cora. "I owe you an apology," she began, her voice trembling. "For everything. For not seeing what Declan was capable of sooner. For... being part of the world that shaped him into who he became."

Cora tilted her head, her brow furrowing. "What do you mean?" she asked carefully.

Nadine's lips pressed into a thin line, her gaze dropping to the table. "The society I was part of—the secret arrangements, the open marriages—" she began.

Cora looked into her eyes as Nadine's voice broke, tears welling in her eyes as she continued, "I saw the way he idolized his father, how he mirrored his behavior. His father was never around, and I let it happen. We became socialites in the community, and everything just sort of escalated. I'm not proud. We were young. I would do a million things differently, Cora. I knew it was wrong, trying to raise a family, three children...I didn't stop it. And for that, I am so, so sorry."

Cora's chest tightened, her hands trembling as she placed them flat on the table. "He made his choices, Nadine," she said, her voice trembling but firm. "He could have found something good to believe in. He could have believed in me. Instead, he took everything I had away from me."

Nadine's breath hitched, her hand flying to her mouth as tears slipped down her cheeks. "I didn't know," she whispered, her voice breaking. "Cora, I didn't know it had gone that far. I... I thought he loved you. I thought he just wanted to protect you."

Cora shook her head, her voice trembling as she replied, "It wasn't love. It was control. And it destroyed everything good in my life."

The two women sat in silence for a long moment, the weight of their shared grief pressing heavily between them. Finally, Nadine reached across the table, her fingers brushing against Cora's.

"For what it's worth," Nadine said softly, her voice filled with quiet resolve, "I'll do everything I can to make this right. You are right, Declan's actions are his own, but if there's any way I can help you rebuild, I will."

Cora hesitated, her gaze locking onto Nadine's. "I appreciate that," she said quietly. "But rebuilding is something I have to do for myself. I've spent so much time living in other people's shadows—Declan's, my grandmother's. Now, I need to figure out who I am without them."

Nadine nodded slowly, her expression softening. "You're stronger than I ever realized," she said. "And I'm proud of you, Cora. Truly."

Cora managed a faint smile, though her chest remained tight. "Thank you," she said softly.

As they finished their tea, the conversation shifted to lighter topics— the shop, Cora's plans for the future, and the small steps she was taking to reclaim her life. By the time they parted ways, Cora felt a strange sense of closure, a quiet acceptance of the past that had once defined her.

They embraced as they stood and pushed in their chairs, and Cora secretly hoped for a real connection with her, one that would become a constant in her life. She had grown to like Nadine, her honesty. She wasn't without fault, and she was willing to stand up and take the fall in her son's choices. For that, Cora found a deep respect.

Later that evening, Cora returned to the apartment, her body tired but her mind alive with thoughts of the future. The journals sat on the small desk by the window, their familiar presence grounding her as she sat down and opened one to a blank page.

Her pen hovered over the paper before she began to write: *Today, I let a piece of the past open a new door for the future. Every step forward feels uncertain, but it's a step nonetheless. And that's enough for now.*

She set the pen down, her head swirling with emotion as she leaned back in her chair. The quiet of the apartment felt like a promise—a space where she could finally breathe, finally rebuild.

As the night deepened, Cora found herself standing by the window, her arms wrapped around herself as she stared out at the darkened street below. The air was cool against the glass, her breath fogging the surface as she whispered, "I'm going to be okay."

The words felt tentative, but they also felt true.

Selah arrived a short while later, her arms full of takeout containers from Mason's Dumpling House and a bottle of wine. "Dinner delivery," she announced brightly, setting everything on the counter.

Cora laughed softly, the sound breaking through the quiet. "You're spoiling me again. I don't think I've ever eaten so well," she said, her voice light.

Selah grinned, her tone teasing. "It's nice to see you getting your appetite back. Get used to it. This is what rebuilding looks like—with food and friends and way too much wine."

The two of them spent the evening talking and laughing, the heavy shadows of the past beginning to lift. As they clinked glasses, Cora felt a warmth spreading through her chest—a quiet hope that maybe, just maybe, she was finally stepping into the life she was meant to live.

The next morning, the soft light of dawn spilled through the windows of the apartment, bathing the room in a warm glow. Cora sat at the small dining table, a steaming cup of coffee in her hands as she flipped through her grandmother's journal. The faint hum of the world outside was a comforting backdrop as her eyes scanned the familiar handwriting.

Her gaze landed on a passage she hadn't read before: *There will always be a moment when we stand at the crossroads of who we were and who we are meant to become. In that moment, the choice we make defines us.*

Her heart soared as she traced the words with her fingers. This was her moment—the crossroads she had been standing at for far too long. For the first time, she felt ready to move forward, to leave behind the shadows of the life Declan had built around her.

The sound of a car pulling up outside broke her focus. Cora stood, moving to the window as Selah stepped out of her car, her usual bright energy evident even from a distance. She carried a bag in one hand and waved with the other, her smile wide as Cora opened the door.

"Good morning!" Selah said cheerfully, stepping inside. "I brought bagels and coffee because I figured you'd need fuel for today."

Cora laughed softly, her heart warming at her friend's thoughtfulness.

They sat together at the table, the scent of fresh bagels filling the room as they ate. Selah leaned back in her chair, her gaze thoughtful as she studied Cora. "Have you thought about what you're going to do with the estate?" she asked.

Cora hesitated, her fingers tightening around her coffee cup. "I don't know," she admitted. "It feels so far removed from the life I want to build. But part of me wonders if there's a way to turn it into something good."

Selah tilted her head, her brow furrowing. "Like what?"

"I'm not sure yet," Cora said softly. "Maybe something for the community—a retreat, a safe space. Something that means more than just... what it was."

Selah smiled faintly, her voice warm as she replied, "That sounds perfect. Turning something broken into something beautiful. That's kind of your thing, isn't it?"

Cora laughed, though her chest tightened with emotion. "I guess it is," she said softly. "It's the only way I know how to move forward."

As they finished breakfast, Selah stood, her hands resting on her hips. "All right," she said brightly. "What's the plan for today? Shop stuff? Apartment stuff? Or are we just going to sit here and admire how far you've come?"

Cora rolled her eyes, though a small smile tugged at her lips. "Let's start with the shop," she said. "I want to meet with the contractor and finalize the layout."

"Perfect," Selah replied. "Let's get to work."

The drive to the shop lot was filled with lighthearted conversation, the two women laughing as they planned every detail of the space. By the time they arrived, Cora felt a renewed sense of purpose, her vision for the shop growing clearer with each passing moment.

The contractor was waiting for them, his clipboard in hand as he greeted them warmly. "Good to see you again, Cora," he said. "Are you ready to make some decisions?"

"More than ready," Cora replied, her voice steady. "Let's do this."

As they walked through the space, the contractor laid out the plans, pointing to where each section would go. Cora listened intently, her confidence growing as she asked questions and offered input. Selah stood nearby, her expression filled with quiet pride as she watched her friend take charge.

"This is going to be incredible," Selah said softly as they finished the tour. "I can already see it."

"So can I," Cora replied, her voice trembling slightly with emotion. "It feels... real now."

Later that afternoon, Cora and Selah returned to the apartment, their energy light and excited after the productive day. They sat on the couch, sipping iced tea as they flipped through design catalogs and discussed ideas for the shop.

"You've got a lot to look forward to," Selah said, her tone warm. "This is the start of something amazing, Cora. And you're doing it all on your own."

Cora smiled faintly, her chest tightening with a mix of hope and determination. "It doesn't feel like I'm doing it alone," she said softly. "Not with you, Jensen, and Dax by my side."

Selah grinned, her voice teasing as she replied, "Well, we are pretty amazing, aren't we?"

That evening, as the apartment grew quiet, Cora found herself standing by the window once again. The journal sat open on the desk behind her, the faint light of the lamp illuminating the words she had written earlier: *The life I'm building feels fragile, but it's mine. And that makes it beautiful.*

Epilogue: A Life Rekindled

"From the ashes of what was, a new life ignites, carrying the promises of tomorrow."

It was December in Colorado, and there was already fifteen inches of snow on the ground. The airports were delayed, the ski hill resorts were booked, and families arrived to witness the Blossoms of Light extravaganza outside of the Botanic Gardens. It was a glorious winter wonderland.

Cora's hand moved instinctively to her stomach, a thought flickering in her mind that she hadn't allowed herself to dwell on before. The possibility lingered, filling her with equal parts fear and hope. She exhaled slowly, her gaze fixed on the horizon as she whispered, "Whatever comes next, I'm ready."

Selah had settled in at her new apartment and her new job granted her flexibility to network with Cora, learning about business at the boutique. Jensen chose a duplex in Boulder, just a short thirteen-minute drive from them. Dax and Nadine both became constant figures in Cora's life, checking in on her routinely, and Sebastian grew fonder of her with each passing day. Cora was grateful to have a support system so strong.

The quiet of the apartment that night felt different—not heavy, but comforting. Cora stood in the kitchen, the faint hum of the refrigerator filling the silence as she poured herself a glass of water. Each moment felt like a step forward, a step away from the shadows of her past.

She carried the glass to the small desk by the window, her grandmother's journal still open from earlier. The pages felt warm in her hands as she turned them carefully, her eyes catching on a passage she hadn't noticed before: Sometimes the biggest risks we take are the ones that bring us home to ourselves.

Cora traced the words with her fingers, her chest tightening as the meaning sank in. She had taken so many risks—leaving Declan, exposing the truth, starting over. And now, with each new step, she was finding pieces of herself she hadn't known were missing.

The air was crisp as Cora walked out to her car. She had spent the better part of the night muffling over designs and layouts.

Selah met her at the shop and handed her a cup of coffee, her smile bright despite the early hour. "One more final meeting with the contractors today?" she asked, her tone light.

"Just one more," Cora replied, her voice soft but steady.

As they walked up the cobbled streets to the building, the streets were alive with the hum of morning activity. Cora watched as shopkeepers shoveled their walks and opened their doors, front windows full of holiday displays. Parents walked their children to school and life moved forward. It was a quiet reminder that the world kept turning, no matter how broken things had seemed.

When they arrived at the shop lot, the contractor was already there, his clipboard in hand. The sight of the building, now taking shape with fresh paint and newly installed windows, sent a surge of pride through Cora's chest.

"It's really happening," she murmured, stepping out of the car.

Selah grinned, her voice warm as she said, "Of course it is. You're making it happen."

The contractor walked them through the latest updates, pointing out where the counters would go, how the lighting was being installed, and what the next steps were. Cora asked questions, her confidence growing with each decision she made.

As they stood by the front entrance, the contractor turned to her, his tone genuine as he said, "You've got a good eye for this, Cora. This place is going to be incredible."

They left the shop that afternoon with a clear plan in place, the next phase of construction set to begin the following week.

"Text me when you get home, Selah," she smiled.

"I will, I promise, C," Selah said, looking over the shoulder at her.

Cora felt lighter as she drove back to the apartment through the slushy streets, the weight of uncertainty slowly giving way to hope.

That evening, as Cora settled into her apartment, the quiet once again wrapped around her like a comforting blanket. She sat at the desk by the window, the faint glow of the streetlights illuminating the journal in her hands.

Her pen floated over the page before she began to write: Today, I saw the future taking shape. It's messy and uncertain, but it's mine. For the first time, I feel like I'm not just surviving—I'm living.

Her words felt like a promise, a declaration of the life she was building piece by piece.

The sound of a knock at the door startled her, breaking the stillness of the room. She stood, her heart racing slightly as she made her way to the door. When she opened it, she found Sebastian standing there, a soft smile on his face and a small bouquet of wildflowers in his hand.

"I thought you could use these," he said, holding them out to her. They were an intrinsic blend of sunflowers, zinnias and cosmos, a perfectly thoughtful palate.

Cora laughed softly, her chest tightening as she accepted the flowers. "You're becoming predictable," she teased lightly, though her voice carried warmth. "They are beautiful, Seb. Thank you."

"Good," Sebastian replied, stepping inside. "Predictable means dependable, right?"

The two of them sat at the small dining table, the flowers now resting in a vase at the center. They talked easily, their conversation drifting between the shop, Cora's plans, and the small joys of everyday life. For the first time in weeks, Cora felt a sense of normalcy—a feeling she had almost forgotten.

As the evening wore on, Sebastian stood to leave, his hand brushing lightly against hers as he said, "You're doing amazing, Cora."

"Thank you," she replied softly, her chest tightening as she watched him go.

That night, as she climbed into bed, the wildflowers on the table caught her eye. Their bright colors stood out against the muted tones of the room, a small but vibrant reminder of the life she was creating.

She closed her eyes, her thoughts drifting toward the future. For the first time in a long time, she felt ready to embrace it.

The bright morning light filtered through the sheer curtains, filling the small apartment with a soft glow. Cora stood in the kitchen, her fingers brushing over the edge of the counter as she sipped her coffee. The room felt peaceful, the kind of peace she had spent years searching for but never truly found—until now.

The faint hum of the city outside reminded her of how much her life had changed. Gone were the quiet, suffocating halls of the estate and the ever-present shadow of Declan's control. In their place was a small but bright apartment, a space that felt like hers in every way.

Cora set her mug down, her gaze drifting again to the small vase of wildflowers on the dining table. The sight of them brought a smile to her face, her thoughts momentarily drifting to Sebastian and the quiet moments they had shared.

She turned toward the living room, her eyes falling on the journals that now sat on the bookshelf. They had been a lifeline during her darkest days, a connection to her grandmother and the wisdom she had carried. But now, they felt like something more—a foundation for the life Cora was building.

Her phone buzzed on the counter, pulling her from her thoughts. She picked it up, her chest tightening slightly as she read the message from Selah:

Heading to the shop now. Bring the plans!

Cora smiled, her heart warming at the thought of another busy day filled with ideas and possibilities. She grabbed her coat and bag, slipping the plans for the shop's layout inside before heading for the door.

The shop lot was already buzzing with activity when she arrived. Construction workers moved efficiently, the sound of hammers and drills filling the air. Selah was waiting by the entrance, her clipboard in hand and a grin on her face.

"Good timing," Selah called, waving her over. "We've got decisions to make!"

Cora laughed, her nervous energy giving way to excitement as she joined her friend. They walked through the space together, pointing out details and discussing the finishing touches that would bring her vision to life.

By midday, Cora felt a sense of pride and anticipation that she hadn't known was possible. The shop wasn't just a building—it was a testament to her resilience, a symbol of everything she had overcome.

Later that afternoon, as the workers packed up for the day, Cora stood by the front window, staring out at the bustling street beyond. The future still felt uncertain, but it was a kind of uncertainty she was learning to embrace.

Sebastian arrived just as she was locking up, his easy smile and steady presence a welcome sight. "How's it coming along?" he asked, his tone warm.

"Better than I expected," Cora replied, her voice soft but confident. "It's finally starting to feel real."

Sebastian nodded, his gaze softening. "That's because it is real, Cora. And it's yours." He leaned in and kissed the top of her head. "Cora, I'd like to officially ask you out on a date, if you'll have me," he said, shuffling his feet.

"I thought you'd never ask," she said with a smile. Her chest tightened at his words, and little by little, she started to feel life falling into place.

That evening, back at the apartment, Cora sat on the edge of her bed, her hands resting lightly on her stomach. Her thoughts had been circling all day, returning to a possibility she hadn't allowed herself to fully consider until now.

The small box on the nightstand felt heavier than it should have, its contents carrying a weight she wasn't sure she was ready to face. But she knew she couldn't avoid it any longer.

With trembling hands, she opened the box, pulling out the pregnancy test inside. The minutes stretched into what felt like hours as she waited, her heart pounding in her chest.

When the results appeared, her breath hitched. Two lines. Positive.

She stared at the test, her emotions crashing over her in waves—fear, hope, disbelief, and a quiet, fragile joy. Her hand moved instinctively to her stomach, her fingers brushing against the fabric of her shirt as tears filled her eyes. Cora stood, moving to the window as she tried to steady her breathing. The city lights twinkled faintly in the distance, a reminder of the life she was creating.

That night, as she lay in bed, her thoughts drifted toward the future. The uncertainty felt overwhelming, but for the first time, it didn't feel insurmountable. She was no longer bound by the chains of her past— she was free, and the life ahead was hers to shape.

Her hand rested lightly on her stomach, a soft smile tugging at her lips as she whispered into the quiet, "We're going to be okay."

And for the first time in years, she truly believed it.

Acknowledgments

Thank you to my two adult daughters for encouraging me to write.

Thank you to my husband for unconditional love and support, for allowing my freak flag to fly and condoning my crazy, made-up plots, for his unwavering encouragement, for giving me a safe place to land, and for making me laugh every single day. I love you, Slade.

Thank you to my family for their love and support no matter what and for never once letting me feel like a middle child.

Thank you to my incredible groups of friends throughout all the years who have entered my life in epic ways and stayed through every stage.....Rachel, Sandy, My Nicole's...you are all my Selah combined into one.

Thank you to my MC College girls: I'm so thankful for our college reunions. You inspired me to show the depth and strength in Cora's college friends.

Thank you to Danielle Steel...you are the reason I fell in love with reading.

Thank you to fellow Fire Girl, Author Samantha Treat, for inspiring me to own it.

And lastly, thank you to my editing team at Hemingway Publishers for guiding me along the way, putting up with my last-minute changes, my 5 am in-the-moment texts and for navigating the course to see my dream come true....

About the Author

Chrissy Curry lives with her husband in Central Illinois but their hearts belong in St. Petersburg, Florida, where they spend their anniversary each year. She has two adult daughters, three adult bonus children, and a beloved golden doodle, Daisy. In her free time, she crochets cuddle cloths for NICU babies in the Midwest. She began her writing career with Children's Books. Her next children's book, ***Listen With My Little Hands***, a sign language book, will be released in March. The next book in this series, OPEN PROMISE, will be released in September.

Children's Books by Chrissy Curry

Daisy Doodle is NOT Tucked in at Night

Wonders of the Sea

Savy Elf Saves Christmas

Just One More

Simply Ask Away

LOVE IS Where You Are

Will You Still Remember

COMING SOON

Listen With My Little Hands

Zadie Zebra Zips Out Another AHHH-CHOO

Madness On the Farm

Adventure Day at CC's

Learning Time at the Zoo

When the Little is No More

The Keeper of Christmas Spirit

Twinning With You

Smoocharoonie

You CAN Do Big Things

All Aboard the Potty Train

It Shaped You

Open Fire Playlist

FRIEND by Benson Boone

MEMORIES by Dean Lewis

FADE INTO YOU by Mazzy Star

BEHIND BLUE EYES by Limp Bizkit

UNDER YOUR SCARS by Godsmack

TANGLED UP IN YOU by Staind

IF OUR LOVE IS WRONG by Calum Scott

FIX YOU by Coldplay

HELP by Anna Clendening

HURTS LIKE HELL by Fleurie

ASHES OF US by Melody Dairies

ANGEL IN THE FIRE by Natalie Taylor

www.ingramcontent.com/pod-product-compliance
Lightning Source LLC
Chambersburg PA
CBHW060426310726

48977CB00001B/72